# Criminal Behavior
### by
### James A. Drexler

To Mary
A wonderful new friend
w/ a somewhat unusual
son
All The very best!
J Drexler
5/00

*authorlink press*
www.authorlink.com

10114 Briar Rose Dr.
Houston, Tx. 77042

Published by Authorlink Press
An imprint of Authorlink!
(http://www.authorlink.com)
3720 Millswood Dr.
Irving, Texas 75062, USA

First published by Authorlink Press
An imprint of Authorlink!
First Printing, July 1999

Printed in the United States of America

ISBN 1 928704 08 5

# Dedication

To Patricia with love

## Author's Notes

This is a work of fiction. All the names, characters, organizations, and events portrayed in this book are either the product of the author's imagination or are used fictitiously for verisimilitude. Any other resemblance to any organization, event, or actual person, living or dead, is unintended and entirely coincidental.

"Conduct which causes any social harm which is defined and made punishable by law."

*Black's Law Dictionary* (Sixth Edition, 1990).

## Chapter One

If I live to be a hundred, I'll never forget that day. Standing with my client, watching the jurors file into the courtroom of the 269th District Court of Harris County, Texas. Eight men. Four women. Three African-Americans. Two Hispanics. Three union members. One postal worker. One unemployed. Definitely the kind of jury that makes a plaintiff's lawyer lick his chops. Since I represented the plaintiff in front of this particular bunch, I was licking away like crazy. Even though I had that jerk next to me, I couldn't help but get excited about those folks. After all, they were about to make me famous and rich. That is, if William Thrasher didn't keep getting in the way.

I'd met him two years earlier, when he strolled into my office to announce he wanted to talk to me about a case. Something having to do with his garbage company being run out of business by an outfit called Waste Disposal Systems, a monster conglomerate from the mid-west that had recently added Texas refuse to its amazingly ravenous appetite. At the time, I wasn't really interested. I didn't know beans about trash hauling and just how lucrative it could be. But when I found out Thrasher was from River Oaks, the only son of a wealthy old-line Houston family, and that his dad was a long-time buddy of Steve Golden's—the truth be told that was probably what prompted Thrasher to come to me in the first place—my interest became suddenly more acute. As for Thrasher himself, he was chubby, short, and bald, and had the unfortunate luck to be saddled with a face that had to remind everyone who met him of Porky Pig. That would have given him an almost comical charm, but William Thrasher was no laughing matter. I don't think I ever saw him so much as crack a smile. Worse than his total lack of

humor, Pig-Boy—that's what I came to think of him as—had
the personality of an angry hornet.

I have to admit, I disliked William Thrasher from the very
beginning, and for that reason alone should have declined his
offer of employment. But the fact is, I got greedy. When I
delved into the facts, his case was almost too good to be true.
Slam-dunk liability. Millions in damages. The kind of deep-
pocket defendant that could easily be portrayed as an out-of-
state bully working over a home-town family business. Trial
lawyers dream about a case like Thrasher's coming to them
just once. So, what the hey, I could put up with Pig-Boy. Of
course, back then, I thought I could get along with anybody.

I had serious problems with Thrasher throughout. Getting
the case ready to try. Selecting a jury that hopefully wouldn't
hate him as much as they could be made to detest the out-of-
town defendant. Putting our evidence on. But so far, I
thought we'd done pretty well, and with that lovely bunch
settling into their places in the jury box, we had more than a
reasonable shot. I stood there telling myself, with all we had
going, maybe Thrasher's going nuts the night before was
actually a blessing in disguise.

What happened—William Thrasher snatching certain
victory from our hands—started after our damage expert, an
economist from U. of H. named Herbert Lyon, testified that
Thrasher Industries had suffered lost profits of slightly more
than twenty million dollars. On that high note, I'd rested our
case. The defendant's attorney, a tall, rail-thin, weasel-faced
fellow from Barrett & Taylor, one of Houston's leading trial
firms, made only a half-hearted pitch for directed verdict.
Judge Otto Loring, a substitute for the regular judge in the
269th, who'd appeared to nap rather soundly throughout
Giles' impassioned plea for justice, muttered he'd take the
motion under advisement. Then, he sent the jury home for
the night.

I was stuffing papers into my trial bag when, out of the
corner of my eye, I spotted Alton Giles sidling toward me.

"Excuse me, Givens, could I have a word with you?"

"Sure. What do you want to have a *word* about?" I couldn't help mocking him. He was a capable, some might say even gifted trial lawyer. But he seemed to take genuine pleasure in convincing normally compassionate human beings to callously turn their backs on widows and orphans.

"Oh come on, Givens," he said, "I was confident Judge Loring wouldn't allow your damage proof, especially when you had the nerve to liken Thrasher to Browning-Ferris in its glory days. And I'm still certain your damage model will never pass muster in the Court of Appeals. That is, if it ever gets there. Just as I know the so-called contract you're suing on will never be construed as allowing Thrasher Industries unlimited access to my client's land-fill."

"So, you want me to non-suit or what?"

"That would be wise, Givens. But I don't imagine your Mr Thrasher would allow it. To put it plainly, my client has given instructions to see if we can find our way to settle this matter before it goes any further."

So. They'd finally had enough. Getting our damages in slick as snot must have done the trick. Instead of continuing to try to piss Giles off, I said, "Sure, I guess we can talk. By the way, that argument you just made for directed verdict? That was nice."

A few hours later—by then it was Allie and Andy who'd come to agreement—I strode into William Thrasher's conference room for what to my immense pleasure would be the last of our end-of-the-day strategy sessions. I couldn't help being just a little bit smug. I carried victory in my pocket.

I briefed Thrasher and produced the settlement memorandum. He read it carefully, took out his pen and was ready to sign. But then, he hesitated. He looked up at me and asked, "What do you think, Andy? Should I take it?"

What did he mean? The offer was for sixteen million dollars, plus unlimited access to the McCarty Drive land-fill

until the city opened its own new solid waste facility. All I
wanted was to have the obnoxious little Pig-Boy out of my
sight forever. Call Monica. Tell her the good news. Go out
and celebrate, then go home and copulate like sex-starved
rabbits.

"Yes sir," I said, "the offer is very fair. It gives you
virtually everything you wanted to achieve going in."

Thrasher frowned and gave me one of his patented stares
of disappointment. *Jesus. Not Again.*

"Now, Andy, let me see if I understand. You come in here
and expect me to take a little over a measly ten mil', that's of
course *after* your firm's taken its share, and you think I'm
gonna fall for this crap when I'm on the lip of the god-
damned cup with really big money just a half a roll away?
What do you think I am? Some kind of fool?"

As a matter of fact, I did. But I didn't say so. Instead, I
tried to explain the advantages of taking the offer on the
table. Thrasher glared at me with angry, beady eyes and
interrupted. "Givens, I've heard enough of your gutless talk.
You go back and tell that sorry piece of shit, Alton Giles, he
can kiss my ass. And Andy, if you think I'm gonna be
suckered into settling this lawsuit for a penny less that forty-
million, then, son, you can pucker up and kiss it too."

When I called Giles and told him the news, he acted more
than just a little bit startled. But he recovered nicely, returned
to his usual arrogant self, and said he'd see me in court.

The jurors finally seated, Judge Loring rapped his gavel,
quieting the murmurs behind us in the gallery and snapping
my attention back to the present. The old boy was more alert
in the morning. He actually appeared to be awake. He leaned
forward and swiveled his chair to face the jury. Frowning
and peering down over the tops of wire-framed glasses
perched on his thin beak of a nose, he began, "Ladies and
gentlemen, at the close of the plaintiff's evidence, the
defendant is permitted to argue that the case has not been
proved as a matter of law...."

*Something's not right. This can't be happening.*

"This means it will not be necessary for you to hear further evidence…."

*You've got to do something! Get up!*

"I am directing a verdict in favor of the defendant…."

I finally managed to get on my feet, but Loring was already on his way off the bench. "Your honor," I said.

The judge paused, looked down at me, and sighed. "Make your motion in writing counsel."

William Thrasher reached up to grab my elbow, squeezing tightly. "Givens, you stupid son-of-a-bitch! I'll have your balls on a plate! Count on it!"

I don't know why, but I chose that moment to glance over in the direction of Alton Giles. He was standing, arms folded across his chest. Our eyes met and his thin, colorless lips curved in a satisfied smirk.

Thrasher released my arm and balled his pudgy hand into a fist. For a second, I thought he was going to punch me. But then, he shrugged, turned away, and waddled out of the courtroom as fast as his fat, stubby legs would allow. I know I probably should have, but I didn't try to stop him.

## Chapter Two

I walked up the street in the steamy, air-sucking heat of the July morning, attempting to make sense of what had just happened. The noxious odors of bus fumes, rancid cooking grease, and garbage, occasionally mixed with the pungent smell of dried urine crusted on the sidewalks assaulted my senses. A young man dressed in grimy jeans and a dirt-smeared tee shirt stepped from the shadows of what had once been the entrance to a stately office building, long-since abandoned, but soon to be rescued by being converted into another of those downtown lofts that have suddenly become so popular. As he approached, he went into his spiel, saying he needed money to help buy a bus ticket home.

"Oh, where's that?" I asked.

He grinned sheepishly. "Man, you and me, we both knows, I ain't got no where to go. I just want to get somethin' to eat."

More than likely, something to drink. That's what we both really knew. All the same, in keeping with my policy to "just say yes," and avoid the guilt that inevitably came with ignoring our city's homeless, I gave him the change from my pants-pocket, along with a crumpled dollar bill. He took the money, mumbled a quick thank you, and headed toward the little convenience store across the street. I continued on to the office, trying to focus on getting Thrasher's lawsuit back on track. I'd already started a mental list. We'd have to try the whole thing over. That meant more time with Thrasher. No way anyone deserved that punishment.

At our reception room door, I met my secretary. "Elaine, please try to get William Thrasher on the line as soon as you can."

She hesitated, glancing quickly over her shoulder. "Uh, before I do, you ought to know, the partners are waiting. I was on my way to head you off. Whitfield has them pretty stirred up, so it might not be a very good idea for you to see them. At least not for a while."

*Great.* They knew already. For a moment, I considered taking Elaine's advice. Reliving the abortion that had just taken place at the courthouse wasn't going to be fun. But my partners had to be worried. We had a hell of a lot riding on Thrasher's lawsuit. They at least deserved an explanation.

When I opened the door to our main conference room, Del Wallace turned to me and smiled. He was a diminutive man, always had a hint of a smile at the corner of his mouth and a mischievous sparkle shining in his eyes. My best friend at the firm.

"We're glad you got back so fast, Andy. We heard what happened."

I smiled at Del and nodded to the others. Then I took a seat across from Fred Whitfield and briefed them on everything. Starting with the juicy settlement Thrasher had rejected the night before, and ending with a quick and dirty analysis of how to get the case against Waste Disposal Systems reinstated.

Whitfield, who was the head of our litigation section, a fact he made sure I never forgot, scowled at me. "Damn it, Andy, this is awfully hard to understand. How can something like this happen? After all the resources we've let you throw at this dog? Directed verdicts aren't easy to overturn. I guess you realize what this might mean, don't you?"

I attempted an engaging smile and tried to play it straight with Whitfield—a real prick of the first order. "No, what?"

Whitfield's face turned purple. "Financial disaster for all of us! That's what!" he bellowed.

"Gee, Fred, thanks for the kind words of encouragement."

He continued to glare at me, the back of his neck now hot enough to fry an egg. "Frankly, I don't care about your

feelings," he said. "What I want to know is what do you
suggest should be done about your draws for the past year?
We've carried you on this Thrasher piece of bull-shit, and
against my better judgment, you know that."

Whitfield seizing the opportunity to inflict as much
damage as he could came as no real surprise. I'd often
wondered how the two of us ever wound up in a partnership
together. To Fred, the practice of law was nothing more than
a business. If someone could afford the firm's fee, Fred
would enthusiastically and capably represent that person's
interests. But woe unto the prospective client whose financial
ability was lacking. Fred regarded people of that ilk with the
detached eye of a scientist observing under his microscope a
species of a wholly unspectacular lower-life form, and would
dispassionately send such a supplicant off to handle his
problem as best he could. Without Fred's able assistance.

On the other hand, I guess I've always thought that being
a lawyer carries with it certain responsibilities. In other
words, times come when some helpless soul really does need
the service of an attorney, but has no way to pay for it. I've
never been able to turn my back.

To say that Whitfield's viewpoint was more in tune with
those of our fellow-partners would be a gross
understatement. I was more or less tolerated by most of them
because of the influence of Steve Golden—the founder of
our firm. His original partners were long-departed, most of
them in fact were dead, leaving Golden, at age seventy-
seven, in partnership with a bunch of self-centered baby
boomers. He often commented on my attitude, saying he
found it refreshing. Whenever I heard him make such a
statement, I felt a warm tingle of appreciation. I'm pretty
sure Steve's words made the rest of my partners cringe.

Del Wallace tried to head Whitfield off, reminding
everyone how we'd voted to take Thrasher's case on a
contingency, and how I'd kept the partnership advised of the
status of the lawsuit throughout its progress, just as I was

supposed to. But Whitfield sensed blood in the water and continued his attack.

"Del, we know how you and Givens are friends, but nothing you or anybody else can say changes the fact. If this case had been properly handled, we wouldn't be in this mess."

"Wait just a minute!" I shouted, feeling my face go suddenly hot. "We'll get this turned around! I promise!"

Steve Golden had been sitting at the far end of the table, well out of the line of fire in a roomful of angry lawyers. A tall, slender man with only a thin fringe of white hair ringing his otherwise bald head, he stood to get everyone's attention. His dark, three-piece suit swallowed him, causing him to appear like somebody's out-of-touch grandfather.

"Andy, I'm afraid we can't be sure of what might happen. Billy Thrasher called me twenty minutes ago. I waited until you arrived to tell everyone. The firm no longer represents Thrasher Industries. We've been discharged. He's sending someone over to pick up the file." Golden paused, looking down, clutching the edge of the table, his knuckles turning white from gripping so tightly in his effort to steady himself. He looked up again, his eyes red and damp. Voice cracking, he said, "I also have to tell you something else that's about to occur. Thrasher Industries will be filing a malpractice lawsuit against the firm."

Everyone groaned in unison. Whitfield wagged a meaty finger in my face.

"Well, I told you. Here it is. I knew we never had any business taking this sort of case on a contingent fee. Givens, we'd be a lot better off if you were someplace else."

Several of the others nodded. My gut was rapidly twisting into a knot, but before things had a chance to turn uglier, Del cut the meeting off, citing how removal of a partner required a recommendation from the firm's management committee.

I trudged back to my office, feeling the stares of secretaries and clerks whose work areas were closest to the long corridor. Del who'd trailed behind, caught up outside my door.

"Buy you lunch?" he offered, displaying his friendliest smile.

"Thanks, but I don't have much of an appetite."

Del nodded. "Well, I just want you to know, I realize you did as good a job as anybody could on that trial. If you'd had Thrasher's father for a client instead of the arrogant ass you wound up with, things would've been a lot different."

The truth of the matter was, Del didn't have the barest notion of what was involved in trial practice. He probably hadn't been inside a courtroom for years.

"I'm afraid Thrasher didn't have anything to do with the judge's decision. He just blew it."

Del looked at me, discomfort glimmering at the corners of his normally cheerful green eyes. "Yeah, if you say so," he allowed.

"Steve was pretty upset."

"Yeah. But not with you. It's just the crazy way things have turned out. He represented William Thrasher, Sr. for years. And they were close friends too. For such a good client, especially one that was founded by a friend, to be planning on filing a malpractice case. That's gotta be a hard one for the old man to take."

I didn't know what to say, so I just nodded and quietly closed the door. After spending the next couple of hours sitting there feeling sorry for myself, I told Elaine I was going home.

On the way out, I met the messenger from Thrasher's office. A young fellow with dreams of going to law school some day, he usually took every available chance to speak with me. This time, he avoided eye contact as he told our receptionist he'd come to pick up a case file. I told Kathy to make sure we had him sign a receipt.

At home, I stopped by the corner of the garage to pick up Ivory. Monica found him one morning hungrily attempting to find a way to pull one of the koi from her lily pond. She sure was stubborn about those fish—kept replacing them time and time again, only to see each fresh batch become another in a long line of late-night snacks for the neighborhood's marauding raccoons. And we never understood why Ivory picked me. After all, Monica was the one who fed him that first time. But from day one, he followed me like a puppy, making his decision clear. He was my cat. I put him down and found a half-full bottle of fume blanc in the refrigerator, poured a glass and headed to the sun-room. A pleasant little spot the previous owners had converted from a back porch into an extra room. I'd claimed it as my at-home office.

Ivory hopped effortlessly onto the top of the desk. I turned on the CD player, selecting an old Jackson Browne recording, *Running On Empty*. I adjusted the volume to just short of what would result in a noise disturbance citation from the West U. cops, removed my cat from the desk, and gazed out the window. Monica had apparently been to the nursery. With the Thrasher trial occupying all of my time, I hadn't noticed. Large clay pots filled with bright pink geraniums surrounded the fountain in the center of the courtyard that served to divide our house into two sections: the 'main' house and 'mother-in-law's suite', so named by the folks who'd built the addition. Water bubbled from the fountain and cascaded over the edges of the circular catch-basins beneath the spout. Monica must have forgotten to shut it off. I always tried to remember to check. The return line had a nasty tendency to fill with debris. If it clogged completely, a burned out pump wasn't far behind.

Then I noticed, across the way, a curtain being closed in mother-in-law's bedroom, causing a chill to run down my spine. I'm normally a cautious guy, and ordinarily would've called 911 to summon the police. But the day's events prompted a bolder approach. I eased through the dining and living rooms to the entryway into the addition, inched open the door, and crept across mother-in-law's living room, keeping an eye on the sliding glass door to the bedroom, which was in plain view through the picture window running across the back of the house.

Rounding the corner, I entered the kitchenette. The door to the bedroom opened a crack.

"Who's there?" I said.

The door opened a few inches more. My wife eased out, a bed sheet wrapped around her like a toga. She saw me and gasped, then stared at the floor.

Monica finally looked at me, biting her lower lip. "Andy..." she started, then stopped, one delicate hand clenching the door knob, the free one trembling.

"What's going on?"

She continued to stand in place, remaining speechless. Finally, it dawned on me. She was blocking the door.

"Who's in there?" I asked, attempting to keep my voice under control.

"Andy," she said, her own voice barely above a whisper, "I'm so sorry. This isn't how I wanted you to find out." She began to sob, tears flowing down her cheeks, but still, she held fast to the doorknob. "His name is Joseph," she finally managed to say.

I shouted, "Joseph who? Who's the son-of-a-bitch hiding behind that door?"

Monica wiped her eyes with a corner of the sheet and sucked in a deep breath. I moved to push past her and she screamed, "Pudge, he's coming! Hurry!"

So, the skunk was out of the box. Joseph "Pudge" Hartson, my wife's boss and the top-gun trial lawyer at Marshon & Davis.

I pulled her hand away from the door. She reached up, grabbing at me, ripping my shirt collar. I threw open the door. The room was empty. The sliding glass door open, the bed rumpled, a tell-tale wet stain on the bottom sheet. An empty bottle of Tattinger's stood on the bedside table flanked by two champagne flutes, both almost empty.

Monica eased past and sat on the edge of the bed. She was crying hard now, tears streamed down her face.

All I could do was stare at her. Finally I said, "How could you do this?"

She shook her head, wisps of blond hair floating around her face. "God, I wanted to tell you a long time ago. But with everything you've had going on it didn't seem fair."

"You call this fair? You and your boss right here in *our* house?"

Monica continued to sob. "Okay. This was wrong, but it's not all my fault. If you'd managed just a little time for us, instead of devoting every waking moment to those damn cases, maybe, hell, I don't know. But maybe it wouldn't have come to this. We weren't always like this. But you've put me last for as long as I remember. And, Andy, I finally got mad."

I shook my head. This couldn't be happening.

"I guess we have a lot to talk about," I said, the words sounding completely dumb, as if spoken by a third-rate actor in some tedious soap-opera.

She looked up at me, her normally bright blue eyes puffy and red. "I can't talk now. Let's take some time. After we've had a chance to think, then, maybe…."

I started to protest, but she cut me off, her jaw clenched resolutely. There would be no arguing with her. "All right," I said. "I'll go. I'll be at the Cornwall. When you're ready, let me know."

Monica didn't reply. She just sat there, stiff as a statue, her gaze fixed on the carpet.

Once out the door, part of me immediately wanted to return, to let her know I still loved her, no matter what had happened. But another part was beginning to feel the hurt and the humiliation of knowing she'd found it necessary to take up with another man. And of all people, Pudge Hartson. The sorry bastard.

Suddenly, the two most important aspect of my life were in jeopardy. Monica, she was the very center of everything. The perfect woman men dream about finding but never do. Tall, willowy, and graceful, long, silk-soft hair, honey streaked to hide the tattles of grayshe was afraid might appear. An inviting mouth full of bleached-white teeth. Sparkling, deep blue eyes. A cute button of a nose. Her finely-tuned sense of humor, intelligence, and, most of all, her inate ability to share her thoughts and dreams and to encourage me to do the same. I couldn't imagine life without her.

And then there was the firm to think about too. Whitfield had been serious at the partners' meeting. After achieving what I'd always wanted—to be a successful member of a well-regarded law firm—I was suddenly faced with the unsettling realization that my position there wasn't at all secure.

At the heart of it all was William Thrasher. When I took him on, I viewed his case as a wonderful feather in my cap. What I'd always hoped for—a chance to join the ranks of the city's top trial lawyers. But I hadn't anticipated how demanding my new client would be. And I never considered what losing his case might mean.

Downtown, I parked in the garage connected to our office and walked to the hotel. A nagging voice kept saying, *Go back. Tell her we can work this out.* But I ignored it. I didn't know the magnitude, or the details, but I knew life was about to take a dramatic, unalterable change.

# Chapter Three

The idea to go to the Cornwall Hotel was probably a subconscious dig at Monica. The place was a favorite of hers. With only fifty guest rooms, it was unique for an up-scale Houston hotel. Bucking the trend of the proto-typical Texan—wanting everything bigger—the owners of the Cornwall were doing quite well, managing to create in the heart of town an atmosphere similar to that of an intimate European hotel. Located just blocks from our office, it provided the perfect setting for client lunches, after-work drinks with colleagues, or with Monica and our friends following opera and theatre performances. I unquestioningly preferred its warmth and charm to the neo-plastic environments of the new downtown clubs that have sprung up like weeds in an untended flower bed to dominate the city's after-hours social landscape.

The hotel was fully booked. But since I was recognized as a loyal regular, the manager at the check-in desk interceded and gave me one of the suites on the top floor. He even gave it to me at a regular room rate. Lucky me.

Up in the room, I tried to decide what to do. No matter what Monica had done, I wanted to save our marriage. But how? The more I thought about her liason with Joseph Hartson, the less I knew where to even begin. Call her in the morning? And say what? Go see Hartson? Demand that he leave my wife alone? Threaten to choke the life out of the little bastard? I didn't have a clue.

And then there was William Thrasher. Convincing Pig-Boy to forget his asinine idea of pursuing a malpractice lawsuit was going to be a tall order. But at least that was a problem I *could* do something to solve.

I hurried to my office where the security guard in the lobby stopped me, pointing to the large wall clock overhead that had just turned seven. Though I was only running up for a file, he insisted I had to sign the after-hours security sheet.

Once upstairs, I quickly located the trial book put together for the Thrasher case, and flipped through to the section containing copies of the reported decisions supporting our requested jury instructions. They'd provide a good place to start the job of convincing Judge Loring how the issues in our lawsuit involved questions of fact that had to be determined by the jury and not the judge.

I knew I was right, but really didn't know how Loring would react. In fact, I didn't know much about the man at all. When our case reached the top of the trial docket, the regular judge in our court was off on vacation. Otto Loring, an elderly retired judge from way out in El Paso, was assigned to fill in. Under most circumstances, I'd never risk trying an important case such as Thrasher's with an unfamiliar visiting judge. But Thrasher Industries was is dire financial straits. We didn't have the luxury of passing up the chance to get our case to trial. That decision was one of the few things upon which my pig-headed client and I had been able to agree.

I tucked the notebook under my arm and switched off the light. In the hallway, Steve Golden shuffled toward me. He spent virtually all of his waking hours prowling around our offices. Though he no longer practiced much law, preferring to leave that activity to younger, clearer thinking minds, he was still totally devoted to the firm—*his* firm.

As he came closer, he waved and said, "Oh, Andy, it's you. At first I thought you were Whitfield." He smiled and continued, "I don't suppose you appreciate me mistaking you for Fred right about now, do you?"

He was right. I didn't. Not then or ever.

He said, "Fred asked to meet after he finished a conference over at Jacob Hardy's."

Hardy headed an investment banking group the firm sometimes worked with when helping energy clients who needed to raise capital. Whitfield didn't do transactional work, but Hardy was his next-door neighbor, so whenever Jacob called, he tried to pretend he was an expert corporate lawyer. We tried to make sure Whitfield always had a competent associate along for those sorts of meetings.

"Andy, maybe we should talk about this situation with Billy Thrasher. I'm sure that's what Fred has on his mind. He's worried about that directed verdict, and I have to say, I am too. That boy has always been impulsive. His dad used to say he was impossible to control. If Fred is right when he says the odds are against us getting a new trial, well, this has all the ingredients for becoming a real disaster."

"Steve, I can reason with the man. Convince him to re-hire us and get his case reinstated. I know I can."

Golden arched his eyebrows. "Maybe you're right. But if you aren't—the publicity of a malpractice suit. I never thought I'd live to see the day when we'd wind up in something like this."

"All I can say is Judge Loring made a serious mistake. I should have been able to make him recognize it on the spot, but he wouldn't even let me make a record. I'll go to work first thing tomorrow to convince Thrasher."

Golden shook his head. "Fred isn't quite as confident as you about the judge being mistaken." He paused, clenching his jaw. "Even if he's wrong and we can't make him see it, the verdict will go up on appeal. Knowing Thrasher the way I do, he'll twist our tail hard. He's not his father, not by a long shot. But the community still respects his name. He can get just about anything he wants published in the *Chronicle*. I can just imagine all the publicity this will generate. And I'll wish more than ever that I'd joined Margaret a long time before now."

I had nothing but respect for Steve Golden. After all, the man was my mentor. Still, what he said made my blood boil.

Whitfield wasn't the one who'd tried Thrasher's lawsuit. I was. Now, here that pompous bag of hot air was, acting like the world's biggest expert. And Golden was listening to him instead of me. I sure as hell wasn't going to wait around to take more grief from that jerk. I told Golden, if they wanted to talk after Fred got back, to call me at the Cornwall. That's where I'd be for a while.

Steve didn't seem to be listening. He stared vacantly into the distance. So I left him there, standing in the darkening hallway.

Back at the hotel, I thumbed through the trial book and marked the cases that needed review. I ordered room service—a steak sandwich and a small carafe of wine. But by the time it came, my appetite was gone. I drank most of the wine and attempted to study the cases from the trial book. No matter how hard I tried to concentrate, I couldn't stay focused. I kept seeing Monica sitting on the bed in the guest room, telling me about her affair with Joseph Hartson. From that scene, my mind raced back to the fiasco in the courtroom and on to the meeting with my partners. When I found myself reading the same paragraph for the third time and still not knowing what it said, I went to the window and pulled open the drapes. Lightning flickered on the skyline announcing an approaching thunderstorm. I forgot about going out and switched on the TV. As always, that did the trick. I fell asleep right there on the sofa.

# Chapter Four

I woke with the phone ringing. The drapes were closed, the room pitch black. The digital clock, glowing on the bedside table read 8:15. It had to be Monica. I answered, trying to sound calm.

"Andy," my secretary said, "I called your house. Uh, Monica told me where I might reach you. I'm sorry to have to call, but this is important. On the way to work I heard on the radio, Bill Thrasher was found in his office this morning. And, Andy, he's dead! He was beaten to death! It's so awful!"

My stress circuits went on serious overload. "Elaine, are you sure?"

"Yes. Del's already checked. It's Thrasher all right. Andy, Del's asking about you. He wants to see you."

"Tell him I'm on my way."

"There's one more thing. I just took a call for you from a lieutenant from the police, I don't remember his name, but I have it written down out at my desk. He wanted to know if I knew where you were and said he wanted to meet with you right away."

"Call him back and tell him I'll be in the office by nine. Tell Del the same."

A quick glance in the mirror said I couldn't spend the day in the clothes I'd just worn as pajamas. I called Elaine and asked her to get the travel bag from my office closet and bring it to the hotel. Then I called the bell captain and ordered shaving supplies, a toothbrush, and toothpaste. When the bell hop knocked on the door, I handed him my rumpled clothes and asked to have them cleaned.

"What about the shirt?" he asked, holding it up to display a badly torn collar.

I shrugged and said, "Do the best you can."

I shaved and showered and, waiting for Elaine, called Monica at her office. Her secretary said she wasn't in. A call home got our answering machine. "Hi, Monica and I can't come to the phone right now," I said. "Leave a message and one of us will return your call as soon as we can," she said. Such a happy couple.

Replaying the past twenty-four hours, I attempted to make a mental list of priorities: Monica having an affair with Joseph Hartson, my partners' reaction to what happened with the Thrasher case and the threat of malpractice, and now, to top it all, Thrasher turning up dead and the police wanting to talk to me. How could I assign priorities to those catastrophes? Throw in being in the path of a force-five hurricane and the list would be complete.

There was a soft knock on the door. Wrapping a towel around my waist, I opened it for Elaine. She handed the travel bag to me as I self-consciously attempted to keep the door between us. Grabbing the bag, I retreated to the bedroom to get dressed. I tried to decide how to handle the police and my partners. And there was Monica to consider too. I needed to contact her more than ever, but, for the time being, that wouldn't be possible. It dawned on me, I was doing what my wife said: putting her on the back burner. Maybe she was right. Maybe I did always put her last.


When we got to the office, two men were in the reception room. One sat in the middle of the sofa across from the receptionist's station. He wore glasses and pretended to read a magazine while peering over the top of his oval wire frames, ogling the woman behind the desk. Kathy was accustomed to having men stare at her and, as usual, did a good job of ignoring the lumpish, balding man. The other fellow stood next to the door leading into our offices. He studied a large framed photograph of a brightly-painted red door set into the middle of a dirty-yellow stucco wall.

"That's good, isn't it?" I asked.

He turned, smiled, and said, "It sure is. I took a course at Rice a couple of years ago. It was taught by the guy who did this."

The man was tall. We looked directly into each other's eyes, making him about six-three or four. He was abnormally thin, had short-cropped steel-gray hair and a long, sad-looking oval face. His pale-white complexion indicated he was either just recovering from a major illness or he didn't get outside much. I guessed he was in his early forties, meaning he had a few years on me.

"Mr Givens," Kathy said, "these gentlemen have been waiting to see you, Lieutenant Puryear and Detective Springer."

"Rupert Puryear," the tall one introduced himself. Nodding toward the sofa, he said, "That's Joe Springer." Springer grinned, a gap-toothed smile. Puryear continued, "I imagine you know about William Thrasher."

"Yes, Elaine, oh, I'm sorry, this is my secretary, Elaine Turner. Miss Turner told me. Please, gentlemen, come on in."

I led them into my office and asked Elaine to take coffee orders. Detective Springer declined. Lieutenant Puryear asked for double cream and sugar. As Elaine left, Del waved at me from the secretary's station. "Excuse me, this will take just a minute," I said, heading to the door.

Del led the way to a small interior conference room across from my office. I'd used it as my war room during the Thrasher trial. The boxes containing our trial preparation materials had already been removed. Fred Whitfield was seated at the now-empty conference table.

Del closed the door, motioned me to sit, and said, "Andy, we hope you understand how concerned we are. Those guys from HPD told me they'll want to interview others in the firm. Naturally, I told them we'll cooperate. But Fred and I thought maybe we should visit before you have your meeting."

"Okay. What is it?"

Del began, "Well, Andy—"

"Come on!" Whitfield interrupted, "Surely you realize there's some reason, apart from idle curiosity, for the police to come asking for you on the morning your former client is discovered murdered in his office."

"As a matter of fact, Fred, I don't. Maybe they think I can help, but I don't see how."

Del leaned forward, his eyes slanting warily in the direction of my office where the officers waited. "Uh, Andy, have you thought about meeting with those guys without another lawyer being present?"

I frowned. "Del, you don't actually think I'm involved with this do you?"

"Of course not," he answered. "It's just that we thought, well, you know, you never can tell where something like this might go. We could probably get Randle Hughes to come over, that is, if you think it might be a good idea."

I shook my head. "Guys, this is real serious, I know that, and believe me, I'm just as shocked as anybody to hear about Thrasher. But I don't see how having Randle come over is going to help."

"I honestly don't know what to think," Whitfield said. "But I do know one thing. We can't afford another problem right now, especially not from you. I think you'd better listen to us, Andy."

I gave Whitfield an icy stare. The dumb-ass. "Look, if that's the way you feel, I'll make sure you don't have another problem, period, from me, or anybody else."

Whitfield, a big bear of a man, leaped to his feet and glared at me. I was a few inches taller than Fred, but he outweighed me by a good forty pounds. Just the same, I pushed my chair back.

Whitfield shouted, "So now you're threatening me, are you? If I was in your shoes, I'd be very careful about making threats!"

"Hold it, both of you," Del said. "This isn't doing any good. Andy, have you decided? What do you want to do?"

What I wanted was to whip Whitfield's ass. But Del was right. That wouldn't help. As calmly as I could, I reminded them of the people waiting in my office. Del got us to agree to get together again just as soon as my meeting was over. By that time, maybe Steve Golden would be in.

Whitfield scowled and said, "Givens, you're ruining this law firm and the reputations of everyone in it. I hope you're satisfied."

But before I could respond, he was out the door, lumbering up the hall.

I paused at my office door and looked out the window. The haze almost completely blocked the view of the street, thirty-two stories below. As I eased into the chair behind my desk, Lieutenant Puryear said, "Mr Givens, we need to learn what you might know about why someone wanted to kill William Thrasher."

"I'm not sure I can help. The only people I met when I worked with him were his employees. He wasn't exactly popular with them, but I can't think of seeing anything to indicate someone wanted to kill the man."

Springer asked, "Were either Thrasher or his company in financial trouble?"

I shook my head. "I'm afraid I can't answer that. It's not that I don't want to, it's just that you're getting into an area that's covered by attorney-client privilege. I can't divulge that kind of information, unless authorized by a representative of the company."

"Wait a minute," Springer said. "You were fired by Thrasher yesterday morning right after you lost a big lawsuit you were trying for his company."

"Yes, " I said, "but the attorney-client privilege survives formal representation of a client. I still can't disclose privileged information unless the client authorizes it."

Springer pursed his fleshy lips and gave me a hard stare. "We'll take that up with the DA," he promised.

Lieutenant Puryear glared disapprovingly at Springer, then said, "Mr Givens, we've heard how Bill Thrasher wasn't the world's most-popular person, and we know you worked with him pretty closely for the past several months. So why don't you let us do our job and tell us who the people were who you met when you were out there working on that lawsuit?"

We spent the next hour going over my list of contacts at Thrasher Industries. For each person I listed, Puryear and Springer probed to determine what I knew about that individual's relationship with Thrasher. Springer took what appeared to be detailed notes. But if he found the exercise as fruitless as I did, he could have just as well been writing a letter to his girlfriend.

Finally, I put a stop to the music. "Gentlemen, any information I've got is way too general to do any good. If you come up with anything specific on any of these people, don't you think that would be a better time?"

Springer grinned. "You might be right. Why don't we change the subject. Like, where were you last night, say, between ten o'clock and three o'clock this morning?"

I told them about spending the night at the Cornwall, but didn't volunteer my reason. Hopefully, we wouldn't have to get into the situation with Monica.

Springer asked if I had been alone at the hotel. When I said yes, he gave Puryear a quick glance. Neither officer asked why I'd spent the night in a hotel just a few miles from home. I wasn't an expert in conducting criminal investigations, but thought they should have asked the question and wondered why they hadn't.

They left and I called Monica again. Same run around. She wasn't in, and her secretary didn't know when to expect her back, nor did she know where Monica could be reached. Likely story. Lucy was a tough-as-nails long-timer, who got off on the power she wielded as gate keeper for the venerable Marshon & Davis. I'd bet my life's savings she always knew *exactly* where Monica was, unless, of course, she was out diddling Pudge Hartson.

Although I wanted another encounter with my buddy Fred Whitfield about as much as I wanted a heart attack, I buzzed Elaine and asked her to let Del know I was ready.


When we moved into our offices a few years ago, all of the partners used their build-out allowances to create contemporary, functional work areas. All of us, that is, except for Steve Golden. His office was an anachronism. Mahogany paneling from floor to ceiling. Oil paintings of his heroes, Thomas Jefferson, Andrew Jackson, and Sam Houston hung on the walls. A dark-stained oak floor, covered by an enormous wine-red and royal-blue Tabriz. A huge, burled-oak partners desk, two matching armoires, one converted into a bookcase that held volumes of early Supreme Court decisions, the other into a liquor cabinet containing an excellent collection of ports, brandies, and Golden's favorite, armagnac. He even had a fake fireplace complete with an ornately sculptured marble mantle-piece. Displayed on top of the mantle were Golden's prize possessions: matched dueling pistols that once belonged to Sam Houston. Chippendale armchairs, a horsehair sofa from the Civil War era, and assorted antique side-tables completed the room's furnishings. The only lighting was provided by table lamps and two polished-brass floor lamps located on opposite ends of heavy, velveteen drapes that remained permanently drawn, as if in denial of the current state of affairs outside the time-warp Golden had created.

Steve was seated behind his desk. In the dim light, I could barely make out Del and Fred standing next to him at either side. That was a bad sign. The managing partners always got on one side of the desk or table or any other sort of barrier that happened to be handy, whenever they wanted to deliver an edict (usually of negative import) to whoever was on the receiving end.

Del wouldn't look at me. Fred was his usual smug self. Steve stared at the papers on his desk. For several moments no one spoke. I wouldn't make it easy for them. They had something to say that I obviously wasn't going to like. Probably they'd decided to let Whitfield take over handling Thrasher's threatened malpractice claim and our part in the investigation of Thrasher's murder. I sat in one of the Chippendales and waited.

Finally, Golden picked up a piece of paper from the stack he had been studying and said, "Andy, I'm very sorry I wasn't here this morning. I arrived shortly after you began your meeting with the police. While you were occupied with that, we, uh, took the opportunity to discuss the Thrasher matter in detail and we reached a decision on a course of action we believe we have to take in light of all of the, uh, circumstances—at least as we presently understand them."

He stopped and looked at me as if he expected me to respond. I stared at him, my eyes suddenly burning.

"Andy," he continued, "I'll make this as brief and to the point as I can. You know me, that's the way I always handle things." He cleared his throat and continued, "The managing partners believe it is in the best interest of the firm to accept your resignation, effective immediately. As I'm certain you know, the Thrasher matter and the resources we devoted to it leave us where our cash position is less than we would prefer. But, we're nevertheless prepared to meet our obligation to you as a withdrawing partner…."

My chest locked in a tightening vice. I struggled to catch my breath, but my lungs wouldn't cooperate. Golden's voice became a distant echo that I was unable to comprehend. First Monica, now my partners. This couldn't be real. I stared at Del. When our eyes finally met, he looked quickly away.

I whispered, "I don't understand how you can do this."

Whitfield smirked. "I'll tell you how," he said. "We took a vote. It's the unanimous decision of your co-managing partners, we'll kick you out if you don't resign. I frankly would prefer to see you expelled. That way, we won't have to pay you as much. But at this stage, Andy, it's entirely up to you. I suppose in all fairness I ought to tell you, if you take this to a vote of the full partnership, I've got the votes. So buddy, either way, you're history."

Golden glared at Whitfield, who gave a contemptuous shrug of his bearish shoulders.

"Andy, I apologize for that," Golden said. "Fred, we agreed I would handle this, so please allow me to do so. It doesn't need to come to expulsion, Andy. We want to help you through this, uh, situation, as much as we can. But we believe it is inappropriate to risk the future of the firm. We have an obligation to our clients and to our employees and their families. I hope you realize, we are very unhappy, but there just isn't any other way."

I suppose he wanted me to say I understood and had no hard feelings. But I just shook my head and stared at the three of them.

Golden was determined to carry on. "I've asked Del to prepare a resignation letter for your signature and our notice to you that we will accept your withdrawal and will continue the firm in the name Golden, Wallace, and Whitfield. As you know, the exchange of those notices will trigger the buy-out clause in our partnership agreement. Accounting is preparing current reports on receivables, work-in-progress, assets, and liabilities. Del will have them to you by the end of the day. That will give us a pretty good idea of the buy-out figure."

I was rapidly becoming numb from shock but could see, trying to change their minds was pointless. The deal was done. I could understand Whitfield. He'd be overjoyed to be rid of me. And I wanted to believe Del's position could be explained by the fact he'd been out-voted. If I got kicked out of the firm instead of leaving voluntarily, I wouldn't receive nearly my fair share of the partnership's assets. But Steve Golden? This wouldn't be happening without his impetus. Did he love his law firm so much that he was prepared to hang me out on the line, just to try to save it? Obviously, the answer was yes.

I stood, feeling dizzy, the inside of my mouth as dry as cooked dirt. Somehow, I managed to ask Del to put the papers in an envelope to be given to my secretary. She'd make sure I got them. Then I left.

Except for one time, many months later, I never went back.

## Chapter Five

I spent the next week at the Cornwall. At first, I was reluctant to go downstairs and risk running into a former partner, someone from Monica's firm, or for that matter, anyone from the legal community, all of whom I was convinced saw me as that dumb-ass who'd lost his case on a directed verdict, was fired by his client, and was now suspected of committing murder in retaliation. But when cabin fever finally got the best of me, after checking with Paul, the bartender who worked the night shift, I ventured down late one evening. Just as he'd said, the place was almost empty. None of the regulars were there, just a couple of out-of-towners. Paul smiled when he saw me and served up a complimentary Remy Martin. He served refills to his other customers seated at the far end of the bar, then returned.

"Andy, I guess you should know, you've been quite a topic of conversation in here."

"Really, what do you mean?"

"Oh, some of your fellow counselors at law have been having themselves a high old time, making bets on when you'd come out of that room upstairs. Apparently, word is out all over town that you've been holed up here."

"Come on, Paul, why would anyone be interested in something as silly as that?"

He grinned. "Beats me. But there's no telling what a bunch of ambulance chasers will come up with to amuse themselves. Maybe they're interested because they figure you're in a fix over that Thrasher guy. You know, the one you used to represent and who now happens to be deader than a post?"

"What's the smart money say?"

He laughed and said, "Never."

When Paul got a look at the dark scowl that broke out on my face, he suddenly found it necessary to busy himself placing glasses in the overhead rack. I finished my drink, and just to show there were no hard feelings, dropped a generous tip on the counter.

Paul's comments had been intended as a joke, but he made a good point. I couldn't hide forever. The next afternoon, I sat at the bar waiting for the regulars to come in. Several folks I knew stopped by and said hello. No one from my old firm. No one from Marshon & Davis. No mention was made about the situation with Bill Thrasher. And of course, not a word about the bets.

That first week, I called Monica repeatedly. The message on our answering machine had been changed. No more cheerful couple, just "You have reached 713-850-1722. Leave a message at the tone and your call will be returned as soon as possible." None of mine were. Her secretary consistently maintained she was "out" and she never seemed to know when Monica might be "in". When I asked if she knew I had been trying to reach her, I got a terse "yes." The ultimate brush off.

It wasn't as if she didn't know where to find me. A clerk from her firm delivered my largest suitcase to the hotel. It was filled with enough of my clothes to permit a prolonged, perhaps even permanent, stay. I've got a thick skull, but the message was beginning to sink in.

The clincher came when Sharon Fielder, one of our mutual lawyer friends, called to say that Monica wanted her to act as her attorney in our divorce. Sharon said she'd do it, only if I said it was okay. I told her it was. After all, what are friends for? As soon as I consented, Sharon dropped her little-miss-friendly act and asked if I would agree to waive formal service of the divorce petition. My stomach went queasy, but I said yes, and she delivered the papers to me at my new temporary office, the bar at the Cornwall. While she was there, I informed her of my 'resignation' from Golden - Wallace and told her about the buy-out agreement, which, under the circumstances, Monica needed to approve. Sharon said Monica wanted us each to sign a disclaimer of any interest in the other's practice. Since she was still an associate at her firm, the offer was a generous gesture on Monica's part. Or maybe it was just her conscience bothering her. Whatever her reason, I agreed and told Sharon to prepare the papers.

Not being able to get through to my wife, and being forced to communicate with her though her lawyer was wholly frustrating. Maybe that was why, after our meeting, I did something down-right dumb. I called Joseph Hartson.

He asked, "Mr Givens, what can I do for you?"

"What you can do Hartson, is stay away from my wife!"

My display of hysteria was met by stony silence. Did he know who I was? My wife was still Monica Bishop at her firm. She'd kept her maiden name for her work, thinking a change would cause too much confusion. Hartson either finally made the connection or figured out what he wanted to say. "Now, Givens, let's don't be ridiculous. Monica is a mature adult. She can make up her own mind who she wants to see, and who she doesn't."

The audacity. "Look!" I shouted, "you're one lucky son-of-a-bitch! If you'd had the courage to face me instead of sneaking out a window, you'd be dead meat right now! I'm warning you, leave my wife alone, Hartson, or I'll kill you!"

Okay, so this was definitely not the thing to say. But that's what I said, and even though the words sounded silly as hell, at the time I really meant them.

Hartson had the good sense not to reply. He simply hung up, leaving me feeling like the world's biggest dumb-ass.

The old saying about things coming in threes? Well, that same afternoon Rupert Puryear showed up. When he sauntered into the hotel bar where I'd remained, with the full intention of getting drunk, as fast as possible, he found me on my second double Tanqueray.

"Mind if I join you?" he asked.

Like I had a choice? "Sure, Lieutenant. What're you drinking?"

He sat on the stool next to mine and ordered a glass of Alexander Valley cabernet sauvignon. "I was sorry to hear about you leaving your law firm," he said.

I shrugged. "These things happen."

Paul brought him his wine. Puryear swirled it in the glass, breathed its bouquet and sipped. "This is quite good."

So the man knew something about red wine. Big deal. I was trying as hard as I could not to like him. "How's the Thrasher investigation coming along?" I asked.

"Oh, we're making progress. Slower than I'd like, but that's nothing unusual. I'm the impatient type."

"So you think you'll catch whoever it was who killed him?"

"Oh yeah, Mr Givens, we'll find the killer, you can count on that." He paused and tapped a finger over his glass. He looked slowly up at me and added, "Look, I can appreciate why you're interested, and want you to understand, we don't do this for everybody, but I'll keep you posted, if you want."

I didn't know what to say.

He finished the wine and said, "That was good. If I could afford it, I'd come in here more often." He looked at me with steel-gray eyes, and nodded toward my glass. "Mr Givens," he said, "if you don't mind me saying so, you ought to think about going easy on that stuff. It's been known to make men do some pretty crazy things."

He dropped money on the bar and ambled away. I hadn't had the nerve to ask if they had a suspect. I guess I was too afraid of the answer.

The triple-whammy effect of the preceding day, combined with a pretty good-sized hangover (no, I didn't take the lieutenant's advice), left me hurting, physically and emotionally. About all I seemed capable of was feeling sorry for myself. At noon, Elaine Turner phoned, surprised to find me in my room. She was calling from a pay phone at Foley's, intending to leave a message that she wanted to talk.

Now here was someone I actually wanted to see. Elaine had been in fairly regular contact with Monica. Maybe she wanted to let me know how my wife had come to her senses and wanted me to come home.

We agreed on seven o'clock at the River Cafe, a popular restaurant and bar down in Montrose.

I spotted Elaine at one of the umbrella-covered tables on the front patio. She was hard to miss. Wearing a white sundress that perfectly displayed her tanned, well-shaped body, her jet-black shoulder-length hair dancing in a cooling breeze that was bringing a merciful end to another sweltering summer day, the woman belonged on the cover of a fashion magazine.

She was drinking Pelligrino with a lemon twist. She gave me what I interpreted as a distinctly disapproving look when I ordered my twist to be accompanied by a double Tanqueray on the rocks.

After my drink arrived, we touched glasses. "Have you spoken to Monica lately?" I asked.

Elaine glanced quickly away. "Uh, yes, I have."

"Well, come on then, what did she say?"

She frowned. "Andy, you really don't want to hear what Monica's been saying these days."

"Of course I do. Why wouldn't I?"

"You just wouldn't, okay?"

So. There wasn't going to be news of Monica wanting me back. "I'm sorry," I said. "This situation, it's pretty hard to deal with."

Elaine touched my arm. "Sure it is. Believe me, I understand. But Andy, all you can do is let everything work its way through."

"I don't understand. What do you mean?"

"This might not make much sense, but believe it or not, Monica feels terribly hurt, maybe even betrayed by what she sees as a whole lot of indifference on your part. She sees what she's doing as totally justified."

She was right. It didn't make sense. "You mean my wife actually blames *me* for her having an affair with a partner at her firm?"

Elaine nodded. "She told me about Mr Hartson. I don't condone what she's done, and she certainly doesn't either, but since you brought it up, I thought you needed to be aware of how she feels. That's all."

"What I don't understand is how can she do this, without even giving us the chance to work things out? Isn't that what you should have the right to expect from the person you've loved and lived with for the last four years?"

Elaine shook her head, causing dark wisps to dance in the breeze. "You've never been through something like this, have you?"

I thought about Martha Jane. "As a matter of fact, I thought I had. But this time, it's different. It came as a total shock."

"Andy, don't you see? Your wife has a heck of a lot of pent up anger and resentment. It simply doesn't make any difference if it's justified or not. In time, she might come to realize it's worthwhile to explore rebuilding your relationship. But you must understand, all she feels at the moment is hurt. And all she wants, at least for now, is to be free to move on with her life."

"I just don't believe it. What on God's green earth have I done?"

"Look, Andy, I told you, this isn't the time to talk about Monica. But if you insist on staying with the subject, you might try to examine what you possibly didn't do."

"Elaine, I still don't know...."

"Let me give you some advice, Andy. No matter how much you want to, trying to determine what to do to get your wife back isn't going to do any good. If she sees value in the relationship, she'll be back. You can count on it. If she doesn't, well, you'll just have to work on convincing yourself things weren't as great as you thought."

I shook my head, not wanting to admit the possibility that the situation was out of my control. "Elaine, I appreciate what you've said, but I'm just not ready to give up."

She pushed a strand of hair away from her tanned forehead. "I didn't say you should give up, but you've got to spend your energy on something more productive than trying to influence your wife's emotions with logic and persuasion. Like I said, maybe you should give some thought to how you acted in the past, and then, if the chance comes, maybe you'll have determined how you might choose to handle certain situations differently. But one thing I'm absolutely certain of is this: you've got to stop wallowing in all of this self-pity. If not for yourself, then realize, you'll never get her back if you allow yourself to fall apart now."

Finally. There was something that made sense. Elaine was only in her mid-twenties, but demonstrated the judgment and maturity of someone twice her age. "I see what you mean," I said. "But I'm not sure how to get over feeling the way I do, and that makes it impossible to do very much about anything."

She took a sip from her drink and looked at me with sparkling emerald eyes. "Well, for starters, what are you doing about your practice? You've gotten quite a few calls from clients who are less than happy you haven't called them back."

I leaned forward. "Yeah. I've been meaning to take care of that."

Elaine stared at me intently. "Andy, forgive me for saying so, but you can't just sit around and do nothing. Do you intend to join another firm or what?"

"I don't imagine there's a lot of interest in somebody facing a major malpractice lawsuit and who's suspected of being a murderer."

She tilted her head and smiled. "You're probably right about the malpractice, but being a cold-blooded killer, isn't that what firms are looking for these days?"

She laughed at her own joke and I joined in. Finding humor in the situation, even if it was of the gallows variety, felt good.

"Actually, I've been thinking about going solo," I said.

Elaine nodded. "I thought that might have crossed your mind. You know, you'll need someone good to run your office, get your work out and keep your books and files."

"Yeah, I guess so. You don't know of anyone like that who might be available do you?"

"As a matter of fact, I do. At least I know she's pretty upset with her boss and she might be looking to make a change."

"Oh, who's that?"

She touched my arm. "Come on, Andy, don't you see I'm sitting here practically begging to come to work for you?"

"Who's the boss that's causing the problems?"

"Mr Whitfield."

I grinned. "That explains everything. I'll probably have to start my own practice just to save you from having to put up with that jerk."

The waiter came and Elaine switched to white wine. I stuck to gin. When I asked her what it was she wanted to talk about, she smiled again.

"I think we just covered it," she said.

The decision to start my own practice was actually pretty easy. For starters, there wasn't any discernable demand for my services. Most lawyers, even the ones who didn't know me from Adam, had heard about Thrasher. If I were Clarence Darrow, they wouldn't be interested in getting involved with that mess.

At least I was in the enviable position of knowing the payments from my old firm would take care of expenses. Truth be known, if not for the money angle, I'm pretty sure most lawyers would prefer to practice on their own. No more office politics. No more having to tolerate partners who turn out to be jerks.

The day after my meeting with Elaine, I called a commercial real estate broker who had a listing on a property that was perfect. Near Hermann Park in an area known as the Binz District, an old two-story brick house on Jackson Avenue, previously occupied by an insurance agency.

The front two rooms, originally the living and dining rooms, became the reception area and a library-conference room. Behind the dining room was a fully modernized kitchen with plenty of cabinet space—ideal for storing office supplies and accommodating a copy machine and document-assembly station. Elaine's secretarial space and our files were set up in what had been a large bedroom on the first floor. My office was in an even larger room that ran across the entire back of the downstairs. On one end we set up my desk and credenza from the old office. On the other, in front of the fireplace that occupied the far wall, we put a work table, guest chairs, a comfortable reading chair, the sofa from downtown, and a floor lamp. Double French doors connected Elaine's work area and my office. A custom-made roman shade over the doors was usually pulled up so we could both enjoy the view of the attractively landscaped backyard, surrounded by a high wooden fence covered with fig ivy and wisteria. The driveway running down the side of the house next to Elaine's office connected the street and a detached garage at the rear of the property. A door from the garage opened into the back yard and a brick walkway wound from there to the back porch leading to my office. The upstairs provided more than ample living space.

A call to Del Wallace ascertained that my old firm would be happy to knock a sufficient amount off of my partnership buy-out to pay for some of their spare office equipment. Del even put me in touch with a bankruptcy trustee buddy of his, who was able to sell an excellent litigation library that formerly belonged to an executive suites for lawyers operation that the trustee was in charge of liquidating. Elaine made arrangements with Sharon Fielder to send movers to Monica's house—I was reluctantly beginning to think of it that way—to pick up the furniture from the sunroom and a spare bedroom.

Less than a week from the day the lease was signed, I had a new office and a new place to live, all rolled into one.

I guess I should have been thrilled. Years earlier, Monica and I shared the dream of someday buying a big old place in a funky neighborhood where we could live and work together. What I'd found would have been perfect. But now, trying to recapture that dream alone left me feeling nothing but profound emptiness and dissatisfaction, just like everything else I'd recently experienced in what I was coming to see as a wholly crummy life.

Although my former partners had been eager to agree on a price for some of their excess equipment, they were less than overjoyed when I called to pick up my case files. Steve was surprisingly cool and flatly refused my request, saying the firm needed to hear from its clients to find out if they wanted their work moved to my new office. I told him I intended to do some contacting of my own. Golden knew my cases involved clients I had generated. Surely he wouldn't try to keep me from continuing to represent them.

A few minutes after my conversation with Steve, Del Wallace called. "Andy, we need to talk about the files you were handling. Steve told me you intend to see if the clients involved will approve a transfer to your office."

"Wait a minute, they're my clients! You know that! What do you expect me to do?"

"Let's not get into an argument about whose clients they are. To tell you the truth, I hadn't even given the question any thought. But I just learned Whitfield has already contacted them and he's gotten most of them to sign new representation agreements with us."

"I'm not going to let him get away with this!"

"Now wait a minute, Andy. I talked to Fred. He believes he was within his rights to contact clients who had fee agreements with our old firm. And let's look at this from the perspective of the clients. Have you given any thought to how much of a problem you might actually have with this Thrasher mess? Believe me, Andy, I don't think you had anything to do with the man getting killed, but apparently there are some folks over at HPD who do."

I didn't like it, not even a little, but saw his point. I told Del I'd hold off on making my calls until I'd examined their new fee agreements. Besides, there were a couple of calls— much more important ones—that I'd put off too long already.

## Chapter Six

I dialed the long-distance number and my father answered. "Hello, Dad," I said.

There was a brief pause, then, "Andy, hi, son. Let me tell your mother who it is so she can get on the other phone. Sarah, it's our boy, pick up the phone!"

Another phone lifted off its cradle and my mother said, "Andy, we've been awfully worried. I know we should have called, but we waited. Your father thought it would be best to talk when you were ready."

So they already knew. That wasn't really surprising. Growing up in a small place like Sandy Creek, Tennessee, a part of each person always belongs to the town. Most of the townsfolk keep up with the ones like me who have moved away. And they don't have to rely on newspapers or television. News concerning one of their own gets back in its own mysterious way. "Mom, Dad, I'm sorry I didn't call sooner. I kept hoping I could get this mess straightened out and spare everybody a lot of worry."

"What do you mean?" my father said. "If we want to worry about you, we will. There's nothing you can do to stop us."

"Oh, Edward," Mom said. "You know what Andy means."

"Son, you must know, we'll help, hell, we've gotta help, any way we can."

"Thanks, that means a lot. And I want you to understand, I haven't done anything wrong."

"Boy, we know that without you having to say so. We raised you didn't we? We aren't worried that you had anything to do with that Thrasher fella. And your Momma will be mad, but I'm going to say it, I never did understand exactly what it was you saw in that wife of yours. I had a sneaking suspicion she'd cause you grief, sooner of later."

So they knew about Monica too. Dad never had really gotten over my break up with Martha Jane. She'd been special to him—went fishing all the time with her father—so what he said I took with a grain of salt. He probably still harbored the hope that someday I'd return to Sandy Creek and get back together with his favorite.

"When do you think you'll have a chance to make it home?" Mom asked.

"Well, I'm not really sure, with everything that's happened. Actually, I was sort of hoping you could come down for Labor Day. That is, unless you're still in contention in the club championships."

"Andy, if I'm still in, I'll forfeit. The way I've been hitting the ball lately, I don't stand to do very well this year anyway. But son, I don't know about your mother. She's been practicing and's determined to take another trophy."

"Ed, will you please? Andy, if you're inviting us down, we accept. That is, if you're sure it won't be too much trouble. I think we can pass on the club matches this year. Give some new flowers a chance to bloom."

"That'd be great," I said. "I think I'll rent a place at Galveston."

"Sounds like fun, son. Just remember, your mother and I, we love you."

"Thanks, Dad. I love you both too."

They told me everything that was happening in Sandy Creek, and I filled them in on where I was living and gave them my new phone number. I promised to keep them posted on developments. The conversation was much easier than I'd expected. It's funny. We spend so much time worrying about problems that turn out not to be problems at all. And in the process we sometimes ignore the things that need our attention the most.

After the call to Tennessee, I phoned Mark Watson. Like many criminal defense lawyers, Mark got his start with the Harris County District Attorney. The last time I saw him was at the Courthouse Club. He'd been giving a spiel to a bunch of us civil trial types, mentioning how he still had friends in the DA's office, so if we ever had a client with a problem, hey, give ol' Mark a call. If any legitimate reason to worry about being a suspect in the Thrasher murder existed, I guessed Mark would know. He wasn't in, so I left a message with his secretary asking him to call back as soon as possible.

When I got off the phone, Elaine was standing in front of my desk. "Lieutenant Puryear is here," she said. "He wants to see you, if you can spare the time."

I had plenty. A lawyer who suddenly finds himself with no clients has lots and lots. After the conversation with Del Wallace, I didn't exactly relish another visit from the police, particularly not until I'd spoken with Mark. Just the same, I couldn't afford to refuse, so I asked Elaine to bring him back.

Puryear went directly to the windows to take in the view of the backyard. After several awkward moments of silence that left me wondering if Puryear wanted to visit with me or had just shown up to consider my house for next Spring's azalea tour, he finally turned and said, "Mr Givens, I was feeling kind of sorry for you, you know, with your moving out of your firm and all, but this set-up sure beats being stuck in one of those glass and steel boxes downtown."

I nodded. "I'm even living upstairs. You may think this is funny, but that's always been something I've wanted to do. Uh, I guess you know, my wife and I have separated."

He folded his long arms across his chest. "Yeah, I heard about that. I'm sorry, too. I lost my wife a few years ago. Cancer. It sure leaves a big hole in your life when it happens."

I came around from behind my desk and sat on the sofa. The lieutenant took one of the chairs at the work table and turned it to face me.

"I'm sorry about your wife," I said.

"Thanks."

"What is it that I can do for you, Lieutenant?"

"Oh, I just happened to be in the neighborhood and thought I'd stop by to see your new digs. I heard from Mr Whitfield how you'd moved out here."

"Now, Lieutenant, I know you're much too busy for a just-drop-in visit." I was beginning to feel like the bad guy in a Columbo episode.

He hesitated, glancing again out the window. "No. Really, there's no reason. I was just at a doctor's appointment at Park Plaza and remembered, your new place was near by...."

Since Puryear didn't seem to be interested in asking any questions, I decided to ask him one. "How's the investigation coming?"

He ran a hand through his close-cropped hair. "Well, like I told you, we haven't gotten as far as I'd like. But we do have a suspect, and the DA wants to indict fast on this one. Probably doesn't want all those fat cats who've been on him to get something done figuring out how imperfect a science a murder investigation really is. The DA and my Chief, even though it's what they get paid to do, they hate handling these things when the PR angle is so big. But, you know, I suppose you can't really blame the folks who're applying all the pressure.

"What do you mean?"

"You know, it makes 'em nervous when they start thinking how there's somebody still on the loose who's killed someone they identify with. And the ones who identify with Thrasher, they have power. Apparently, they've been using it, putting on heat, demanding progress, which, by the way, means an arrest, and fast, too."

"That's too bad," I said.

Puryear nodded. He stared past me, momentarily lost in thought, as if trying to make up his mind about something. He looked at me again and said, "Mr Givens, I suppose I should tell you. Some of the folks working on this case think that you might be involved with this. It would be very helpful to our investigation if you could clear up some questions we have."

My heart skipped. "What do you mean, Lieutenant? There are people in your department who actually believe *I* killed William Thrasher?"

Puryear nodded. "Mr Givens, this is never easy. I thought, maybe, you know, with you being an attorney, you'd want to straighten this out on your own. But I realize now, that wasn't such a good idea. We'd better just play it by the book."

My stomach wrapped in a queasy knot. "Wait a minute, what is it you're saying, Lieutenant?"

Puryear stared evenly at me with steel-gray eyes. "I don't believe we should talk about this until you've taken the opportunity to consult with an attorney." He stood and glanced toward the door. "And Mr Givens, if I were you, I'd make sure he's good."

With Puryear gone, I called Mark Watson again. He still wasn't in, but this time his secretary promised to try to reach him and have him call right away. While I waited, I read the fax Elaine had received from Del and compared names with my list of active client files. The vast majority had signed new fee agreements with Golden, Wallace & Whitfield. What had that jerk done to turn so many of them against me?

At least Mitchell Starlarski hadn't signed. That would have been more than I could take. Making sure Mitchell intended to stay with me was vital. I called his office, but he wasn't there. His secretary suggested I try him on his cell-phone.

Mitchell answered with a nearly inaudible, "Yeah?"

"Mitch, this is Andy. How are you?"

"Good to hear from you pards," he whispered. "I was just thinking about you. We need to talk."

"What's wrong with your voice, Mitch?"

"There's nothing wrong," he murmured. "Louis is...." His voice returned to normal. "Oh, that's too bad, Louis. Sorry, Andy, but Louis was trying to sink a putt worth three hundred dollars. I wanted him to at least have a fair chance, you know how he always accuses me of cheating?"

I knew. Louis was Mitchell's cousin. They played golf together almost every day. It never ceased to amaze me how a person like Louis, who played so much, could still be so bad. He usually lost several hundred dollars to Mitchell every round, making one crazy bet after another. What amazed me even more was how Louis always enjoyed himself tremendously. Maybe that's because he knew, more times than not, he'd win his money back at the card table after the golf was over.

"Where are you guys?" I asked.

"Out at Bentwater. You've been out here haven't you?"

"Yeah, they've got a couple of great courses. But what are y'all doing way out on Lake Conroe?"

"Oh, Louis bought a piece of property up here. His kids like to ski and he's planning on starting a house this fall, after things settle down a little. Hey, I bet him another hundred he'll put at least two balls in the water on number fourteen. What do you think?"

"The Weiskopf course?"

"Yep."

"Gee, that's tough to call. That hole doesn't give you much chance to play safe."

"You want in on it, Pards?"

"No thanks, I'll pass."

"Listen, Andy, I gotta let you go. Louis is getting impatient. But we do need to talk. Can you bring your sticks and join us out at Kingwood tomorrow, say at about one-thirty?"

I was irritated that Mitchell hadn't even given me the chance to say why I'd called. Still, I took him up on his invitation. A chance to see Mitchell and Louis and the show they put on would be welcome after the past few days.

I was about to go for a run to stretch out the kinks when Elaine came in to say Mark Watson had called while I was on the phone. He would be over to meet first thing in the morning.

Nothing really needed doing at the office, so I gave Elaine the rest of the afternoon off. She said she was meeting some friends and asked if I wanted to join them later for a drink. I appreciated the gesture, but took a rain check. I wasn't in the mood.

After she left, I went upstairs to change into my running gear. Puryear's words echoed in my head. Was I really in as much trouble as it seemed? Downstairs the phone rang. I hadn't gotten around to getting a phone for my bedroom and started not to answer, but it kept ringing. Finally, I went down to my office and picked up the receiver.

"Yes?"

"Andy, is that you?"

It was Monica.

## Chapter Seven

"Hi, Andy, how are you?"

"Well, okay, I guess. How are you?"

"I've been better. But, you know, what can you expect?"

"Monica, I'm glad you called. I guess you must realize, I've been trying to reach you."

"Yes, I know. I just wasn't ready to, you know—"

"Well now you must be. Anyway, we're talking, right?"

"Andy, the reason I called, I was wondering if, well, do you think we could get together this evening, or some other time, if you're busy tonight?"

"No, I mean yes, tonight is good for me. Do you want me to come over?"

"That might not be such a good idea. Why don't we meet someplace instead."

"Fine.You name it."

"How about the Mediterranean?"

"Great," I said, realizing I sounded way past the point of too eager. What the hell, I was. After all, she had called. *Finally*. And when she did, she'd suggested one of our special restaurants. That had to be a good sign.

"Is seven-thirty good for you?"

"Sure, I'll meet you at seven-thirty." We hung up and I looked at my watch. It was already six-fifteen. I took a quick shower, and shaved, succeeding in giving myself a nasty cut. I couldn't make the bleeding stop right away, so I tore off a square of tissue and stuck it on. Then I got dressed, selecting the suit Monica had given as a birthday gift the year before. Perfect.

When I arrived at the restaurant, she was already seated near the back. She wore a plain pale-green sleeveless dress.

Her hair was pulled back tightly with a bow in back that matched the dress. No jewelry, almost no make-up. Still, she was as attractive as I'd ever seen her. I got to the table and she hesitated, uncertain of how to greet me. Finally, she opted for the cool approach and angled her face away from mine, offering her cheek for one of those fake, no-contact kisses reserved for people you either don't like very much or fear they might be contagious. I did my best not to show my irritation at being placed in either category and obligingly brushed my cheek against hers.

Monica already had a glass of white wine. I ordered a gin martini, very dry.

For several moments, neither of us spoke. Monica kept looking down at her lap as if she'd lost something from the table and thought she might find it there. But then she raised her head, looked at me and said, "Andy, I don't know, maybe this wasn't such a good idea. I'm so nervous, I don't know why, but I am."

"I'm just glad you've at least decided it's time to get together. There's nothing to be nervous about."

"This has to be hard for you. Mr Thrasher. Your firm. And me. All of it coming at once."

"Please, Monica, let's not get into that. There are a lot more important things we need to talk about."

"You don't need to say that, Andy."

"I just wanted you to know, how I feel, that's all."

Monica looked away. I finished my drink in one large swallow. The waiter came and replaced it with another.

My wife looked at me and said, "I keep thinking, if I'd said something earlier, maybe none of this would have happened. I don't think I'll ever forgive myself."

I shook my head. "I've already said it and I meant it. It won't do any good to focus on what happened. But I have to say, what I don't understand is, after you found out about Thrasher, why did you wait so long to call? I've been going crazy worrying. The way you just cut me off, do you really hate me that much?"

She winced. "Andy, I don't have a good answer I don't like to think I hate anyone."

"You don't *think* you hate me? Well, that's nice to know. Monica, I'm relieved." I was being an ass, and I don't know why, but I couldn't seem to stop. "How on earth did it come to this?"

"You have every right to be angry, Andy, but I can't say exactly how or why, it just has."

"But, we've meant so much to each other. Don't you see, we owe it to ourselves to try to fix this? Don't you see, we belong together?"

She didn't respond. She just stared past me. Finally, she said, "I'm sorry, but our relationship is beyond fixing as far as I'm concerned. It wouldn't be fair to say I want to try to work things out when the fact is, I don't. Andy, I'm sorry, but it's just too late."

Too late? What did she mean? We *had* to try. She owed at least that much. But instead she just sat there, detached from all emotion, calmly eliminating the last vestige of any hope that we could start over.

"Why don't you tell me why you wanted to see me?" I asked.

Monica looked at me, her blue eyes suddenly gone glacier cold. "I'm not sure," she said. "I guess I wanted to see if we can agree to keep things civil. I don't want to fight with you, and I wanted you to know that."

"Monica, I'm not going to fight. I promise I won't do that. If you'll just promise you won't cut me off again, that's all I ask."

Tears suddenly welled in her eyes. Her bottom lip quivered, and I was afraid she was going to cry at any second, but she managed to hold it in a little longer. "Andy, don't you understand? We aren't going to be together anymore. I'm not going to be available to answer to your beck and call. I'm not willing to promise a part of my life to you. I'm not willing to promise that to anyone right now."

Who was this stranger sitting next to me? Certainly not the woman I'd so happily married. The one who shared absolutely everything with me. How could we ever have been that close and now be so far apart? Sitting with her in that crowded restaurant, seeing the way she was, I suddenly felt more alone than ever.

We picked at the tapas I'd ordered and left most of the wine untouched. Neither of us spoke. Finally, our eyes met. Monica's flat, matter-of-fact gaze, devoid of all emotion, communicated the awful truth. It was over.

Monica glanced quickly away, folded her napkin, and put it on the table. I kept staring at her. I didn't know what to do.

She gave a thin little half-smile and said, "I want you to realize, I don't feel right about a lot of things. I'd appreciate it if you could arrange with Sharon Fielder to come to the house to pick up whatever else you might want. I'd feel better if you would."

I wasn't in the mood to be accommodating, and had no interest in making her feel less guilty. Still, I said I'd call Sharon. It wasn't the gentlemanly thing to do, but then I got up from the table and left Monica sitting alone.

When I stopped to pay the waiter on my way out, he thanked me and said, "Uh, sir, excuse me, but you've got something on your chin. I have been wanting to tell you, but you and the woman, you seemed to be, well, you know, you were having a private conversation."

I pulled a piece of crinkled tissue from my chin, a dark circle of dried blood in the middle.


When I got back to the house on Jackson Avenue, I took the photograph of Monica that I kept on my desk out of its frame and burned it in the fireplace, staring at the low flicker of blue and orange flames as her image curled, turned black, and floated bit by bit up the chimney. How could this have happened? Despite what she'd done, and how she felt, I wanted her more than ever.

I slumped onto the sofa and eventually fell asleep. I had a weird dream about Monica, Thrasher, and my former partners. They were a happy bunch, dancing in a circle atop a grassy hill underneath a large oak tree, all of them enjoying being rude and nasty to me. Then I noticed the back of Thrasher's head. It was a bloody mess. Pieces of it kept falling off. Monica, Fred Whitfield—and I'm not sure, but I think Joseph Hartson was there too—all took turns helping him put the pieces back in place.

I woke with someone shaking my shoulder. Light streamed in. My office was hot, the air heavy and stale. Elaine peered down at me, offering a glass of juice. "If this is a new way you've come up with to try to make a favorable impression on your clients, demonstrating you never sleep while you're working on their cases, you'd better think again. You look awful."

I forced myself to sit. "I had a bad night. I saw Monica, and you were right, there's nothing I can do about her wanting a divorce. In fact, she has me convinced, she hates my guts."

Elaine nodded sympathetically. "Maybe you can't do anything about her, but you can't afford to be down. Mr Watson will be here any minute and you're going to have to help him, if you expect him to be able to help. Why don't you go upstairs and clean up? I'll let you know when he gets here."

She went to the thermostat and lowered the setting. The compressor switched on and cool air flowed from the ceiling vents. I didn't feel like meeting with anyone and was about to ask Elaine to find Mark's home number to head him off, but when I looked up he was standing in the doorway between my office and Elaine's.

"Can a poor ol' cowpoke get a cup of coffee?" he drawled as he walked into the office. He wore his customary western suit, string tie, and boots. Having grown up on a ranch out in West Texas, he worked especially hard at demonstrating his cowboy heritage.

Elaine smiled and said, "Sure, I'll get you a cup, or better still, why don't I show you where we keep the pot? Andy was just on his way upstairs. You don't mind, do you?"

"Mind? Darlin', it will be an absolute pleasure to follow you anyplace you want to go. By the way, who are you?"

"Uh, Mark," I said, "this is my secretary, Elaine Turner."

"Why, Miss Turner, ma'am, it is indeed a pleasure. Andy, you go on and do whatever it is you need to do. And take your time. I'll still be here."

When I got back, they were seated at the work table, Elaine laughing uncontrollably, Mark smiling broadly, displaying gleaming white teeth, waving his arms, making emphatic gestures as he spoke, engrossed in telling my secretary one of his famous tall tales.

Elaine stood to leave, but I asked her to stay. "You might as well hear it from the horse's mouth," I said.

"Now, Andy, I guess I don't mind being called a horse, as long as you're talking about the whole animal and not just the back part. And you know me, I'm always happy to have such a pretty lady as Miss Turner around."

"Mark," I said, "I suppose you know I'd like to discuss your helping me with this Thrasher thing, that is, if you're interested."

He grinned. "I sort of thought that was why you called, Andy. William Thrasher's a hot topic at the courthouse. You can bet somebody in the DA's office is counting on making a name for himself with this one."

Elaine said, "We understand that. But what we don't know is if anyone really thinks Andy might be involved."

Mark leaned back and looked at both of us, arching bushy eyebrows over wide-set blue eyes. "I'm sorry, I guess I'd just assumed you knew." He paused and brushed back the shock of rust-brown hair that had fallen over his forehead. "The grand jury will probably indict by the end of the week."

"Mark, this is ridiculous," I said. "I hope you believe me, I wasn't involved."

"For what it's worth, which unfortunately isn't much, I do. But as far as the indictment goes, I'm afraid there's not much we can do to turn that pony around."

"How can you be so sure they're going after Andy?" Elaine asked.

"Sorry, darlin', can't reveal my sources, but they're reliable, you can count on that."

"I just don't understand," she continued. "What is it that makes them think it was Andy?"

"Now, there's a question that maybe I can answer. I don't know how, I'm going to have to work on that little detail, but supposedly, the police think they can place Andy in Thrasher's office the night he was killed. That, coupled with the fact they think Andy has a pretty good motive for getting rid of his former client, who'd just threatened a big, messy malpractice lawsuit, is evidently what has them convinced. There's one other thing too. And it just might be the most important factor of all. Pure and simple, they don't have anyone else to accuse."

"But Mark, I wasn't even near Thrasher's that night! I don't see how anybody can possibly say I was!"

Mark shrugged.

Elaine glared at him. "What's this about accusing Andy simply because there's nobody else to blame? They can't get away with that can they?"

"It happens," he said. "It shouldn't, but it does, especially when the dead guy is a big shot from River Oaks. It wouldn't look good for the boys at HPD, or that prick we have for a DA, for a case like this to go unsolved. And the word I hear is there's been plenty of pressure on those guys to get this one wrapped up pronto."

"Lieutenant Puryear said the same thing," I offered.

Mark stared at me as if I were the world's biggest moron. "You mean you've been talking to the police?"

I nodded, suddenly embarrassed.

"Andy, that's got to stop."

I felt my face turning red. "Okay, anything you say, Mark. I realize, I've been pretty dumb, but will you take the case?"

"Of course I will, Andy. I have to tell you, though, it doesn't give me a lot of pleasure. I don't enjoy my cases as much when I believe my client is innocent."

I asked where we needed to begin and he suggested we should start with a fee arrangement. He gave me one hell of a break. We both knew that. And when I asked if there would be an adjustment if I wasn't indicted, he laughed and said he'd charge me double.

I asked Elaine to make out a check. It would take just about all of my available cash, but with the payments from my old firm scheduled to start coming in, I could still get by. Mark slipped the check into his jacket pocket and we went to work.

Our first step was to call Albert Anderson, the assistant DA who was handling Thrasher. Elaine and I listened on the speaker phone while Mark explained to Anderson who he represented and asked if I would be permitted to appear before the grand jury. Anderson said he'd think about it, but didn't believe my appearance would be necessary.

"You're going to have some fast talkin' to do, if you indict my man and lose, which I promise you, you will," Mark said. "Especially when it comes out how we offered to go in front of the grand jury and save everybody a lot of time and trouble, but Albert Anderson wouldn't let us."

"Mark," came Anderson's raspy voice, "I appreciate your advice, but I'll run this case the way I see fit, if you don't mind. I know you've got me on one of those damned speaker phones and Givens is probably listening to this, so let me say for both your benefits, we have a case that's strong as a garlic pie and there's nothing either of you can do to change that. It wouldn't help and will probably wind up hurting you a hell of a lot more if Givens comes down here to testify."

"If that's so, you should be eager to have my man in front of the grand jury," Mark said.

"Like I told you, if I decide that would be helpful to the investigation, I'll let you know."

Then, the line went dead.

"What do you know about this guy, Anderson?" I asked.

Mark pulled at his string tie. "Oh, he's a career prosecutor, really enjoys the power. He has pretty good courtroom skills, not as good as mine, if you're interested."

I was. Very.

"This kind of case is right up his alley," Mark added.

"Then why won't he let us cooperate and have Andy appear before the grand jury?" Elaine asked. "It doesn't make any sense."

"I imagine just the opposite of what he said, you know, about how strong his case is, is probably a lot closer to the truth. He might be more than just a little bit worried about how those folks might react if Andy goes in front of them and does a good job convincing them he doesn't deserve to be charged. Besides, darlin', my offer to let your boss go and testify in front of a grand jury was just for show. I'm not about to let them have a free shot."

"You mean Anderson is so set on charging Andy, he doesn't want to risk letting him clear his name? Mark, that can't be right."

Mark shook his head and smiled. "Darlin' forgive me for saying so, but I don't think you've been listening very carefully to what I've been trying to say. Or, maybe I just haven't done a very good job with the telling part. Anyway, I'll try again." He paused to push that unruly shock of hair from his forehead, sighed and continued, "The DA's office can't afford to have this case go unprosecuted. And they're afraid they're sunk, if they don't go with the best they've got. The decision has been made, and Andy's it.

"Just look at their choice for a prosecutor. Albert Anderson, he's a career man at the DA's office mainly because he's never been able to make a decision on his own. He has to have that big Harris County machine behind him, or he wouldn't be worth ten cents. A man in his spot with even the smallest streak of independence could cause the DA real problems on a case like this one. That's why Albert is so perfect, at least for their side he is."

Listening to Mark explain the facts of life, particularly what he said about the DA pursuing a case against me simply because there wasn't another convenient suspect, it all seemed so absurd. To make things worse, I was beginning to realize just how out of my element this was. I was accustomed to being in control of everything. I was the one to whom others came to solve their problems. Now, all of a sudden, things were different. Criminal law and the politics that went along with it were new and unfamiliar territories. Even though Mark was as good as they came, I didn't like in the least the idea of having to put my fate in someone else's hands.

Elaine looked at her watch. "Andy, are you still going to keep your appointment with Mitchell Starlarski?"

"No, for some strange reason, I don't feel much like golf right at the moment."

Mark raised a wind-weathered hand like a traffic cop's. "Wait a minute," he said. "If you take my advice, you'll go ahead. This is the perfect opportunity to show the prosecution we're not worried. You know, we can't afford to have you behaving like some criminal who's afraid to be seen out in public. I'd go with you, but I need to do some more checking with my sources before they dry up. I want to know as soon as possible what they have to link you to Thrasher's office on the night of the murder. Besides, golf's not my game. I've always found it a mystery how you people find any fun in chasing a little white ball around in a field. Even after you're finished beating it to death with all of those clubs you carry, I hear that sucker is still way too tough to eat."

Going seemed ridiculous, but I'd just agreed to follow Mark's advice. "Okay, I'll do it," I said. "But other than my playing a round of golf, what's the next step?"

Mark pushed away from the table. "In addition to checking on what they've got on the crime scene, and I'm going to do that just as soon as I get back to my office, I'll call Anderson and make sure he understands I don't think he has any cause to ask for an indictment. But what I'll really be trying is to get him to agree, if one is returned, to give us a chance to go in on a no-arrest at the DA's. We don't want to give him a chance to grandstand and have you collared at one of your court hearings or something like that."

Being arrested. Now there was a pleasant thought. I couldn't help wondering, what other new and exciting experiences were in store?

## Chapter Eight

It took almost an hour to drive up the East-Tex Freeway to Kingwood, one of the first of the now-numerous "planned" communities that ring the city. I've often wondered about the people who choose to live in those sorts of places, thinking they're so smart, in their safe, sterile surroundings, convinced they have the world's problems licked. No poverty, very little crime. No drugs, well, maybe just a few, but certainly not as bad as everyplace else. That they've got things taken care of, leaving everybody else to fend for themselves. The attitude of these people—who could do so much, but don't—is what allows the rot and decay of modern-day America to continue to spread unchecked.

As I drove, I kept imagining myself in a courtroom, hearing a jury foreman pronounce me guilty. When I got to my exit, I had the urge to keep driving, find some little East Texas hole in the wall and disappear.

Mitchell and Louis were already on the putting green when I arrived. From my vantage point at the window in the pro shop, they were impossible to tell apart. Two stocky, barrel-chested men, almost the same height, a little under six feet, they walked with identical, jerky, waddling motions, using almost no arm movement, reminding me of two giant penguins. They were wearing identical Panama-style golf hats with the word "Ping" printed on their cloth hat bands. Mitchell's concealed a full head of carrot-red hair. Louis was as bald as a billiard ball. But with the hats, they could pass for identical twins.

I paid my guest fee and went outside.

Mitchell looked up from a putt, saw me, and said, "Andy, it's about time you got here. I was beginning to worry I'd be stuck with nobody but poor Louis. That's worse than having to play by myself."

Mitchell's voice, high-pitched and, raspy, didn't fit his robust appearance. People meeting him for the first time, were usually thrown off balance.

"You mean playing *with* yourself don't you, Starlarski," Louis replied. "You do that several times a day."

Mitchell shook his head and grinned. "Pards, you put your clubs on with me. We'll make Louis ride alone. If we can manage to keep upwind of him most of the time, we might make it through the day without having to puke."

They were at it already.

I'd never had a bad time on a golf course. But being out there just didn't feel right. My mind kept wandering back to the problems facing me in town. After six holes, Mitchell was up by four on our original bet. We played automatic two-downs, and he was up two on the first press, starting another bet. It stood to be an expensive day.

As we rode to the seventh tee, Mitchell said, "Pards, something's wrong. You've barely said two words all day, and I've never seen you hit so many indifferent shots. I guess I should be pleased to be taking your money, but just the same, why don't you tell me, what's going on?"

I looked at Mitchell and said, "I suppose you've heard about me leaving my firm."

"Of course, that's what we need to talk about."

"Do you want to know why I left?"

"Not really. That's between you and a bunch of folks I don't have nothin' to do with. But if you want to talk about it, well, you know me, Andy, I'll do anything I can."

"That big case I mentioned a while back? The judge kicked it out—after we'd been in trial for almost three weeks. The night that happened, my client was murdered. Then, my partners asked me to leave. Said it was in the best interests of the firm."

Mitch stared at me. "Good Lord, Andy, I heard about that Thrasher guy gettin' killed. And I thought you'd mentioned you were working on something for him. This explains why I got that call from one of your partners, a guy by the name of Whitfield."

"What did he say?"

"It was real strange. Said you might not be able to handle my business any more, and he asked if he could send out some sort of new agreement for me to sign with his new firm. I told him I'd need to visit with you, before doing anything like that. It was a pretty weird request he was making and I figured you'd be able to let me know what was goin' on. Andy, they don't actually think you had anything to do with that Thrasher guy gettin' killed, do they?"

So, that was why so many of my former clients had elected to switch. If I were ever guilty of committing a murder, there was no doubt, the victim would be Whitfield. "I don't know what they think," I said. "But I might as well tell you, the police think I did. My lawyer tells me I'm probably going to be charged any day now. Anyway, Whitfield might be right. You might need another lawyer before too long."

Mitchell steered the cart off of the path and Louis drove past us.

"Andy, this is serious isn't it? No wonder your head hasn't been in the game. Pards, believe me, I don't see how anyone would actually believe you might have killed somebody. You're joking, aren't you?"

I shook my head. "Wish I was, Mitch, but this is no joke."

A dark cloud of worry cast a shadow over my friend's normally cheerful face. "Andy, if you want to stop, and go in, we can. I didn't know about any of this and, well, why didn't you tell me this was happening?"

Up ahead, Louis paced back and forth on the tee box. He saw me looking in his direction, and shouted, "Hey, Andy, is Mitchell finished sucking you off yet? If he is, let's get going. I have better things to do than to wait for that deviant pervert."

I smiled at Mitchell. "If it's okay with you, let's keep going. That way we can talk. Besides, I feel like I'm about to get hot."

I hadn't really meant that last part, but having the problem out in the open helped and I actually did play better. By the eleventh hole, I was ahead on the second press and tied on the first. As we started to play our approach shots, Mitchell asked, "How's Monica holding up through all of this mess?"

I gave him a lame smile. "Oh, I imagine she's okay. Mitch, I'm sorry I didn't tell you, but when all of this other stuff happened, she let me in on the fact we're getting divorced."

His jaw dropped. "Pards, is there anything else you've forgotten? You and Monica? I don't believe it."

I saved the juicy details and just told him I'd come home to find Monica waiting to tell me she'd fallen in love with one of the lawyers at her firm. That really shook Mitchell up. He was always mentioning how lucky Monica and I were to have each other. His wife and seven-year-old son had been killed in a car wreck two years earlier. Mitchell was driving and had to veer suddenly to avoid a pickup truck that crossed the center line. He'd lost control. Their car flipped over in a ditch and was demolished. Lu Ann and little Mike were killed instantly. Miraculously, Mitchell got out without so much as a scratch. He was past the worst of his grieving, but still, every now and then, he'd get that far-away look in his eyes. It made my heart ache.

At least he'd started dating, that's what Louis announced that afternoon, devoting most of his teasing to speculating about what sorts of deformities Mitchell's mystery woman must have. But I knew where my friend's heart still was and whom he still blamed for what had happened. After I mentioned the situation with Monica, he stopped joking around and was quiet for the rest of our game.

The round finished, we went into the locker room to the card table in the corner where Mitchell and Louis each kept a locker. Mitchell had to buy the drinks. He'd won a little over four-hundred dollars from his cousin. By the time we'd finished our first round, Mitchell was recovered from his melancholy. He and Louis were back at it, swapping insults harder than ever. Floating on their banter, I was actually able to relax and have a good time.

The locker-room attendant was delivering our second round when a short, stocky man with dark olive-colored skin, salt and pepper close-cropped hair, and one of the weirdest goatees I've ever seen walked past. He nodded to Mitchell and Louis and Mitchell said, "Hey, Vince, wait a minute. There's somebody I want you to meet. Andy, do you know Vincent Caponi?"

I said no, introduced myself, and stood to shake hands. Caponi peered at me through dark-framed coke-bottle lenses as he cinched his towel around his waist and took my hand. He had a grip like a vise and apparently enjoyed showing it off. He nearly broke a couple of bones with that handshake. Judging from the weather lines protruding from the corners of the frames, I guessed he was in his early fifties. By the looks of the rest of him, he kept in pretty good shape.

Mitchell said, "Vince has a problem you might be interested in hearing about, Andy. He mentioned it to me the other day. You do still have that problem don't you Vince?"

Caponi's pleasant smile faded." Yes, I'm afraid it's not going away, no matter how much I wish it would."

"Well, then, you and this guy ought to get together. Andy's been my lawyer for years, and believe me, Vince, he's the best there is in the whole damn town."

Caponi said, "Mr Givens, Mitchell is correct when he says I have a problem. I would like to set up a time to come to see you when it is convenient."

"Sure," I said. Although I didn't know why. I didn't even know if I would still be practicing law the next day.

"Do you have a business card?" he asked. I fished around in my wallet and found one of my old ones. I wrote my new address and phone number on the back and handed it to him "Now, gentlemen, please excuse me," he continued, "I am having dinner at home this evening with my wife and our son, so I must hurry on."

After Caponi left, I asked Mitchell what he knew about him. Mitch said he had some kind of beef against some banks over in the Beaumont area. He suggested it would be worth my while to meet with the man, and then, if I was interested, he volunteered to check him out. I almost told him not to bother. It was typical of Mitchell to want to help out, but it was preposterous to even consider taking a new case. Things were way too uncertain for that.

The conversation shifted back to Mitchell's new girlfriend. Mitch denied it, but Louis swore he had one. My involvement was distracted by thoughts of what was waiting in town, so I passed up Louis's offer to join them for dinner and headed back to the city.

I dreaded the unknown, knowing, no matter what, I was going to have to face it. Suddenly, I was in some other, far and distant place, hurtling across a dark, barren plain. The lights of distant pursuers glowed dimly on the horizon. There was no place to turn. No place to go but straight ahead, into an increasingly strange and hostile land. The lights became brighter, my pursuers were closing in. I was overcome with an intense feeling of impending catastrophe.

When I returned from wherever I had gone, I found myself in my driveway, behind the wheel of my car, the motor running. How I managed to get there, I haven't a clue.

## Chapter Nine

The next morning, I got down to my desk early. For the first time since Thrasher's death, I felt like trying to get some work done. Thanks to Fred Whitfield, I only had a handful of fairly routine cases but they'd been neglected for so long, there was plenty to do.

Requests for admissions in an employee wrongful-termination case were due by the end of the week, so I started there. By the time Elaine got in, I'd already placed several notes giving instructions on correspondence that needed to go out and calls to make and a dictation tape in the out-box on the corner of my desk.

She claimed the contents of the box and went into the kitchen to start the morning coffee.

A moment later, she was back holding Ivory. "Didn't you hear him scratching on the kitchen door?" she asked. "He's been trying to get out to see you, probably ever since you got home last night."

I frowned. "Of course not. Do you think he'd still have been in there if I had?"

She laughed and said, "No, I suppose not. You mustn't've noticed the note I left last night. Monica had him delivered after you left. She sent a message along saying she thought he'd be happier with you, and she hopes you won't mind taking him."

Mind? It was good having my old friend with me again. When Elaine put him down, he immediately jumped onto my lap. He rubbed against me and presented his chin for a good scratching. Then he hopped onto the floor and systematically circled the perimeter of the room, carefully inspecting all of its corners. Satisfied that the office was secure, he curled up behind my desk, where a shaft of sunlight provided a warm spot suitable for his morning nap.

While Elaine and I worked, Ivory finished his nap, then disappeared to explore the rest of the house. Every now and then, he returned to make sure I was still where he'd left me.

I was thinking about lunch and possibly asking Elaine to join me, when the front doorbell rang. Elaine returned from the door, pale as a ghost.

"That Detective Springer is here. He says he has a search warrant to serve."

So this was what Lieutenant Puryear meant when he said he would go by the book. I told Elaine to call Mark Watson and went to see Springer. He stood just inside the front door, two uniformed officers at his side. He looked as if he'd put on weight since I'd seen him up in my old office. Or maybe I just hadn't been very observant that first time.

He handed me the search warrant and said, "Mr Givens, while the officers conduct the search, I'd appreciate it if you and your secretary would just stay out of their way and don't give them trouble."

"What are you looking for?" I asked. "I can assure you, I don't have anything to hide and if you'll just let me know, I'll try to point you in the right direction."

Springer rolled his moon-shaped eyes. "*Sure* you will, Givens. You just do as you're told and stay out of the way."

My cheeks flushed with heat. "Wait a minute, I have a right to know what you're looking for."

Springer grinned maliciously. "That's right. You do. It's in the warrant." He pushed past me and began to direct his men.

I watched with Elaine as the police systematically turned my office and my rooms upstairs upside down. After nearly three hours, they wound up taking my personal working file on the Thrasher case, and several items of clothing from my upstairs closet.

Just when I thought they were finished, a platform tow truck with an HPD insignia pulled into the driveway. Springer handed me a second warrant. This one authorized the impoundment of my car. When I asked what they wanted with it, Springer gave me another of his stupid grins and said, "Sir, you'll have to take that up with your lawyer." He told me he'd be seeing me again, "real soon," and he and the rest of his crew left.

The driver loaded my Mazda onto the towing platform and backed out the drive-way, stopping to let one of the uniformed officers climb in on the passenger's side. As they drove away, the driver stuck his head out the window and smiled broadly, clearly enjoying giving some smart-ass lawyer a hard time.

At a little past three o'clock, Mark returned my call. I started to fill him in about the search warrants, but he said that could wait until I got to his office. I needed to meet him there right away. We were expected at the DA's by three-thirty.

Elaine drove me downtown. We didn't say much. I guess we were both too nervous.

Mark's secretary ushered us into his office and informed us that he would join us in a few minutes. Elaine paced back and forth on the Navaho rug in front of the desk. I stared out the window, taking deep breaths, concentrating on remaining calm.

Several minutes later, Mark popped his head inside the door. "I've been on the phone with Anderson," he said. "He's waiting for us, so we need to go. Elaine, dear, if you could be so kind as to drive us over, I'll explain things on the way."

"Have you seen the indictment?" I asked.

"Yeah. Murder in the first degree."

Elaine looked at me, alarm registering in her glistening green eyes. "Is that capital murder?"

"Mark glanced quickly at me, then nodded. "Yeah, but even though we're at the top when it come to giving folks the lethal needle, there actually are only a limited number of situations in the penal code that allow imposition of the death penalty. So far, this case doesn't fit any of them. I'm pretty sure the State's not gonna try."

*Pretty Sure.* The shock of those words numbed me.

The ride was short. Mark sat in the middle of the back seat and leaned forward so we both could hear. "Now, Andy, when we get in there, don't say anything unless I say it's okay. You'll have to go over to 42 San Jacinto to be processed. Finger printed, photographed, all that stuff. I won't go with you. It's more important that I make sure Judge Garza will be available to set bond this afternoon. We wouldn't want you to have to cool your heels over-night in the county lock-up."

"What'll happen after I'm processed?" I asked, suddenly feeling like a canned ham.

"They'll put you in a holding cell until the judge is ready for the hearing. You just keep your mouth shut over there and you'll do fine."

Elaine parked at the side of the DA's building. As Mark and I got out, she looked up at me, tears running down her cheeks.

Mark leaned inside the window. "Hey, pretty lady, don't you worry. He's going to be okay. I'll make sure he gets home this evening."

"Feed Ivory for me, will you?" I asked.

She managed a smile. "Sure. I'll be happy to."

I reached inside the open car window and squeezed her hand.

"Call me?" she asked.

Feeling my throat catch, I nodded. Then I watched her car ease into traffic and head out Fannin, back toward the office.

We entered the building and took the elevator up to Anderson's floor. A uniformed sheriff's deputy led us into an interior room across the hall from a door that had Anderson's name on it. Anderson, Lieutenant Puryear, and Detective Springer were waiting. Springer still wore that stupid grin, looking like the Pillsbury Doughboy in a cheap suit.

Mark shook hands with Anderson and said, "Albert, this is my client, Andrew Givens."

Anderson looked to be pushing fifty, and had obviously long since given up any hope of retaining any semblance of youthfulness. His face was round and fleshy and his thinning hair was completely white. His body was flabby and soft, and he held himself in a stooped, rigid posture that suggested he had a painful physical disability. Without preamble, he nodded in the direction of the police officers standing behind him on the other side of a well-used metal table positioned in the middle of the room.

Springer stepped forward and, adopting the laconic style of Joe Friday, read me my *Miranda* rights. As he finished, Lieutenant Puryear glanced quickly over to Anderson. Did either of them have anything to say about the indictment? If so, they kept it to themselves.

Puryear motioned to Springer who summoned a uniformed officer into the room. Looking at me for the first time since the meeting started, he said, "Mr Givens, you need to go with Deputy Henry. After the booking procedures are finished you might have to wait a while, but as soon as the judge is ready to see you, you'll be taken to the courthouse. You'll see Mr Watson again then."

Henry looked at me with flat, expressionless brown eyes and nodded toward the door. We took the elevator to the basement where I was hand-cuffed. Another first. Then we rode in silence over to the County jail where Henry helped me out of the van and led the way to Central Intake. The handcuffs were removed and I was photographed and finger printed. I filled out a form describing my medical history and another acknowledging that the only personal property taken from me was my belt. Then, Henry took me upstairs to the holding cell. The whole process took less than thirty minutes. Very efficient. But that opinion changed during the next two hours, as I waited in the lock-up cell, a large square room with a grimy, plexi-glass wall across one side and cement walls painted a sickening yellow on the other three. At least two dozen other men, most of whom were either drunk or spaced out on drugs filled the cell. As Mark instructed, I kept my mouth shut.

Finally, one of the deputies who'd been doing nothing for the past half-hour other than drinking coffee and shooting the breeze with his co-workers, picked up a piece of paper from his desk, examining it with a puzzled expression as if he was attempting to read ancient hieroglyphics. He walked to the cell and shouted, "Andrew Givens!"

I identified myself and he opened the door and motioned me out. After being re-hand-cuffed, I was led through a labyrinth of corridors to another sheriff's van. The driver of the van took us to the Criminal Court Annex, where another deputy took me in the elevator to the fifth floor and through a rear hallway to the courtroom. Randle Hughes, the attorney my former firm retained when one of its clients needed a criminal lawyer, was in the hallway speaking with an assistant DA. They tried to act as if they didn't notice me being escorted by the sheriff's deputy. An embarrassing situation for Randle, a humiliating one for me.

To my relief, before he took me into the courtroom, the deputy un-cuffed me. Mark Watson and Albert Anderson were waiting. Mark came directly over. Smiling, he said, "Hey, pal, you don't look too bad for the experience. They treat you okay?"

"What I look like doesn't begin to show what I'm feeling."

Mark said, "Judge Garza should be in any minute. This shouldn't take long."

Before I had the chance to say how interested I was in making sure I didn't have to go back to jail, a deputy came in followed by the court clerk and the judge. Garza, a Mexican Indian, wore his hair long. It was streaked with silver, hinting his age might be more than the baby-smooth skin of his face indicated. He had a wide nose and prominent raised cheekbones, and was small and wiry, standing only about five-foot-six. In his black robe, he looked a lot bigger.

"Counsel, what do we have here?" he asked.

Anderson stood. "Judge, this is a bail hearing in the State of Texas versus Andrew Givens. The defendant has been charged in an indictment returned by the Harris County Grand Jury with murder in the first degree."

Garza nodded. "What is the State's position on the issue of bail?" he asked.

Anderson shifted his weight from one leg to the other. His back still bent, he craned his neck to look up to where the judge sat. "Uh, Your Honor, the State does not absolutely oppose the defendant being released on bond—provided the amount is appropriate. The Court needs to be aware in that regard, that this is a serious case. A well known member of the community was the victim of an extremely violent and brutal homicide. Also, the defendant is quite well-off. Although he is a member of the Texas Bar, we have to consider him a serious flight risk. Under these circumstances, it would be inappropriate to release him for any amount less that one-million dollars."

Wealthy? Me? The thought that I'd be cooling my heels in jail unless I came up with that kind of money caused my insides to twirl.

Mark reacted swiftly. "Judge, I can assure you, Andrew Givens is definitely not a flight risk. That's just wrong. And nothing else the District Attorney said has one whit to do with the amount of bond that should be set. As your honor knows, bond must be determined in this state solely to insure that the defendant will appear at trial. Mr Anderson admits the State doesn't oppose bond. He also realizes that my client is a well known member of the Houston legal community. His roots are deeply set and the chance that he might flee the jurisdiction of this court to avoid the baseless charges that have been brought against him is nil. The very idea that this man should be required to post the preposterous sum of a million dollars is repugnant to the entire bail system."

Judge Garza scowled at Mark and said, "Mr Watson, did I hear a request for a lower bond than the amount the State has requested in that speech you just made?"

"No, Judge, you didn't, and I apologize. We ask that Mr Givens be released on his personal recognizance, which, under the circumstances, is entirely appropriate."

Anderson stood again, but the judge cut him off before he could speak. "Mr Anderson, I believe the points made by Mr Watson are well taken. Now, I want everyone to understand. I'm not suggesting I'm in favor of some kind of double standard or anything like that. But I do believe Mr Givens can appreciate, perhaps more than most people, the importance of the issues with which he is faced. It should not be necessary at this time to set a monetary bond to insure his participation in these proceedings. Therefore, I am going to order that the Defendant be released on his own recognizance."

Albert Anderson's milk-white complexion turned crimson. How was he going to explain this development to his boss? He laboriously pulled himself to his feet, to try one more time, but the judge waved him off and focused his gaze on me.

"Mr Givens," he said, "I hope you don't disappoint me. If I get even the slightest inkling that you might cause me problems, I won't hesitate to lock you up until this case is over. Do you understand?"

"Yes, sir. You don't have to worry about that."

The judge's clerk handed me a form to sign, and I was free to leave. Just like that.

We rode down in the elevator in silence. When the door opened, the lobby was packed with people. What were they doing, milling around the courts this late in the day? Suddenly, blinding lights flashed on. Mark grabbed my arm and we fought through the throngs of reporters who blocked our path, most of them shouting unintelligible questions. A woman I recognized as working for Channel Thirteen News stepped directly in front of us and asked, "Mr Givens, did you kill William Thrasher?"

What did she think? That I'd give her the scoop of a lifetime, saying, "Sure, I killed the son-of-a-bitch"?

With Mark in the lead, we finally managed to push past the crowd and out the door. Mark's clerk had his car parked at the curb waiting. We quickly jumped in, avoiding the swarming hoard that followed.


At his office, Mark asked me to stay for a few minutes. He took the chair behind his desk and fished from an expandable red pocket folder two sheets of paper. Staring at me, he said, "Andy, I can't tell you where I got this, but we need to talk about it. If anyone ever asks, you didn't see this tonight, understand?"

I nodded.

"They have a video camera in the parking garage at Thrasher Industries. Did you know that?"

"No, I didn't, but why are you asking?"

"Take a look at this, then maybe you can tell me what's going on." Mark slid the papers across the desk. His thick eyebrows crinkled as he frowned at me and drummed his fingers on the desk top.

I examined the top sheet, a cover memo from Detective Springer directed to Albert Anderson, the style and number of my criminal case on the reference line. On the second sheet were the notations:

July 16th

1:35 a.m. in
1:58 a.m. out
TX RVK-747
VID windshield glare

"That's my license plate number on the next to last line," I said.

"That's right, Andy, it is. Now, can you please tell me what your car was doing in Thrasher's garage on the morning your ex-client was busy getting himself killed?"

My car? In Thrasher's garage? Impossible. "If that's what this is supposed to mean, I have no idea. I sure as hell wasn't the one who drove it there. I promise you that."

Mark leaned forward. "Listen, Andy, if you're hung up on the idea that somehow I'll do a better job if I believe you're innocent, or if this is some kind of pride thing, and, you know, you think I might think less of you if I know you're guilty, you've got to understand, none of that matters. Not in this kind of work. What is vitally important is letting me in on whatever you know. I can't defend you if you're not able to do that. It just won't work."

I felt my face flush. How could he think I'd been lying?

"Mark, I haven't told you some cock-and-bull story just so you'll think I'm a good guy. I'm not lying. I simply have no idea what my car was doing in Thrasher's garage. That's all I can say."

He loosened his string tie. "Okay, Andy, I hear you."

Maybe, but he still didn't sound as if he necessarily believed what he heard.

"Do you see the bottom line on the report?" he continued. "I don't know what it means, but I do know the police have a videotape from the garage with a time sequence on it. That's why they're able to say your car was there. Even if you weren't at Thrasher's that night, now, with this tape, Anderson has some pretty strong circumstantial evidence that says you were. We're getting damned close to a *prima facia* case."

"You mean, because there may be evidence that my car was in and out of Thrasher's parking garage, even with no proof of who was driving it, the DA has enough to get his case to a jury?"

"Who's to say Albert doesn't have proof of who was driving? They got the license plate off of the videotape. Maybe they've got the driver on there too."

I glared at my lawyer, trying to control my anger. In a slow, even voice I said, "I hope to God whoever that person is shows up on that tape. One thing's for sure, it won't be me."

Mark nodded. But his normally warm demeanor had turned icy and his silent gaze was unsettlingly impassive.

# Chapter Ten

The first thing I did when I got home was check the middle drawer of my desk. The extra car key was there, right where it belonged. As promised, I called Elaine. On the first ring, a man answered.

"Is Elaine Turner there?" I asked.

"Sugar, it's for you," he said.

"Andy, is that you?"

"Uh-huh."

"It looked pretty bad on TV."

I took a deep breath. "It's already made the news?"

"Yeah. I'm afraid so. A special report from the courthouse on Channel Thirteen. By her account, the judge made a mistake letting you out."

I should have known. Still, the thought of being hounded by a bunch of overly-aggressive reporters was a bitter pill. The action of my former partners, distancing themselves from this disaster, was beginning to make sense.

"Elaine, I, uh, realize you're busy, but I'd appreciate it if you could come in early tomorrow. It's pretty important."

She said okay, and was about to hang up, but then she said, "Oh, I almost forgot. A mister Caponi called after I got back from dropping you and Mark off. He said he met you recently and you invited him to come in to see you about a lawsuit he might have. He made an appointment for ten-thirty tomorrow."

*Great.* Just what I needed. A meeting with some odd-looking guy who got his grins breaking bones. Probably wanted to sue some banker for loaning him too much money. Just the same, Elaine couldn't be blamed. She'd simply followed one of my cardinal rules: No matter what, *always* make time to discuss new business.

Although past the point of exhaustion, I found sleep impossible. Who could have taken my car? Obviously it had been done in an attempt to throw suspicion on me as Thrasher's killer. Whoever it was had to be pretty damned proud. And what about the key? Only two existed. Neither could be duplicated without going through the manufacturer. The one I always used was on a ring along with my house and office keys. The spare stayed in a box in my desk drawer, right where I'd just found it. The only ones who knew about it being there were Monica and Elaine. Neither of whom was a likely candidate for being involved in Thrasher's death.

Ivory jumped onto the bed and climbed up on my chest. He curled into a comfortable position and tucked his head under my chin, purring noisily.

Well before dawn, I finally concluded sleep wasn't in the picture. Ivory gave a mournful stare for having disturbed his rest, but joined me in the kitchen as soon as bacon began sizzling in the pan. I was cleaning up and making fresh coffee, whistling in a concerted effort to cheer up, when Elaine arrived, earlier than expected.

"You seem to be in a fine mood for somebody who made the front page," she said, tossing the *Chronicle* on the counter. "Hey, something smells good. You didn't by any chance save some did you?"

I shook my head. "I was hungry. Guess spending a day in jail has that effect."

She nodded toward the paper. "I'll take care of feeding myself. You ought to read this while you're still in such a good mood."

The story of my arrest was indeed on page one. Related articles about the bond hearing and highlights of the background of William Thrasher—confusing his supposed benevolent acts with the actual good deeds of his deceased father—headlined the Metropolitan Section. The lead story placed emphasis on my representation of Thrasher Industries in a significant lawsuit, that I lost right before the night when Thrasher was murdered. The way the article went, the verdict was in: Andy Givens was guilty as sin.

I tossed the paper into an empty chair. "We might as well start a scrapbook," I said.

Elaine arched her dark, pencilled eyebrows. "That's pretty rough stuff. You sure are taking this in stride."

Compared to what? The way I'd fallen apart over Monica? I shrugged. "I'm not so sure how I'm taking it. Maybe I'm just numb."

Elaine finished eating. She gave Ivory a piece of bacon to quiet the loud meows that emanated from beneath the table. I asked if anyone other than herself knew about where I kept my spare car key.

"No, is it missing?"

I filled her in about the camera in Thrasher's garage and how it apparently showed my car going in and out of the garage on the night Thrasher was killed.

As my story unfolded, shock registered in her emerald eyes. "Andy, as far as I know, I'm the only person from the old office who knew where that key was kept, or that it was even there." Suddenly her mouth flew open. "You don't think I had anything to do with this, do you?"

I smiled. "Of course not. But somebody did. And whoever that was, had to have known about the key."

"Couldn't they have hot-wired your car, you know, the way they do on TV?"

"Not without setting off the alarm," I said. "There's no way around it. Whoever got the key from my desk used it to drive my car to Thrasher's office. Then, somehow, managed to return it to the drawer before I missed it."

Elaine's eyes narrowed to slits. "Maybe we're approaching this from the wrong angle. Do you have any idea who actually killed Mr Thrasher?"

I shook my head. "I've thought about it, but haven't come up with anyone. Now, after the business with my car—I just don't know what to think."

She walked to the window, turned, and looked at me. "Well, I've thought about it too. I don't know why, but I keep thinking Fred Whitfield. He was awfully upset about the malpractice lawsuit still going forward after Mr Thrasher died."

What a nice, simple world it would be if my nemesis turned out to be the killer. "Don't you imagine you're suspicious about Fred because you don't like the man?"

Elaine tilted her head toward me. "Sure, that might have something to do with it. But there's more to it than that. That man positively can't stand the thought of spending money, much less losing any he already has. He'd probably sell his soul to keep from paying the deductible on the firm's malpractice policy. Maybe he was willing to do worse than that."

I was about to ask if she had any other ideas when the doorbell rang. It wasn't quite ten o'clock. Vincent Caponi was early.

Elaine cleared away the leftovers while I went to the front door. Caponi was dressed in an expensively tailored suit of dove-gray silk, a necktie with alternating stripes of gray and burgundy, and a matching silk handkerchief in his breast pocket. His tasseled black loafers were perfectly polished.

"Mr Givens, I hope I'm not too early. I gave myself plenty of time to get lost, but didn't need it. Miss Turner gave excellent directions."

"Don't worry," I said. "You're fine. Please, come in."

I reached to shake his hand, this time ready for his vice-like grip.

We sat across from each other at the work table, a thermos of coffee and fresh cups in the middle. "Mr Caponi, I'm afraid you might have made a wasted trip. I need to fill you in on a problem."

He waved his hand dismissively. "I watched the news and read the paper. The matter with that fellow, Thrasher, is of no significance, unless, of course, you tell me the situation makes it too difficult to undertake representing a new client. But let me say, I hope that is not the case. I've checked and know you have the qualities I'm looking for."

He poured a cup of coffee and waited for my reply.

"Sir, I'm not certain how this is going to play. I've never been is a situation like this. I really do appreciate your interest, and, if you'd like, I can help find you somebody else."

Caponi put his coffee down. "Why don't you just listen to my story. Then, maybe we'll see where to go from there."

What the hell. Listening couldn't hurt. "Okay," I said.

Caponi gave me a big, toothy smile. "Thank you, Mr Givens. Let's see, where to start?" He gazed out the window, turned back to me, and asked, "First, do you know anything about me and my family?"

"Well, I guess I really don't, other than the fact you happen to be a member of the same country club as my friend, Mitch Starlarski."

"Then that's where we'll begin. You see, I've only lived in Houston for a short while. Until six months ago, we lived in Port Arthur. My wife, Sylvia, and my son, Roberto, we had to move to get away from all of the harassment. We got calls around the clock. Some of them pretty frightening."

"I don't understand. What calls are you talking about?"

"I'm getting to that, Mr Givens. I've gotten ahead of myself already and I apologize."

I held up my hand. "No need. And please, call me Andy."

"Very well, uh, Andy, I was about to tell a little about myself. I'm sure you can tell from my name, my family is Italian. My father has lived in New Orleans all his life. His father immigrated from Salerno when he himself was a young man. Grandpa came to America just before the turn of the century, poor as a mouse, but with a lot of hard work, he became quite well-off. Got into the import business. At first, with olives and lemons from our family home in Southern Italy. Later on, he began importing wine and much later even fine Italian fabrics. By the time my father was ready to take over the business, our family was what most people would think of as wealthy.

"Today, my older brother, Alphonso, is in charge. I worked in the business for years, but when he took over and made changes I couldn't live with, I left and started out on my own. Something totally different. I became a builder. Houses and apartments, in New Orleans mainly. When I started to do pretty good, Alphonso suddenly got real interested in what he could do to help. I wasn't about to let that happen, so I moved my base of operations to Texas.

"I guess that was seven or eight years ago. That was when I decided to do my own developing. Build decent low-cost housing. Living in this great country, it has always been hard to take seeing the way some people have to live. Trying to raise their families in little more than card-board shacks. I wanted to give them an option. Something a lot better. The funny thing was, I discovered most conventional lenders weren't at all interested in those sorts of ventures. So I came up with the idea of starting my own savings association."

"Why didn't you just borrow from your family? At least let them back your notes?"

Caponi sighed. "Like I said. My brother and I, we don't get along." He gazed out the window again. "This isn't something to be proud of, and I wouldn't say anything about it except it has a bearing on my situation today. Anyway, it's like this. Shortly after Alphonso took over our operations, he started doing deals with the Mancusos. You know about them?"

I nodded. They were one of the largest organized-crime families in the South.

He slowly shook his large head. "Now, I'm sad to say, there are a lot of people who believe the Caponis are all a bunch of gangsters. I don't know about my brother, he might be in pretty deep. But, Andy, I want you to know, I personally have never had time for those people. I hate them and everything they stand for."

"Vincent, I'm confused. Are you saying your company has been damaged because someone accused you of having ties to the Mafia?"

He nodded emphatically. "Yes. That's definitely part of it. But just bear with me. You'll see precisely what the problem is." He paused to take a long sip of coffee. "To get to the bottom line, Andy, the major banks from the Golden Triangle tried to run me out of business. After I got Centennial Savings up and running, the banks weren't coming close to matching the interest rates we offered. Pretty soon, we'd taken a sizable share of their depositors." He stopped and looked at me, dark eyes questioning.

"Go ahead, I'm with you," I said.

"Well, our business did even better than I'd even dreamed. We were building the kinds of projects I wanted. And I can tell you, there was a fantastic demand. We never had a problem keeping our units full. And we diversified, safeguarding against any sudden downturn in a local economy. That was my son's idea. Thanks to Roberto, we had developments in Houston, Austin, Nashville, Gainesville, and Tallahassee. Our largest project was under construction in Little Rock when the problem hit. We'd almost completed when the permanent lender went belly-up. Closed its doors just like that. That's another case to look at, after we finish this one. Those guys up in Arkansas, their accountants *and* their lawyers all lied through their teeth about the excellent shape their bank was in.

Roberto and I were confident we could handle the problem. All we needed was a commitment from another lender. Until then, we'd arranged financing locally in the community where the project was going in. But after our experience with that bunch of crooks in Little Rock, we decided to steer clear. We couldn't let it happen to us again."

"So what did you do?" I asked.

Caponi shook his head and looked at me gravely. "We made an even more serious mistake. I realize that now, but we decided to go to a bank from our own home base. I actually was foolish enough to believe it would be good for relationships in the community if we let a local bank in on one of our deals. I called Carroll Carter, president of First Texas Republic, and explained what had happened to us up in Arkansas. He said our needing twenty-million in permanent financing might be a shade too strong for his bank to take on alone, but he asked if we'd be willing to consider meeting with representatives of several of the area banks about them possibly participating in a loan.

"Wait a minute. You mean several of your competitors, all of whom were taking a beating from Centennial because of your interest rates, were actually interested in making a loan to you?"

Caponi gave me a sheepish, uncomfortable smile. "I realize how that sounds now, and I'm embarrassed to admit how naive I was."

"I assume the meeting took place?"

"Oh, yes. It took place all right. I wouldn't be here if it hadn't. I went with Roberto. Mr Carter was there along with representatives from most of the other banks in the area. I explained the situation up in Little Rock and let Roberto fill them in on Centennial's operating history. Then, Mr Carter asked what would happen if they decided they wouldn't be able to help. I said we'd simply go elsewhere, maybe to the East Coast. The representative from Commercial Bank asked what would happen if we couldn't arrange a new loan from any source. I tried to explain how that was never going to happen, but when he persisted, I thought he was just being dense, so to get him off the subject I finally said if that happened, we'd be in some trouble. All of our personal assets were tied up, pledged for the construction financing up in Little Rock.

I shook my head. *Man, this was getting interesting.*

"Andy, you must understand, until that point, the meeting was very cordial. Everyone genuinely seemed interested in being involved in the financing we needed. But after we left, supposedly to let them talk about structuring the loan package, instead they went to work figuring out ways to do us in."

"How do you know?"

"Uh, you know Tom Davis, the attorney from Port Arthur, don't you?"

"Sure. We had a case against each other a couple years ago. Good lawyer, and seemed like a neat guy too."

Caponi gave me another grave look. He thinks well of you, too. In fact it's really his recommendation that caused me to seek you out."

This was getting more confusing by the minute. "What does Tom Davis have to do with this?"

"Andy, Tom attended the entire meeting, acting as counsel for First Texas. After Centennial went under, he called and told me what happened."

I leaned forward. "Sir, don't take this the wrong way, but I find that pretty hard to believe. Tom isn't the sort of lawyer who goes around revealing privileged communications."

Caponi dismissed my statement with a shrug. "When was the last time you spoke to Mr Davis?"

I thought for a moment. "I guess it has to be more than a year."

"Then I guess you don't know. He's very ill. Cancer. Doesn't have much time left."

"What?"

He nodded. "And that was why he called me. He said people in his position sometimes realize they have a higher authority to answer to than the bar association. So he told me about Carroll Carter and that bunch he rounded up to attend that meeting. As soon as we left, they went straight to work figuring how they could hurt Centennial the most. Ultimately, they decided to spread word that Centennial was about to go under and its customers would probably be left holding worthless certificates of deposit. They always used to say our depositors were taking a large risk because our certificates weren't federally insured. But this time, they embellished the story, saying Centennial was controlled by the Mafia, who'd been siphoning off assets to the point our certificates were worthless. That our ability to satisfy paying off withdrawals was based on nothing more than a pyramid scheme. And, Andy, those folks didn't waste time. They spread their pack of lies so effectively, by the end of the day we had a full-blown run in progress."

I propped my elbows on the table, by now all ears. If what I was being told was true, Vincent Caponi had a damned good case. "So what happened next?"

Caponi smiled. He could see he'd gotten my attention. "Well, then the papers, the *Enterprise* and the *News*, each ran stories saying there had been a large number of Centennial depositors who were making withdrawals due to lack of confidence in the company's operations. The *Enterprise* even did a story *confirming* my link to the New Orleans Mancuso family. That was the kiss of death. After that, the situation snowballed. We tried to find interim financing, hoping we could ride things out. But we discovered no bank would touch us with a ten foot pole. That left no other choice. We filed for Chapter Eleven here in Houston."

I'd long since stopped taking notes. The picture was clear. Was I interested? With what I faced, I still wasn't sure. But despite those misgivings the juices were definitely beginning to flow.

"Andy, I'm prepared to give you a check for your initial expenses. Actually the money is my wife's. She's been selling off antiques and jewelry at a little shop she opened up in Humble. As for your fee, I'll assign a third of everything you recover for Centennial. Our bankruptcy attorney assures me she can get the judge's approval. And Roberto and I will assign forty-percent of our personal interests. Together, we had over fifteen-million dollars invested. But before you say anything, I urge you, please confirm what I've told you."

"I intend to," I said. "Who is it you have handling your Chapter Eleven?"

Her name is Rebecca Zimmerman. I have her card if you need her number."

"No, that's okay. I know her." I guessed Caponi already knew that. She was another friend who started at Marshon & Davis at about the same time as Monica. She opened her own shop after determining she didn't fit the big-firm mold.

He smiled broadly. "Andy, I'm pleased. We are going to make a great team." That said, he got up and walked to the door, turned and nodded formally.

Moments later, Elaine came in. "How'd it go?"

"I'm not sure. We might be getting into something I'm not prepared to handle."

"Well, he sure seemed pleased when he left. He gave me something to give to you."

"What?"

Elaine held out a plain-white letter-sized envelope.

"I think I can guess, but let's see."

She opened it, looked inside, and whistled softly. She withdrew a cashier's check. "Pay to the order of Andrew Givens, fifty-thousand dollars. Has a nice ring to it, doesn't it?" she asked, smiling at me.

"You'd better put it in a safe place."

"You mean you don't want it deposited?"

"Not now. I have some calls to make first. For the time, let's just put it away. Then, if you can join me, I'd like to take you to lunch. I have a story to tell about a man named Vincent and a company called Centennial Savings Association."

## Chapter Eleven

The day after my meeting with Vincent Caponi, I called Rebecca Zimmerman. She was expecting me. Caponi had already instructed her to disclose any information I wanted. According to Rebecca, Centennial wouldn't come out of Chapter Eleven alive, unless Caponi succeeded with his lawsuit. The bankruptcy judge understood the score, and that's why she was certain my fee arrangement with Caponi would be approved. She also confirmed that the company's last financial statement, before the run by its certificate holders, stated Centennial's net worth at just a little over eighty million dollars.

When I asked her opinion about Caponi, she assured me he could be trusted. "You'll be dealing with a real rarity," she said. I asked what that was and she replied, "A truly decent man."

My next call was to Mitchell Starlarski. In addition to operating his thirty-odd convenience stores and playing more than any man's fair share of golf, Mitchell also managed to find time to serve as one of the directors of the Bay Shore Bank, a nifty little jewel operated by one of his pals out on the east side. Mitchell said he could probably find out what the banking community thought of the Caponis and Centennial and promised I would hear back from him by the next morning. By the enthusiastic tone of his voice I could tell he was pleased that I was considering Caponi's case, and that he'd turned Caponi on to me. I didn't say a word about Tom Davis.

My last call was to Tommy Jackson. Tommy was one of Del Wallace's old clients who I'd met when Del was helping him with a public stock offering for his marine ventures.

Tommy hadn't gone through with the offering. In fact, he pulled the plug right in the middle of the deal, one that was virtually guaranteed to make him a very wealthy man. The problem was, Tommy and the world of corporate finance just didn't mix. He couldn't get used to the idea of having all of those accountants and lawyers and other assorted hangers-on living with him for the rest of his days.

He was in his early fifties, and those years had been tough ones. His rugged, weather-beaten face had more lines than a Tennessee road map. His most prominent physical feature was an ugly purple scar running vertically down his bulbous whiskey nose. He got the scar jumping from the deck of a push boat that crashed into the railroad bridge at Baton Rouge. Tommy insisted the accident happened because of a heavy fog that night. Others, including the investigators from the Army Corps of Engineers, thought alcohol had a lot to do with the accident. Although Tommy admitted he once had a problem with the bottle, he swore he never let anybody drink on one of his boats, himself included. To prove the point, he kept what little hair he still had slicked down with baby oil, a habit he developed as a young deck hand when he discovered one of his fellow crew members drinking his Vitalis.

Tommy owned several businesses, a barge-towing company, a drilling mud company, an off-shore rig supply business, and his pride and joy, the best seafood restaurant on the Texas Gulf Coast. He knew practically everyone who lived in that part of the country. And though a lot of people who belonged to the so-called upper-crust of East Texas society didn't care much for Tommy, considering him an uneducated, uncouth scoundrel, he'd always shot straight with me.

When he answered the phone, and recognized my voice, the needling began immediately. "Well, Andrew, my, my. What'cha got yourself into, boy? The papers say you killed a client. Now ain't that somethin'? You, a big shot lawyer, and now you're in more trouble than me. I guess that's just about the only thing I ain't never been accused of. Son, you can tell me, did you really do what they say?"

"It's good to talk to you too, Tommy."

"Andrew, allow me to give a piece of advice. Ya gotta remember. They can kill ya, but they can't eat ya. Understand?"

I wasn't sure what the lesson was that I was being taught, but said, "Thanks, I'll try to remember that, Tommy. But the reason I really called is I need some information and thought you might be able to help."

"Andrew, that's gonna cost ya. Ya realize that don't ya?"

Tommy enjoyed baiting lawyers and accountants and, I suppose, all of the other people who charged fees for their time. He always tried to negotiate his own fee for any requested favor by one of us 'parasites.'

"That's fine with me, Tommy. I'll give you credit on the next invoice I send at double my hourly rate. How's that?"

"Andrew, my boy, you're gettin' creative on me now, ain't ya? A trade sort'a. I guess that's okay, but I still gotta bill ya. My accountants make me send them things."

"What can you tell me about a fellow from over in Port Arthur by the name of Vincent Caponi?"

"Ya mean the fella who used to run that savings association that went bust?"

"Yes, he's the one."

"Well there's not much I can say. I met him a few times over at my restaurant. Liked him okay. He ought to get rid'ah that stupid little beard. Makes him look like some kind'a odd duck, if ya know what I mean. He had hisself a good thing in that savings company, and was for damn sure causin' the bankers over here more than their fair share of migraines. But now, there's a bunch'a folks over here who think he's the devil hisself. The talk is, he's some kind'a mafia don. I kind'a doubt that. But who's to say? What really has everybody so pissed at him is that when his company went into that Eleven, a whole lotta folks lost every damn cent they had to their names. It always comes down to money, don't it?"

"Everybody over there sees it that way?"

"Damn it, Andrew, wha'da'ya think I am? Some kind'a mind reader? I dunno. But that fella ain't gonna' win no popularity contest, not around here."

"Tommy, do you know, did Caponi do anything wrong, you know, like cheating his customers at Centennial?"

"Well, Andrew, *everybody* does things wrong. You know that don'cha? But did he *cheat* anybody? Hell, I dunno. I really don't. I heard some rumors that maybe some of the financial wizards at the banks over in Port Arthur put the screws to the poor bastard. He's probably still trying to figure out what hit him. Lemme put it to you this way, everything I know about Caponi is he and that boy of his were runnin' a square operation. But Andrew, what I know ain't worth much."

"What sort of rumors are out there about the banks?"

"Oh, nothin' more'n they were lookin' for a chance to pop it to Caponi and when it came along they gave it to him, big time. Say, Andrew, if you're callin' to find out if I think Caponi's worth gettin' involved with in some kind of lawsuit against them sorry bloodsuckers, I can't say. Personally, I think anybody that'd try what Caponi was doin' deserves a god-damned medal, but he probably needs a little extra in the brain department too, for ever tryin' to be such a do-gooder in the first place. I'll just say this, if ya do take a case against them guys, I hope you tatoo 'em good. Them wise asses need it, bad."

"Have you seen Tom Davis lately?"

"Guess ya ain't heard," he replied, "Tom's real sick. Gettin his lungs chewed up by the big-C. I heard they put him in St. Elizabeth's and now he's in a coma. The docs don't expect him to wake up."

"I knew he was sick, but I didn't know it was that bad."

"Yeah," Tommy said, a new tone of sincerity in his fog horn voice. "Too bad about that boy. He's a pretty decent human. For a lawyer, that's saying somethin' ain't it?"

"I guess so, Tommy."

"Andrew, you be careful, ya hear?"

"You know I will."

As I hung up, Elaine popped her head in the door. She wore a bright red dress with gold embroidery on the cuffs and sleeves. A pretty fancy outfit considering the casual dress code we adopted when we opened the new office. She said she had a lunch date. Must be her new boyfriend. I reminded her that Mark was coming out later that afternoon. She promised to return before he arrived.

I spent my lunch hour working on a draft of a complaint to file in the Centennial case. I was already thinking of it in those terms. Though I still hadn't decided to take it and wouldn't until I talked with Mitchell Starlarski. Just the same, tinkering with a draft couldn't hurt anything. And it kept my mind occupied with something other than speculation about the quality of prison food, what my cell mate might be like, and all sorts of similar questions that kept running through my mind.


Elaine and Mark arrived together. She was giggling, probably at another of his cowboy jokes.

"Why don't we meet in the conference room where there's space to spread out?" I suggested.

"No need for that, at least not right away," Mark said. "We have to be out at Thrasher Industries in thirty minutes."

"What on earth for?"

"We have a right to examine the crime scene. It won't do nearly as much good for me to go alone. They have to leave everything in place until we've had the opportunity to take a look."

I frowned." Are you sure this is a good idea? I mean, is this really necessary?"

Mark nodded emphatically, "Yeah, it's a very good idea, and it's absolutely necessary, too."

Elaine asked, "Do you want me to come along?"

"Sure," Mark said. "In case your boss hasn't told you, you're working as our legal assistant, darlin'."

The idea of the three of us traipsing into Thrasher's office still made me uncomfortable, but Mark was insistent. We took his car, Mark insisting that I sit in back, in case the parking garage camera was rolling. He didn't want to give anybody the chance to compare images on different video tapes.

My old friend, Detective Springer, was waiting in the lobby when we arrived.

He nodded and said, "When you go up to the office, don't disturb anything. I'll be with you to make sure you don't."

A uniformed officer waited at the elevator. Springer gestured to him and he let us get in. We all rode up together to the top floor, to what had been Thrasher's private office. Even though the Thrasher Building was only six stories high, it seemed like a long ride.

We had to wait until the receptionist behind the locked double-glass doors noticed us and pressed the button on the console.

In a low whisper, Mark asked, "Was this in place when you were up here working with Thrasher on his lawsuit?"

"Uh-huh," I whispered back. "Thrasher told me his father had it installed when he was in charge."

We followed Detective Springer and the other officer through the conference room that led to the entrance of Thrasher's office. The glass door between the conference room and the office was propped open with a chair, and a yellow plastic strip was taped from one side of the opening to the other with stenciled black lettering: "HOUSTON POLICE DEPT. DO NOT CROSS." Springer stopped just inside the doorway, blocking us. He seemed intent on keeping us from examining the room from any vantage point other than where we stood.

Mark immediately got in the detective's face. "You know I'm entitled to view this as thoroughly as I want. I can assure you I'm not interested in merely taking a peek from barely inside the door. And you also must know, I'm entitled to and I need to be able to consult with Mr Givens and our assistant while we're here, so why don't you and your friend wait in the conference room. You can watch us from the other side of that glass wall."

Springer grinned. "No way, Watson. You don't like it, take it up with the DA."

Mark turned to me. "Andy, you and Elaine stay here. I'm gonna call Albert Anderson."

"There's a speaker phone inside the credenza in the conference room," I said. "I'd like to hear what Anderson has to say, if you don't mind."

"That's a fine idea," Mark said. "Springer, why don't you join in. That way, you can explain why you and your sidekick are so intent on violating my client's rights."

We didn't have to bother. His bluff called, the Doughboy backed down. He shrugged indifferently and left us alone in Thrasher's office.

The first thing I noticed was a chalk tracing like the ones I'd seen in films outlining the position of Thrasher's body. He'd been seated at his desk, head and shoulders atop it, arms flung out in front. A dark, rust-colored stain ran off the corner and the rear of the desk top. Similar stains covered the plush beige carpet at the front and behind the desk. A lot of blood had been spilled. A chill ran up my spine and I became suddenly queasy at the thought of streams of red cascading into slippery, glistening pools on the once pristine carpet.

But I suppose it could have been worse. Apart from the stains and small flecks of dried blood on top of the desk and on the far wall, Thrasher's office appeared pretty much the way I remembered it. Ornately upholstered velvet arm chairs next to the windows with the Galleria view. Elaborate displays of photographs and memorabilia. Mark sketched a diagram of the room and had Elaine help with dimensions using the tape measure Mark brought. I left them to it. I'd already seen more than enough.

"What about the stains," Elaine asked. "There sure must've been an awful lot of blood."

Mark shook his head. "We're almost done, darlin'. Let's talk after we're out of here. There's no point tempting Springer to eavesdrop. Andy, do you have everything here pretty much in mind?"

"Yeah," I said, though all I could really think about was the image of Thrasher lying there with his skull smashed in and blood all over the desk and the floor.

"Come over here for a minute will you?" Mark asked. "Is this the way the office always looked? It's awful neat in here."

I started to say how Thrasher treated his secretary like a maid, but Mark stopped me.

"Outside," he whispered, gesturing toward the open door where Springer was edging ever closer. "Let's get out of here," Mark said.

That was fine by me.

## Chapter Twelve

On the ride home I couldn't get the images of those blood stains and the chalk outline of Thrasher's body out of my mind. Even Mark was subdued. The three of us made the trip in silence. Now, we sat together at one end of the long polished walnut table in the conference room.

"Well, where do we go from here?" I asked.

"I'm not sure," Mark answered. "Let's start by reviewing the case we know the prosecution has. First they have Thrasher, killed in his own office by multiple blows to the back of his head. The word is, the killer used a baseball bat that Thrasher kept in his office as part of his collection of sports memorabilia. We'll know for sure when I file a motion for disclosure of a list of the State's physical evidence. You know anything about a bat, Andy?"

"Yes. I didn't really think about it not being there, but it wasn't. Thrasher was proud of that bat. One of the Astros gave it to him a couple of years ago."

"How did he come to have something like that in his office?" Elaine asked.

"Oh, his family once had a small interest in the Houston Sports Association," I said. "That was the outfit that used to own controlling interest in the Astros. I don't think it still has anything to do with them, but Thrasher always acted like *he* owned the team, and he liked to collect things from the players. Must have made him feel important."

Mark went to the flip chart clipped onto a portable easel in the corner of the room. At the top of an empty sheet he wrote with a red marker:

Victim - Thrasher

Location - Thrasher's Office

Murder weapon - Baseball Bat?

"What sort of evidence will they be allowed to present about the condition of Mr Thrasher's body?" Elaine asked, leaning forward in her chair. "I see a lot about criminal cases on television and they always show a lot of awful pictures of the victim. Mark, does that really happen?"

"Yeah, 'fraid it does. We always offer to stipulate to facts that will keep 'em out, but there's not a prosecutor in Harris County who's stupid enough to agree. There'll be plenty of blood splattered all over everything, including the recently departed William Thrasher. It'll all be there, in full color, for the jury's viewing pleasure."

I swallowed, my throat gone dry. "Another thing's just as sure."

"What's that?" Mark asked.

"By the time those folks finish looking at that stuff, they'll be ready to crucify the sorry son-of-a-bitch who did it."

"Yeah," Mark agreed, "we might as well get used to that."

Elaine propped her head in her hands and looked at Mark."Isn't there any way at least some of the pictures can be eliminated?"

Mark sighed. "Darlin', Albert Anderson will have so many reasons for presenting what he wants shown to the jury, we'll be seeing lots of pictures, you can count on it. There's simply no way to keep 'em out."

"It seems to me we're best off by conceding the murder was violent and gruesome," I said.

Mark nodded. "You're absolutely right. We have to be prepared to go into court just as interested as the State of Texas in meting out harsh punishment to whoever had the audacity to commit such a despicable act."

Elaine sat up straight. "You know," she said, "just because what happened out at Thrasher's was so awful, doesn't mean Andy is guilty. While we were there, I kept asking myself, who could possibly believe Andy Givens could do something like this?"

Mark grinned. "That's real good. Darlin', you get a gold star." He turned his attention to the flip chart. "Now, what about Thrasher's office? Andy, you notice anything that seemed unusual?"

I shook my head. "No, not really. But I didn't even notice the bat was missing. Thrasher kept it next to the window behind his desk. He paced around during our meetings and sometimes he liked to pick it up and carry it around with him. It's strange. When he was angry, I worried someday he was going to hurt somebody with that bat."

"The office was pretty tidy. Nothing seemed out of place," Elaine observed.

Mark wrote 'Tidy' next to the words, 'Thrasher's Office', on the flip chart. "Well, the State'll probably use the over-all appearance of the office to support the theory that the killer knew Thrasher and that Thrasher let him in that night. And they won't have any trouble proving you were a regular guest up there, either."

"Wait a minute," Elaine said. "Aren't you overlooking the fact that somebody could have gotten into the office without Thrasher knowing?"

"Darlin, I suppose anything's possible," Mark replied. "But did you see that security system out at the elevator? You can't get past the lobby on the top floor without somebody on the other side letting you in. I think it's most likely Thrasher did let his killer into his office that night. And that means he knew whoever that was."

Elaine persisted. "Even so, Mark, Andy wasn't the only person who Thrasher ever met with. How can anyone say who it was that Thrasher had up there?"

I knew the answer to that one. The videotape. "How many cars were in and out of the garage that night?" I asked.

Mark's bushy eyebrows arched. "We sure as shootin' wanna find out."

We could have continued, but the meeting broke up shortly after my question about what might be on the videotape. Mark was interested in getting back to his office to make sure our discovery motion included a request for videotapes, even though we weren't supposed to know one existed.

Until the trip to Thrasher's, I'd still harbored a slim hope that, somehow, the DA would conclude that putting me on trial for Thrasher's murder was a big mistake. I envisioned Albert Anderson and Lieutenant Puryear coming to me and apologizing for all the trouble they'd caused. Fat chance. Their evidence definitely pointed in my direction. Sure, the State still had to prove its case beyond a reasonable doubt, but maybe that wasn't as impossible as I'd first believed.

The key was the videotape. My car shown entering and leaving the garage at the approximate time of the murder. Were any other cars shown entering or departing Thrasher's garage that night? Hopefully, the video would have something on it that Mark could utilize to at least raise the question of whether anyone else with a motive to kill Thrasher was there that night too.

Eventually my thoughts turned to Centennial Savings. What was I doing, taking on another one of those cases of a lifetime, when all of my energy needed to be devoted to staying out of prison?

Elaine returned from showing Mark out and asked if I needed her for anything else. I told her no. Anything we had could wait. I didn't feel like trying to work that afternoon anyway. What I did feel like was having a drink.

I got in the little shit-box on wheels—all the rental agency had available when my own transportation was waylaid by HPD—and drove to Spec's for a quart of Gordon's. Back home, I sat at my desk, pondered the sorry state of my life, and attempted to drink my problems away. Sitting in the quiet stillness of the early evening, watching the shadows lengthen as dusk turned to night, I thought about Monica. What could I do to convince her it was still worth trying again? I just didn't know. As the room grew darker, I couldn't get the thought out of my mind. What had I done to deserve the rotten hand I'd been dealt?

When I woke up, the sun was shining through the window in my bedroom. I was on my bed (how I got there, I don't know), still dressed. My mouth was dry and tasted bitter. The faintly sweet aroma of gin made me gag. I made a feeble effort to get up, but the slightest motion delivered incredible pain, right between the eyes. Ivory rubbed against me and licked my cheek with a sand-papery tongue, an impatient reminder of my most important function—serving him his Friskies Gourmet. As foggy memories of the preceding night began to emerge, I blamed my sorry condition on Ivory. He hadn't lifted a paw to stop me. He'd just have to wait. That would teach him. Somehow, I managed to ease under the comforter. Lamenting my party with Mr Gordon, I pulled a pillow over my head.

When I hadn't ventured down by mid-morning, Elaine came upstairs. "Andy, are you all right?"

I peered out from under the pillow, the sunlight still blinding. My secretary stood in the doorway, hands on her hips, definitely unamused.

Her voice as hard as flint, she said, "Well this isn't going to help anything, now is it?"

"Elaine, I think I've come down with some kind of a bug," I mumbled.

"The only bug you've got came from that gin bottle downstairs. You know, the one that's almost empty?"

*Funny, I thought it was empty.* "Yeah, well maybe that could have something to do with it. They say that stuff is bad for your resistance."

She frowned. "It's also bad for your liver, your heart, and a lot of other important things. Like brain cells for instance." She took a small step toward me and stopped. "Andy, you're a great boss and I practically begged to come back to work for you. You know that. But I'm not going to sit by and watch you self-destruct. I'm saying this for your own good and I hope you realize that and take it the way it's intended." She came closer and pulled the comforter onto the floor. "Mister," she said, "you get yourself into the shower pronto. I'm bringing coffee and toast up in a few minutes, so you'd better hurry."

I managed to force myself into a sitting position. A few painful moments later, I stumbled toward the shower.

Elaine was speaking with someone downstairs. I clutched the knob on the bathroom door and tried to listen for who was there. No use. My head pounded too hard.

Three extra-strength Excedrin and a tepid shower helped. By the time I dressed and got downstairs, I was beginning to think, just maybe, I might actually live to see another day.

Elaine was seated at her desk opening and posting the morning's mail. "A fresh pot of coffee's on. It should be just about ready," she said.

I smiled as brightly as I could in a vain attempt to demonstrate normalcy. Not very many people out there were on my side. Without question, Elaine was. I couldn't afford to lose her support, and vowed to stop acting like such a weakling.

I picked up the mail and took it with me into the kitchen. "Want a cup?" I shouted, causing my head to throb.

"Yes, thanks."

I poured two steaming mugs and put sweetener and a stir stick in Elaine's. Taking the opposite way around, I passed through my office and dropped the mail on the desk. When I got back with her coffee, I asked, "Who was here a while ago?"

"Oh, that was Sharon Fielder," she said, her cheeks turning crimson.

I was light-headed and my legs shook from the exertion of standing. To conceal how bad I still was, I sat on the edge of her desk. "What's wrong? You're blushing."

She looked away, her face flushed an even deeper shade of red. "Well, Andy, I could tell, by the sort of look I got from her, she was pretty curious about why I was coming down from upstairs. As a matter of fact, she acted as if she'd just caught me in your bed."

Oh *right*. Who would seriously think a sweet kid like my secretary would have anything to do with me? "Elaine, I'm sorry if Sharon upset you, but you shouldn't worry what she thinks. I sure don't."

"Andy, this isn't funny. The woman happens to be your wife's divorce lawyer, you know."

"What did she want anyway?"

"She dropped off drafts of a property settlement and decree of divorce. You know, she was sort of upset that you weren't available to see her and asked me to let you know her client is interested in finalizing the divorce as soon as possible."

I remembered last night's goal—getting Monica to come to her senses. So much for that. I felt like a dog that keeps getting kicked for no reason. "Where are the papers?" I asked.

Elaine searched the top of her desk and shrugged. "You must have picked them up with the mail. They should be at the bottom of the stack, in a white envelope with Ms Fielder's mailing sticker on the outside."

They were. I didn't take a lot of time reading what they said. Reviewing the documents that spelled the end of the most important piece of my life was simply too unpleasant. But I did skim through enough to see that Monica proposed selling the house and splitting the proceeds. A house. That's all it was. At one time, I thought it would be our home for the rest of our lives. Now, it was just another piece of real estate. I sure didn't want it. Obviously, Monica didn't either. She and Joseph Hartson probably planned on making a fresh start someplace else.

The agreement went on to state we both were to keep the personal property in our present possession and that we'd each relinquish all interest in the other's professional practice. That's what we had agreed earlier. My first impulse was to throw Sharon's drafts across the room. But I resisted. I wasn't about to let Elaine see me acting like an ass again. Instead, I went out back and sat on the steps.

The air was heavy, the heat absolutely oppressive. A typical summer day in Houston. My headache still raged, but I didn't care. I just stared vacantly at the dull green shine of the lawn, enjoying again feeling sorry for myself.

Ivory was crouched in the bed of ferns that grew along the fence, still as a black marble statue. Muscles quivering, he raised on his haunches and leaped onto the fence where he deftly snatched a chameleon from the fig ivy. He popped the lizard into his mouth, its skinny tail protruded from between his jaws, wiggling desperately as it turned from bright green to ashen gray. Ivory saw me and trotted over. He dropped the now black chameleon, badly mangled but still alive, at my feet and gazed up at me, seeking approval for his hunting prowess. The lizard attempted to limp away, but Ivory deftly planted a paw on its back, holding it in place.

I picked up my cat and held him on my lap, stroking his coat and giving him a good scratching under his chin. He purred loudly, and didn't seem to notice as his prey slipped into the grass.

In the sunshine, the gin slowly sweated out. Rivulets of perspiration ran down my face and neck, and my shirt soaked through. Eventually, the headache got better. Life didn't seem quite so hopeless.

Elaine came outside and sat beside me. She scratched Ivory's ears and ran her fingers along his spine, causing him to arch his back in appreciation. "Mitchell Starlarski called a few minutes ago," she said. "He asked if you could have lunch with him tomorrow. He said he has the information you asked him about. He has a bank board meeting at ten o'clock and wants to eat at the Cornwall at twelve-thirty. He's reserved one of the private dining rooms, so whatever he wants to say must be pretty important, huh?"

"You never can tell with Mitchell, but I hope so. I asked him to do some research about our friend, Mr Caponi." I put Ivory down and we went inside. Ivory followed. He'd had enough of playing the great jungle cat for one day.

Perspiration still dripped into my eyes. I wiped my forehead with my sleeve. "Uh, Elaine, there's one thing I would like you to do. Could you get Sharon Fielder on the phone?" If this was really what Monica wanted, I was going to have to get used to it.

Sharon seemed relieved to hear from me. Apparently, Monica had been putting the pressure on, wanting to make something happen. She explained how uncontested proceedings like ours were usually handled by a special assistant of the Family Court Judge called a Master, and suggested it might be best for everyone if I wasn't there for the hearing. I told her that was fine with me. I didn't relish the thought of standing in front of a judge, a master, or anyone else, with Monica and her lawyer putting the finishing touches on the last chapter of our marriage. That was one scene I would be more than happy to avoid.

## Chapter Thirteen

When I got to the Cornwall the next day, a new attraction graced the restaurant. A stunningly beautiful woman, in her early thirties or maybe a little younger, was working as hostess. Her long, wavy brown hair, enormous dark eyes, full, soft lips and prominent, high cheekbones gave her an exotic, seductive look. She wore a colorful floral print dress that fit pleasingly on a figure that I'm pretty sure made other women envious and I'm certain made red-blooded males take special interest. When I asked for Mitchell, she smiled and said he was waiting upstairs.

The private room was a little on the side of over-kill. But, as a kid who'd grown up on Houston's rough and tumble east side, Mitchell was insecure about his pedigree and always strove to do things right.

I took the chair across from him and said, "Well, Mitch, did you have fun this morning, foreclosing on little old ladies or whatever it is you guys do at your board meetings?" I didn't know why, but whenever Louis wasn't around, I found it necessary to fill in.

Mitchell frowned in mock protest. "Pards, that's not nice. Here I am, trying to do you a favor, buying your lunch at your favorite place, and this is all the thanks I get?"

"Mitch, don't get me wrong. It's just that you look so much like a banker, I guess I just can't help it. You know how everybody feels about people in your profession don't you?"

"Yeah, a whole lot better than they do about attorneys." Then, without giving me a chance to reply, he turned suddenly serious. "I see they're actually charging you with killing that client of yours."

I waved my hand, as if shooing a fly. "Not to worry, Mitch. I've got a good man representing me and we're working hard. I'd rather this had never happened, but when it's over, it'll be okay." I didn't know what my chance of winning *really* was, but what else could I say? It was awkward for Mitchell, not knowing what to say to a friend with a problem like mine. He smiled with relief when I shifted the conversation to the purpose of our meeting. "Mitch, did you learn anything about Vincent Caponi?"

"Yeah," he replied, brightening. "I got one of our officers at Bay Shore to do some checking. Had him say we were considering a request to participate in a financing for Caponi's company. Caponi had quite an operation going with that private savings association. But something happened. One day his credit rating was an A-plus and the next, it was an F."

"When was that?"

"The change came at the same time Centennial had a whole bunch of withdrawals by its certificate holders. Apparently, Caponi had most of his own money tied up in those certificates and when Centennial went in the drink, so did he."

I leaned forward. "Your guy find out why the withdrawals were made?"

"Yeah. I asked him about that. He wasn't really sure. All he could find out was it had something to do with one of Centennial's projects going south. You know, it wouldn't take much to start a run on an outfit like that. I'd be willing to bet my house Centennial's certificate holders heard plenty about the lack of safety in their investments from the banks over in Beaumont and Port Arthur. Centennial was beating their interest rates by a mile and they wouldn't have let the chance pass to pile on when somebody like Caponi found himself in a jam." Mitchell paused to sample the wine I'd selected. He screwed up his face in disgust. "Don't see how you can stand this stuff. It's so damned sour."

Attempting to get Mitchell to enjoy good wine was something I'd worked at on and off for years. But still, he'd never learned, preferring *Boone's Farm* over anything else. "What about Caponi?" I reminded him.

"Well," he continued, "you know, Andy, I don't see how the boy was doing it, but those interest rates he was paying, they were almost high enough to make me want to invest in his company instead of risking my money building more stores."

"Did your guy learn anything else?"

"Yeah. There's a couple of things. First, when he called those other banks and they found out that Bay Shore was thinking about participating in a financing for Centennial, he was told, more than once, that Centennial is most likely a Mafia front organization and the suggestion was made it'd be best to steer clear of gettin' involved with those boys. And they asked him, more than once, who the other banks was that might be thinking about doing a deal with Centennial."

"Is that right?"

Mitchell grinned. "Is the Pope Catholic? I'm sure all right. And there's another thing I'm just as sure about."

"What's that?"

"Just this, Andy. Vincent Caponi don't stand a chance of borrowing a nickel from anybody. Not with the mess he's in."

"Did your man keep notes, like for instance, who it was that he talked to?"

Mitchell shrugged. "I don't know."

"Do me another favor, Mitch?"

"You name it, pards."

"If your guy did keep notes, I'd like to see copies of them, make sure he keeps the originals. I might want to talk to that bank officer myself pretty soon."

Mitch chuckled. "Why? You thinking about taking out a loan? Word is, you might not be as good a credit risk as you was a few weeks ago."

I ignored Mitchell's last remark and thanked him for his help. When lunch arrived, the conversation shifted to Mitchell's business, which, as usual, was doing better than ever, and when we might have the time to get out on the golf course. I told Mitchell that might have to wait.

After we ate, I headed out the front door, ready to give my claim ticket to the valet, but Mitchell stopped me.

"Andy, do you have another minute to spare? There's someone who, as long as we're here, I'd like you to meet."

I said, "Sure," and we walked around to the restaurant.

The same attractive woman was still at the reception desk. Mitchell went directly to her and said, "Uh, Andy, I'd like you to meet a friend of mine, Susan Knight. Susan, this is Andy Givens. Uh, he's my lawyer, but don't hold that against him, he's a good friend, too."

She smiled and held out her hand. "It's a pleasure to meet you, Mr Givens."

The three of us stood there. Mitchell, having turned temporarily speechless, grinned like a farm boy showing off a prize heifer. I managed to say something inane about how much I enjoyed the hotel. Mitchell finally recovered enough to inform me that Susan was the hotel's new food and beverage manager. I said that was "nice." Then, before I had the chance to make an even bigger fool of myself, I said I had to go. Mitchell stayed. I didn't blame him in the least.

As I drove back to my office, I thought about what Mitchell had come up with. It confirmed everything I'd heard from Caponi's lawyer, from Tommy Jackson, and from Caponi himself. And Mitchell's information underscored just how far the banks were willing to go to keep Caponi on the carpet. The man was a pariah in the banking community. But he had one hell of a lawsuit.

It wouldn't be easy. But I knew I wanted his case. If Vincent Caponi still wanted me, I was in. As for my own problem, I had one of the very best criminal lawyers in the city representing me. It didn't make sense, putting my career on hold, and just sitting around wringing my hands waiting until the day my case came up for trial.

The decision made, I called Vincent Caponi and told him. He was happy. I was happy. One kicked dog deserves the help of another.


On Thursday afternoon, with a draft of the complaint ready, I called Caponi to invite him to my office. He had a creditor's hearing in Centennial's bankruptcy, so our meeting would have to wait until the weekend. But he did have good news to report. The bankruptcy judge had already approved my fee agreement. Right after our conversation, I called Mark Watson to check on where things stood.

"Andy, I start a drug trial in federal court down in Brownsville on Monday. That's gonna have me tied up for a while. I realize it might be inconvenient, but, if this sucker takes as long as I'm afraid it might, I may have to file a motion for a continuance in your case. We're on the December trial docket in case you've forgotten."

I hadn't. Mark had explained how he liked trying cases in December. Juries were usually less willing to convict around Christmas time.

"Anyway," he said, "I don't know, but with this trial starting down in the Valley, that might not give us enough time to get ready."

"Actually, a continuance might not be bad," I said and told Mark about the new case I was about to file and how it might keep me pretty busy, especially at first, when the defendants would file their inevitable preliminary motions, trying to knock us out of the game before it really started.

Mark seemed pleased to hear about my case. He thought it was important to keep working and not let myself "get all hamstrung" by what was happening in the criminal courthouse. Before we got off the phone, I asked him about his case in Brownsville.

"It's one of the easy ones," he said. "My man's guilty as sin."

On Saturday morning, Vincent and Roberto Caponi arrived promptly at eight-thirty. Vincent introduced me to his son with obvious pride. The younger Caponi shared his father's dark complexion and eyes. But all similarities in appearance ended there. Roberto was extremely thin, almost fragile, with delicate, almost feminine features. One thing was certain, no one needed to worry about being hurt shaking his hand.

Both men wore business suits, something of an oddity for a weekend morning. I wore my usual Saturday clothes, jeans, crew-neck cotton knit shirt, and running shoes, no socks.

I brought coffee and pastries from the kitchen and gave them each a copy of the complaint. I munched on an almond croissant while they reviewed the pleading.

After several minutes, Vincent put his copy down. "Andy, you have done a fine job telling the story. Don't you agree, son?"

Roberto smiled at his father, and said, "Yes, I sure do." But he glanced nervously in my direction and continued, "Please forgive me if this is not appropriate, but there are a couple of questions I have, Mr Givens. You should understand, I don't know much about lawsuits, so what I want to ask might seem pretty stupid."

"The only thing you can do that's stupid at the beginning of something is to have questions and not ask," I said.

Roberto's dark eyes darted quickly to his father. The older Caponi wore a perplexed frown. The young man hesitated.

"Well, go ahead," Vincent huffed.

Roberto looked at me, smiled a tight, nervous smile and said, "Mr Givens, if we are able to prove everything that is stated in the complaint you have prepared, what amount of money can we realistically expect to recover?"

"That's a good question. We don't want to lock in on a specific amount until we're a lot further along. As a matter of fact, if we were in state court, it wouldn't even be appropriate to ask for anything other than an amount which exceeds the jurisdictional minimum. But let me assure you, Roberto, we are going after every last cent when it comes to recovering Centennial's losses, whatever they might be, and you and your father's personal losses as well."

"What about punitive damages?" Vincent asked. "What can we expect to recover in the form of punishment for what has been done to us?"

I nodded. "Another good question. I'm glad you raised it. You shouldn't go into a case like this expecting to recover punitive damages. That doesn't mean we won't ask for them. We will. And it doesn't mean a jury isn't ultimately going to award them. Just don't get your expectations up and expect a windfall."

Vincent said he understood. But I wasn't so sure. Once into a big case, most clients find it impossible to resist the temptation of dreaming about having all of life's problems solved at the courthouse.

When they finally ran out of questions, I described the problem I saw about deciding the best place for filing the lawsuit.

Vincent Caponi said, "Andy, my son and I have argued about this. I'm worried about the people in the Golden Triangle. In case you've forgotten, we moved away from Port Arthur for our safety."

Roberto walked to the windows and looked outside. When he turned to face us, his thin lips were drawn tight. "Yes father," he said his voice rising in an exasperated tone. "That's true. But you know what I think. If we can change perceptions, win those people over, then a Beaumont court will be the very best place for our case."

Vincent Caponi's face turned dark. "Roberto, you know how those people feel. I'm not going to risk our chances. Not when there is already so much hate."

I swiveled in my chair, facing Roberto. "You see an opportunity to alter how Centennial's viewed over there?"

He nodded.

"How would you propose going about it?"

Roberto looked questioningly at his father who was continuing to stare at him harshly. He sighed and said, "Mr Givens, the certificate holders are an extremely diverse group. But they are controlled by a steering committee that was formed to see what could be done to recoup the money that everyone lost. The decision the committee made was to file a lawsuit against my father and myself. Rebecca Zimmerman has gotten their claims against us removed to the bankruptcy court. But if we can convince that committee that the certificate holders stand a better chance if they align themselves with Centennial instead of fighting against us, Beaumont would be the very best place imaginable for our lawsuit."

"I agree with you," I said. "Who serves on the committee?"

Vincent Caponi shook his head slowly and chuckled a wry, humorless laugh, making no effort to conceal his displeasure. "Oh, yes. I know them all. But the only one you would have to convince is Ronnie York. He's the one with the influence over the others. And I believe he's who hired Nathan Junell to file the lawsuit on behalf of the certificate holders."

I whistled under my breath. Junell spelled real trouble. The man was a state senator, his legislative district included Beaumont and Port Arthur. Before going into politics, he'd made a sizable fortune representing refinery and factory workers in asbestosis litigation and class-action lawsuits dealing with issues of safety in the work place. A case like the one against the Caponis was right up his alley.

"Vincent," I said, "do you have any objection to my at least having a meeting with Mr York and his attorney? Like politics, lawsuits sometimes make strange bedfellows."

Caponi's expression softened. "Mr Givens, I have hired you to represent us. I have confidence in your judgment and I intend to follow your advice. If you believe it might be worthwhile, I certainly have no objection to your meeting with those people. I would suggest though, that, if you do, you and Roberto should attend such a meeting without me. I have a temper and I am worried I might not be able to control it, especially if I find myself in the same room with the people who have had such insulting things to say about my family and our integrity."

I nodded.

Vincent asked his son to go out to their car and bring in the files on Centennial that I had requested.

"He's quite an impressive young man, you must feel very fortunate to have him as your son," I said.

Caponi beamed. "Yes. He's worked very hard. Graduated with honors from Tulane with a degree in economics. That only took him three years. Then he went on to the Wharton School in Philadelphia and got an MBA The day he joined me in my business was the happiest day in my life, next to the day when I married his mother, of course. But, Andy, I worry about him. He is so intense, and I know, he wants to please me, I'm afraid, sometimes a little too much. I wish he would take more time to enjoy life, maybe have a girlfriend, something other than always being so consumed with his work. But now that this catastrophe with our company has happened, there isn't much choice."

My first thought was that I wasn't at all sure that Roberto would be interested in girls. But what the heck, what did I know?


Early on Monday I called Nathan Junell. His office in Port Arthur was closed, but a message on the answering machine informed me he could be contacted in his Houston office. At the Houston number, a secretary answered. She said Junell was in conference. But he called back only a few minutes later. I explained who I was and asked if he and the head of the certificate holders committee would be willing to meet. He said they probably would, and we set a tentative meeting date for Thursday evening over in his Port Arthur office. That way, it would be easier for him to round up an appropriate representative from the steering committee. Later, I confirmed the meeting with Roberto. After I got off the phone, Elaine informed me Junell's office called saying we were on.

## Chapter Fourteen

We rode to Port Arthur in Roberto's Jeep Cherokee. Other than by their reputations, neither of us knew the men we were going to see. Junell was practically famous, a master politician and a skilled trial lawyer with a well-publicized flair for eccentricity. As for Ronnie York, Roberto said his father was correct in saying the man was respected. From what Roberto knew, he was a no-nonsense, crusty sort, who was accustomed to having things go his way.

We agreed the best way to handle the meeting was for me to make our pitch, which essentially was that the certificate holders were wasting their time beating up on the Caponis. If they wanted to really do something to recover their investments, they needed to work *with*, not against Centennial. Roberto's main function would be to field questions concerning the details of the company's operations. Seeing the way Roberto's hands trembled on the steering wheel, I tried my best to put the young man at ease. But after a couple of fruitless attempts, I gave up and we rode the rest of the way in silence.

Junell's office was in a one-story brick building located on the Port Arthur - Beaumont highway. The asphalt parking area in front was deserted. The heavy glass door at the entrance was locked, but a piece of paper torn from a yellow legal pad was taped to the inside of the door instructing us to go around to the back. Roberto followed as we waded through knee-deep weeds littered with trash, paper, and beer cans along side the building. An El Dorado and a Dodge pick-up with dealer's plates were parked near the back door.

Before I could knock, the door opened and an enormous figure appeared, motioning us in. I took a step inside and was hit by a chilling blast. The place was cold enough to hang meat. The only light in the long hallway came from a low-wattage bulb encased in a yellow-tinted plastic light fixture at the far end of the corridor.

The fellow who'd let us in wasn't the sort of person you would enjoy meeting in a dark alley, or in a dimly lit hallway, for that matter. He didn't say a word. He simply motioned with a wave of a massive paw that he wanted us to follow.

I was beginning to suspect this hadn't been such a hot idea, but after Roberto and I exchanged brief questioning glances, we followed down the linoleum-tiled hallway staying a few steps behind our guide. When he stepped under the shaft of light emanating from the overhead fixture, I could see he wore light-weight khaki shorts, a tank-top, and sandals. Here I was, practically freezing to death and this guy was dressed for a day at the beach.

From a few steps behind, Roberto whispered, "Andy, that guy, he is some sort of animal."

If the Incredible Hulk heard, he ignored the comment and leaned his considerable weight against the wall on the right side of the corridor. A door opened and we were motioned inside. This was getting more bizarre by the second. Roberto and I went in and the door closed behind us. We found ourselves in a windowless room with a long, beaten-up wooden table in the middle, surrounded by an odd assortment of chairs, none of which seemed to match the others. The walls were covered with cheap plywood paneling that had been painted, by the looks of things, a long time ago, in a depressing shade of industrial green. An old VISTA poster tacked into the plywood proclaimed, "If you're not part of the solution, you're part of the problem." The place reeked of stale smoke. Cigarette butts littered the floor. Someone had swept hundreds of them into piles in the corners.

Roberto's lips were drawn tight and, despite the cold, his face glistened with sweat. "Andy, maybe this wasn't such a good idea. I'm for getting the hell out of here right now."

I checked the door. Locked. I started to knock, but heard a loud scraping noise behind me. A section of the paneling on the opposite wall opened inward and a shaft of bright light flooded in.

A deep voice boomed, "Gentlemen, please come in."

We didn't wait for a second invitation.

A huge man, who I took to be Nathan Junell, was seated in a high-backed leather chair behind an enormous mahogany desk covered with mountains of paper. Another man sat in an armchair facing the senator, drinking a Pepsi from a can.

Junell stood and said, "Mr Givens, Mr Caponi, I apologize for making you come in through the back. But at this time of day, if people spot cars out in my lot, they'll come in and insist that I see them. I can't seem to ever get any work done around here anymore, what with all the damned interruptions. Brad—he's the fellow who let you in—informs me you must have left your Jeep parked out front. If you don't mind, why don't you let him take your keys and move it around back?"

Roberto frowned. But he must've realized refusing the offer meant another tour with the Hulk through the fun-house behind Junell's office. In any event, he produced his keys.

Well into his sixties, Junell was at least six feet tall and easily weighed three hundred pounds. He had an enormous head with cartoonish facial features. A wide mouth with full, fleshy lips that protruded like those of a fish. Elephantine ears, and a nose that would have put Jimmy Durante to shame. His eyes were dark close-set, intelligent, and active, almost animal-like as they darted from one side of his range of vision to the other, following every movement around him. His wide forehead slanted away from his nose to the point where his hair line began. He wore his yellowish-white hair in a sweeping, somewhat greasy pompadour. His white linen suit was rumpled and decorated with large coffee stains and was made out of enough fabric to make a two-man tent.

Junell said, "Well, Mr Givens, Mr Caponi, I apologize again but you have to admit, it's pretty interesting back there isn't it? I took this office over from a former client, the local of one of the unions I used to represent. I dropped those boys like hot lead when the president and two of the top stewards were indicted for racketeering. Their lease was paid up for the next couple of years and it was the only way to collect my fee." He shook his head and chuckled. "Those boys, they weren't convicted, but that would have been a whole lot different if the feds had ever found out about that room back there and what was in it. I sat at this desk for months, not knowing. Found it by accident. All the records of how those guys had been shaking down local contractors. Who was paying and who wasn't. By the time I made my little discovery, the trial was over and they couldn't be tried again. Mr Givens, I'm sure you can appreciate how that kept me out of one hell of an ethical dilemma. Gave me the perfect excuse to keep my mouth shut and keep a clear conscience at the same time. Only reason I'm telling you about this is one of the stewards is writing a book, one of those 'assisted by' things you see when the one with the story can't even spell his own name. A guy who used to write for the *Beaumont Enterprise*, so help me, he came in here the other day wanting to see the secret room. Said he's writing a friggin' book with this dumb-ass." He wiped his brow with the back of his hand and continued, "That's probably going to get them both in a hell of a lot of trouble. But I checked, and sure enough, they're actually writing the sucker. Don't that beat all?"

"Trouble, my ass," the man in the other chair said. "They'll be dead meat."

"Uh, gentlemen," Junell said, "this is Ronnie York. He's head of the steering committee for the class of certificate holders I represent."

York moved his chair around so he could see the two of us and Junell. He nodded, but didn't bother to stand. Older than I'd imagined, probably in his mid-sixties, he had a hawk-like face with angry, fighter's eyes, a thick white mustache and short white hair that grew flat against his head. He was thin, almost scrawny, with weather-worn features. In his younger days he was probably thought of as tough and wiry. Now, he just looked like some old, worn-out cowboy. His white western shirt, faded jeans, and dusty boots added to the image.

He stared at us, cool and impassive. It was plain to see, as far as he was concerned, we were about as welcome as two skunks at a picnic. I shook hands with Junell and held my hand out for York. He snorted and gave me an angry stare. Finally, he grudgingly took my hand.

Junell nodded toward the two empty chairs across from his desk. "Well now, gentlemen, exactly what is it that you want to discuss?"

"We want to show you how Centennial's certificate holders can get their money back," I said.

"That would be a neat trick," York retorted. "The Caponis are busted, at least that's what they're swearing to over in that damned bankruptcy court. If that's how it is, I don't see how we've got much to say to each other. I want you to know, no offense to that kid you brought with you, I aim to see that whole family behind bars before this is through. Just like that damned Keating bunch."

Roberto's face turned red. The veins in his slender neck bulged. Before he could say anything, Junell interceded. "Now, Ronnie, that's not what this is for. I told Mr Givens he should come over because we wanted to hear what he has to say. Why don't we give the man a chance?"

York folded his arms and grunted. "Okay, Junell. I still don't see why you're insisting on this, but let's hear it."

The big man turned to me. "Well, sir, how do you propose to go about doing that?"

I told them, trying to make it good.

As I made our pitch, York stared at me with growing irritation. Finally, he apparently had enough. "Mister," he hissed, "if you're suggesting that you want us to lay off the Caponis while you go on a wild-goose chase, trying to deflect attention off of your clients and onto people over here who are responsible, productive members of our community, well, sir, that ain't gonna' happen."

"Look," I said, "if you keep after the Caponis, none of the certificate holders are going to get anything. Surely you must recognize that by now."

York looked at me as if I was the most stupid person he'd ever met. "We ain't buying that bull. You're the one who needs to open his eyes. We got your boys by the balls. And we ain't about to turn 'em loose. Sooner or later, they'll start to holler 'cause it hurts so bad and those family folks, you know who I mean, the real nice ones from over in New Orleans, they'll come runnin' to the rescue."

Junell shouted, "Ronnie, that's enough!"

Roberto, who had said nothing since we entered Junell's office, touched my arm, leaned toward me, and whispered, "My father was right. We'd better go."

York glared at Roberto and said, "Look you little wop, if you have something to say to me, say it. Or does that Mafia mouthpiece you brought with you have to do all your talkin'?"

Roberto lunged from his chair. I grabbed his arm, pulling him back.

A livid Nathan Junell shouted again, "Ronnie, I think it's best if you leave." Turning to Roberto, he continued, "I apologize, Mr Caponi, for my client's behavior. He's upset, but that's no excuse to act the way he has."

"*Apologize*? For *me*?" York thundered." I ain't apologizin' to nobody. And Nathan, you ain't neither. What the hell is goin' on here?"

Nathan Junell laboriously pushed himself out of his chair, pulled himself erect, and in a calm voice said, "Ronnie, you and I can discuss this later. I have asked you to go. Now, I am telling you. Leave us, Mr York."

The old man's jaw dropped. He stared at Junell wild-eyed as if he'd just been shot and didn't believe it. But he recovered quickly. Glaring at Junell, he got up and stormed out. Doors slammed loudly outside. York was going to be hard to deal with. I was glad he was Junell's problem.

Junell flopped his massive body into the huge burgundy leather chair behind his desk. He rubbed his florid face with a meaty hand, his features contorting grotesquely. He sat for several minutes, holding his head in both hands. He seemed to have forgotten we were still there.

When he finally looked up, I said, "Mr Junell, thank you."

Junell waved his arm, dismissing my comment, and said, "No problem, Mr Givens. Ronnie and I go back a long way. Sometimes, you have to treat him rough or he'll get himself and everybody else with him in trouble. I can assure you that's not the first time I've had to kick him out of a meeting and it probably won't be the last. But he helped get me elected the first time I ran for the state legislature. And he's been involved in all of my campaigns since. I've helped him in lots of ways too. Taking on this lawsuit against your clients is just the latest in a long line of pay-backs."

Roberto edged forward in his chair, anger flickering in his dark, shining eyes. "Mr Junell, I want you to know, my father was against this meeting. He has been forced to put up with men like Mr York on too many occasions. This has all been so unnecessary. I am sorry, but it is best that we go back to Houston. I just want to say, what your client said about us is wrong. You are a fool if you believe him."

Junell stoked his chin and looked at Roberto. He broke into a wide grin and said, "Young man, don't you worry about me being a fool. I might be, but there's one thing you need to know. I don't get involved in lawsuits for the fun of it. I do it to make money. So I can assure you, I won't take any pleasure getting a judgement against you and your daddy, if it's of no more value than to use as a wall decoration. Your lawyer's the same. At least he is if he's any damn good. So, son, if you can show me a way to do what Mr Givens suggested, which, by the way, would happen to be in my client's best interests too, then I'm all for it."

"We came here hoping to get a feel for whether we have a reasonable chance to sway public sentiment over to the Caponis," I said.

Junell sighed. "I'm afraid what you just saw in Mr York's attitude is pretty much the way things are in the whole community. That might be next to impossible."

"Well, we might as well head back," I said. "Roberto, do you know of a good place around here to have dinner? It'll be late by the time we get back."

"Uh, Mr Givens," Junell said, "if you don't mind some friendly advice, if I were you, I'd just go on to Houston. I'd hate to hear that you had a run-in with somebody else over here. People are pretty mad right now. It would be best if you don't give anybody the excuse to do something stupid."


It was after eleven when Roberto dropped me off. I called the answering service for my messages. There was only one. Nathan Junell had called at ten forty-five. He'd left a number to call in the morning. I was exhausted and depressed. Water hauls had that effect on me. I kept asking myself, why hadn't I paid more attention to Vincent Caponi?

## Chapter Fifteen

When I called Vincent the next morning, he must have known I was calling to eat crow. He answered on the first ring. "Have you had a chance to speak with Roberto?" I asked.

"Uh, no, Andy, I haven't. He's moved into a new apartment down in your part of town. How did your meeting go in Port Arthur?"

"Well, I have to admit, Vincent, it was about the way you anticipated. One thing's certain. We don't want to file our lawsuit over there."

"I could have been more insistent that you not waste your time meeting with those people, but thought you needed to see for yourself. At least now you have a greater appreciation for what we are up against."

"True," I said.

"When will we file our lawsuit?"

"Everything is ready. I'll take it down to the courthouse this afternoon."

After the experience the night before, I wasn't eager to speak with Junell either. But since I was still in the medicine-taking mood, I called the number he'd left. A woman's high-pitched voice answered, "Jew-nell res-ah-dence." I asked if the senator was there. "Ah, one mo-men, ah'll go an' see," came the reply. There was a loud clatter on the other end of the line as the phone was placed on a hard surface.

Moments later, Junell came on the line. "Yes?"

"Senator, this is Andy Givens. You called my office last night after our meeting."

"That's right. I just want you to know, I think you might be on the right track with the lawsuit you're getting ready to file."

"I sure think so."

"I hope you understand, there isn't much I can do on a public level. I'm not about to take on the entire banking community. But the people who invested in Centennial Savings need their money back. If that doesn't happen, there's going to be one hell'uva lotta suffering. If I can help prevent that, I will. From time to time, I hear things. People come to me with all sorts of information. If I come up with anything that you might be able to use in your case, I'll let you in on it, that is, if you can agree to keep your source confidential."

Junell's offer was highly unusual to say the least. Here the man was, on one hand, representing people who openly admitted to wanting to see my clients behind bars, and, on the other, offering his assistance in helping them win their lawsuit against a bunch of powerful bankers that Junell wasn't willing to attack himself.

"Senator, I sure won't turn your offer down. But if you don't mind me asking, how can you help if your clients expect you to destroy the Caponi's in that lawsuit you have going?"

Junell chuckled. "The governor's calling a special session of the legislature this fall. The regular session starts after the first of the year. That takes us all the way through next summer. That case against the Caponi's isn't going anyplace for a while, and that's even if I wanted it to. In the meantime, if you get somewhere with your lawsuit, I won't have any problem calling off the dogs."

I thanked Junell and we promised to stay in touch. Then, I went to Elaine and asked if all of the copies of the complaint were ready. She said they were, so we packed my trial bag and headed downtown.

I left my car with the valet at Clive's, where I planned to buy my secretary lunch, and we walked the short distance to the courthouse. When the clerk stamped our pleadings, I learned the case was assigned to Judge David Lowenstein, one of the more experienced of the federal judges in Houston. He had a reputation for never playing favorites and for enjoying high-profile cases, attributes that could serve us well.

As we walked back from the courthouse, I shared my thoughts about the judge with Elaine. We were within half a block from the restaurant when I saw them, walking together, coming from the opposite direction, so wrapped up in each other they didn't notice me standing not twenty yards in front of them. Joseph Hartson stopped at the door to allow Monica to enter. She looked at him, smiled, and went inside.

I just stood there on the sidewalk. Elaine went straight to the valet and spoke to him and then came back to me. She touched my arm and said, "Andy, I don't feel like eating a big lunch today. Why don't we stop on the way back to the office and pick up a couple of sandwiches. I'd prefer that if you don't mind."

All I could do was nod.

The day had turned suddenly dark. A thunderstorm was rapidly moving in from the Southwest. We almost made it to Butera's before the sky opened up. A crackling bolt of lightning struck close by, followed instantly by ear splitting thunder. Then, rain came down in a blinding torrent.

I parked near the side entrance, and decided to make a run for it. "Wait here!" I shouted.

By the time I got inside, I was soaked. Waiting in line, water squishing in my shoes, angry for leaving Clive's, having been run off just by the mere sight of Monica and Pudge Hartson, I tried my best to put those thoughts out of my mind and ordered sandwiches and a half dozen of Butera's special oatmeal cookies. While one of the women behind the deli-counter prepared the order, I went to the cooler and picked out a cold bottle of chardonnay.

Outside, it was still pouring. Elaine held the door open and I made a dash for the car. She giggled as I handed her the wet paper sack and slipped inside. Although we had less than a mile to go, getting there became an ordeal. We had to detour off of Montrose before we got to the museum. High water was already causing cars to stall out there. I didn't want to risk the same fate, especially in an unfamiliar rental car, so I tried to make it home by meandering through South Hampton. We headed down Sunset, but had to turn back at Hazard, a street with an appropriate name for the day. Eventually, we were forced to circle back almost all the way to downtown to get onto Fannin which finally got us through. When we pulled into the driveway, rain was still falling, not nearly as hard as before, but it could still be classed as a downpour.

"Wait just a minute and I'll run upstairs to get an umbrella," I said.

Elaine wrapped her arms around the sack and said, "Don't be silly. It's just a little rain. You open the door. I'll be right behind you."

I hurried to the front door and slipped the key into the lock. But by the time Elaine made it inside, she was soaked too. Her silk blouse had become transparent, clinging to her like an extra layer of skin. Our eyes met in the reflection from the mirror over the fireplace. Elaine gasped, then turned beet-red. I put our lunch and the wine in a chair and headed upstairs to get some towels. By the time I got back, she was in the bathroom. I left a large towel and a pair of my cotton warm-ups outside the door.

Back upstairs, I changed into jeans and a worn, faded-blue Memphis State sweat shirt. When I entered the kitchen, I found Ivory sleeping peacefully on the hard linoleum floor next to the copier. It didn't look like a very comfortable place for a nap, but then I've never been able to figure out what makes that cat do some of the things he does. I opened the wine, got glasses from the cabinet and carried our lunch into my office. After a while, Elaine appeared, her foot bare, dressed in my warm-ups. Her hair was wet and her make-up was gone, but at what most women would consider their worst moment, she was still absolutely stunning.

We sat across from each other at the table. I poured the wine and gave her a glass.

"This is pretty good," she said.

"I need to apologize for causing this whole mess in the first place."

"What do you mean? It wasn't your fault it rained."

"You know what I mean. If I hadn't allowed the sight of Monica and her boyfriend to run me off, none of this would have happened. I have to admit, though, no matter how hard I try, I can't get her out of my system. And I just can't tell you how bad it makes me feel whenever I think about her and realize it's never going to be the way it used to be."

She swirled the wine in her glass. "My shrink told me being rejected by the person you love is like experiencing the unexpected death of a close family member. I don't really know about that, since I don't have anything to compare it with. The initial pain, that's what you're going through right now, it gets better after a while. It never really goes away, but you just get used to it, and then, it doesn't seem quite so bad.

"You mean you've been through this?"

She brushed a loose strand of hair from her face and her lips curved in a wry smile. "It's been a while. Over a year as a matter of fact. Everything was so perfect. And I thought we were both happy. I *know* I was. When Rob came home that night and told me he was moving out, it was so out of the blue. I hurt so much I didn't think I would live through it. If it hadn't been for my brother, I don't know what might have happened."

"What I find so hard to understand, and it makes me feel pretty damn guilty, is the fact that I didn't know."

"Well, in case you've forgotten, a year ago, you were already up to your ears in the Thrasher case. You didn't have your antenna out for picking up on that sort of thing."

"But why didn't you just say something?"

She sighed. "Andy, you're my boss. I wasn't about to trouble you with my problems."

"But we're friends too. At least I hope you see us that way. If there's ever anything I can do to help, you have to promise, you'll let me know."

Her lip began to quiver and she looked quickly away. "Okay, that's a deal. But we were talking about your problem, and, since we're friends, I want to tell you something. A lot of people wind up destroying themselves because they never get past the stage that you seem to be stuck in with this business with your wife. You know what you should do don't you?"

I shook my head. "I'm afraid I'm the one who doesn't have a clue."

She reached across the table and touched my hand. "It's time to get angry about what that insensitive bitch did. Excuse the language, but that's the word that fits, and it's time you use that anger to get over the worst of the hurt. Believe me, you've got to do that, if you're ever going to start feeling good about yourself again."

I shook my head.

She leaned back. "You're a nice man. You need to remember that and then, start acting like it."

The rain had stopped and the setting sun broke through soft cottony clouds, the last rays of light casting long shadows across the wet lawn. Ivory meowed, asking to go out. I opened the back door and he raced past. The air smelled of rain-washed plants and trees. Elaine came and stood next to me. I looked out into the yard where Ivory happily played his game of jungle cat.

"Thanks for the advice," I said.

She leaned against the door frame, her arms behind her back. "Thanks for being a friend,"

I was about to ask if she wanted another glass of wine, when she remembered, we hadn't mailed the service copies of the complaint. She hurried to her car to try to make the last pick-up at the Hyde Park Station.

"If these envelopes don't fit through the slot in the box outside, I'll be back," she said. "I'm not about to be seen in a sweat suit and high-heels."

I sat in the chair next to the windows and watched as dusk turned slowly into darkness. That special time of day when the world becomes quiet and peaceful. I had the unsettling impression though, that this was merely the calm before the storm.

## Chapter Sixteen

The sun was coming up as I dressed in light-weight nylon shorts, tee shirt, and running shoes and headed for Hermann Park. I started out slowly, letting my muscles warm up. Running three to six miles each day had once been a morning ritual. One that had come to an abrupt halt back in July, along with just about everything else. I'd been away for over six weeks, a fact that became painfully apparent in the steamy heat of the August morning. By the time I got to the jogging path around the golf course, I was already sucking air, and was soaked with sweat. I stopped, recovered my breath, and stretched until I spotted him, running with his usual easy, fluid motion. I got back onto the track and started running again.

It didn't take long until I heard his voice coming from close behind. "Hey, fella, what're you doing out here? Man, it's been a while."

I looked over my shoulder and said, "Hi, Del. I figured it was about time. If I didn't, I was afraid I never would."

Del Wallace caught up and then slowed his pace to match mine. "Yeah, this would be a pretty easy habit to break. First time I roll over and stay in that nice, soft bed instead of getting out here will probably be all it takes to make me quit."

It would take a lot more than that. That Winter, Del had completed the Houston Marathon. A special project he undertook after celebrating his fortieth birthday. His time hadn't been spectacular, but just finishing was quite a feat, especially for a forty-year-old first-timer. Now, he was hooked. Del giving up running was as unthinkable as someone voluntarily giving up an arm.

"How far you going?" he asked.

"Oh, I thought I'd make it once around and back to the house. That'll be a little over four miles. But the way I feel, I'm not too sure I'll make it."

Del grinned. "It's all that rain we had. Hot as it is, the steam just rises up out of the ground and saps the air right out of you. In a few more weeks, when it cools off some, we won't have to worry about that for a while. Let's see how it goes."

As Del gradually picked up speed, I dropped a couple of steps behind, and concentrated on maintaining his pace. For the first ten minutes, I didn't see how I could go another step, but somehow, I blocked out the burning sensation in my lungs and finally was able to relax and feel a rhythm in my stride. We glided around the park loop until we were back within a quarter of a mile from our beginning point. Del lengthened his stride and we finished at a full-out run.

He slowed to a trot, turned to grin back at me and said, "See? You can still do it."

My legs felt like heavy pieces of rubber and the coppery taste of blood welled in my throat. I held my arms up over my head, trying to take in as much oxygen as possible. "I did it all right," I said. "Now, the only question is, will I live to tell about it?"

Del wasn't even breathing hard and he laughed and began jogging in place on spindly legs that didn't look strong enough to support a fly. A few minutes later, we jogged out of the park, just like old times, as if none of the events of the last several weeks had ever happened.

As we approached my place, Del asked, "How are things going? I've been meaning to call to have lunch or something."

I smiled and said, "Del, I'm fine. It's not much fun, going through all of this, but then, I guess I really don't have much choice. Have time for coffee?"

He smiled, appreciating the fact I apparently didn't hold hard feelings, and said, "Sure, I'd like that."

I invited Del to look around while I got the coffee started. I brought a pot and fresh bagels into my office where Del sat, holding my cat. "At least it appears you're adjusting to life as a bachelor without much trouble," he said.

"I don't know about that. To tell you the truth, the situation with Monica, that's been harder to handle than anything else."

Del's eyes twinkled and he smiled, conspiratorially. "Then everything else must be pretty damned good. I honestly don't know what Charlotte would do to me if she came home and found a lady's under-garments in the guest bathroom. Obviously, you don't have to worry about that."

"What are you talking about?"

He rolled his eyes. "You mean to say, you actually don't realize you have a woman's underwear on the towel rack in the bathroom? You must be doing even better than I imagined."

*Oh, God.* I did my best to explain.

Del nodded, chuckled and said, "So those items belong to Elaine, do they? I guess I shouldn't be all that surprised. Did I ever mention to you that after the Christmas party we had for the firm's staff last year, Charlotte came home telling me that girl had her eyes set on you?"

"Del, that's ridiculous."

"Have to give her credit, the lady works fast. And, Andy, I have to say, you're a lucky dog. Just about every male associate we've got and, if the truth be known, probably more than one or two of your former partners, have tried to get in her pants. Hell, if I wasn't so scared of Charlotte, I'd probably have tried myself."

There was no sense attempting to dissuade him. Anyway, he was just teasing. I was at least a dozen years older than Elaine. Game playing and running kept me in reasonably good shape. But Elaine Turner? No way. She was definitely out of my league. I changed the subject by asking Del how the firm was getting along.

He became suddenly serious. "Andy, I'd be lying if I told you everything is fine. Whitfield has been on an absolute power trip. He thinks he won a big victory when you, uh, left. Now, he's trying to actually implement those billing quotas he's always favored. If we do that, we'll be the biggest sweat shop in the city."

"Steve Golden won't let him get away with that, will he?"

Del paused to take the last bite of a bagel. "I don't know. Steve's taken this whole deal awfully hard. He just doesn't seem to care any more. It hurts to see this happening to him. Almost as much as it hurts having to live with the fact that we turned our backs on you when we shouldn't have."

"Del, I want you to understand, I don't blame you."

He put Ivory down and went to the window. "No? Well, you should. With everything that's happened—Thrasher, Monica, us at the firm—Andy, I've felt like a traitor ever since that day in Golden's office. I'm sorry."

"You know, I thought my life was pretty damn good. Thought I had it all. But all it took was one bad day and everything changed. Let's just leave it at that, okay?"

Del swallowed hard. "Andy, if there's anything I can do to help, I want to know about it."

"As a matter of fact, I do need a favor."

Del's somber expression brightened. "What can I do?"

"You're going to find this hard to believe, but I have a pretty good reason to know someone, most likely someone from the firm, drove my car to Thrasher's office the night he was killed. I want to find out who."

Del stared at me wide-eyed. "Andy, that's pretty far out, isn't it?"

"Yeah," I answered. "About as far out as the fact that, as of this very moment, I stand accused of murder."

When I came downstairs after cleaning up, Elaine was at her desk. "You haven't happened to go into the downstairs bathroom since yesterday afternoon, have you?"

"Why, no, I sure haven't," I replied.

"Oh, good," she said with obvious relief.

I didn't have the heart to tell her.

It didn't take long that morning before the phone started ringing. Apparently, the *Centennial* lawsuit had struck a nerve. The first call was from the courthouse reporter from the *Chronicle*. She didn't really want to know about the lawsuit. She was more interested in finding out if my clients were connected to the Mancusos from New Orleans and if I was the same Andrew Givens who was charged with murdering William Thrasher. On the first question, I told her no, they were not. On the second, I confirmed that I was *the* Andy Givens.

The next call came from a reporter from the *Beaumont Enterprise*. He asked pretty much the same questions. *Texas Lawyer* even called. Everybody seemed to be working the same angle and it was one I didn't like: 'Members of reputed Mafia crime family, facing accusations of operating bogus savings association and stealing millions from unwitting investors, hire accused hit-man attorney to represent them in damage action against competitor financial institutions.'

I had just about decided to tell Elaine to hold all of my calls for the rest of my life when she came into my office and said, "Andy, there's a call from Joseph Hartson's office. He wants to talk to you."

I guessed he wanted to say something, man to man, now that I'd caught him out in public with the woman who, for the time being, was still my wife. Maybe he was worried that I'd follow through on my stupid threat. I picked up the phone and tried to sound as casual as possible, as if my wife's lover calling was an ordinary event.

Hartson's secretary answered. She instructed me, "One moment for Mr Hartson," and immediately put me on hold.

Feeling like an absolute fool, I held the receiver and waited. Several minutes passed until Hartson finally came on the line.

"Mr Givens, I have called because I represent First Texas Republic Bank. I understand you have filed a lawsuit on behalf of Centennial Savings Association and certain of its owners. Their names are Caponzi, I believe."

"Caponi," I corrected. "Are you telling me you intend to represent Texas Republic?"

"Yes, that is exactly what I am telling you." His voice dripped with arrogance.

"Hartson, don't you think you have a little bit of a conflict here?"

"I certainly am not aware of one. Marshon & Davis has an excellent system for determining those matters. I can assure you, we don't have one with this case."

"Look," I said, "I'm not talking about any conflict that your firm might have. I mean, don't you think, you and I might have more than the usual difficulty working on this, in light of the fact that you and my wife...."

"Oh, I see what you mean. No, Givens, that won't be a problem, at least not for me. Texas Republic has been a client of this firm for at least the last thirty years. When someone stands by us for all that time and comes to me with a problem, I assure you, I can keep my personal life separate from my professional one. I trust you can do so as well. If you have a problem with the situation, well, that's just too bad."

In the dictionary under the word pompous, the definition would have to say "Joseph Hartson." I struggled to maintain my composure. "Hartson, I have to say, I believe you are making one very serious mistake."

But he didn't seem concerned in the least. He treated me like a teacher with a slow student, not bothering to conceal the exasperation in his voice. "Givens, you will learn this about me: I do not often make mistakes, especially when it comes to trying lawsuits. In fact, the reason I called was to point out to you, lawyer to lawyer, you are the one who has made a serious mistake."

My grip on the telephone receiver tightened to the point I was afraid it might splinter in my hand. "Why don't you just tell me then, why did you call?"

"I've reviewed the allegations in your complaint and have discussed them with the President of Texas Republic. Your pleading contains the most scandalous, utterly false statements I have ever seen. Givens, you and your clients had better be able to prove every word. You and I know you can't do that, so I'm giving you a break. You can withdraw your pleading now, or you know what will happen, if you don't."

So, the big man from the big firm was going to try to intimidate me into quitting before the contest even started. Fat chance. "Hartson, I can assure you, I don't make it a practice to file frivolous pleadings, but if you want to move for sanctions, you just go ahead and do whatever you think you need to."

"Now, you listen to me, Givens, with all the trouble you've got, I'd have thought you would appreciate some friendly advice."

"Do you have anything else to say?"

Hartson didn't reply. Instead he simply hung up.

The last call that day came from Vincent Caponi. The press had gotten his phone number and he had received several calls. So far, he hadn't spoken to anyone. He said it was too much to ask of Sylvia to have her keep acting as a buffer, so he wanted to know how he should respond. That was easy. I told him to be his normal, gracious self, and tell everyone who called that he wanted very badly to tell his side of the story, but his lawyer insisted that all questions from the press had to be referred to counsel. I also told him to get in touch with Roberto to relay the procedure.

People enjoy blaming lawyers. Every now and then we can actually come in quite handy. This was definitely one of those times.

## Chapter Seventeen

The first item of business in *Centennial* was arranging with the defendants to exchange all documents that might be relevant to the issues involved in the case. I still intended to send formal discovery requests, just to make sure they understood what we wanted. Elaine volunteered to stay late on Thursday to get the final work product completed. The next morning, I was scheduled to pick up my parents at Hobby. If we finished everything that night, I could take them straight from the airport to the beach house I'd rented for the weekend, allowing us to miss a lot of the traffic headed to the island for the Labor Day weekend.

At almost eight o'clock the requests were finished. Elaine placed the stack of bulky envelopes containing the document requests and interrogatories on her desk to be delivered to the offices of the defendants the next morning. As we wrapped things up, I asked if she wanted to go get something to eat.

"Andy, that would be nice and I appreciate you asking, but look at me, I'm not dressed to go out." She wore a tailored, navy-blue skirt, a white cotton blouse, and navy-blue pumps. She looked more than dressed to me. But then, I've never been able to appreciate the female psyche.

"Well, we could stay here. There's probably something in the kitchen that I can whip together to make a decent meal."

"Oh, you don't need to go to the trouble. Besides, I almost forgot, I'm supposed to have someone coming over to my place."

She straightened the things around her desk and picked up her purse. I thought she was about to leave, but then she looked at me and said, "Why don't you come over? You're going to take off for a few days and there's someone I'd like you to meet."

"Thanks, but I don't want to be in the way."

"Andy, that's nonsense. I really would appreciate it if you'd come. Just give me half an hour's head start."

I needed to pack for the weekend, and I didn't look forward to playing the role of third wheel. But for some reason I found myself wanting to meet whoever Elaine had been seeing. Maybe, I just didn't feel like another evening of Lean Cuisine for one. In any event, I found myself saying okay.

Elaine lived in a four-plex on Miramar in the section of Montrose nearest the museums. Huge live oaks grew out in front. A tall, wrought-iron gate painted dark green bordered the far end of the parking area. It opened onto a long, narrow courtyard with New Orleans-style townhouse apartments on one side and a high, cedar fence covered with jasmine vines on the other.

When I rang the bell, a tall, slender young man, who I guessed was about Elaine's age, opened the door, smiled, and said, "Hi, you must be Elaine's boss. Come on in, she's upstairs changing, but she shouldn't be long." He had a full head of dark hair, combed straight back. A handsome guy, casually dressed in tan cotton slacks, a blue oxford cotton shirt with the top two buttons undone, and well-worn L. L. Bean moccasins over white cotton socks.

We shook hands and went inside. A flight of stairs and a corridor leading to the rooms on the main floor were immediately inside the door. He stood at the foot of the stairs and shouted, "Hurry up, Sugar, the rest of your company is here and we're starving." He led me down the hallway to a combination living and dining room. A white leather sofa, a matching easy chair, and a tan Eames chair filled the living area. Shelves made from cement blocks and boards lined the far wall and held a good-sized paperback library, tape cartridges, CD's, and what looked to be an expensive stereo system. On the opposite side of the room, was a rectangular dining table with a glass top and chrome base. Four directors chairs were positioned around the table, the seats and backs made of chocolate brown leather and the arms and legs of chrome.

My host offered to fix a drink. I asked for a beer.

"By the way," I said, "I didn't catch your name."

He laughed and said, "You mean Elaine didn't bother to tell you?"

"No. As a matter of fact, she didn't."

He laughed again and headed to the kitchen. He leaned through the pass-way and said, "I'll have to have a word with her about that, and Mr Givens, I apologize for my poor manners as well."

Just then, Elaine came down the stairs dressed in faded jeans and a mint-green long-sleeved cotton pullover with a v-neck. "Andy, you've met Eddie?"

I nodded and she said, "He's really something, don't you think?"

Eddie returned from the kitchen with two Heinekens. He handed one of them to me and put an arm around Elaine and asked, "What're you drinkin' tonight, babe?"

She ducked her head and slipped away from him, laughed and said, "Oh Eddie, will you stop it?"

It was plain to see they shared special feelings.

"How 'bout one of these?" he asked, nodding toward his bottle. She replied that she'd prefer wine and said there was a bottle in the refrigerator. When he returned and handed her the glass she said, "Andy, I'd like you to meet my brother, Eddie Turner."

"That's more like it," he said. "Mr Givens told me you hadn't said who it was you wanted him to meet."

"Oh, didn't I?" she asked, a little too much innocence in her voice. "Andy, I'm sorry."

I smiled and shook Eddie's hand again.

Dinner, it turned out, had been picked up at Hunan River by Eddie on his way over, Almond chicken, jumbo prawns, snow peas, and steamed rice. A lot better than your average Chinese take-out.

While we ate, Elaine and her brother gave a thumb-nail history of their experiences growing up together. Eddie was older by only eighteen months and, as kids, they moved frequently from place to place compliments of the U.S. Army. Their father was now a retired Army colonel. The moves afforded them few opportunities to make lasting childhood friendships. Little wonder they were so close.

From some of the stories they told, I reached the conclusion that life apparently hadn't been easy for the Turner kids. Their father was seldom home, but his absences hadn't been a cause for sorrow. Though his intentions had been good and he'd done the best he could, he'd approached the task of parenting with the mentality of a drill sergeant. Neither said much about their mother, other than she had been sick a lot when they were young. When Eddie went to high school, it was Elaine who attended all of his basketball games. And Eddie had been his sister's main support as she grew up too. Her most difficult years were in high school when Eddie was away at college. Her decision to leave the University of Illinois, where she was on a full academic scholarship, and to move to Houston at the end of her sophomore year was based largely on the fact that Eddie had a job in Houston in the Marketing Department of the Coastal Corporation.

Over his sister's loud protests, Eddie even filled me in on Rob Warren. According to Eddie, I got the condensed and censored-for-table-conversation version. Elaine had been working on completing her degree at the University of Houston when she met him. He was charming, brilliant and, according to Eddie, a "hunk." At the time, Warren was completing his doctorate in biochemistry, and taught a biology lab as part of his duties as a post-graduate assistant. Elaine had to take the lab to fill out the requirements for her degree. His offer to go for a cup of coffee led to a casual date. Within three months, Elaine had her degree and something else too. She'd fallen in love for the first time in her life. It wasn't long until they got an apartment together. She took the job at Golden-Wallace so Rob could devote his energy to completing his thesis.

According to Eddie, Warren's announcement a year later that he was moving out was the biggest shock of his sister's life. And to make matters worse, instead of simply leaving, Rob evidently thought he had to justify his decision by putting all of the blame on her. He said she wasn't intellectually stimulating, and his friends found her boring. He even claimed he was worried that continuing their relationship would reflect negatively on his judgment, and could hurt his chances of getting the assistant professorship he was pursuing.

Naturally, Rob's "justification" just about destroyed Elaine's self-esteem. Eddie moved in with her temporarily until the worst was over. And they still reserved Thursday evenings for each other. "Unless," according to Elaine, "Eddie has a hot date."

I helped Elaine finish what was left of the wine and remarked that it was still difficult to believe she'd gone through such an experience without me having an inkling that anything was wrong.

"I have to admit, it wasn't easy," she said. "But I needed to work. Eddie kept emphasizing the importance of that. If I'd lost my job on top of everything else, I don't want to even think about that."

"What ever happened to Rob?" I asked.

"Why should we care about that jerk?" Eddie replied.

"I'm sorry I asked. Just curious."

"That's okay," Elaine said. "As I understand, Rob Warren still hasn't completed his doctorate. I think he's teaching high school chemistry at one of those private Christian schools out around Katy."

Eddie laughed and said, "I doubt it if he'll keep that job too much longer, once his employer finds out he's living with a dancer from the Hot Lips Cabaret."

Elaine gave her brother an annoyed look and said, "Eddie, this isn't the time to start that silly game again."

Eddie's eyes twinkled as he broke out in a broad grin. "Why, Sugar, I know we used to make up all sorts of horrible stories about good ol' Rob, but this time, I'm only reporting the news. Had to take a customer there just the other night, company business you know. Anyway, there he was, walking out the door with this really outrageous looking young lady. Man, what a set she had. When I asked the girl at the hostess station, she told me Rob's friend worked as a dancer at the club. Said her old man had come to pick her up because she was feeling too sick to dance that night." Eddie held his hand over his heart. "That's the truth, Sugar, I promise."

"I thought you said he was only interested in the intellectual types," I said.

Elaine dead-panned, "She must be working there to pay her tuition at Rice."

At a little past midnight, Eddie said he had to leave. Sharing the evening with Elaine and her brother had been more fun than anything I'd experienced for weeks, and I was reluctant to see it come to an end.

On the way to our cars, Eddie stopped me. "Andy, my sister thinks a lot of you. Don't get me wrong. I think that's fine, the two of you becoming friends. Just remember, she's been through a lot. As far as I know, tonight is the first time since that asshole screwed up her head that my sister has let a man in her apartment, other than me."

I wasn't sure what Eddie meant. Elaine inviting me to have dinner with them had been perfectly harmless.

"Eddie, everything will work out for her. I'm sure of it."

He nodded. "Just one more thing. I don't know if she'll ever risk being in love again. But if she does, you can know, she'll never stop."

I didn't know what to say about that.

# Chapter Eighteen

The day after I took my parents to the airport for their flight back to Nashville, Del Wallace called, asking if we could meet for breakfast at a restaurant near the Galleria. He had to see a client in the Post Oak Plaza Building that morning. I left a note on Elaine's desk, letting her know where I'd be, and asking her to set up a meeting that afternoon with Mark, who hopefully was back from the Valley.

The drive out Westheimer took twenty minutes. I could have saved time by using the freeway, but avoided those things whenever possible. Way too many maniacs out there.

Del was waiting at a table near the back of the restaurant, a long, narrow building covered on the outside with shiny aluminum and simulated passenger car windows designed to make it look like a railway dining car. There wasn't much of a crowd. Just a couple of lonely looking customers seated at the counter and an obese fellow at a table near the front door. He held the front section of the newspaper in one hand and mopped up egg yolk with a slice of toast with the other. He had coffee stains on his shirt and what looked like grape jelly smeared on his sleeve. The restaurant's owner probably paid him to sit there to give the place color.

Del wore a green-striped seersucker suit, a pale-green button-down shirt, and a paisley bow tie. He teased me about wearing jeans and running shoes on a work day.

"Whitfield would probably make you go home and change clothes," he said.

He'd already ordered—three scrambled eggs, buttermilk pancakes, and sausage links. For being so small, the man could eat like a linebacker. I ordered toast and juice explaining that I needed to cut back after being subjected to my mother's attempts to fatten me up.

Del swallowed another mouthful and said, "I've finally been able to get the records you wanted. It took a while, because the DA subpoenaed the originals. I had to get the duplicate copies the building kept."

"Anything interesting?" I asked.

He reached into his portfolio and pulled out a thin stack of papers. "I don't know. None of this makes much sense."

He handed me the pages, copies of our building's after-hours sign-in and sign-out sheets for the month of July. I found what I was looking for on the two sheets that contained entries for July 15th. Near the bottom of the first page, my printed name and my signature next to it, indicating I had signed in and out of the building on that date. The sign-in space read seven o'clock, the approximate time I'd gone back from the Cornwall to my office to get the trial notebook.

But what appeared in the sign-out column made my gut knot. Twelve-fifty-five. Impossible. I'd been there only long enough to have a brief conversation with Steve Golden and to retrieve the trial book. Ten minutes, fifteen at the most. I quickly scanned the other entries for July 15th.

His name was there too, just as I suspected. Fred Whitfield had signed in at eight-fifteen and back out at ten-twenty, right after Steve Golden who'd signed out at ten. That gave Whitfield plenty of time to search my office and find my spare key. It also gave him the opportunity to alter the time of my departure on the building log. The sorry son-of-a-bitch. I looked up from the papers, my blood boiling.

Del's eyes were wide with concern. "Andy, you look like you've seen a ghost. What's the big deal with these things anyway?"

I frowned. "I'd better not say anything just now, Del."

He held up a hand in protest. "Damn it, you're not going to do that to me, Andy. Not after I went to the trouble of getting these for you in the first place. I deserve to know.

How can you expect me to help, if you don't let me in on what's going on?"

He was right, but I still couldn't afford to tell him.

"Look, I really do appreciate what you've done. You just have to trust me. It's better if I don't say anything about this until I've had the chance to figure a couple more things out, that's all."

He wasn't pleased, but grudgingly said, "Okay, Andy, have it your way."

"Thanks," I replied. "You still willing to help, even if I can't fill you in on all the reasons?"

He frowned and said, "Sure, I guess I am. What do you need?"

"Didn't you say that the DA subpoenaed the building logs?"

"Yeah, that's right. I was afraid I wasn't going to be able to get them at all, until the building manager finally let me in on the fact that a duplicate of each day's record is made and sent to an off-site service bureau where they prepare microfiche of the records. He said it really cuts down on the volume of paper they have to keep track of."

"Well, did they subpoena any records from Golden-Wallace?"

"As a matter of fact, Andy, we've gotten a couple of subpoenas."

"What did they ask for?"

"The firm's billing records on the Thrasher case. All of our investigative files on the case, too. And one other thing, all of our telephone reports and phone bills for the last six months."

I smiled and Del said, "Don't tell me, let me make a wild guess, you'd like to know what they got."

I continued to smile and said, "Yep, and copies of what you produced would be nice, too."

He threw up his hands and gave me an exasperated, 'I should have known,' look. "I'll see what I can do," he said.

When I got back from my meeting with Del, Mark Watson was in the office waiting. He and Elaine were in the conference room watching the TV. Nothing much was happening. Just a grainy, black and white image of the inside of some sort of building, illuminated by overhead lighting that caused a glare on the top of the screen.

"It should be any time, now," Mark said.

"Is this it?" I asked.

"Yeah," Mark replied. "First thing I did this morning was call our public servant, lawyer Anderson, and ask him where in the hell was the tape. At first, he acted like he didn't know what I was talking about. But I reminded him about my discovery motion and told him the word was, they had a tape. He got madder'n hell when I suggested he was holding out on me, but what really must have upset him is now he knows, they have a leak at the DA's. I picked up a copy of this a half-hour after my little talk with ol' Albert, saddled up and headed over here." He grinned and motioned for me to take a seat. An automobile appeared on the screen, coming up the incline of the ramp on the inside of the garage.

"Stop it right there," he said.

Elaine pushed the freeze button on the remote, a band of snow oscillated through the middle of the frame.

"That's your car, isn't it?" he asked.

The image wasn't very clear, but it definitely was my Mazda. I could read the number on the license plate. The windshield was partially obscured by the snow in the middle of the screen. To compound matters, the light from the overhead fixtures in the garage caused a reflection on the glass making it impossible to see inside.

"Does that get better?" I asked, pointing at the windshield.

"Afraid not," Mark replied.

Elaine continued the tape, confirming what Mark said. She played it repeatedly as we looked for something we might have missed. As the tape ran, Mark pointed out the time sequence indicator that appeared in the bottom corner of the screen. As my car went past, it read: 7/16 - 01:35. Mark asked Elaine to fast-forward. A few seconds later, my car appeared on the tape again, this time headed out of the garage. The sequencer read: 7/16 - 01:58. We played that segment over and over. Elaine thought she could see a person's image through the glare of the reflection on the windshield. Mark and I disagreed, but he said he would see what could be done to enhance the image.

"I can't see why they're saying I was driving. You can't see a damn thing inside the car window," I said. Yeah, that's a shame," Mark agreed. "You'd have the killer, right there, if those sorry lights hadn't screwed things up."

"What about the rest of it?" I asked.

"That's it," Mark replied. "Anderson promised me, there was only one car in or out of that garage after ten o'clock, which by the way was when Thrasher went back to his office that night. Andy, I'm afraid we struck out on that one, pal."

Another good idea down the tubes.

For more bad news, I told Mark about my meeting with Del Wallace and showed him the copies of the building logs that Del had given me earlier that morning.

He whistled. "Somebody has it in for you, pal."

"Yeah, it looks that way."

"Got any idea who?"

"I'm beginning to get one," I answered.

He stared at me intently. "Well, do you want to let me in on it?"

"Let me do some more thinking," I said. "I don't want to send you off on a tangent based on any half-baked suspicions."

Mark shrugged. If that's the way I wanted it, fine with him. "What about the person at the security desk that night? You don't happen to recall who that was, do you?"

I tried to remember. "No. Not really. But it probably was the regular guy who works there. I don't recall him ever not being there. Anyway, the guy I'm thinking about, his name is Carlos."

"Will he be able to help?" Mark asked.

"I don't know. I guess I'll be pretty amazed if he can. He never impressed me as being very attentive. Some of the people at the firm used to joke about how lax our building's security was, compared with some of the other downtown office buildings."

"What do you mean by that?"

"Oh, nothing much, I don't suppose. I do know that Whitfield called it to the attention of the partners at one of our meetings several months ago. There were complaints from the building's management that people were signing in and out on the security sheets using phony names."

"Like what?" Mark asked.

I smiled and replied, "Oh, Boris Yeltsin, Bill Clinton, Elvis, stuff like that. It was all pretty juvenile. Whitfield even thought it was funny, and he has about as much of a sense of humor as you'll find in a cancer ward."

Mark paced slowly around the room. He turned back toward me and said, "Andy, there's more than one way to skin this cat."

"What do you mean?"

"What I mean, is I'm about to let you buy me lunch."

"Fine with me. Where do you want to go?"

"The restaurant at the Cornwall," he answered, heading out the door.

I switched from Nikes to a pair of tasseled loafers, grabbed my navy blazer and followed. Why did he want to drag me all the way down there?


On the ride downtown, Mark wouldn't explain anything. Maybe he was paying me back for not telling him about who I thought might have set me up with the building logs and my car. We arrived early enough to beat the noon traffic and got a good table next to a window.

After we were seated I asked, "Okay, what's going on?"

"Didn't you tell me, the night you spent here when Thrasher was killed, you ordered room service?"

I nodded.

Mark leaned forward. "Well, if the DA takes the position that you were up in your office from seven until almost one o'clock in the morning, won't the hotel's records establish you had food delivered to your room during the time you were supposed to be someplace else?"

Ah. "I sure hope so."

I asked our waiter if the restaurant manager was in the hotel. I told him I was a friend of Susan's and asked him to let her know I wanted to say hi. While we waited, I asked why the DA needed to prove where I was at all times that night in the first place.

"He really doesn't," Mark replied. "But he might not be aware of the significance of what we might have here. We know somebody phonied-up those logs to make it look like you were up there in your office, brooding about Thrasher until you decided to go out to his place to solve your differences with him, permanently. Anderson might not focus on the room service order. If he doesn't, we can spring it at trial, and show how somebody wanted the world to believe you were someplace you really weren't that night. Even if we don't find out who that somebody is, in fact, come to think about it, even if the DA never even uses the logs to try to show where you were that night, we can use the discrepancy in the building logs and what we're hopefully going to find on the hotel's records ourselves. Either way, we'll have gone a long way toward making the jury wonder why somebody wanted people to think you were in your office that night when you weren't."

Mark leaned back, wearing a big, catfish grin. A low, husky woman's voice came from behind me. I looked over my shoulder. Susan Knight was speaking to a customer. She saw me and waved. She was even more attractive than I remembered from our first meeting. When she came to our table, I introduced her to Mark.

"Andy, you seem to know the most beautiful women in town. If you don't mind, I'm going to have to figure out a way to hang around with you more often."

I grinned at Susan and said, "Don't mind him. He's harmless." Then, for my absent friend's benefit, I asked Susan if she'd seen Mitchell lately and jokingly commented that he didn't seem to have as much time for golf as he did just a few weeks ago.

Susan said, "As a matter of fact, I expect him to drop in any time now. His bank meetings are usually on Tuesdays. If yesterday being a holiday doesn't change their schedule, he should be here."

I asked if she could spare a few minutes and quickly explained what we needed.

Susan frowned. "If you wanted that sort of information for any date one month later than July, there wouldn't be a problem. But I'm afraid the records we kept earlier won't do much good."

Mark furrowed his brow. "Wait a minute. I don't understand. Don't you keep records for longer than two months? You must have to keep 'em for all kinds of reasons."

"I'm sorry," she replied. "Mr Watson, you are absolutely correct. We keep those records. But you see, it's the kind of information we had on them back in July that's going to give you a problem."

"You mean, the hotel isn't going to be able to refer to its records to determine if Andy got room service back in July?"

"No we can tell you if he did or not, but from the way Andy described it, you need to know *when* he ordered and *when* his service was delivered. That's what our old records won't show, not unless the server made a special note on the ticket. Ninety-nine times out of a hundred, all I'll be able to tell you from our old system is what was ordered during a particular shift and where it was delivered. And in case you're wondering, what we refer to as the evening shift runs from six in the evening until midnight. Other than what I've just told you, I'm afraid the only other thing I'll be able to give you under our old system is the name of the server."

Mark's face became dark. "Andy, when did you check in that day?"

I thought for a moment. "I think it was a little before seven. The hotel should have a record of the time I signed in shouldn't it?"

Susan nodded. "Yes, the front desk keeps that. They always have from what I understand."

"Damn," Mark said. "That means we can't use the room service records to prove you weren't at your office all night. They'll probably say you could have ordered room service as soon as you checked in and then you went out right after it was delivered." Mark stared out the window, the first time I'd seen him take his eyes off a pretty woman in all the time I'd known him.

I asked Susan to locate the records for us, if she could. At least we could find out who made the delivery. She said she'd have them as soon as possible. I thanked her and nodded toward the bar. Mitchell Starlarski was standing at the rail, a drink in his hand.

As Susan left, I waved to Mitch and tried to motion to him that I wanted to talk, but his attention was riveted on the beautiful woman moving gracefully toward him. Mark offered to drive me back to my office but I said not to bother. I had someplace to go. It was time to pay Fred Whitfield a visit.

## Chapter Nineteen

I used a pay phone in the hotel lobby to call my old office. According to Kathy, Whitfield wasn't there. She said he was in court. Our confrontation would have to wait. Then again, maybe not. It *was* Tuesday. Unless my ex-partner had changed his habits, which was highly doubtful, Fred being a plodding, methodical man, I'd find him at the City Club. He played racquetball there with Judge Julian Campbell every Tuesday afternoon whenever they both weren't in trial. Fred never lost the chance to leave the world the message he was engaged in court, even when it wasn't true. And since Judge Campbell wasn't seeking reelection, he frequented his courtroom only on the rarest of occasions. Even money said I'd find them at the club.

I borrowed Mitchell Starlarski's Suburban, promising to bring it back in time for Susan's scheduled golf lesson later that afternoon. Apparently, Mitchell had grown tired of playing exclusively with Louis.

I parked in the visitor lot between the Compaq Center and the twin office buildings that faced onto Richmond Avenue and took the elevator up to the club level. A scrawny kid named Johnnie, who looked to be no more than seventeen, but was billed as one of the assistant tennis pros, was working the front desk at the pro shop.

"Is Fred here?" I asked.

"Whitfield?"

"Yeah."

Johnnie scanned the reservation calendar. "Yep, sure is. Let's see, he's on Court Number Two. Should be just about finished. Even if they're not, they have to give the court up in another fifteen minutes."

I thanked the young man and took the corridor to the west-wing courts where an observation deck afforded spectators a spot for watching the courts below through plexi-glass back walls. Whitfield and Judge Campbell were a sight. Both men slashing at the ball, banging clumsily into walls and diving desperately for shots. What they lacked in ability, they made up for with sheer determination. They were big men and I could feel the building vibrate whenever one of them slammed into a wall.

Judge Campbell strained for every shot, his large face the color of a pickled beet. When he bounced off a wall, sweat showered off of his head like water off the coat of a wet dog. Fred executed a perfect roll out, less than an inch from the bottom of the front wall, and the judge bellowed in rage, loud enough for those of us on the observation deck to know that Whitfield's ancestry had just been placed in question.

Merely watching their efforts made me thirsty. I went to the counter at the grill, bought a bottle of Calastoga Water and asked the attendant if she'd noticed the way Whitfield and Judge Campbell were going after each other. She smiled and confided that the people who assigned courts usually tried to put them further away from the grill because of their disruptive antics.

Finally, they appeared at the top of the stairs. Judge Campbell was smiling and Whitfield wasn't. Fred received quite a few barbs from the spectators, most having to do with letting an old man beat up on him like the judge had just done. Nearing sixty and a heavy, beefy man, Campbell was in surprisingly good shape. Losing to him was nothing to be ashamed of. Everyone knew that, but that didn't stop them from razzing Whitfield.

When Whitfield noticed me, his demeanor suddenly changed. No longer the grim loser, he suddenly became Judge Campbell's best buddy. He put his arm around Campbell's shoulder and fixed all of his attention on the judge. I walked quickly toward them, blocking the way leading into the locker room.

Whitfield glanced at me and quickly looked away. He wiped his face with his towel and mumbled, "Hello, Givens."

He tried to slip past me, but I moved with him, continuing to stand in his way.

"Now, wait a minute," he said.

"No, you wait. We need to talk."

"I'll be happy to, as a matter of fact there *is* something we need to discuss. But you've picked a bad time. At the moment, I happen to be busy."

"Look," I said, "We need to get this cleared up now."

Whitfield peered at me, eyes narrowed into slits, a puzzled expression on his still florid face. "I don't have the slightest idea what you're talking about, but I've told you, I don't have the time. Call me tomorrow and maybe we can arrange something. Now, please, I have to go."

He tried to push past me, but I grabbed his shoulders and shoved him against the wall. The same people who had been watching the racquetball match crowded eagerly around.

"You're not going to set me up for killing Thrasher and get away with it!" I shouted.

Whitfield glared at me, and struggled to pull away. "Givens, you fool, I don't know what you're talking about! If you don't take your hands off me, I promise, you'll regret it!"

I was about to punch him in the mouth, but Judge Campbell grabbed my arm. "Andy, you stop this right now! If you'd pulled this stunt in my courtroom, I'd have you locked up for contempt."

I released my grip, pressing Whitfield against the wall as I did. "Okay," I said. "I'll go. But Whitfield, I'm not going to let you get away with this. I don't care what it takes. You'd better watch out."

Fred made a lunge toward me, but Judge Campbell held us apart. I stormed out of the club, feeling the astonished stares of the people I passed. Once again, I'd managed to make a genuine mess of the situation and I knew it. I decided to go home before I made the day worse than it already was.

By the time Mitchell dropped me off at my office, I had calmed down but was still on edge. A note from Elaine reminded me of our meeting the next day with the Caponis. I gave Ivory his supper and went to my desk to read the mail. First Texas Republic's answer was in the stack. Hartson had been true to his word. His pleading included motions to dismiss for failing to state a claim entitling my clients to their requested relief and one for sanctions against the Caponis and their counsel for filing a patently frivolous pleading.

I took a recent bar journal article on sanctions upstairs with a half bottle of chennin blanc. After finishing the article, which advised how important it was to avoid even the possibility of giving a federal judge the chance to levy sanctions, I picked up a new novel I had been meaning to read—another one of those lawyer books. A story about an idealist trying to defend an innocent man, who the legal system seemed determined to find guilty of having committed horrible sins. Pretty tame stuff compared to what I was going through.

Even though I'd succeeded in making an ass out of myself with the little show at the City Club, a night's sleep left me convinced I still needed to have a serious talk with Whitfield. If I let him know I'd figured out his scheme to blame me for Thrasher's murder, maybe he'd panic and make some sort of mistake. Fred was far from dumb. In all probability he'd remain cool as a cucumber. Just the same, I had to try. Even if he didn't fall apart and confess, maybe he'd still reveal something I could use to expose him as the real killer.

I called him early that morning determined to convince him to meet. As I expected, he didn't take my call. Instead, I got stuck with a girl who hadn't been with our firm when I was there.

"Mr Whitfield told me you might try to contact him," she said, her voice dripping with arrogance. "I've been instructed to inform you, he does not wish to speak with you." What a tight-ass. Fred had finally discovered his perfect match.

"Just let him know I called. And you might tell him, one way or the other he's going to have to deal with me."

By lunch time he still hadn't called. I guessed he never would.

That afternoon, we spent several hours re-visiting the Caponis' meeting with the bankers and going over the details of what they knew, and what they'd heard or suspected concerning the run on Centennial, and what was said and by whom concerning their alleged ties with the Mancuso family. We'd notice depositions as soon as the written discovery responses and initial document productions were in. Any information my own clients could provide would be useful in determining who we needed to depose and in preparing deposition questions.

Our session ended not because the Caponis had run out of things to say. They had both been full of ideas, some of them really good. And on top of that, they had one hell of a lot of pent up frustration from having to suffer as the result of wrongful accusations—something I could readily relate to. They were obviously enjoying having the chance to tell their story, even if it was only to an audience of one. I was the reason we had to call it quits that afternoon. My mind kept wandering back to Whitfield.

As The Caponis were leaving, Elaine stuck her head in the office. "Andy, if you can spare it, I need to see you when you have a minute."

"What is it?"

"Fred Whitfield's secretary called, oh, maybe thirty minutes ago. She said Fred wants to meet with you in the morning. He'll be at the Buffalo Grill at seven-thirty."

I nodded.

"What's this about? You and Whitfield?"

"I'll tell you later. Just call her, before she gets away, please?"

"You're going to confront him about Mr Thrasher, aren't you?"

"I don't know if confronting him is exactly the right way to put it, but I do intend to speak with him about it."

"So you think he did it too?" Elaine asked, a hint of a smile forming.

I grinned. "Maybe tomorrow we'll find out."

That night, I stayed up late, playing out imagined scenarios for next morning's meeting. I had the feeling I sometimes get when something really significant is about to happen. I was right about that. Only not in the way I could have ever imagined. Not in a million years.

# Chapter Twenty

Trying lawsuits for a living, it's not unusual to wake up with your gut in a knot. Small wonder so many people in my line of work wind up screwing up their lives, becoming alcoholics, drug abusers, or worse. I got up with all of the familiar symptoms. Cotton mouth, dull headache, and a flip-flopping stomach. In a word, I felt lousy. I'd have preferred to stay in bed, but couldn't. The time had come to make something happen.

I was dressed and on my way downstairs when the door bell rang. I opened the door and there stood, Lieutenant Rupert Puryear and Detective Joseph Springer.

Puryear said, "Mr Givens, we apologize for coming by so early, but something has come up. Do you have a few minutes to spare?"

I frowned. "Sorry guys, anything you need to discuss with me, you'll have to take up with Mark Watson."

"This doesn't have a thing to do with Thrasher, you know that," Springer blurted.

Puryear flashed an angry glance at Springer. "The fact is, Mr Givens, we don't actually know if this has to do with the Thrasher case or not."

"Well, I'm not saying anything without Mark being present," I explained.

"I suppose that can be arranged," Puryear replied. "We just thought you might be able to shed some light on the reason one of your former partners was shot a little earlier this morning."

A wave of nausea struck. "What do you mean?"

"Oh, Givens, that's very convincing," Springer said, smirking.

"What happened, who was it that was shot?" I imagined Del lying on the jogging path at the park. Although officers regularly patrolled the area, there had been several nasty incidents involving joggers being assaulted. We'd often commented how something really bad was bound to happen, sooner or later.

Springer rolled his eyes. "Lieutenant, this guy is really good, don't you think?"

Puryear frowned at Springer and said, "Mr Givens, it was Fred Whitfield who was shot."

My heart caught. "How is he?" I managed to ask.

Puryear looked at me and said, "I'm afraid he's dead, Mr Givens. Shot, in the back of his head. He was gone before he hit the ground."

I asked the officers to come inside. While they waited in the front room, I went to my office and called Mark Watson.

When Mark came on the line he said, "Andy, have you heard about Fred Whitfield? It's on the news right now! He was killed outside his front door early this morning."

"That's why I'm calling. The police are here. Lieutenant Puryear and Detective Springer. They want to talk to me about Whitfield. I told them I wanted you present."

Mark said to tell Puryear that he was on his way, but not to say anything else until he got there. That would be easy enough. I didn't want to talk to anyone, least of all to anybody connected with the police. Whitfield, shot and killed. Just before our meeting. I couldn't believe it.

Mark got to my place in less than fifteen minutes. He asked Puryear and Springer to wait and we went back to my office. He paced around the room, more nervous than I'd ever seen him.

"Want me to make some coffee?" I asked.

"Yeah, that would be a good idea. You don't have some made yet?"

"No, I was on my way to a breakfast meeting, and didn't take the time."

I headed into the kitchen. Mark followed along.

"You might want to call whoever it was you were supposed to meet. This is probably going to take a while," he said.

"That won't be necessary."

"Oh?"

"My meeting this morning? It was supposed to be with Whitfield."

Mark's mouth fell open. He walked slowly back to my office. When I brought the coffee in a few minutes later, he was seated at the work table. I sat down across from him and handed him a mug.

"I think you'd better tell me, why were you going to see that guy? From everything I know, he was just about the last person you'd be having breakfast with."

I met Mark's intent stare. "Well, somebody killed Thrasher. He sure as hell didn't beat himself to death. And whoever that somebody is went to a lot of trouble to make it look like I did it. The only person I could think of who would do something like that was Whitfield."

Mark shook his head. "Even if he did, what did you expect to accomplish by meeting with him?"

"Mark, it's my neck that's in the noose. I thought, just maybe, I'd get him to say something we could use to prove he's the one who's guilty."

Mark stared at me, eyes wide. "Andy, assuming you're right, what I don't understand is why would Whitfield have anything to do with you?"

"I guess I sort of forced him into it," I replied, beginning to realize the mistake I'd made.

Mark's shoulders sagged and he let out a deep sigh. "Oh? How'd you manage that?"

"I went over to the City Club, after we had lunch. I figured Whitfield was there and I went looking for him. He was, and, well I guess I made it pretty plain we had a score to settle. He probably realized he couldn't duck me forever, so he decided to meet with me."

"Andy, this is important. Did anyone see you with Whitfield?"

"I'm afraid so," I said. Then I told about the altercation and what Judge Campbell said.

Mark listened quietly, occasionally shaking his head.When I finished he let out another long sigh and said, "Pal, you ain't makin' this easy. The next time you feel like playing Perry Mason, Matlock, or whoever it is you've been watching to make you behave so foolishly, do me a favor and resist the urge."

"I'll try."

Mark pointed a thick finger at me. "Do better than try. Make sure you don't."

I deserved the criticism. I started to apologize and to explain why it had seemed the right thing to do. But Mark stopped me before I got very far. "Andy, I have to ask. Other than what you've already told me, do you know anything about the Whitfield shooting?"

I shook my head. "No. I promise. I'm probably more confused about Fred's death than anyone. I was counting on proving he killed Thrasher."

Mark gazed out the window. "You know, maybe Whitfield didn't have the guts to kill Thrasher himself and hired somebody else to do it. Maybe that somebody was afraid that Whitfield's conscience was starting to bother him."

"He'd have to have acted pretty quickly to arrange for somebody else to kill Thrasher," I said. "Until Judge Loring granted that directed verdict, against us, what reason would Whitfield have had for wanting Thrasher dead?"

Mark nodded and said, "Yeah, I see what you mean." He looked at his watch and said, "We've kept the Lieutenant and his side-kick waiting long enough. Andy, I don't want you saying anything to those hombres until we know a little more about what's going on." He stood and straightened his string tie. "I just want you to realize, not speaking to them might cause them to start assuming things they shouldn't."

I hadn't had much luck trying to be cooperative with the police and told Mark I agreed with his point of view. He went out front to tell them that unless they intended to arrest me, they might as well leave. When he came back, Elaine was with him.

"What did they say?" I asked.

"Oh, they acted more than just a little pissed that we'd kept them waiting so long," Mark replied. "Springer seemed like he'd enjoy the chance to arrest me just for bringing them the news. Puryear, I think his upset was just a show. You know, he's a pretty cool customer. Before they left, he even mentioned how you can go down to the impound lot and pick up your car. Apparently, the lab boys are finished with whatever they were doing for all this time."

Mark said he had to get back downtown. He had a sentencing scheduled in federal court. I went with him to the front door. I knew I'd screwed up again. This time worse than ever. I felt crummy about it, but what could I do? "Mark, I really am sorry about this," I blurted. "What do you think is going on?"

He faced me, the color drained from his face. He looked as if he'd aged a good ten years right in front of me. He pushed his hands deeper in his pockets, looked at me, and shrugged. "I don't know. I've never considered it useful to try to do the state's investigative work. Defending somebody usually doesn't require it. But maybe this time we should. Maybe you're right about Whitfield. Or maybe something else is goin' on. Have you given any thought to whether anyone connected with that defendant in the case you were trying for Thrasher might be involved?"

I shook my head.

"Well maybe you should. Anyway, we'll talk later. Right now, keep that chin up, pal. I'm afraid I've got to run."

"Okay, Mark, I will."

"And Andy?"

"Yeah?"

"This time, just think, don't try to go out and play hero, okay?"

He didn't have to worry. I'd learned my lesson.

When I returned, Elaine was still seated at the work table, her elbows propped on the table top, her head held in her hands.

"If you want to start looking for another job, I'll understand."

She looked up at me, and a single tear rolled down her cheek. She sniffed and said, "Not unless you want me to."

"No, I'd like you to stay. I just don't want you involved with something where you might wind up getting hurt."

"Let's not worry about that. You're going to beat them. I know you are." She bit her lip, fighting back more tears. "What's going on? Whitfield? Shot? I'm still convinced he's the one who killed Thrasher, but this doesn't make sense."

I nodded. "That's what Mark thinks, too. But he came up with a new angle. Suggested somebody from the other side on Thrasher's civil case might be involved."

"What do you think?"

"I'm not sure what I think."

"Will they accuse you of Whitfield's murder?"

"It's a possibility."

"Isn't there anything we can do?"

"About that? I'm not sure. I promised Mark I'd leave the detective work to somebody else. I guess we need to focus our attention on getting ready for our discovery conference with the banks."

"You mean you can actually think about working on that with all of this other stuff going on?"

I shrugged. "I'm afraid we have to. The only other option would be to quit. And I'm not going to do that."

She managed a weak smile. "No, I know you're not."


No matter how much effort I put into trying to concentrate it didn't do any good. Could I be wrong about Whitfield? If he didn't kill William Thrasher, then who did? A hit man from W.D.S.? I put the papers I'd been trying to review back in their box and went in to see Elaine.

"You're right. I can't do this. I'm going to go out for a while. Want to come along?"

"No," she said. "You were right when you said we needed to work. Somebody had better try. You go ahead."

Outside, a good-sized congregation of reporters and camera crews were gathered on the front lawn. I was beginning to understand why some people view those folks as little more than vultures, the way they wait so anxiously for some mishap or tragedy to strike and then spring into action, refusing to go away until the bones have been picked clean. I wasn't about to allow them to make me a prisoner in my own house. I went out the back door and made a dash for the rental car parked in the side driveway.

There was a little bar over in the Heights where I still might be able to have a couple of drinks in peace.

## Chapter Twenty One

The next morning, I forced myself out of bed before Elaine arrived. I didn't want her discovering me nursing another hangover. My head throbbed and my stomach was in a nasty, rebellious state, but I managed to fix breakfast for myself and Ivory. The food helped and okay, I admit it, I did put a pretty good shot of brandy in my first cup of coffee. That helped too, and I was able to turn my attention to trying to catch up with the work that should have gotten done the day before.

Elaine walked in just as I was finishing the first box of documents. We spent all day reviewing records and getting them ready to produce to the defendants.

By late afternoon, I'd returned to normal. I called Del Wallace and found out that Fred's funeral was scheduled for the following day. He sounded more than a little surprised when I told him I'd see him there. I didn't look forward to having a confrontation with anyone. But I was still convinced Whitfield was the one who'd put me in this mess. The way I saw it, I didn't really have a choice. I had to go.

The Methodist Church on University Boulevard was nearly full. I took a seat on the back pew next to a plump, gray-haired woman seated next to a man who could of passed for her twin. Another fellow sitting in the pew ahead of ours turned around and stared at me. I didn't know him either, but he must have recognized me. He gave me a hard, unpleasant stare, as if I were the lowest scum on the face of the planet. He whispered to the woman seated beside him and she started staring too. A few minutes later, they got up and took seats on the other side of the aisle. The whole area probably would have vacated, if the service hadn't started.

The minister told us what a fine, decent man Fred Whitfield was. He emphasized how much Fred would be missed by the members of his church, by the legal community who knew and respected him and, most of all, by his family who Fred had loved and who had loved Fred so deeply. The flowers at the front of the church were beautiful and the woman who sang "Nearer My God To Thee" brought many in the gathering to tears. I almost had to remind myself we were there to put to rest the man I was convinced was William Thrasher's cold-blooded killer.

The procession to the cemetery took almost an hour. Whitfield grew up in Pasadena and since his father was buried out there, I guess Fred's choice had been to do the same. I drove by myself and was close to the end of the long line of cars following the hearse out the Gulf Freeway.

The Whitfield family plot was at a far corner of the cemetery, only a short walk from the drive where an attendant from the funeral home directed us to park. The day was scorching hot, the sun glaring down from a white, hazy sky. The air was completely still and the leaves on the line of red buds that ran along the boundary of the cemetery hung limp, desperate for relief from the withering heat. There wasn't any shade for those of us who couldn't squeeze under the open-air tent that covered the grave site.

As the minister began to speak, the crowd at the rear pushed forward. As people shifted to accommodate the press of those standing behind, I found myself next to Steve Golden. He looked much older than I remembered, and extremely frail. I touched his arm to get his attention and he turned, shielding his eyes with a hand and squinted up at me. His face was ashen and he was perspiring heavily. At first, he wore a puzzled look, as if he didn't recognize me. But when he did, his look turned to one of contemptuous anger. He stared at me for several seconds. Then he turned away and eased past the people next to him.

Golden's reaction stung. The man had been my mentor, the one who gave me the opportunity to develop and prove my professional skills. He'd introduced me to his best clients and to his fellow lawyers facilitating my acceptance in Houston's legal community. In the process, we became personal friends. I stood there unable to believe what was happening. I didn't even realize the service was coming to an end until some of the people standing around me began to recite the Lord's Prayer.

Darla Whitfield and her two teenaged daughters each placed a single red rose on top of Fred's casket. Then, his remains were lowered into the ground. Darla and an elderly woman, probably Whitfield's mother, each dropped a clump of earth into the grave. The minister gave the benediction and the people slowly began to disperse. Golden and several others, including most of the members of the firm, went up to Fred's family. As Golden spoke to Darla, she looked past him to where I stood at the back of the tent.

After Golden and the others left, I went to her. "Darla, I'm sorry this happened," I said.

She glared at me, her eyes puffy and red. "You have some nerve showing up here."

"Darla, please, don't think for a minute that I had anything to do with Fred's death."

Hatred emanated from the woman's every pore. "That's not what I heard. I was told you threatened Fred at the City Club and made some wild accusation that he was responsible for you being accused of killing William Thrasher." Her youngest girl began to sob. Darla put an arm around her and hugged her close. "You know," she continued, "it's so unfair. Fred actually said you deserved the benefit of the doubt. He wasn't as sure as some of the others seemed to be that you killed Mr Thrasher. Then Fred gets shot. I'll see you pay for this, Andy Givens. You'd better believe I will."

Maybe it was the heat, or the charged emotions of the moment, or some combination of both factors, but just then, Fred's mother fainted and fell in a heap on the ground. It happened so suddenly, no one was close enough to catch her. For an instant, she looked as if she was going to slide right into her son's open grave. The minister rushed to the fallen woman's side, reached beneath his vestment and pulled out a plastic vial that he cracked open and held under the elderly woman's nose. Darla and the girls ran to her too. They all began crying as the minister supported the old woman's head under one of his arms and continued to give her periodic whiffs of ammonia. She began to come around and softly moaned as she lay on the ground.

Darla Whitfield stared up at me, tears streaming down her face. "Andrew Givens, we don't need to be tormented by you. Please leave us alone."

The minister glared at me. I walked away, feeling like a complete ass. Showing up had been a terrible mistake.

When I got to my car, Del Wallace was there, leaning against the hood of his car which was parked behind mine.

"Nice wheels," he said, motioning toward my rental.

"Yeah, thanks, I'm considering keeping it and getting rid of my old one."

"Got time for a drink?" he asked.

I thought briefly of the night before. Was a trend developing? But then, I said, "Sure, where do you want to go?"

"There's a little place up on the freeway, that's not too far."

I followed Del to a run-down seafood restaurant opposite the Hobby Airport exit called Davy Jones' Locker. Cool and dimly lit, the place was a lot more impressive than it looked from the parking lot. When my eyes became accustomed to the darkness, I could make out attractive underwater murals decorating the walls.

Del was greeted by the proprietor, whose name actually was Dave Jones. He was a short stub of a man dressed in a black shirt and trousers. His skin was pink and virtually wrinkle free. He had pudgy, short fingers and a full, round belly that hung over his belt. A ring of white fringe surrounded his otherwise bald head. He wore oval wire-rimmed glasses that pinched a red, heavily veined bulbous nose. He led us into a small bar that had even less lighting than the restaurant and to a booth at the rear of the narrow room.

"Haven't seen you for a while," he said to Del.

"Not much chance to get out this way lately," Del answered. "This is a friend of mine, Andy Givens. We, uh, have some business to discuss, Dave."

Jones nodded to me and said, "Nice to meet you Mr Givens. You know, I've heard about you and was wondering...."

Del cut him off with a hard stare. Jones held up his hands and backed away. "Okay, I'll leave you alone, and I won't come by to bother you with stories about your brother, either, Del."

Del smiled and said, "We appreciate that, Dave."

"Just one thing, though, are you gents here to just talk or are you plannin' to have something to drink?"

"I'll have a Bud-Lite," Del said.

I said I'd have one too. When Dave came back with two ice-cold bottles, he grinned and stepped back from the table, not saying a word.

"Did you say he knew Raymond?" I asked.

"Yeah, Dave and Ray were in business together. It was quite a few years ago. They had a restaurant out on Hillcroft. It didn't last very long. I might have mentioned, how Raymond never could seem to get along with anybody from a business standpoint. Well, that's why they split up. But he and Dave remained friends, even after they'd gone their separate ways with the restaurant. I got to know Dave and I like him. I guess, mainly because he was just about the best friend my brother ever had. Anyway, I try to stay in touch with him by dropping by every now and then."

I'd never met Del's brother, but I'd heard about him. He'd owned several small restaurants in Houston, none of which had ever been all that successful. Finally, he'd quit the restaurant business and became a rep for a manufacturer of a line of restaurant equipment. He died in a motel fire up in Lufkin shortly after beginning his new career.

I looked at Del and suddenly felt sorry for him. "There were a lot of people at Fred's funeral," I said, trying to divert his attention from his brother.

Del sipped his beer. "Yeah there sure were."

"I saw Steve Golden. He acted like I've got leprosy."

"Well, Andy, there's a lot of talk going around. Judge Campbell must've told everybody at the courthouse about your little set-to. You know just before Fred's killed, it doesn't look very good."

I felt that now-familiar knot in my gut begin to twist. "That's true," I admitted. "But anybody who knows me has to realize, this is all just so much horseshit."

"Yeah, well I know that. Fred even mentioned to me, the day before he was shot, he was beginning to think there was something peculiar going on and maybe you weren't guilty."

"He really said that?"

Del nodded. "But Andy, that doesn't change how things look to an awful lot of people. I might as well let you know. With all the talk that's been flying around, some of the younger partners are thinking about leaving. That's probably what Golden is so upset about. If the firm folds, it'll probably kill the poor man."

"What do you think?"

He sighed heavily. "I'm afraid it'll happen. Even if we bring in somebody from outside, with all the talk and the attitude of the younger guys, I don't see how we can make it."

"I'm sorry. I feel like I'm responsible for all this mess."

"Hey, we're the ones who didn't stand beside you, remember?"

"I don't know. I just keep thinking, if I'd handled the trial differently, if I'd been able to make that judge understand the mistake he was making, then all of the rest of this, maybe it wouldn't have happened."

Del sighed. "You know, it's strange. Another thing Whitfield told me. Something he said he'd found out about that judge in the Thrasher case, Otto Loring?"

"Yeah?"

"He and Fritz Taylor went to college together. They were roommates at Baylor."

I stared at Del. "Fred didn't know about that during the trial?"

"No. When he told me about it, that was just a few days ago, he said he'd just found out. He thought it really stank, you know, that the judge and the boys over at Barrett and Taylor didn't bother to mention it to anybody on our side. Fred was even thinking about going to the judicial commission about it.

"I've got a case going with Taylor right now," I said. "Him and that prick of a partner of his, Alton Giles."

Del nodded. "Yeah, that's right, they represent one of the banks, don't they?"

I didn't know what to make of that piece of news. Something wasn't right, but for the life of me, I couldn't put my finger on what. We finished our beers in silence. "I guess I'd better be getting back," I said.

"I'll probably stay a while and visit with Dave," he said. "But Andy, I want you to know, I don't hold you responsible for any of this."

As I walked to the parking lot, it occurred to me there were a lot of people out there who did. And I thought about Fred Whitfield, too. Had somebody else been in on killing Thrasher and then gotten rid of Fred to make sure he didn't have a chance to develop a case of the guilts? And why had Fred told his wife and Del Wallace he wasn't sure I was the one who killed Thrasher? After going to all of the trouble to set me up, why would he do something like that? The more I thought about it the more confusing everything became.

One thing was certain. Fred Whitfield's death was going to make finding answers to my questions much more difficult.

## Chapter Twenty Two

Mark Watson called the day after the funeral saying the skinny at HPD on Whitfield's murder was I was their boy. But so far, they had zilch to prove it. They'd have to get a big break if they were going to make a case. Mark said they realized the chance of that happening was someplace between slim and none. The way they saw it, unless they got a conviction on Thrasher, there'd be no justice done.

Knowing what those people thought was depressing, but this wasn't the time to let feeling sorry for myself get in the way. And no time for more Phillip Marlow impersonations either. I'd made a commitment to handle the Caponis' case and I was determined to see it through. I even swore off the booze. That's how serious I was. For the remainder of the week, Elaine and I worked shoulder to shoulder, plowing through box after box of Centennial documents, numbering and copying all of the ones the defendants were entitled to receive. On the eve of our scheduled meeting with the lawyers representing the defendants, we'd managed the impossible. We were actually ready.

Marshon & Davis occupied the top eight floors in the newest building in the Houston Center complex. Our meeting was in the main conference room on the top floor. A polished mahogany table large enough to seat at least thirty grossly-inflated egos dominated the room. An original Remington, portraying Texas Rangers locked in battle with a band of surrounding Comanches was mounted on the wall at one end of the room. The opposite wall was paneled in mahogany matching the table, and hid a sophisticated, state-of-the-art imaging screen and control panel for video, overhead, and slide presentations.The entire entry wall was made of glass, bringing into the interior reception area a spectacular view of downtown Houston afforded by floor-to-ceiling windows that ran the length of the outside wall.

They were all waiting. Joseph Hartson and his associate, Carl Hopgood, for First Texas Republic. William Mossberg and Connie Sullivan, a young woman associate from Lathwell & Mossberg, representing Port Arthur Commercial. Three attorneys from a Beaumont firm, including Nelson Tucker, the recognized dean of trial lawyers from that part of the state. Tucker and his bunch represented the *Beaumont Enterprise*, one of the papers that printed the false statements about Centennial's precarious financial position, and the Caponis' supposed links to the Mafia. Fritz Taylor, from Barrett & Taylor was there, representing Groves State Bank, and, to my extreme displeasure, he had Alton Giles with him too.

When I walked in, everyone stared at me as if somebody had just let in a giant cockroach. I went to the opposite side of the table and sat next to Fritz Taylor, who promptly got up and moved, leaving William Mossberg seated nearest to me, three empty chairs away.

"Hello, Mr Mossberg," I said.

With up-turned nose, he looked away, as if even acknowledging the presence of someone of my ilk was offensive. His gaze shifted to the end of the table where Hartson stood, speaking to his associate. "Joseph, why don't we begin. I believe everyone is here."

I should have guessed. This was going to be Hartson's show. He looked around the table, his steel-gray eyes meeting mine for only the briefest instant. He wore an expensive suit of dark charcoal wool, tailored to make him appear taller than the he was (he was five-eight at the most) and to hide the extra pounds that were creeping around his gut. His light, sun-bleached hair was long over his collar. He had an unusually fair complexion that made him appear almost ghost-like, and a firm jaw and cold, impassive eyes. I had the sudden image of this self-styled modern-day gladiator in bed with my wife, and I wanted to hurt the son-of-a-bitch so badly I could taste blood in the back of my throat.

Hartson got right down to business. Looking around the room he said, "Thank you all for coming. As you know, this is the preliminary meeting required by Judge Lowenstein. We are here to discuss exchange of documents and discovery scheduling. Uh, Mr Givens, am I correct in understanding you still are handling this case on your own?"

Trying to needle me already. "Yes, that's right."

"Then may I presume you are prepared to discuss our exchange of documents?"

"That's what we're here for isn't it?"

Hartson frowned. "Well, on behalf of all of the defendants, we wish to repeat what I have already conveyed to you. We believe this case has no merit, and, as I have put to you before, our clients are offended, indeed, they are extremely angry to stand accused of the wrongs alleged by you and your clients. We intend to give this case our highest priority, and I assure you, we *will* dispose of this and then we will pursue whatever remedies are available to us at that time."

We were headed no place and getting there fast. "You guys can cut all the sanctimonious bullshit. I talked to Tom Davis. He told me what your clients cooked up."

The room became ominously quiet. They knew. And now they knew that I did too.

"The ravings of a sick man," Hartson countered, recovering as smooth as glass. "If you rely on anything that poor man told you, you'll make a very large mistake."

The others around the table chimed in, chorusing their agreement with nods and murmurs of approval.

"Hartson, I assure you, I am not making a mistake. If you don't already realize that, some day you will. But I didn't come here to try to convince you of anything. Why don't we get to why we're here? When will you guys be ready to exchange documents?"

Hartson returned my gaze with a contemptuous stare. "Oh, we're ready. We're ready, this very minute. I told you we intend to be vigorous in handling this case. We are prepared to ship copies of our documents to you as early as this afternoon, provided, of course, that you and your clients are prepared to do the same."

I smiled as I looked around the room. All of these bright, creative legal talents lined up and all they'd come up with was the old steam-roller approach. "Good, we can do that," I said.

Mossberg, Taylor, and some of the others shot uncertain glances toward Hartson. But he didn't seem to notice. "We'll send a truck over right away," he said. "But, Mr Givens, I must warn you, it is a rather large truck. I'm not sure, you might not have the space. Your complaint is incredibly broad and now, I am afraid you're going to suffer the consequences."

"I'm pretty sure we can find room," I said. "How many documents should I expect?"

Hartson turned to the legal beagle sitting next to him. "Carl, how many records will the defendants be producing, all told?"

Hopgood fished a paper from the folder in front of him. Glancing at it he said, "There are 327 boxes, sir." Grinning, he continued, "Our last page number is 654,507."

Most of the other lawyers sitting around the table broke into broad smiles. They reminded me of school children proud of their latest classroom prank. Trying to swamp us in paper would make our job more difficult, but it was, just the same, surprising that they'd take this tack. More times than not, I've seen those who tried come to rue the day.

"If you have your delivery people wait, they can pick up Centennial's records when they've finished delivering yours," I suggested.

Fritz Taylor glared at me. "See here, young man," he said, "we don't intend to do anything of the sort. You should realize, we aren't on the same side. You can make your own arrangements for delivering your documents to us, which by the way, I might remind you, we each expect to receive our own individual copies of all of Centennial's records."

I'd never had a case with the man, but just from this first encounter, it was easy to see where Allie Giles had gotten his training on how to be a pompous ass. "I don't believe that's what the judge's pre-trial order says. It reads furnish *a copy* to the opposing *party or parties*."

Taylor smirked. "Young man, I have tried many cases in Judge Lowenstein's court. I am wholly familiar with his standing pre-trial order and I assure you, he requires a copy of *all* documents to be delivered to *each* party."

"Well, that's not what the order says," I replied. "If you want to interpret it that way, I guess that means you guys'll have to produce four sets of all of the defendants' records— one for Centennial, one for Vincent Caponi, one for Roberto Caponi, and one for Sylvia Caponi—they're all individually named parties."

Taylor's eyes bulged. "Now see here, Judge Lowenstein would never require us to do that!"

"Let's call the judge. He'll probably tell us what he wants," I replied.

Taylor gave me a hard, flinty stare. This was starting to be fun.

Nelson Tucker said, "Fritz, I was thinking, because of the volume of records involved, maybe it'd be preferable to have a repository for all of the documents the defendants need to keep up with in this case." An obvious attempt to toss his colleague a life-line.

A couple of the others nodded. No dummy, Joseph Hartson jumped on board too. "Sure, that's an excellent idea, Nelson. And our firm will be happy to assume the task of setting it up. Even though Fritz is obviously correct, the judge won't mind us doing it this way, if we all agree to it."

Taylor wasn't happy, being shown up, but he was smart enough to allow his compatriots to afford him a way to save face. "Okay, Pudge, if Marshon & Davis is willing to serve as repository, we'll go along."

"I'll send our records over this afternoon, right after we get yours," I said.

Carl Hopgood asked, "How many documents will you be producing?"

Not nearly as many as it looks like I'll be getting," I answered. William Mossberg, turned to me and asked, "What about depositions, are you prepared to agree on a schedule for taking them? I'd like to get started right away."

"I'm not prepared to address that until I've seen your records," I replied.

Taylor's face turned beet-red. A purple vein bulged in the middle of his forehead. He'd already begun to sputter something, but before he had a chance to say anything intelligible, Nelson Tucker interceded again.

"Mr Givens, I believe we can agree with you," he said. Examining his calendar, he continued, "The initial conference with Judge Lowenstein is scheduled for the first week in October. That's a little more than two weeks from now. Why don't we target having a tentative agreement about depositions before that first hearing?"

Two weeks wasn't much time, but Tucker's suggestion wasn't completely unreasonable and I didn't want to risk taking the wind of reason from his sail, so I said I'd try. Hartson attempted to reassert his leadership, saying there was nothing further we needed to discuss.

As the others left, Hartson stood at the door, shaking hands with his colleagues. Even though I'd gotten through our first face-to-face encounter, I still worried that I might hit the sorry son of a bitch, so I waited, hoping he'd go back to his office, leaving a clear exit. But as the last of the other defense lawyers left, Hartson glanced in my direction, spoke briefly with Carl Hopgood, and stepped back inside the conference room and closed the door. He took a seat across from me.

"If you have another minute, I think we should talk," he said.

I stayed put, not speaking.

"Uh, Givens, I think you might be right about this case presenting special problems."

"What do you have on your mind?"

"Givens, I've checked into your background. Until this Thrasher matter, your reputation was quite good."

"You've had a pretty good source of information," I said, glaring at him.

Hartson shifted in his chair. "Monica says she believes you weren't involved with William Thrasher's death and she says she's equally confident you had nothing to do with Fred Whitfield being killed either."

"I'm touched," I said. I still had the almost uncontrollable urge to break the man's nose.

"Naturally, I really don't know about any of that," he continued. "But this Centennial matter, that is something with which I am intimately familiar. Don't believe what you've been told by Tom Davis. We can prove the man was mentally imbalanced. Such a tragedy. At one time, Tom was a splendid lawyer. Givens, I assure you, you will never get any place with the Caponis. In light of all of your other problems, it would be a real shame to see you get hurt by representing the kind of people they are. Take some friendly advice and bow out of this now, before you get in too deep."

"Hartson, you and I aren't friends. But as long as you're in the mood for advice, let me give you some. You're the one with the problem here. If anybody needs to get out of this case, it's you."

He shrugged, not bothered in the least by having his hand called. "Like I said, I won't do that, Givens. I am sorry you and Monica had problems. I can assure you, I was not the cause of them. Perhaps it might help if you realize, she came to me. It wasn't the other way around."

"You're a damned liar!"

Hartson stood and backed away from the table. "Monica Bishop is not the issue," he said. "I wanted to speak with you simply because I see a lawyer with so many personal matters to deal with, he's made the mistake of becoming involved with people like the Caponis. If you don't recognize the blunder you're making and recognize it right away, you're going to pay and pay big."

I shook my head. "No, Hartson, you're the one who's wrong here. My wife will always be the issue between you and me. As for my clients, I'm comfortable with them."

"You know about their connection with the Mancusos and you sit there and say you're *comfortable* with them?"

"I'm not aware of any so-called connection between either Vincent Caponi or his son and the Mancuso family."

Hartson shrugged. "Well, you'll be finding out pretty soon then, and when you do, it'll be too late. My client isn't going to sit still for being sued by a bunch of gangsters."

I stood. Hartson edged closer to the door. "I don't know if you actually believe what you've said or not, but just so you know, I've done my homework. My clients are in no way connected with the Mafia. In fact, they've gone to great lengths to avoid being sucked into that mess. The ones who've made the big mistake are your client and the other defendants, and they made it when they started spreading their malicious rumors."

Hartson opened the door." Very well, Givens, if that's the way you intend to handle this, I can't keep you from it. Just remember, when it falls on your head, I warned you."

I didn't favor Hartson's last remark with a reply. Instead, I resumed packing papers into my briefcase. He watched for a few seconds, then slipped quietly out the door.

That afternoon, Elaine and I watched the messenger service's van pull out of the driveway, leaving with our document production—thirty-eight boxes, containing the story of a once-successful, now bankrupt business. Back in the conference room, boxes of the defendants' documents were stacked from floor to ceiling.

"This is about half of it," Elaine said. "The rest of them are upstairs. We'll have to work on some of them up there or we'll wind up wearing ourselves out bringing them up and down."

To say we were in big trouble would be a gross understatement. Making sense of everything we'd just received would take a lot more than two weeks.

Elaine slumped, hands deep in the pockets of her jeans. She looked at me and said, "Andy, I almost forgot. Mark called. He asked me to tell you, Judge Garza has set your trial for November thirtieth. He wants it completed before Christmas."

I felt another all-too-familiar surge of panic. The end of November. That was getting pretty damned close.

Chapter Twenty Three

The morning after my meeting at Marshon & Davis, Roberto came over to lend his aid to the task of analyzing the mass of paper. Vincent called to offer his help too, but sighed with relief when I said we could manage without him. Actually, I was less than confident that we'd be able to make much progress even if we had another dozen skilled document examiners working with us. And while normally, I'd have been more than happy to put a client to work, the catch with Vincent was he was simply too impatient to sit still for the tedious task of pouring over box after box of paper. The probability was, he'd miss something important—a risk I was unwilling to take.

Roberto, on the other hand, was perfect for the job. He performed even the most mundane tasks with unfailing diligence, and he demonstrated a superior intelligence that made me certain his work could be counted on. And something else emerged from having him in our office every day. Something that was quite unexpected. At least by me. Once outside his father's immediate sphere, and given the opportunity to be around us and get to know us better, Roberto dropped his reserved, cautious formality and relaxed, allowing his real self to come out. He and Elaine quickly forged a friendship, swapping war stories about their similar experiences growing up under the influence of disciplinarian fathers, dubbing Vincent "Benito," and Colonel Turner "Adolph."

He also revealed himself to be an excellent impressionist. From the ill-fated occasion of our meeting in Port Arthur, he vividly portrayed the roles of Nathan Junell, Ronnie York, and even Brad, the Amazing Hulk. Naturally, he had Vincent down cold.

We were two days into the project when I received a call from Travis Ball, an accountant who worked for Thrasher Industries and whom I'd met several times during preparation of the W.D.S. case. I'd heard from Del that Travis had assumed the role of acting C.E.O. at Thrasher, though he probably wouldn't have the job very long. Del also understood that Western Waste was actively pursuing acquiring the company.

To say the least, I was uncomfortable taking his call. After all, Thrasher had just sued my former firm for my alleged malpractice. I hadn't seen the petition yet, but according to Del, I was a named defendant too. Although Travis and I had always gotten along well, I didn't give him the chance for any of the usual chit-chat.

"Hi, Travis," I said. "What can I do for you?"

"Uh, Andy—thanks for taking my call. I spoke to Steve Golden a little while ago. Has he called you yet?"

"No, but what's this about, Travis?"

"Well, I guess if you haven't talked to him, you wouldn't know. I wondered if he'd place the call. Anyway, I've got some pretty interesting news. There might be a chance we can settle with W.D.S. They're apparently concerned we might get swallowed up by Western. And, well, I was wondering if you'd be willing to go up to Chicago and negotiate for us."

"If this is some kind of joke, Travis, I don't appreciate your humor."

"Hey, I'm serious. I realize you think you have the right to be pissed at us. But I'm telling you, this might be too good an opportunity to pass up. W.D.S. is hot to trot. They see a chance to get rid of a lawsuit, and avoid Western setting a hook in our butt to boot. The only thing is, with Bill Thrasher dead, you're the only person we know who has enough background about our claims."

"Yeah, and I'm the guy you've just sued for supposedly screwing up your lawsuit and who also happens to be under indictment for killing your ex-boss. Don't you think you'd better find yourself another negotiator?"

"Andy, for what it's worth, I want you to know I think the charges against you are a bunch of bull. And as far as the malpractice claim goes, if we can get the case settled, that'll be a dead issue."

"I'll think about it."

"Well, think fast. They want to meet tomorrow afternoon."


It was almost eight-thirty when I finally left the headquarters of Waste Disposal Systems, Inc. Despite the hour, traffic on Michigan Avenue was still heavy and the sidewalks were crowded too, causing slow going as I made my way to the hotel. Even though the calendar said mid-September, a surprisingly cool breeze blew in from the lake. Coming from stifling heat and humidity that showed no signs of ending in Houston, the evening was absolutely invigorating.

The folks from W.D.S. never explained why, but apparently the lawyers from Barrett & Taylor hadn't been invited to participate in our settlement talks. Their regular counsel, some corporate types from Kirkland & Ellis, had been called in to carry the ball instead. At first, they did a lot of posturing and arm-twisting, but by merely being patient, I finally managed to get them to make a realistic proposal. When they did, it was even better than I'd hoped.

Travis Ball was back in Houston, eagerly waiting for my call, so I headed straight to the Hyatt to fill him in on the details. He'd been right about W.D.S. wanting to settle. When I said the offer was more than I anticipated, and although when they made it, it didn't make a lot of sense to me, they wound up renewing the same offer that was on the table before the directed verdict: $16 million, plus unlimited access to their landfill on McCarty Road. I'd always thought that was fair. Unfortunately, William Thrasher had thought otherwise.

Under the circumstances, the deal was so sweet, Travis Ball was certain to jump at it. That's why I'd decided to wait to call him until I could get away from the enemy camp. If they were unethical enough to monitor our discussion, they might find out how desperate Travis really was. In our short session the night before, I'd come to understand that Travis had grown quite fond of being a top dog, even if it was at a down-at-the-heels outfit like Thrasher Industries. He'd do anything to keep Western Waste from buying him out of a job. I didn't want those sharks at W.D.S. to find that out and try to renig on their offer, making Travis squirm enough that he'd start bidding against himself.

I pushed the hotel room door open and flipped on the light. A floor lamp at the far end of the room came on, emanating a feeble glow. I put my briefcase down on the table next to the telephone and pulled back the heavy black-out curtains capable of keeping the room as dark as a tomb at any hour.

A narrow plaza separated the Hyatt from a neighboring building and, in the office directly across from my room, a thin, balding man sat at his desk, tie askew, shirt sleeves rolled to his elbows, talking on the telephone. While I was still standing there, he looked out the window and seemed to stare directly at me.

I took a step back from the window and was about to wave. Out of the corner of my eye I saw a reflecting image in the window. My heart raced. Someone was edging out of the bathroom. A short, stocky man, dressed in black, arm crooked, hand poised above his shoulder, holding something—a pistol—pointed at the ceiling. He eased closer and leveled the handgun. The man in the office jumped to his feet and ran to the window, frantically waving his arms.

I grabbed the briefcase. Pivoting, as if throwing a discus, I hurled it at the intruder. A deafening blast roared. Something hot stung my head. My legs buckled and I fell to the floor.

The man who'd just shot at me rolled onto his feet. My throw had been on target. Something warm and sticky ran into my eyes. The gun lay on the middle of the bedspread. He lunged to reach it. I dove at his legs. We went down, my arms wrapped around him at his knees. He kicked free and we both struggled to our feet. He stared at me with flat, emotionless eyes. I glanced at the pistol. It was closer to me than him. I reached for it and he charged at me, arms outstretched. Stepping backward, I stumbled over the briefcase. I was already falling when he got to me. I grabbed his wrist and pulled as he hurtled past. He stumbled, shoulder down, straight into the floor-to-ceiling window. He hit it moving fast and gave a brief, startled cry as the glass shattered and he toppled through the opening. Wiping blood away from my eyes, I pulled myself up and staggered to the window.

Across the way, the man in the office stared wild-eyed with shock. Eighteen floors below, my attacker lay grotesquely sprawled on the brick pavement.

Moments later, shouting echoed in the hallway. I opened the door and caught a brief glimpse of several uniformed policeman. That's when the room began spinning and I guess that's when I passed out.


The bullet fired from a distance of less than ten feet only brushed my temple, resulting in a nasty scalp wound and a headache that went well beyond the severity and the persistence of those I'd experienced after my worst encounters with Mr Gordon. Just the same, I wasn't in any position to complain. If my briefcase hadn't hit its mark, I wouldn't have had the chance to even think about it.

When the boys in blue found out who I was (thanks no doubt to Rupert Puryear or Albert Anderson) they initially operated on the theory that I'd invited my attacker up to Chicago to plot our next criminal act. The man's name, by the way, was Charles Lucas, or, as his former pals in the

Banditos used to call him, Dog-Man. The Banditos were a particularly nasty motorcycle gang that had once regularly wreaked havoc from El Paso to New Orleans. After most of his compatriots wound up either dead or permanently behind bars, Dog-Man moved on to bigger and better things, such as serving as contract labor for various organized criminal enterprises in Texas, Oklahoma, and parts of the Southeast.

Mark Watson, who, along with Elaine Turner were my only welcome guests during my hospital stay, filled me in on the depth of my problem, which centered on the fact that the gun found in my hotel room was the same one that was used to murder Fred Whitfield. Fortunately, my prints weren't on it and Dog-Man's were, but that didn't keep the local authorities from pursuing the case from the angle that I was the simple victim of a business deal gone sour.

Fortunately, this time there was an eye witness. When the police finally got around to taking his statement, the fellow from the office in the next building prevented me from being locked up on the spot.

I suppose this development should have left me thrilled, or, at the very least, relieved. But for some strange reason, I was incapable of mustering a single positive thought. Some guy, who'd once run with the Banditos, had murdered Fred Whitfield. And then trailed me all the way to Chicago to do the same to me. If I hadn't been luckier than the last ten lotto winners combined, he'd have succeeded, no sweat.

The more I thought about this bizarre sequence of events, the more convinced I became: Dog-Man had, without doubt, been hired by Whitfield to kill William Thrasher. Then, apparently Whitfield had become spooked, or maybe he'd refused to pay for the contract. Fred had certainly been cheap enough and dumb enough to try to pull a stupid stunt like that. And then, after the news reports all but announced I was responsible for Fred's murder, as well as Thrasher's, Dog-Man had apparently decided to try for a trifecta, and, in the process, make sure all outstanding investigations ended with my death. The reason he tried to get so close before pulling the trigger was to make my murder look like a suicide.

My most depressing thoughts were the realization that I couldn't prove any of my suppositions not a single one— and the knowledge of what all of this had to look like to an objective outsider. Here I was, facing trial for murdering a client, then threatening my former law partner with bodily harm and the next day his wife finds him shot dead in their front yard. Finally, this. A fatal tangle with an ex-Bandito turned known hit-man in my hotel room where the weapon used to murder my ex-partner just happens to be found. In combination, the events had all the ear-markings of rank criminal behavior. And even though I was totally innocent, I was beginning to wonder, did that really make a difference?

# Chapter Twenty Four

After forty-eight hours in bed and another day and a half spent putting the finishing touches on the W.D.S. settlement, and in the process making a friend for life of Travis Ball, I was finally able to leave Chicago and its not so fond memories behind. But what I'd just gone through up north was a piece of cake compared to tackling the task of getting a handle on the mountain of paper the *Centennial* defendants turned over.

Almost all of their records were nothing more than filler designed to give us a hard time. To make matters worse, they'd done their best to hamstring us, producing the records in a disorganized jumble. Elaine and I, along with Roberto, went back at it, pouring over paper, box after box of it.

Counting the down-time caused by my trip, we were a full ten days into the process, with only four days remaining until the hearing with Judge Lowenstein. We'd worked as hard and as long as we could, living off of fast food and caffeine. Elaine and Roberto even stopped bothering to go home. Catnaps—not the endless ones enjoyed by Ivory—just grabbing a couple of hours here and there were the only rest any of us got.

Mark was about to go crazy, trying to schedule trial preparation with a client who was too busy to give him any time. I finally promised he'd get my undivided attention the day *after* the hearing with Judge Lowenstein. The problem was, we'd already pushed ourselves to the outer limits of physical and mental endurance. I wondered if I'd be much good to Mark by then.

Late in the afternoon, a steady rain driven by a sudden thunderstorm splattered against the windows. The mood in my conference room was as grim as the weather. I was on my sixth or seventh cup of coffee since lunch. Even the jag from the caffeine wasn't keeping me alert. But Elaine and Roberto still were going strong. How they could do it was beyond me.

Roberto looked up from the stack of papers in front of him. He was smiling.

"Have either of you seen one of these?" he asked. He slid a sheet of paper across the table so Elaine and I could see:

PRIVILEGED AND CONFIDENTIAL
ATTORNEY WORK PRODUCT

| | |
|---|---|
| HOT DOCUMENT | X |
| PRODUCE | — |
| DO NOT PRODUCE | X |
| PRIVILEGED | — |
| DUPLICATE | — |
| OTHER | X |

"Nope," I said. "They must've used sheets like this to flag special documents and then missed pulling this one before they made their production."

Elaine picked up the sheet of paper. "What a goof up. Was this attached to anything?"

"Yeah and it's pretty interesting," Roberto said, his lips curving in a sly grin. "It's the Mason memo, only this one has handwriting in the margin."

We'd already found several copies of the Mason memo. Mason was Anthony Mason, the president of Groves State. He'd written it the day after the Caponis' ill-fated meeting at Texas Republic, instructing all of the bank's employees to find out if their customers held Centennial Savings certificates, and if they did, to encourage them to transfer their savings to the Groves bank because of the institution's "outstanding record of growth and stability." By itself, the memo was strong circumstantial evidence that Groves State was involved in a scheme to get Centennial's customers to pull their investments. By far, it was the best single thing we'd discovered from the blizzard of paper the defendants had produced.

"Let's see," I said.

Roberto handed it over, now smiling from ear to ear. He had good reason. Someone had written in the top right margin "Tell all Centennial certificate holders the Caponis are owned by Mafia—all of Centennial's money has been pulled out by the Mancusos."

Roberto and I shook hands across the table.

Elaine leaned over my shoulder, taking her first look. She whistled softly. "Who do you suppose wrote this?"

Roberto laughed. "I'm pretty sure it's Tommy Duncan. He's a vice-president at Groves and he's undoubtedly one of the stupidest human beings alive in the world today. He probably was the one Mason gave the job to of putting out the real message he wanted our certificate holders to hear. Duncan's so slow, he had to write it down just to remember it."

"Is that what 'TBD' stands for?" I asked, pointing at the initials on the copy line that had been marked with a high lighter.

Tears ran down Roberto's cheeks he laughed so hard. It took a while but he finally gasped, "Yeah, Tommy Boyd Duncan. Folks call him 'Tommy Boy' after the character in some stupid movie that big guy from *Saturday Night Live* made a few years ago. You know, the one who died?"

Elaine and I both nodded.

"Anyway, you'd have to know him, he's actually that dumb."

"What do we do now?" Elaine asked.

"Well, I'm going to take you and Roberto out for dinner. This calls for a celebration. Tomorrow, we'll get a deposition notice ready for Mr Duncan. He might make a pretty good place to start."

Elaine sighed. "If there's any celebrating to do, I'm doing it in bed. I think I'll sleep for three days."

Roberto sat back in his chair and continued to smile. I was happy for him. He'd worked long and hard, adding immeasurably to our progress. Now, because of his efforts, we had a valuable weapon to use in our battle with the Defendants. I didn't want to admit it, but during the preceding days I'd begun to wonder if we hadn't bitten off substantially more than we could chew.


Judge David Lowenstein was next in line for senior judge of the Southern District of Texas. His rank earned him one of the largest courtrooms in the federal building. The place was, if nothing else, impressive. An enormous raised dais that compelled everyone to gaze upward to the bench. A ceiling that was a good twenty feet high. Taking up the space roughly equivalent to a tennis court. The whole effect gave the impression that, very possibly, God Himself presided on the bench.

The same gang who attended the meeting in Hartson's office sat at one of the large tables inside the bar. The other counsel's table was mine for the taking. Waiting for the judge, I tried to keep from worrying about how badly out-numbered I was by calculating how much the defendants were spending on the hearing. Eleven lawyers, with hourly fees probably ranging from around $500 for folks like Hartson, Mossberg, Tucker, and Taylor, maybe even that little weasel Alton Giles, down to maybe as low as $175 for mere drones like Hopgood. I guessed in total they were billing at least $2,500.00 an hour.

My mathematical calculations were interrupted by a loud rap from inside the door leading to Judge Lowenstein's chambers. Everyone stood as Lowenstein entered the courtroom. To meet the man on the street, he was small and unassuming, but his regal bearing in those long, dark robes justified the way his clerk announced his presence as if he were a monarch.

The judge surveyed the scene and motioned us to our seats. "Gentlemen," he announced, "this is our first pre-trial conference. We will establish a schedule for discovery and for filing any dispositive motions which you may need to file. What I intend to do is propose a schedule. But first, have all potentially relevant documents been exchanged?"

I stood. "Andrew Givens for the plaintiffs. Yes, your honor."

Hartson also was on his feet. "Judge, Joseph Hartson for First Texas Republic Bank. I have been appointed spokesperson for the defendants for this hearing and I concur with Mr Givens' statement. We have exchanged all of what each side believes are potentially relevant documents."

Lowenstein nodded. "Good. Is there any reason why we can't begin the deposition phase of discovery in ten days?"

That was fast for my side. We'd barely gotten through a fairly cursory review of the defendants' document productions. But I didn't have much choice. "That will be fine," I said.

Hartson also voiced his approval. They were going to try to push as hard and fast as they could. Try to keep us from ever getting a foothold on the mountain of paper they'd produced.

Lowenstein glanced briefly at his docket notes, obviously determined to keep things moving. "Why don't we alternate weeks. Plaintiffs take the first week and defendants take the second and so forth. This clearly is a Track Five case. But for any of you who might not know, I don't believe in lengthy depositions. The issues are fairly straight forward, and even though I realize you may need to be fairly intensive in your development of the evidence, unless someone can convince me otherwise, I'm going to include in the pre-trial order the provision that no deposition will last longer than two days. And gentlemen, don't try to get cute with this. That's two days, from 9:00 a.m. to 5:00 p.m., with an hour's break for lunch."

Short depositions would help. The last thing we needed was to get pinned down in lengthy depositions of the Caponis.

Hartson was back up. "Judge, on the subject of depositions, there is one other matter we need to discuss. A rather large number of documents have been exchanged by the parties. We believe it would be most efficient for the party noticing a deposition to be required to pre-designate all documents that are going to be used with the witness."

Judge Lowenstein turned to me. "Counsel?"

"Judge, I can't agree. You need to understand, the defendants dumped a mountain of paper on us, hoping they could smother us with it. Now they want us to pre-identify what we've found so they can coach their witnesses. That's not fair."

Hartson stared at me, his face turning red. The other lawyers glared at me too. Hartson cleared his throat. "Your honor, may I reply?"

Lowenstein nodded.

"We merely produced the documents required by the allegations made in the complaint. The over-breadth of plaintiffs' own pleading is what has Mr Givens in trouble."

"Well, Mr Hartson, I'm sure you folks, with all of your computers and data bases can adequately prepare witnesses to be deposed without making the plaintiffs reveal their work product. That request is denied."

"But your honor—"

"That's enough, counsel. You have my ruling."

Lowenstein consulted his docket notes again. "Oh, yes. There are two other things. Defendants' motions to dismiss for failure to state a claim and their motions for sanctions have been denied. You will soon receive my written order on those subjects. Finally, either side may move for partial or complete summary judgment at any time. However, the party opposing any such motion will have twenty days from the conclusion of discovery to file a response. I will consider shortening that time for good cause shown. The order I am about to enter provides that all discovery is to be completed by next August first. Your proposed pre-trial order will be submitted to me by September Fifteenth. Final pre-trial will be conducted on next September Thirtieth and trial is set for October Fifteenth."

The lawyers at the defense table were stunned. Hartson stood again, this time walking around the table to go nearer the bench. "Your honor, this is a very large, exceedingly complex case. I'm afraid you might not be giving us enough time to prepare it properly."

"Oh, I'm sure this is plenty of time," Lowenstein said as he smiled down from the bench.

"But you honor, with all respect, some of us have other cases already set. We won't be free to work exclusively just on this one matter."

"Now, Mr Hartson, you know I've heard that argument many times. I'm not going to tell you what to do about handling your respective dockets. You don't need my help doing that with all of those highly skilled lawyers you've got waiting back at your office. And gentlemen, don't think I'm trying to prevent any of you from being able to participate in this case. I recognize the right of each party to have the assistance of a lawyer or firm of lawyers of his or her own choosing. What I'm doing here, gentlemen, is simply making sure that cases in my court move quickly to conclusion. Most of you have tried cases with me before and you know how I feel about that."

Hartson remained standing. "Your honor, there is one more thing. I didn't want to have to be the one to bring it up. Frankly, I'd hoped Mr Givens would see fit to address the issue himself, but since he hasn't, well, Judge, we don't want to get into the middle of this proceeding and then have the

Plaintiffs complain they need more time because their lawyer can't represent them."

Judge Lowenstein looked at me. "Do you understand what this is about, Mr Givens?"

"Oh really, your honor," Hartson continued, "we all realize Mr Givens faces murder charges. His trial starts in just a few weeks. What are we supposed to do under your schedule while he's on trial himself? Better yet, what's going to happen if he's convicted?"

I leaped up. "Wait just a minute, Hartson, that's not going to happen. I guarantee it!"

Lowenstein stared at me. "Mr Givens, kindly address the court, not opposing counsel."

"Sorry, your honor. I am scheduled to begin trial on November thirtieth. The case should carry through until the Christmas holiday."

The judge nodded. "I'm aware of the charges you face, Mr Givens. I want all of you to know, I will not allow any comment by any of you in this court concerning the fact that Plaintiffs' counsel is under indictment. Also, in the event Mr Givens is convicted, and please understand, Mr Givens, I have no idea what might happen in your case, I will not tolerate any remark about the plaintiffs' lawyer being convicted of a crime. Now, Mr Givens, I am instructing you, inform your clients that your personal circumstances will not be considered by the court in granting any continuance of the schedule I have just ordered. If that means they need to go out and hire someone else, or if you need to associate co-counsel, then that's what you'd better do. Do all of you understand? This is the last I want to hear about this."

He didn't give anyone a chance to respond. He took a few seconds to fill in the blanks on the scheduling order. Then, he left the bench. His clerk directed us to come up to her desk to pick up copies of the order.

That afternoon I briefed Elaine, Roberto, and Vincent Caponi about what had happened. We were on a fast track with a judge who'd made it plain he wasn't going to play favorites. We couldn't ask for more.

After the Caponis left, I had Elaine call a messenger to hand deliver the Tommy Duncan deposition notice. Lowenstein had afforded us the opportunity to strike the first blow. I planned to make it a good one.

# Chapter Twenty Five

"It's not going to be easy," Mark said. We were in his office, just the two of us, winding up our meeting on how to try the Thrasher case. The DA could put my car in Thrasher's garage on the night he was killed. The doctored security sheet from my building said I'd been there until shortly before the murder. To make matters worse, Del Wallace had struck out in his attempt to get copies of the firm's phone records. Anderson must've gotten the word about somebody leaking the building logs to us. The office manager at Golden - Wallace had been ordered by Mr Golden, at the DA's insistence, to keep them under lock and key. For more going against us, Susan Knight's efforts with the room service records hadn't helped. She'd found the delivery ticket, but as she suspected, it didn't show a delivery time. And the waiter? He'd disappeared, gone back to visit his family someplace in Central Mexico. His friends weren't sure where that was. Mark had an investigator trying to find him, but so far no luck.

But by far the most devastating blow was something Mark had just learned. Albert Anderson made a supplemental production in response to our *Brady* motion, an obvious effort to keep us from scrutinizing their evidence.

"It stinks to high heaven, but they do it all the time," Mark explained.

"What can we do?" I asked.

Mark stood and jammed his hands in his pockets. "Oh, I'll go to Garza, and scream like a stuck pig, but nothing'll happen. Anderson'll be chided for the delay, and that's about all. We'll just have to try to get our guy to get his analytical work done as fast as he can."

Our guy was Desmond Cutler, a former F.B.I. agent and one of the best forensic specialists in our part of the country. He could handle a last minute job like this, no problem. We knew that. What had us steamed, not to mention worried no end, was the evidence itself. Blood—William Thrasher's blood—had been found on the carpet of my car. We were, of course welcome to send the carpet samples to our own expert for verification.

"They can get to a jury with this, can't they?"

Mark nodded. "Yeah, I'm afraid so."

We sat in silence for several minutes. I found myself concentrating on the patterns in Mark's Navajo rug.

"If they didn't have that damned videotape of your car entering and leaving the parking garage, and now, Thrasher's blood inside your car, I'd say we stood a pretty good shot," Mark said.

"That's like saying if there hadn't been so many Indians, Custer might have stood a fighting chance."

"Andy, if they didn't have that stuff, Judge Garza might have seriously entertained a motion for directed verdict. And even if he wouldn't, we might've risked not putting you on the stand."

"You mean you'd be considering not having me testify?"

"Yeah. They don't prove their case if they don't put you at Thrasher's office that night. What's the point of putting you on if we don't have to? As it is, we're left with the tape showing your car and just the shadow of a person hidden behind the reflection of those lights shining on the windshield. That's reasonable doubt stuff—but not directed verdict material, understand?"

"Yeah. Reasonable doubt. It's more like a *shadow* of doubt, don't you think?"

Mark pursed his lips in a wan smile.

"You know, it's such a shame we haven't been able to develop anything on Whitfield," I said.

Mark rocked back on his heels. I'd raised a sore subject. Since my trip to see Whitfield at the City Club, even after what happened up in Chicago, I'd kept my promise and left the investigative work to Mark and his folks. So far, nothing had developed.

Turning toward me he said, "Andy, you know I've got people on it. Fred Whitfield might have paid that Lucas fella to kill Thrasher. But we have to face the fact, we're not going to be able to prove it. We don't even have anything we can use to suggest to a jury that he did it."

"What about W.D.S.? I liked your idea about that outfit being involved. And I *was* up in Chicago when that guy tried to kill me."

Mark shook his head. "I'm afraid we came up with zilch on them, too. Those boys play rough, but did they bump off Thrasher? If they did, you have to give them credit, they did a damned good job of hiding their tracks."

I slumped in my chair. "We're in a box, aren't we?"

"Afraid so, pal. We'll have to defend the old fashioned way, punch holes in Anderson's presentation. Demonstrate how thin their case is. It's gonna to be tough, but there's a lot of room to build reasonable doubt. We've got a good shot."

"Do we still want to set that deal up with Del Wallace?" I asked.

Mark smiled mischievously. "Yeah, we might as well."


We took the video deposition of Tommy Duncan in the main conference room at Marshon & Davis. The same eleven lawyers who'd attended the scheduling conference ten days earlier were there for the defendants. God, how those folks liked to make money. Since I was such a terrible paper shuffler, I brought Elaine along to help with the exhibits. Admittedly there was another reason. Her presence might distract some of the lawyers on the other side of the table.

Vincent and Roberto attended too. They had personal insights concerning Duncan and we thought it would be good to have them there so they could pass them along. Also, I wanted them to become familiar with the deposition process.

The time would soon come when each of them would have to take a turn in the witness chair.

Duncan was a large, boisterous man. At least six-six, he must have weighed a good three hundred pounds. He was affable and gregarious, and reminded me of a younger version of Willard Scott. He showed up dressed in a loud plaid sports coat, maroon slacks, and an open-collared white shirt. He wore huge diamond rings on two fingers on his left hand and his large, gold nugget bracelet kept trying to slip over a fat paw of a hand. He seemed absolutely relaxed with the surroundings smiling broadly every time anyone said anything to him.

Even the lawyers on the other side of the table were amused by his appearance. I could see them thinking, "What is Givens doing wasting his time with this oaf?"

I spent the morning plodding laboriously through Duncan's background and his responsibilities as a vice-president with Groves State Bank. As the questioning went on, I saw the conclusions I'd hoped for being drawn by my opponents. They could relax. The witness was a nice guy, but a dolt who didn't know a thing. They could put it on cruise control for the afternoon, and enjoy the thought of all that money they were making doing absolutely nothing.

By the afternoon session, the only ones still paying attention were Arthur Cannon, the young associate who was assisting Alton Giles in representing Groves State, and Carl Hopgood, who was turning out to be a compulsive son of a gun, full of so much energy he probably wouldn't be able to stay still at his own funeral.

I kept it up a little longer, just to be sure, stumbling around with one innocuous question after another—most of which weren't comprehended by the witness on the first go around. I'd even heard Cannon, who'd taken over from Giles the task of representing the witness, mutter under his breath that my clients probably wished they'd hired somebody who knew how to take a deposition.

I waited until after the final break of the day. By then everyone was thinking, "Good, just another forty-five minutes of this garbage and we can go home." That's when I had the court reporter mark as an exhibit the Anthony Mason memo, the one with Duncan's marginal note on it. I slid a copy of the exhibit across the table for Arthur Cannon's inspection. Boredom having won out over the prospect of a few hundred dollars more easy money, the weasel Giles wasn't around. He'd apparently called it quits at the last break.

The court reporter handed the marked exhibit to Duncan.

"Have you seen this document before?" I asked.

"Uh, sure I've seen it," Duncan replied.

"There is some hand writing in the top right hand margin. Do you see what I'm asking about?"

"Yes, I see it."

"Is that your handwriting?"

"Yeah, it's mine all right."

"Now the document itself, is a memo from Anthony Mason the president of your bank, right?"

"That's correct."

Heads started to perk up on the other side of the table.

Arthur Cannon said, "Uh, counsel, I don't believe we've seen this before. It doesn't have one of our production numbers on it."

Carl Hopgood stood and eased behind Duncan's attorney. He took a brief look at the document and hurried out of the conference room.

"I'll represent to you that it is, indeed, a document which was produced to us by Groves in this case. Maybe you guys just forgot to put a number on it, or maybe there's another explanation, but I'll get to that later." I forged ahead, trying to keep Duncan's lawyer from calling time out. "Now Mr Duncan, this memo from Mr Mason, it instructs Groves employees to encourage customers of Centennial Savings to cash in their certificates and to deposit those funds with Groves doesn't it?"

"Objection. Lacks foundation. Calls for a conclusion. Vague and ambiguous. The document speaks for itself," Duncan's attorney said. If he could have thought of more objections, he'd have made them too.

"Answer the question," I said.

Duncan looked at his lawyer. "What do I do?"

"You know I'm entitled to an answer unless you're instructing him not to," I said.

"Uh, I'm not instructing him not to answer, but it's just I don't know about this particular document."

A crowd of defense lawyers had gathered to stand behind Cannon. They strained to get a look at the exhibit in Tommy Duncan's hand.

William Mossberg said, "Mr Givens, I believe we should take a break and get to the bottom of where this document came from."

"There's a question pending. There won't be a break until I've gotten an answer to my question," I replied.

What Arthur Cannon was thinking about, the Lord only knows. An experienced lawyer on his side had just told him what to do, but he ignored the advice and said, "Mr Duncan, you may answer just the question pending and then we may want to take a break."

Mossberg threw up his hands and headed for the door, no doubt to try to find Joseph Hartson.

Duncan smiled broadly. "With all this arguing goin' on, I've plumb forgot what the question was."

I restated it. "Mr Duncan, the memo prepared by Mr Mason instructs the employees of your bank, Groves State, to encourage all of the Centennial Savings certificate holders they can identify to pull their money out of Centennial Savings and to deposit those funds with Groves. Isn't that right?"

"That's right it does," he said, still smiling broadly.

"Now the handwriting in the upper right corner of the document, that you just said is in your handwriting, it reads: 'Tell all who have Centennial certificates the Caponis are owned by the Mafia and all Centennial's money has been pulled out by the Mancusos.' Why did you write that on this memo Mr Duncan?"

"I thought we were going to take a break," Cannon said, his voice going up in a high whine.

I shook my head. "Not with a question pending. Answer the question, Mr Duncan."

Cannon sat, frozen in his chair. "Let's break," Connie Sullivan said.

"Answer the question," I repeated.

Incredible as it may seem, Tommy Duncan continued to sit there and smile like an idiot. "You want me to go ahead and answer?"

"Yes," I replied.

Arthur Cannon sat next to his client, a bewildered look on his ghost-white face. I was witnessing an early end to the young man's career as a trial lawyer. He'd probably be back in the office drafting wills after this performance, that was if he wasn't fired on the spot.

"Well," Duncan said, "Mr Mason came by and told me this was what he'd learned at the meeting he'd just attended—the one you asked me if I attended and I told you I didn't get invited to? Anyway, uh, Mr Mason told me to pass the word that this was the real reason people needed to get their money out of Centennial just as fast as they could. Now, you need to understand, he was just trying to help make sure a lot of good folks didn't get hurt."

*The real reason.* His statement was so absolutely perfect. I couldn't believe it. I sat there for several seconds, considering if there might be any way to improve on it.

Suddenly, Joseph Hartson rushed into the conference room, followed closely by Carl Hopgood and William Mossberg.

I handed the court reporter the Hot Document sheet and had it marked as the next exhibit. "Mr Duncan, I will represent to you that this exhibit is a copy of a sheet that was produced to us attached to the preceding exhibit. Have you ever seen this before?"

"No," Duncan answered.

Hartson snatched the sheet of paper out of Tommy Duncan's hands. "This is work product," he snarled. "You don't have the right to make this an exhibit or to ask any further questions about it. I demand that you withdraw the exhibit." A purple vein bulged on Hartson's forehead. The wholly satisfying thought of Monica some day being his widow flashed through my mind.

"I'm not prepared to withdraw it, but I don't have any further questions about it, not right now anyway. In fact, I guess I can say I don't have any more questions for Mr Duncan. I'm finished with him."

Hartson led Cannon and Duncan out of the room. For the first time that day, Tommy Boyd Duncan wasn't smiling.


That evening, we celebrated at Montesano's. Vincent and Sylvia were the perfect host and hostess, ordering special Italian delicacies, keeping the Chianti flowing, taking turns recounting their family histories, meeting as young adults in New Orleans, helping Vincent's father build the family business, even the recent past, the bitterness of leaving it all behind to avoid the corrupting, lethal influences of the New Orleans Mafia. They told it all with passion, pride, and eloquence. Elaine and I laughed until both of us had tears running down our cheeks as Sylvia told the story of how she managed to catch Vincent.

Even in his father's presence, Roberto loosened up, abandoning his cautious, calculated speech and reserved manner and revealing a sense of humor that was both entertaining and refreshing. He sent all of us into hysterics with his flawless imitation of Tommy Duncan, who was, after all, responsible for our party in the first place.

# Chapter Twenty Six

Sunday, the first of November. Mark and I should have been working together, but to his chagrin, my day was devoted to Vincent and Roberto. Vincent's deposition was scheduled for Thursday and Friday. After the disastrous experience with Tommy Duncan, the defendants apparently intended to go directly for our key witnesses, trying to put us on our heels before we had a chance to hit more pay dirt. We spent the better part of the morning covering the basic elements of defamation, business interference, civil conspiracy, and the Sherman Anti-trust Act. The Caponis had to understand those laws before being deposed.

That afternoon, we practiced. I assumed the role of the opposition, peppering Vincent with questions like pellets from a twelve-gauge, showing him what to expect and then discussing the best way to answer particular questions, and how to avoid being forced into taking positions that could prove to be detrimental to our case.

My chief concern was his temper. He'd warned me about it when we set up the meeting with Nathan Junell and Ronnie York. At first, almost anything would push him over the edge. And the mere mention of the Mafia, or pointing to the fact he was presently living off of the income that Sylvia managed to bring in with her antique consignment shop up in Humble sent him ballistic. But eventually, he was able to cover even those sensitive topics without losing his composure.

At a little after three o'clock, Elaine brought in deli sandwiches and soft drinks. As if on cue, Mark Watson just happened to drop by. He'd spent his day with Desmond Cutler working on how best to attack the State's forensics. I introduced him to the Caponis and invited him to stay to eat.

Vincent had often inquired about Mark and Mark was painfully aware of the big case that kept diverting my attention from preparations for the Thrasher trial. The occasion afforded the opportunity for the two of them to finally meet.

As we sat around the table, munching on the sandwiches, Vincent asked Mark if he'd ever represented a lawyer in any of his other criminal cases.

"Oh, it's happened occasionally," Mark said.

Vincent arched his eyebrows and gestured in my direction. "Were any of them as, uh, challenging as the one with our friend?"

Mark leaned back and took a sip from his Dr. Pepper. Elaine started keeping our refrigerator stocked with the stuff when she found out it was Mark's favorite. "Yeah," he said. "As a matter of fact, it probably was the most interesting case I've ever handled."

"Would you tell us about it, Mark?" Caponi asked.

Mark gave me that sly grin he displays when he's about to spin one. "Well it was a case involving a fellow who had been practicing law, but I believe by the time his case came up on the trial docket, he'd already had his license suspended…."

I'd heard this one before. Many times. It involved a sot of a lawyer named Jack McNamara, who was banished for life from a local watering hole for scamming the proprietor, and who later came back disguised as a woman and while he was there, all decked out in his dress, high-heels, and wig, managed to get in a fight with the bartender and wound up stealing the poor guy's wooden leg. Mark felt obligated to defend McNamara because he'd bet him fifty dollars he'd never get served in the place again.

By the time Mark finished, Vincent and Roberto were both in stitches. "What happened at the trial?" Vincent asked, gasping to catch his breath.

Mark grinned again and looked at me. "Oh, there wasn't a trial. Jack was guilty as sin. We plea bargained. He made restitution and got six months probation."

Everyone laughed some more. Mark apologized for taking up so much time with his story, then he said he had to go. The Caponis had had enough coaching for one day too. Before they left we set up a time to meet again on Tuesday.

Alone in the office, with no one but Ivory to keep me company, I made some phone calls. The first one was to Tommy Jackson. He hadn't heard anything more about Centennial. Just the same, he said he'd send me a bill for the consultation. Next, I called Nathan Junell. Like Jackson, the senator didn't have any useful information. But he seemed pleased that I'd called and promised to stay in touch.

On the morning of Vincent's deposition, my conference room was filled to capacity. Though we'd be cramped, with most of the defendants' boxes still stacked high on one end of the room, I'd insisted on the defendants coming to my office. Alton Giles and even the little snot Carl Hopgood acted genuinely offended when they asked if I really intended to allow a cat in the room during the deposition and I answered that I did.

I have to admit, I was more than just a little nervous, but Vincent was terrific. Calm, thoughtful, articulate. Our hours of rehearsal paid off as he kept his temper in check throughout the day, even when Giles, who'd taken first crack for the defendants, brought up the question of Caponi's supposed affiliation with the Mafia.

By the time we called a halt that afternoon, the boys on the other side of the table were a discouraged bunch. Caponi had proved himself highly knowledgeable about his business and genuinely concerned about the catastrophic effects Centennial's failure had caused to its depositors. Anyone with half a brain could tell he was credible. In short, they hadn't laid a glove on him.

I saw no need to work more with Vincent that evening so I gave him the night off, asking both Caponis to be back at seven-thirty the next morning. I'd asked Elaine to bring in breakfast. We could go over the meeting at Texas First Republic. That was the only major subject Giles hadn't gotten into.

Elaine was busy reorganizing the conference room when I got back from showing the Caponis out. Her normally vibrant face was drawn and dark circles ringed her eyes. With all that'd been going on, it was no wonder.

"Uh, Andy, you had a couple of calls this afternoon."

"Who from?"

"Mark called. He wanted to remind you that we need to meet again this weekend. He sounded nervous."

"Oh? Did he say what he's nervous about?"

"No. He didn't. But I imagine he's getting pretty concerned about the trial and us being so busy."

I winced. "Yeah, I guess he is. We've just got to do the best we can to handle both situations. I'm sure Mark understands."

Her normally cheerful eyes suddenly sparked with anger. "Mark needs more of your time, Andy. He thinks you've got your priorities seriously out of kilter. You know, your whole future being at stake. That puts a lot of pressure on him."

Elaine was right. Centennial's chances looked a lot better now than when we started. We had Tommy Duncan and Arthur Cannon, wherever that poor boy was, to thank for that. I could still bring in someone to take over for the Caponis. Now, there'd be plenty of folks willing to take their case. Maybe after Vincent's deposition, I'd talk to them about it.

"Who else called?" I asked.

She looked down at the floor avoiding my gaze. "Uh, it was Monica."

My heart skipped a beat. "What did she say? Did she leave a message?"

Elaine looked at me, her eyes flat and expressionless. "She told me to tell you she's sorry."

I felt a surge of excitement. She'd come to her senses. "What else did she say?"

Elaine shrugged and turned away. "That's it."

"Didn't she want me to call?"

In a soft quiet voice she said, "I don't know. She didn't say." Without another word she picked up a stack of file folders from the conference room table and walked past me.

I could barely contain my excitement as I hurried to my office and dialed our old number. It was no longer in service. I called Marshon & Davis, the after hours operator told me Monica no longer worked there. I'd need to call back during normal business hours to find out how to contact her.

Not being able to reach her was frustrating beyond belief. At least her message was encouraging. I went to ask Elaine to go for a drink. Maybe she'd have more advice on what to do, now that my wife seemed ready to talk. But when I got to her desk, she was gone.

That morning, the season's first norther had barreled into town. It was chilly outside, so I made a fire. As usual, Ivory curled up as close to the blaze as he could manage. Baking his brain, I called it. I daydreamed about being back with Monica. What that would mean. Then, I must have dozed off.

I found myself walking in the hilly woodlands near Sandy Creek. I was headed home, following a trail I had gone down many times before. Mockingbirds and blue-jays kept me company, chattering overhead. I came to a lively, spring-fed stream that meandered through sun-dappled hickories, sweetgums, and dogwoods. I had been away for a long time and I was hot and tired. At the sight of the water, I became filled with eager anticipation. I was almost home.

Suddenly, the forest grew dark and ominously silent. The stream widened into a deep pool, and the once-crystal water went muddy and dark. The change happened so fast, it caught me completely off-guard. Then, I saw it, only for an instant, a large, menacing shape darting in and out of view, on the far side of the black, oily water, its presence warning me, don't go on. You won't like what you'll get if you do.

# Chapter Twenty Seven

As was their custom, the Caponis arrived the next morning several minutes early. We rehearsed one last time the events surrounding the meeting at Texas Republic. Vincent had it down cold. He would do fine, I was confident of that. Roberto was the one who puzzled me. Just when I thought he was finally comfortable with the lawsuit, with everything going so well, he showed up acting as nervous as a first grader on his first day at school, fidgeting, unable to remain still, pacing nervously back and forth in front of the windows. Vincent attempted to find out what was bothering his son, but Roberto wouldn't say. One thing was certain, though. He seemed particularly annoyed with his father.

To make matters worse, when Elaine finally arrived she showed up in a foul mood. Not so much as a "good morning" did we get from her. I followed after her to find out what was wrong. She was at her desk busily arranging papers for the start of the day. A pencil fell to the floor. She picked it up and snapped it in half. Her nose was red and her eyes were swollen.

"Elaine, what's wrong?" I asked.

"Nothing," she answered, glancing up at me and then quickly turning her attention back to her work.

"What can I do to help?"

A single tear rolled slowly down her cheek leaving a glistening trail. "Andy, I'm fine, really I am. I've just got a lot to do, that's all."

"Something's wrong and I want you to tell me about it. Remember what you promised?"

"You've got a lot to do and so do I. We'll talk later. I promise."

I was about to protest but the phone rang. Elaine took the call, one of the defense lawyers hassling us about something. Whoever was on the line was a talker. Elaine shrugged, and motioned for me to go back to join the Caponis.

Back in my office, Roberto was still staring out the window. Vincent was seated at the table. I sat across from him and poured a cup of coffee.

"This day isn't starting so well, is it?" he asked.

"No," I agreed. "All of us are under more pressure than we realize. I guess that's it."

Vincent looked past me to where his son stood. "I hope you're right."

Roberto ignored another request from his father to join us. His thoughts had apparently taken him some place far removed from my office.

Moments later Elaine buzzed in. The court reporter and the videographer were set up. The defendants' lawyers were waiting in the conference room. Even though they'd received a serious blow at Tommy Duncan's deposition, and Vincent Caponi had already proven himself an excellent witness with a compelling story to tell, to a man, the defense lawyers acted more pompous and arrogant than ever. Like condemned men, spitting in the face of their executioner, they showed complete and utter disdain for Caponi. They obviously had gotten together about this and I actually found their little act quite remarkable.

Just the same, when the session got underway, Vincent continued his admirable performance. Thankfully, Roberto appeared to have calmed down. He sat next to me and took detailed notes of the questions and the answers his father gave.

Mid-way though the morning, Allie Giles announced he had no further questions and passed Caponi to the next defense attorney. Under Judge Lowenstein's order the defendants only had another five hours to complete Vincent's examination. By noon, William Mossberg was finished too. His questions were nothing more than harmless follow-ups. Even eager-beaver Carl Hopgood had apparently become discouraged, leaving before the morning session was completed.

Just before the lunch break, Joseph Hartson announced he would go next. I cautioned Vincent—one more time—to be careful. Despite my intense dislike of the arrogant son-of-a-bitch, I readily conceded he was smart and dangerous. If there'd be any serious problem presented for our side that day it would come from Hartson.

I took Roberto and Vincent back to my office. Elaine was already setting out the lunch she'd ordered from Butera's. I was preparing my plate when Roberto said, "Excuse me, Andy, but there is an important matter I must attend to during the lunch break. I'm sorry, but I must do this."

"Okay," I said. "Just be back for the afternoon. It's important that you get a chance to see Hartson at work. You know, you'll probably be next, after they finish with your father."

Roberto glanced over to where Vincent sat, filling his plate with pasta salad, thick slices of provolone cheese, and an enormous mound of black olives. That same agitated, almost angry expression he displayed earlier that morning reappeared. He nodded to me, said, "Yeah, sure," and hurried past me.

I took the opportunity afforded by our break to try to contact Monica again. The people at Marshon & Davis told me they'd been instructed not to provide any information concerning her new address to anyone who wasn't on Ms. Bishop's approved list. Needless to say, I wasn't. And I ran into another road block when I called Sharon Fielder. It turned out she was at a seminar in San Antonio and wasn't expected back until Monday. I could leave a message, but her secretary wasn't authorized to tell me how to contact Monica. I couldn't even get her to say that she would try to contact her to tell her I'd called.

To my extreme displeasure, Roberto didn't make it back as he'd promised. But I was perhaps even more disappointed with Hartson's examination. I'd expected more from the man. He seemed to be holding back or maybe, for some reason, his heart just wasn't in it. Did it have something to do with Monica? Maybe she'd given him the news about wanting to get back together with me. Whatever the reason, Vincent Caponi handled Hartson's soft-ball questions with ease. He even kept his cool when Hartson grasped at a straw and asked one of those "isn't it a fact you had sex with your pet parrot" questions, modifying it to: "Isn't it true you paid Tommy Duncan to give false testimony during his deposition in this case?"

That one hit me so out of the blue, I didn't even have a chance to object. Still, Vincent handled it well, giving a straight forward, simple "No," and keeping his cool.

Hartson, ever the arrogant one, smiled and seemed to regain his air of confidence. "Are you sure about that?"

"Wait a minute," I said. "I'm not going to sit still for you asking that kind of question, and then have you try to intimidate my client."

Hartson stared at me in mock disbelief. "Are you instructing your client not to answer? I'm only offering him an opportunity to correct his testimony, if he needs to."

I returned Hartson's stare. "No, I'm not going to instruct him. I'll let him answer, but just this once."

Caponi looked at me and I nodded. "Yes, Mr Hartson I am sure. The answer to your question is no, I did not pay Tommy Duncan to lie in this case."

Hartson smiled again and said, "Very well. Those are all of the questions I have. I believe I can speak for the others, we are finished with this witness."

Good. The others weren't even going to bother. Caponi could handle all of them and they knew it. As the defense bunch filed out, I congratulated Vincent and asked him to have Roberto call. "I don't know what's wrong, but it's important that we get it straightened out right away," I said.

Caponi nodded gravely. "Andy, I agree completely. I will speak with him, get to the bottom of what's going on, and then, I'll make sure he calls."

With Vincent gone, I asked Elaine into my office. She sat in one of the chairs across from my desk.

"You promised to tell me why you were so upset this morning," I began.

Her green eyes glistened. She looked across the desk, lips pursed. "Andy, I've had a lot on my mind, you know, worried about you, worried about getting all of my work done."

I wasn't buying it. "Did any of this have to do with the call you took from Monica?"

"Well, like I said. I worry about you, and part of it is worrying about you getting hurt if you get back together with someone who might not be good for you and who it seems to me certainly doesn't deserve you."

"Is that it?"

Tears suddenly rolled down her cheeks. She took a deep breath and said, "Well, I might as well say it. I have to wonder how our friendship might be affected if you and Monica are together again."

I smiled. "Elaine, dear, after what we've been through, if there's anything I'm sure of, you have a friend for life. There's nothing that I'd ever allow to interfere with that."

She forced a small, tight lipped smile. "Look, let's just drop it. I'm fine. I really am."

She was anything but. But before I could think what to say, she hurried to her car. I stood at the front door and watched her drive away, then waited as a beat-up delivery van stopped in front.

A young man got out and walked to the door. "You, Andrew Givens?" he asked.

"That's me," I said and signed for the envelope he held out. It was from Marshon & Davis.

Back in my office, I opened it. The motion was short and sweet. Tommy Duncan had recanted his deposition testimony and signed an affidavit saying the Caponis bribed him to testify falsely and that I assisted them in falsifying the version of the Mason memo we'd used during his questioning. The defendants sought sanctions of a million dollars against all of us and dismissal of the lawsuit. An expedited hearing was set before Judge Lowenstein on the twentieth of November.

My gut had been in a knot before but not like this. Vincent and Roberto, bribing a witness and telling Tommy Duncan I was in on it too? No wonder Hartson and the others acted so smug during Vincent's deposition. They'd had us right where they'd wanted us.

I tried reaching Roberto but he didn't answer. Next, I called Vincent, but didn't have any luck there either. I left a message on his voice mail saying he needed to call me back immediately. Then, I sat and waited. How in the world had I managed to get into such a mess?

Hartson's words of warning kept flashing in front of me, as if printed on an enormous neon sign: "Bow out of this now, before you get in too deep."

## Chapter Twenty Eight

No matter how hard I tried, I couldn't get anyone's attention that weekend. No contact with Roberto, Vincent, Elaine, or Monica. Even Mark Watson, who'd been eager to see me for days, had an emergency. Some sort of special hearing on a last minute appeal for a convicted cop-killer, necessitating postponement of our Saturday meeting. Of course, Ivory was around, but, after a while, my agitated demeanor made him so uneasy, he even wound up avoiding me.

The recent developments in *Centennial* were almost worse than what I was up against with the Thrasher murder trial. Had Roberto and Vincent actually paid a bribe to Tommy Duncan? Did that explain why Roberto had been so nervous? It certainly didn't seem like something the young man would do. That is, unless his father put him up to it. I didn't want to believe that. If Vincent Caponi was actually capable of enlisting his son in that sort of conduct, then anything was possible. And if the Caponis had done it, why would they find it necessary to tell Tommy Duncan that I was involved?

By Monday morning, I still hadn't gotten through to the Caponis. And at eight-thirty, Elaine wasn't in. Maybe she'd had it and was quitting. I was about to call her apartment when the phone rang.

Del Wallace said,"Morning, Andy, you got a minute?"

"Sure."

"Golden just told me he spoke with Monica. He wants me to come down to his office to discuss it."

"Where are you now, Del?"

"Just back from running. Got a little carried away and did a double turn around the park. You need to get out there, fella."

"You know why she called him?"

"Nope. I called to see if you might know."

"Well, she called and left a message for me saying she's sorry."

"Yeah?"

"Let me know what's going on as soon as you can, okay?" Out of the corner of my eye I saw Elaine standing at her desk. Another line lit up and she answered it.

"Sure," Del replied. "Hey, you think Monica wants to try it with you again?"

"That's what I thought at first, but now I'm not so sure. I've tried, but I haven't been able to get in touch with her. And then something happened late on Friday that diverted my attention. So I just don't know."

"What happened, Andy?"

I started to tell him about the Duncan deposition and the Defendants' motion for sanctions but thought better of it. I was too embarrassed to admit that on top of everything else, I now stood accused of bribing a witness and falsifying evidence.

"Look, Andy, I've got to go. Golden wanted me right away. I'll call you back in a little while, okay?"

Elaine stuck her head in. "Vincent called. He asked you to call him. He sounded funny and he said it's urgent."

Caponi answered on the first ring, his voice muffled, and his speech thick and slightly slurred, like his throat was clogged with oily mud.

"Vincent," I said, "I've been trying to reach you all weekend."

"I know. Uh, Andy, something's happened. I need to see you as soon as possible."

"Good. When are you coming in?"

There was a long pause before he answered, "I'd appreciate it if you could come out here. I don't want to leave Sylvia."

"What's happened, Vincent?"

"I'll tell you when you get here. And Andy, please understand, this is important. I need to see you right away."

If Vincent wanted to play mystery man, that was okay. He had a lot of questions to answer, regardless of what his problem was. I put a copy of the motion for sanctions in my briefcase and headed for my car, stopping at Elaine's desk on the way out.

"I've got to go meet Vincent."

"Is there anything particular you want me to do while you're gone?"

"Yeah. Get on Lexus and pull up the cites on all the sanction cases decided in the Fifth Circuit for the past three years. You can query on Rule 11."

Elaine nodded. "Would you like me to print out the abstracts too?"

"Sure, that'd help. And Elaine, I don't know how long I'll be, but I'd appreciate it if you'd wait for me. We need to talk."

She looked up at me. "Sure, if that's what you want."


It was already dark by the time I got back to town. Rain had fallen all afternoon and the pavement was wet, casting bright reflections from the streetlights. Elaine's car was parked in the driveway. At first, I was surprised to see it, but then remembered, she was waiting for me. I went into my office and sat next to the fireplace, staring into the crackling flames.

"It was getting awfully chilly in here," she said, following me. "I hope you don't mind."

I didn't reply. I just sat there and continued to stare at the flames, my emotions welling up, ready to burst in a flood of bitter frustration and pent up anger.

"I read the Defendants' motion. I don't believe a word of it. But what did Vincent say?"

I looked at her and slumped further down in my chair. "Roberto," I said. "He's dead."

Elaine lurched backward, eyes wide with shock. "Andy! What happened?"

"I'm not really sure. I only know what Vincent was able to tell me. Roberto's housekeeper couldn't get in on Saturday morning. The chain latch inside the door was fastened and she couldn't get him to come unlock it. She got worried and wound up calling Sylvia and Vincent. They came into town and Vincent broke the chain so they could get in. They found him in the bathroom, hanging from an over-head pipe in his shower."

I got up and poked at one of the logs, igniting the unburned side. Ivory pressed closer to the blaze, mesmerized by the motion of the flames and the sounds of hissing, popping wood.

"The police are certain it was a suicide. The door was locked from the inside. There's no other way in or out of that apartment other than the front door."

Elaine sank onto the sofa. "How are Sylvia and Vincent?"

"About like you'd imagine. Devastated."

"What are you going to do?"

"I really don't know. Roberto's suicide, that's terrible enough, but on the day the sanction motion was filed? It doesn't look very good."

Tears ran down her cheeks. "Roberto would never bribe a witness. And never in a million years would I think he was capable of killing himself."

I nodded. "That's what I think too. Nothing makes any sense."

She sighed. "That's not true," she said. "There's one thing I'm absolutely certain of. You're going to come through this. And in the end things will be better for you than ever before."

I smiled. "That doesn't seem very realistic."

"Wait and see."

I leaned forward and took her hand in mine. "Well, I guess we'll find out pretty soon. Our hearing on the sanctions motion is set for next week. We'll need more time and the judge will probably have to grant our request for it, especially now, but we can't count on it. And then, right after that, the Thrasher trial starts."

Elaine wiped a tear from her eye. I still held her hand. I found myself saying, "Will you stay with me tonight? I'd like you to." It's funny, I didn't even think about it. It just popped out.

She answered by guiding me down next to her. She rested her head on my shoulder and nuzzled against my neck. I put my arm around her and held her close. We gazed into the flames, every now and then looking at each other and smiling. I cupped her face in my hands and we kissed. Then, we melted together, in an almost desperate embrace.

Slowly, the fire burned down until only glowing embers remained. I helped her up and we walked, arm-in-arm, up the stairs.

# Chapter Twenty Nine

The sun was coming up, Elaine nestled next to me. I kissed her forehead and she opened her eyes, smiled sleepily, and held her arms open. Any fear that she would regret last night evaporated.

It was almost noon by the time we made it downstairs. I prepared lunch while Elaine retrieved phone messages.

"Anything important?" I asked as she came into the kitchen.

She picked up one of my salami and mustard sandwiches, frowned, and put it back on the plate. "Mark called. He's sorry about the weekend, but you need to get together with him as soon as possible. He also said, in case you've forgotten, you stand trial for murder in just over two weeks."

*Great.* "What else?" I asked.

"Del called—twice. Once yesterday afternoon. I must've been out bringing in fire wood, then he called again this morning saying you need to get in touch with him right away."

I went to the phone and dialed. "Del it's me," I said.

"Yeah, Andy. Uh, I told you I'd get back in touch after my meeting with Golden."

"Right. And?"

"Well, I told Steve he'd have to tell you himself, but I was just angry at the time. You're going to find out anyway so you might as well hear it from me."

"What is it?"

"I'm sorry, but late last Friday we got a hand-delivered letter from Monica saying she's claiming her community interest in your partnership share. She says she wants her accountant to go over our books and intimated she might not be in agreement with the buy-out figure."

My jaw dropped. So this was why she was sorry. "Del, that can't be. We had an agreement. I told you about it."

"Yeah, I know. She said she's had second thoughts after everything that's happened."

That bastard Hartson. This had to be his doing. "Look, I'll try to talk to her and see what I can do."

"That's good. Golden's firm on deferring further payment until things get resolved. And pal, that includes the fee you just got us on that W.D.S. settlement. So the sooner you can get this situation ironed out, the better."

I hung up and looked at Elaine who stood at the pantry door. "Monica wants one-half of my interest in Golden–Wallace. It looks like we won't see any of that W.D.S. money anytime soon."

Elaine nodded. "Andy, I'm sorry. But at least, now she's shown her colors, maybe you'll see her for what she really is."

I smiled. "You seem to be taking the fact pretty well that your employer can't afford you anymore."

She tilted her head and smiled coyly. "Oh, I think we'll be able to work something out."


On the morning of Roberto's funeral we flew to New Orleans, Vincent, Sylvia, Elaine, and I, passengers on a private plane that Alphonso Caponi sent for his brother's use. I wondered if Vincent had encouraged me to accompany him as a way to admit that he and Alphonso were closer than he'd previously allowed. Maybe close enough that Vincent followed his big brother's practices, such as bribing witnesses and co-opting his own lawyer.

During the short flight, Elaine tried her best to get Sylvia to recall the good times that she, Vincent, and Roberto had shared. An elegant woman, through all of their previous adversity, Sylvia had demonstrated remarkable courage and grace. Now, she carried the look of a stunned, wounded animal. She listened to Elaine for a while but then turned away, staring out the window at the quilted pattern of swamps, grasslands, and streams meeting a thin ribbon of gray sand along the coastline.

As the plane made its approach into Lakeside Airport, Sylvia finally spoke. Looking into her husband's eyes, she said, "I keep thinking this is all some terrible mistake. Pretty soon someone will come in and tell us that everything is all right and when we get home, my son will be there, waiting."

"I know," Vincent said, his voice choking. "But dear, we must be strong. God's will is a mystery."

Sylvia glared at him, a sudden angry fire raging in her eyes. "This was not *God's* will. Those evil men who made it their business to ruin our lives, they are the ones who are responsible."

Vincent nodded and put his arm around her. He looked across the aisle to where Elaine and I were sitting. "My wife is right. You have my promise, one way or the other, those people will pay for this. I assure you, they will."

I wasn't sure what Vincent meant. But this certainly wasn't the time to find out. Elaine took my hand and held it tightly.

Alphonso Caponi was waiting on the taxi-way, standing next to two black stretch limousines. He was a short man with a blocky, powerful build accentuated by a bulky black cashmere coat worn over his charcoal-gray suit. His complexion was dark, and his hair was salt and pepper, just like Vincent's.

A strong, chilling wind gusted from a high, slate-gray sky. A few heavy drops of icy rain began splattering the concrete. I pulled my suit collar up, put an arm around Elaine, and watched as Alphonso embraced Vincent and then put an arm around Sylvia, speaking quietly and earnestly to her for several moments. I was too far away to hear what he said, but for the first time that day, I thought I saw a glimpse of a smile on Sylvia's lips.

Alphonso turned to where we stood. "Mr Givens, Miss Turner, I am Vincent's brother. It is my pleasure to meet you."

I nodded and took his offered hand, wondering uneasily if any photographers might be in the vicinity.

"Miss Turner," he said, "if you don't mind, I suggest you ride with Sylvia and Vincent to the cathedral. I need to have a few private words with Mr Givens."

Elaine nodded and hurried into the front limousine with Sylvia and Vincent. I followed Alphonso into the second limo. The windows were heavily tinted making the gloomy scenery outside appear as dark as night. Alphonso sat across from me and remained silent for several moments into our ride, studying me. Finally, he said, "Mr Givens, Vincent told me about the accusations of bribery and subornation of perjury that are being made by the banks you are suing. He is convinced it is the reason his son is dead."

"Look, Mr Caponi, I don't know why you're telling me this."

He shrugged. "Vincent is worried that maybe you believe the accusations. I'm talking with you because there are some things I want you to understand. First, I don't see eye to eye with Vincent. But he is my brother. Naturally, I want to help him any way I can. Now, I am trying to do that by speaking with you to give you my assurances that my brother's business has never had any involvement with my personal pursuits. And, second, Mr Givens, I know my brother. He would *never* become involved with a scheme to bribe a witness. I'm also confident his son would never do that either."

"How can you be so sure?"

A hint of amusement flickered in Alphonso Caponi's dark eyes. "Vincent doesn't have the stomach for something like that. I admit, sometimes I've laughed at him for being so squeamish." He took a cigar from his inside pocket, clipped the end and clinched the cigar between his teeth. "He would never do it," he added.

"Would you?" I asked.

Alphonso smiled. "Me? If I had to? The answer is, of course."

"What about Roberto? What makes you so sure about him?"

Caponi waved his arm dismissively. "Roberto, he was a very peculiar young man. But he wasn't stupid. He was, in fact, very bright. I'm sure you must already realize that. He never would've done anything so dumb."

"What do you mean by dumb? Didn't you just tell me that you would bribe a witness if you had to?"

Alphonso nodded. "That's right, I did. And mind you, I'm not saying I've ever done it, but if I did, the person would have so much fear in his heart, if not for himself, for a member of his family, a child, a wife, even a lover, it wouldn't make any difference. But you can be sure, he would *never* admit to anyone that he had accepted money from me."

Listening to him, I got the clear impression, Alphonso Caponi spoke from personal experience.


On the flight back to Houston I asked Vincent to sit next to me. His face was drawn and haggard. "I talked to Alphonso about what's going on."

He nodded. "I know."

"Before we left, I filed a motion for additional time to gather evidence for the sanctions hearing. Judge Lowenstein's trial coordinator called. The judge will hear oral argument on our motion for an extension on November twentieth. That's the date when the motion was to be heard. It's been taken off calendar, so we know we'll get some time."

"Will it do us any good?"

"I don't know. I hope so. But we've got to come up with something to use at that hearing."

Vincent grasped my arm and stared at me intently. "Andy, I will do everything possible. I know why Roberto died, and now, if it is the last thing I do, I intend to punish the people who are responsible for his death."

"Just don't do something stupid."

Vincent didn't reply. He just stared at me displaying the same anger glowing inside him that his wife had shown earlier in the day.

I went back to sit next to Elaine. She was asleep. I gazed out the window. We were flying on top of a long blanket of soft, billowy clouds. The sun was beginning to set, and the sky displayed a striking panoply of color, bright orange shading down to dark purple.

I kept wondering, what was in store? With Elaine there next to me, all of a sudden the stakes seemed a lot higher.

# Chapter Thirty

Judge Lowenstein's courtroom was jammed. The Defendants had their regular gang there. It even looked as if they'd invited a few more along for the show. And the seats behind the bar were filled too, mostly with attorneys, many of whom I knew. But they weren't in court to offer their moral support. Like a crowd assembled for a hanging, they were there simply because they wanted to watch.

I went inside the rail and took a seat at my usual table for one. Hartson looked over in my direction, shaking his head in a gesture of disgust.

Moments later, Judge Lowenstein entered the courtroom. He surveyed the crowd and a deep frown formed on his round, normally impassive face. He looked down to his courtroom clerk seated in front of the bench and asked, "Have I missed something? This looks like a docket call. All I've got on my calendar is a hearing on a motion for more time to respond to a motion."

"No, that's it, judge," the clerk replied.

"Well let's go ahead," Lowenstein barked.

I stood and said, "Your honor, I've filed this motion because extremely serious charges have been made by the Defendants. Now, I assure the Court these charges are untrue and they will ultimately be shown to be completely baseless. However, one of the persons against whom these charges were made died only a few days ago. His death will make it much more difficult to gather the evidence we need to address the motion. That is why Plaintiffs must request a ninety day delay of the hearing on Defendants' motion for sanctions. Under the circumstances, our request is justified and I respectfully ask your honor to grant it."

Noisy murmurs came from the defense table. Fritz Taylor in particular looked as if he was about to blow a gasket.

Lowenstein glared down from the bench, silencing the lawyers seated at the defense table. "Is that all, Mr Givens?" he asked.

"Yes sir," I replied as I took my seat.

"Mr Hartson, the defendants' motion for sanctions was filed by your firm. Do you want to respond?"

Hartson leaned forward, rising half-way out of his chair. "Carl Hopgood will argue the motion, your honor."

"Very well," Lowenstein said.

Hopgood took his place at the lectern. As he opened his notebook and peered down at the pages, his slender frame quivered. He glanced briefly back in the direction of Hartson, tiny beads of perspiration forming on his rapidly reddening cheeks.

"Counsel, any time you're ready," Lowenstein prompted.

Hopgood gave the judge a nervous grin and cleared his throat. "Excuse me, your honor, we oppose the plaintiffs' request for more time. The very idea that they want to take more discovery to try to obtain evidence that will some how justify what they have done is ludicrous. They *and* their counsel have abused the discovery process enough as it is."

"Counsel," Lowenstein asked, "are you aware that a hearing on a motion for sanctions entitles the non-movant to an evidentiary hearing?"

Hopgood stood at the lectern, wearing a blank, uncertain look. Was it possible he hadn't anticipated even this basic question? Could he actually think Lowenstein would do whatever he wanted, simply because he was from Marshon & Davis?

"Counsel are you going to answer my question?" Lowenstein prompted.

"Uh, yes sir," Hopgood replied. "The answer is, yes, we are aware. That is normally what is required, but this is a special case. Under the circumstances, having already been shown to have abused the discovery process, the Plaintiffs

shouldn't be permitted to have any discovery, so they don't
need more time."

Lowenstein stared at Hopgood and shook his head.
"Young man, tell me. Do the Defendants want a hearing on
their motion for sanctions or don't they? I've read the motion
and the affidavit of Mr Duncan. These are extremely serious
matters, and if I determine that what Mr Duncan says
happened is true, I will have no problem granting the relief
you've requested in your motion. But, Mr Hopgood, I'm not
going to conduct a hearing of this nature without affording
the Plaintiffs and their counsel an adequate opportunity to
obtain and present evidence."

Hopgood glanced back to his boss and Hartson nodded to
him.

"Very well, your honor. We will agree that Plaintiffs be
given time to prepare, but ninety days is too much time."

"Counsel, I don't need your approval to grant a motion!"
Lowenstein thundered. "And I am going to grant it. But
ninety days does strike me as being too long." Lowenstein
consulted his calendar. "Can the parties be ready for a
hearing on January Fourth? I have that day clear, subject to
one or two minor matters that shouldn't cause too much of
an interruption."

I guessed by that time I'd either be in jail or not, so I told
the judge the date was good for the plaintiffs.

Hopgood still didn't get it. "January Fourth is acceptable
to defendants," he said.

Lowenstein glared at him, got up, and stormed off the
bench.

After the hearing, I called from a pay phone to give
Vincent Caponi the news. Then, I headed for Mark Watson's
office where he and Elaine were waiting. The Thrasher trial
started in ten days.

## Chapter Thirty One

The early morning's darkness was just giving way to the first feeble glimmerings of dawn. The house was still and quiet. Rolling over onto my side, I reached across the bed. No Elaine. She wasn't comfortable staying, now that my parents were in the house.

Having them attend the trial wasn't exactly my idea. Just the thought of them sitting in the courtroom, hearing me accused of committing the murder of William Thrasher, was enough to make a guilty plea look appealing. But everyone insisted. Elaine reminded me how important family was in times of trouble. Mark wanted them in court for strategic purposes. But I had to wonder, was demonstrating that I was a nice guy with a respectable mother and father really that important? What the hell, he probably intended to call my first-grade teacher and my boy-scout troop leader as character witnesses. But even if I could have convinced Mark, it wouldn't have made a difference. I couldn't have kept my parents away with a truck load of dynamite.

I pulled on warm-ups, and laced my running shoes, then went quietly downstairs. Mom was already in the kitchen getting breakfast underway. She was in her element, like a bird tending its nest, as she fussed over her preparations, wanting everything to be up to her self-imposed standard of perfection.

I gave her a big hug and kissed her on the cheek. She smiled happily, poured a mug of steaming coffee, and handed it to me. By her cheerful demeanor we could have just as easily been off for a vacation to the south of France.

"I'm going out for a minute," I said.

"Don't be gone long. Breakfast's almost ready, and I want you to go upstairs to see if your father is up yet. That man. Ever since he retired, the way he sleeps."

"I'll be right back," I said as I headed outside.

The sky was a dark, steely gray. A brisk, bone-chilling breeze carried the scent of approaching rain. I walked to the back fence. Brittle leaves rustled in the sycamore tree in the next yard. Inside, a warm glow emanated from the hallway leading from my office to the kitchen. A light came on in the bathroom upstairs. Dad was up.

I tried to tell myself to stay calm, everything was going to turn out all right. I tried to fend off the queasy-sick feeling of a stomach tied into knots. I tried to ignore the fact that I was scared as hell.


For weeks, the papers contained nothing about the up-coming trial, and I'd developed the secret hope that maybe the media had grown disinterested and my little event would proceed in relative anonymity. Talk about being an optimist.

When we arrived at the criminal court annex, even though a steady drizzle threatened to turn into a down-pour at any second, reporters, camera crews, and technicians swarmed impatiently around the front of the building. The instant we stepped out of our car, a cry went up and Mark and I were mobbed. Thankful for Mark's suggestion that Elaine take my parents in through the entrance at the side of the building, we waded into a teeming sea of cameras, microphones, and lights.

The reporter from Channel Thirteen blocked our path, grinning in anticipation as our eyes met. Waving her microphone in my face, she shouted, "Mr Givens, can you receive a fair trial in Harris County, given the charges you face?"

Mark eased between us, smiled and said, "Andrea, you know better than that. Mr Givens won't have anything to say until the trial's over, that's the way it's got to be."

We squeezed past the reporters and eventually managed to make it inside the courthouse. We jumped onto an already crowded elevator, avoiding more folks with cameras and lights who were trailing close behind.

Upstairs, Judge Garza was on the bench conducting a sentencing hearing. Albert Anderson sat at one of the tables inside the bar speaking intently with a skinny young man with a bobbing adam's apple and bulging eyes.

"Who's that?" I asked.

"That's Arnold Weiss," Mark whispered. "He's going to second chair. We might have some fun in the next few days after all."

"Why's that?"

"Oh, if Albert is dumb enough to let Weiss take a witness or two, you'll see."

Mark led the way to the other counsel's table. I glanced over my shoulder to Mom, Dad, and Elaine who were seated on the first row outside the bar. They looked as nervous as three staked-out goats waiting for the lion to show up.

When Judge Garza finished his hearing, he looked down from his bench and said, "In the People of the State of Texas versus Andrew Givens, are the parties ready to proceed?"

Anderson and Mark stood and in turn announced that they were.

"Counsel will please come up," the judge said, summoning the lawyers with a wave of his hand. I had to catch myself to keep from going up too. A few minutes later, the bench conference broke up and the lawyers headed back. Mark detoured to lean over the rail to say something to Elaine, who in turn whispered to my parents. Dad gave one of his patented shrugs of displeasure. Mom frowned too, but she nodded to Mark and said something to Dad. Then, they followed as Elaine led them out of the courtroom.

"What's happening?" I asked when Mark came back to sit next to me.

"Garza's worried he won't have enough room for the panel he's calling in, he's asked for sixty, so he's keeping spectators out during jury selection. I've got Elaine taking your folks back to your place. They'll be more comfortable there anyway."

I turned and waved to my parents who were following Elaine out of the courtroom.

"What else happened up there?" I asked.

Mark grinned. "Oh, Weiss asked if we intend to call either of your parents as witnesses. If we do, he wants the judge to invoke the rule and keep them out of the courtroom until they're called to testify. I said we didn't think it would be necessary. But it's funny after he went to the trouble of mentioning it, Weiss didn't invoke the rule. Anderson didn't either."

Jury selection in a murder case usually is a long, tedious process and our case was no exception. It took ten days to select a jury of twelve and three alternates, both sides trying to learn everything they could about each person on the panel. Anything that might cause someone to be for or against. Unlike most murder cases, mine presented its own peculiar problems. Mark pointed out months before that normal stereotypes for evaluating juror tendencies might not be meaningful in my case. For example, African Americans and Hispanics were viewed by many criminal trial lawyers as generally reluctant to convict. People of all races who have incomes near the poverty level generally don't like to return guilty verdicts either. On the other hand, most Whites and high-income earners, regardless of race, tend to convict much more readily. But with a white, relatively affluent lawyer on trial for killing one of the silk-stocking set from River Oaks, would poor and minority jurors maintain their usual tendencies? We simply didn't know.

Just the same, after Anderson exercised the State's pre-emptory strikes, the ones that can be used to eliminate prospective jurors for reasons other than an individual's bias or prejudice, we decided to make a *Batson* motion to try to seat two black jurors who Anderson had knocked off, despite the fact he'd asked them only benign, meaningless questions.

No prosecutor enjoys a *Batson* hearing and Albert Anderson was no exception, seeming to actually become angry when he was asked to state his nondiscriminatory reasons for striking those two prospective jurors.

Mark became equally upset when the judge accepted Anderson's explanation that he didn't like school teachers on juries because of their tendency to attempt to dominate fellow jurors. At least Garza didn't buy Anderson's story that he found funeral directors unduly sympathetic to the accused in a homicide cases. That one *was* overturned and we got Lonnie Morris, owner of the Garden Trail Funeral Home, seated as our twelfth juror.

Perhaps of greater significance, in the process of seating Mr Morris, an oil company accountant was bumped off the jury down to alternate number one. That was quite a coup for us. In addition to bean counting, the guy looked as if his favorite hobby was pulling the wings off of flies.

With the jury in the box, Judge Garza sent them home, announcing opening arguments would begin at nine the next morning. Mark and I headed to his office, but my legs became suddenly heavy. A strange tingling sensation ran down my fingers and a lead-like weight pressed against my chest. For a minute, I was afraid I was having a heart attack. Then, I realized, what I felt was raw fear. I tried to ignore the sensations, and took several deep breaths trying to calm down.

Mark looked at me and punched my shoulder. "We'll get 'em," he said.

All I could do was hope he was right.

# Chapter Thirty Two

An expectant hush fell over the courtroom as Albert Anderson rose to state what the prosecution intended to prove. He stood directly in front of the jurors, hands in pockets, shoulders hunched, occasionally pacing from one end of the jury box to the other, assuring them he'd do his job. That he'd prove beyond reasonable doubt that I was William Thrasher's killer. The seven men and five women who were to decide my fate hung on Anderson's every word. A couple of them even nodded forgiveness when he apologized for having to take up so much of their valuable time.

As the theme of the State's case emerged—that I was guilty of the brutal murder of a man who once had given me his complete and absolute trust—papers rustled and pens and pencils scratched among the reporters crowded into the first row behind the prosecutor's table. Tomorrow's headlines in the making.

True to Mark's assessment, Anderson worked at an irritatingly deliberate pace. Like a snail inching its way across a sidewalk, he made me wonder if he was ever going to reach his intended destination. But by the time he sat down, the somber expressions on the faces of several jurors said he'd made his position clear.

I turned and whispered to Mark, "This isn't going very well, is it?

He looked at me and shrugged. What could we do?

Anderson's first witness was Margaret Staples, Thrasher's personal secretary, a frail, unattractive woman, forty-ish, wearing drab, nondescript clothing, no jewelry, no make-up. The perfect camouflage for preventing people from noticing her existence. William Thrasher once mentioned, as far as he knew, the woman had virtually no life outside of her employment at Thrasher Industries. And that was just the way he liked it.

Staples was the last person, other then the murderer, to see Thrasher alive. As was her custom, she worked late at the office the night of July Fifteenth, assisting her boss until eight-thirty, when he finally let her go. By then, even the cleaning crew had come and gone. According to Staples, Thrasher stayed on, pouring over the case file he'd picked up from my office, earlier that day.

"Did you see Mr Thrasher again after you went home that night?" Anderson asked.

Staples sniffed." Yes. I came back at 6:30 the next morning and found him in his office. He was slumped over his desk and there was a lot of blood. I knew he was dead."

"What did you do when you found him?"

"I ran back to my desk and dialed nine-one-one. Then waited until the police came and I let them up in the elevator and inside the security door at the elevator lobby. They asked me a lot of questions first and later they even made me go back inside Mr Thrasher's office." She grimaced, and continued, "That part was awful. All that blood. And the smell. I thought I'd get sick."

"You said you had to let the police up in the elevator. Why was that?"

"Oh, it's part of our security system. You can't access the elevator to our floor from the lobby without calling up first. That is, unless you know the access code and how to key it in on the phone in the elevator."

Anderson nodded gravely. He glanced into the jury box, making sure they were listening. "Also, you said you had to let the police inside a security door at the elevator lobby on your floor. How did that work?"

"We've had that here ever since the days of Mr Thrasher's father being in charge. Nobody can get inside the main door on the top floor unless they're let in by the receptionist. There's a button on the console at the reception desk that releases the lock. Our receptionist and I, we have special keys to open the door from the other side. Mr Thrasher had one too, but we were the only ones."

"Was that system in operation on July Fifteenth?"

"Yes, it was."

"Now Ms Staples, do you know, did William Thrasher have a private phone in his office that wasn't tied into the company's switchboard?"

She arched her eyebrows in surprise. "Why yes, he did. How did you know?"

"Do you know why he had a private phone line installed in his office?"

Mark looked at me. What was this about? I shrugged. I didn't know. He stood up. "Objection. Lack of foundation. Calls for speculation."

"Sustained," Garza said, pleased to finally have something to do.

"Did you observe William Thrasher using that private line?"

"Yes, I did."

"Did he use it frequently?"

"Objection," Mark said. "Calls for a conclusion."

"Over-ruled. The witness may answer."

"I'd say not very often."

"Do you know, Ms Staples, if that line was used for business calls?"

"Well, sometimes it was. On rare occasions, Mr Thrasher gave the number to business associates who could call him on it, usually after normal hours."

I began to understand where this was headed. I scribbled a note for Mark.

"Ms Staples, do you know, did Mr Thrasher give his private office number to Andrew Givens?"

Mark was on his feet. "Objection, leading."

Garza sighed. "Over-ruled. Answer the question."

"Yes. Just before the trial started, Mr Thrasher had me give Mr Givens the number on a card he had printed up with just the number on it."

"Do you remember the number?"

"Yes. But I don't see why you need it. It's private."

"Your honor?" Anderson looked to the judge.

"Please answer the question," Garza instructed.

Staples crinkled her brow and gave the Judge an angry stare. "Well, it's 713-850-1687."

Anderson wrote the number on a blank sheet of poster-sized paper at the easel next to the jury box. Beside it he wrote 'Private Phone Line—William Thrasher.' Then, he walked to the witness box.

"Ms Staples, when you went back inside Mr Thrasher's office with the police on the morning of July Sixteenth, what was your understanding of what, if anything, the police officers wanted you to do?"

"Well, they wanted me to look around with them to see if anything was missing from the office."

"What did you determine in that regard?"

"Uh, I really didn't find anything. I'd never seen Mr Thrasher's office in such a mess. He was very much a stickler on neatness. And I couldn't really tell about the papers that had been on his desk. Some of them were scattered on the floor and a lot of them had blood on them."

Anderson smiled and went back to his seat. "That's all I have, Ms Staples. Thank you."

Mark quickly examined his notes and the ones I'd made too.

"I have just a few questions, Ma'am. First, do you know what the code was back in July that could be entered to activate the elevator to allow it up to your floor?"

"Yes, it was a five-digit number."

"Ms Staples, how long was the access code for the elevator in use? I'm talking about the same one as the one which was in use back on July Fifteenth and Sixteenth?"

"Why, it was the same for as long as I worked at Thrasher Industries."

"And that was, I believe you said for over fifteen years?"

"Uh, that's right. Actually Mr Thrasher's father was the one who had the system installed. He did it when we first moved into the building."

Marked smiled. "Thank you for that information," he said. "Now, how many people worked for Thrasher up on the top floor?"

"Well, let me think. I believe there are six of us with offices on the executive floor. There were seven, counting Mr Thrasher."

"And all of you who have your offices up there have the access code, right?"

"That's correct."

"As a matter of fact, all of Thrasher's employees on the floor below the executive floor, they're about a dozen of them down there aren't there? They all had the access code to the top floor too, didn't they?"

Staples stared at Mark and gave a loud, indignant sigh. "Well, of course, they needed it, so they could use the elevator."

"Is it correct, Ms Staples, that over the fifteen years while you've worked for Thrasher Industries you do not know how many people actually were given the access code to the elevator?"

Staples arched her eyebrows in alarm. "I never gave it to anybody, if that's what you're trying to imply."

"No, ma'am, I'm not suggesting you did, but my point is, you don't know if anybody else gave that code out or not, do you?"

"No, I guess I really can't say."

Mark took a step closer to the witness. "Now, earlier that day, did your boss have anyone visit him in his office?"

"Well, yes. After he got back from the courthouse, he spent most of the day with Travis Ball. Travis went home, probably at around six-thirty or so, and after that, the attorney who represented Waste Disposal Systems came in to see Mr Thrasher.

"That was Alton Giles?" Mark asked.

"Yes, that's correct."

"When did Mr Giles arrive?"

"Like I said, it was late, probably eight or eight-thirty."

"Ms Staples, do you know what Mr Giles and your boss discussed?"

Margaret Staples shook her head. "No. Like I told Mr Anderson, they met with the door to Mr Thrasher's office closed."

Mark cut his eyes to the prosecutor's table where Anderson sat, stone-faced, staring straight ahead.

"Your Honor," Mark said, "may we approach the bench?"


Mark emerged from Garza's chambers wearing a deep frown.

"What happened?" I asked as he sat down.

"Anderson says they checked with both Giles and Staples. Giles was only there for a few minutes. Staples went to the ladies room right after he arrived and by the time she got back, he was already gone. Thrasher told her he let him out. Under the circumstances, he didn't think he needed to disclose the meeting to us, and he didn't bring it up on direct testimony because he didn't want to confuse the jury with unnecessary facts."

"Did you get into what Giles was doing there?"

Mark nodded. "Apparently, William Thrasher wanted to see if W.D.S. still would be willing to settle. According to Giles, he told Thrasher to forget it."

"I think we might have something here. Giles is a total snake."

Mark nodded again. "I hear you, pal, but before we decide to put him on the witness stand, we need to decide how it might shake out. So far, they don't have a lot they can say about the way you handled Thrasher's civil case. If we open the door, we're liable to give Anderson the excuse to turn this into a real three-ring circus."

Garza took the bench and called the jury back. Mark wrapped up his cross examination of Thrasher's secretary. And Albert Anderson announced his next witness as Joseph Springer. I barely took notice. I was still focused on the fact that Alton Giles had met with my client on the very evening that the W.D.S. suit was dismissed. What had they been up to?

## Chapter Thirty Three

Joseph Springer still looked like the doughboy as he waddled to the witness stand. If somebody poked him in the ribs, no doubt we'd have heard his trademark giggle. But once he was sworn in, he let everyone know this was no laughing matter. He was the big cheese detective responsible for the Thrasher investigation. Using a to-scale poster board diagram of Thrasher's office, the adjoining conference room, secretarial space, and reception area, Springer meticulously described the scene as he'd found it. Thrasher slumped onto the desk, the back of his head revealing multiple blows. A large pool of partially congealed blood running from the side of the desk away from the door down onto the carpet. Another similar pool running from Thrasher's head onto the carpet at the front of the desk. A series of what Springer took to be splatters of blood on the desk top, on the carpet, and on the wall nearest the front of the desk. Some of them on the papers that were found scattered on the carpet. Others found on the documents on the desk. Still others on a photograph on the far wall. He also described a baseball bat found on the floor between Thrasher's chair and the credenza behind his desk. He immediately noticed streaks of what appeared to be blood on the wide part of the barrel.

Anderson retrieved the bat from the evidence cart, handed it to Springer, and asked, "Is this the bat that was found in Mr Thrasher's office as you just described?"

Springer took it from Anderson and ran his hand over the surface. "Yes this is it," he said.

Anderson returned to the cart and picked up a large manilla envelope. He took the envelope to Springer and asked him to identify the contents.

"These are the photographs that were taken on the morning of last July Sixteenth, by a HPD photographer. The photographs were taken at my direction."

"Do they accurately depict the scene as it existed at the time the photographs were taken?"

"Yes, they do."

Anderson handed the photographs to Mark who scanned through them. Everyone in the courtroom strained to get a look.

"Can we approach the bench, judge?" Mark asked.

Garza said to the bailiff, "Why don't you take the jurors to the jury room? This probably is best taken up without trying to do it all up at the bench."

After thirty minutes of argument, Garza allowed all of the pictures in, except one close-up showing a very dead, William Thrasher staring vacantly from a half-open eye.

With the jury back, Garza nodded to Anderson.

"Judge, the State asks that it be permitted to display to the jury the evidence just admitted," he said.

"You may proceed," Garza replied.

Anderson took his time, starting at one end of the jury box and moving slowly, pausing along the way to make sure that each juror got a good look. An eternity passed. Three jurors became visibly upset. Two of the them stole glances at me while the pictures were being displayed. Not a pleasant situation.

To make matters worse, when Anderson finished, Garza adjourned for the day, leaving those vivid, grizzly pieces of evidence the last things the jury would have to think about until trial resumed in the morning.


Back in Mark's office I paced the floor. My lawyer sat feet propped on his desk top, occasionally turning to toss an orange nurf ball at a miniature basket mounted to the wall. He was a lousy shot.

"How'd you think it went?" I asked for probably the tenth time that afternoon.

"I told you, Andy. We did okay. Those pictures were rough stuff. But at least we planted some questions. You know, how *anybody* could have been up there that night?"

"What about Steve Golden? Did your investigator get in touch with him?" I'd pestered Mark about contacting him even though Mark's source at the DA's assured him Golden was going to testify for the State and what he was going to say wasn't going to help our side one bit.

Mark took another shot. He missed again. "Yeah we went up to see him. I have to tell you, Andy. Your former partner was less than cooperative."

"He'll have to admit, I was only up there for a few minutes," I said, pleading a case I knew Mark already considered a lost cause.

Mark said, "Look Andy, the word I have is Golden believes you did it. He also thinks you arranged for the hit on Whitfield and that you and Charles Lucas were up to more no good when you got into a fracas with him in Chicago. With that attitude, I suppose he could hurt you a lot more, but supposedly all he's gonna say is that he did see you up there in the office that evening and he had a brief talk with you, but he doesn't remember seeing you leave. And that, my friend, is not going to help."


The next morning, Joseph Springer was back on the stand, eager to continue the task of hanging me out to dry. Anderson questioned him about the collection of physical evidence at Thrasher's office, launching Springer into a seminar on how blood samples and carpet samples were collected, how finger prints were isolated and sent for analysis, and how all pieces of potential evidence were labeled with identifying numbers recording their location to establish a chain of custody for every piece of potentially significant evidence.

Then, Anderson shifted topics. "Detective, following your activities at Mr Thrasher's office on the morning of July Sixteenth, did you collect evidence at any other site?"

Mark objected. "Evidence isn't evidence until it's admitted by the Court, your honor."

Garza nodded. "Please re-phrase that last question, counsel."

"Yes, your honor," Anderson said. "In your investigation, did you collect any items from any other site?"

"Yes, we did."

"How did you do that?"

"By executing search warrants and by issuing subpoenas," Springer replied.

"Was a search conducted at the office and home of Andrew Givens?"

"Yes, we searched the home and the offices, both the one on State Street and his new office on Jackson Avenue, that's where he lives too."

"Were any items taken into police possession as a result of those searches?"

"Yes sir, there were."

Anderson walked to the witness stand, several pieces of paper in hand. He gave the papers to Springer. "Do you recognize these?"

Springer put on a pair of glasses, peered at the paper and said, "Yes, these are inventory sheets that I prepared, listing all items taken at William Thrasher's office and at the office of Golden, Wallace, Givens & Whitfield, and at the office and residence of Andrew Givens. There is also a sheet listing items and samples taken from a Mazda automobile registered to Andrew Givens."

"And all of these items were labeled for identification purposes as indicated on the lists?"

"Yes, that's correct," Springer replied. He looked up at the jury and smiled.

"After collecting the items and samples referred to on these lists, what happened to those items?"

"All of them have been maintained in the custody of the police department. There have been occasions when some of the items, particularly blood samples, and fingerprints which were lifted at William Thrasher's office, were checked out to another agency, but on those occasions entries are made on the inventory sheets. Those people have to sign them in or out, so the chain of custody for each item is always preserved."

Anderson turned to face the judge. "Your honor, we may want to get into additional aspects of the investigation with Detective Springer at some later point, but subject to our need to do so, that's all we have for him right now."

"Very well," Garza replied. "Mr Watson, do you wish to cross examine?"

We'd discussed the night before what to do with Springer on cross and decided to stay away from a fight about evidence handling. We were giving up a potentially valuable area, one where there was usually room to punch holes in the prosecution's presentation by pointing out sloppy, unreliable procedures. But we couldn't get around the fact that the State had solid evidence of my car going in and out of Thrasher's garage, and traces of his blood underneath the seat of my car. We'd look guilty as hell if we started picking fights with the way the investigation was conducted in light of that sort of proof.

Mark decided to ask just one line of questions.

"Detective Springer, you said you found finger prints belonging to Mr Givens in Mr Thrasher's office. Where did you find those prints?"

"Well, Springer started, eyes narrowed to slits, squinting toward the ceiling, "let's see, I believe they were found on the arm of one of the chairs next to the windows."

"Do you recall finding Mr Givens' fingerprints anyplace else in Mr Thrasher's office?"

Springer shifted in his chair. "No. We, uh, we did find his prints on several of the leather chairs in the adjoining conference room."

Mark smiled. "Thank you for the information Detective. Do you know, when those fingerprints were left there by Mr Givens?"

Springer looked up at the ceiling and sighed. Finally he said, "No, Mr Watson. You can't tell when any particular print was left."

"Am I correct in my understanding that those prints of Mr Givens could have been there many days prior to July 15th?"

Springer gave Mark a hard, icy stare. "Yes, I suppose that's possible."

Score one for our side.


After the morning recess, Anderson called Thomas Heintz, the Harris County Medical Examiner. Heintz was a stockily built man with rubbery facial features and a pasty complexion. His suit was baggy and rumpled and the straw-like thatch of hair that grew atop his head stuck up like a clump of unruly weeds. The M.E. was new to his position, leaving him still relatively unacquainted with the art of testifying in murder trials. Mark said his predecessor was to blame for that. He'd held the position for over twenty years and during that entire time he hogged the ball when it came to going into court. No one ever understood why. Maybe he was a masochist.

Anderson had to lead Heintz like a dog on a short leash, but ultimately got him to say that William Thrasher died possibly as early as ten-thirty on the night of July Fifteenth and possibly as late as two-thirty on the morning of July Sixteenth. The cause of death—a crushed skull, and severe trauma to the occipital lobe, the medulla, and the upper spinal cord. The injuries the result of multiple blows with a heavy, blunt object.

When Anderson let him go, Mark went back to work trying to demonstrate almost anyone could have killed Thrasher.

"Dr. Heintz, do you know, is there anyone here in the courtroom who would be incapable, from a physical standpoint, of delivering blows with a heavy, blunt object with sufficient force to cause the types of injuries that resulted in William Thrasher's death?"

Anderson stood. "Objection. Calls for sheer speculation."

"Over-ruled," Garza said. "Answer the question, doctor."

Heintz fidgeted. "Well, I'm not sure. That's something that I haven't really thought about."

"Well, doctor, please think about it now. Is the type of injury which caused William Thrasher's death an injury which could have been inflicted by the use of a heavy, blunt object by any person sitting here in the courtroom?"

A flush of embarrassment spread on the medical examiner's face. He looked at the prosecutor's table. But Anderson studiously avoided him.

"Yes," he finally answered. "Virtually anyone could have generated the force necessary to cause the injuries that resulted in the decedent's death, provided, of course, the object that was used wasn't so heavy that it couldn't be handled."

"How about this?" Mark asked, picking up the bat from the evidence table. "Little boys and girls who play little league can swing these things can't they?"

Anderson shouted an objection.

Mark stood holding the bat, smiling at Dr. Heintz. "I withdraw the question," he said. "Thank you, doctor, that's all I have."

Anderson next called David Matthews, a criminologist who worked homicide investigations for HPD. Matthews explained the significance of blood-splatter patterns, and how those patterns in relation to the position of Thrasher's body revealed how Thrasher had been killed. One blow, almost certainly the first one, had been administered with the perpetrator standing behind Thrasher and striking him in the back of the head with a sharply descending swing. There had been at least three additional blows, all administered while

Thrasher was slumped forward with his arms outstretched and the right side of his face resting on the surface of the desk. He was certain of at least four blows because he had been able to identify four distinct splatter patterns on the desk, carpet, and walls in Thrasher's office.

"What were you able to determine from your analysis of the blood splatters?" Anderson asked.

"Well, as for what I believe was the first blow, the splatter pattern indicates the victim was sitting up, fairly erect in the chair behind the desk, just as the blow was administered. Because we know with reasonable certainty the instrument used to administer the blow was the bat found in the room, we have been able to calculate, based on the angle of that first blow, again as revealed by the blood splatters, that the person who administered the blow was relatively tall."

"What do you mean by relatively tall?" Anderson asked.

"I meant that in relation to the total population. Actually, the person had to be at least six-feet tall."

"Thank you," the prosecutor said. "No further questions." He gazed over at me, reminding the jury, with his stare, 'This man is over six feet tall.'

Mark was on his feet immediately. "There was a lot of blood in that room wasn't there?"

"Yes there sure was," Matthews replied.

"The person who was swinging that bat, was swinging it pretty hard isn't that right?"

"Yes, the splatters reached the far wall. Those blows were delivered with a lot of force, I agree."

"With all of that blood, all over the place do you think it is more probable than not that some of that blood would have wound up getting on the perpetrator or on the perpetrator's clothing?"

Matthews shot an uneasy look over to Anderson. "Well, I'm not sure about that."

"I didn't ask you if you're sure, Mr Matthews. I'm asking, based on your professional experience, is it more probable than not that whoever killed William Thrasher in this violent, brutal manner, would have gotten some of the victim's blood on his or her own person?"

Anderson stood to object, but Garza waved him away.

"That's a proper question. The witness will answer," he instructed.

Matthews frowned. "I would have to say it would be pretty difficult to have gotten out of there without taking away some of the victim's blood."

"A little or a lot?" Mark asked.

"Objection!" Anderson shouted.

"Sustained," Garza responded. "Move along, counsel."

"That place was a bloody mess wasn't it?" Mark demanded.

Matthews stared incredulously. "Yeah it was a mess all right."


We met at Mark's office to sum up where we stood.

"That was pretty good with Matthews don't you think?" I asked.

Mark shrugged. "So far, they've proved that Thrasher's dead and how he died, but not a lot more. Our job is to keep reminding the jury that anybody could have killed the man."

I resumed my pacing—something I'd never done before. "Do you think they'll actually believe the prospect of a malpractice lawsuit is a sufficient motive for killing somebody?"

"I don't know," Mark admitted. "More important is how are they going to take the evidence from this point on? This is where Anderson has to give them something to prove you're the man."

"That's the videotape, right?"

"Yeah, and your car with the blood in it, the sign out log, and whatever else they've got. We still need to talk to your buddy about those records."

"I'm seeing him tomorrow morning."

Mark nodded. "I'll be here pretty much all day. It will go pretty fast from here, so we'll have to be ready with our case. This'll be our last weekend to work, so I'm going to need you."

"I know."

"How's the case for Caponi? He going through with it after what happened with his son?"

I stopped and shook my head. "Vincent's upset for me even considering Roberto actually doing what they say he did. Of course, they say Vincent was behind it and you know I'm implicated too, so it's pretty ticklish."

Mark turned in his chair, tempted to take a shot with the nurf ball, but he must have realized this wasn't the time. He swiveled back to face me. "Any chance you can ease your way out, say you've got a conflict with your client?"

"Sure, I could do that, and then the whole thing would come crashing down. You've heard the saying, we hang together or separately, we'll be hanged?"

Marked nodded uncomfortably.

Chapter Thirty Four

The eyes of the jurors were riveted to the video screen. The glare from the overhead light still prevented seeing the person behind the wheel. Anderson had the videographer freeze the screen to show the times of entry and departure displayed on the lower right corner of the screen and to show my license plate number, a little fuzzy, but still readable. For emphasis he wrote all of the information down on the flip pad:

Date: July 16th
Time In: 1:35 a.m.
Time Out: 1:58 a.m.
License Plate No: RVK-787

Next, the custodian of records from the Department of Public Safety informed the jury that license plate RVK-787 was assigned to a Mazda 929 which was registered to Andrew C. Givens, a resident of Harris County, Texas.

Following a brief recess, Anderson called Larry Komansky, a white-bearded gnome of a man who operated the special forensic lab for the state of Texas.

"Dr. Komansky, were you furnished certain samples for your lab's analysis in connection with the investigation of the death of William V. Thrasher, Jr.?"

"Yes, Detective Joseph Springer of the Houston Police Department's Homicide Division sent samples to me for our analysis." He consulted the slim black notebook he'd brought with him. "I received pieces of carpet labeled as coming from the office of Mr Thrasher, and I received pieces of carpet identified as coming from a Mazda 929 automobile registered to Andrew C. Givens. In addition to the samples furnished by Detective Springer, I received a blood sample from the Harris County Medical Examiner identified as coming from the body of William V. Thrasher, Jr., taken during autopsy."

"Did you conduct an analysis of any of these samples?"

"Yes. We did typing and DNA profiles on the blood recovered from the carpet samples and compared them with the same tests run on the blood sample identified as having been taken from the body of William Thrasher."

"Doctor Komansky, you mentioned that one of the tests you conducted involved an analysis of DNA Can you tell us, what that is?"

"Certainly. DNA is the abbreviation for a chemical substance called deoxyribonucleic acid. This substance is in all of us, in every single cell in our bodies. We often refer to it as the building block of all living things. It carries the special genetic fingerprint of each of us. By analyzing samples of blood or body tissue, we can make comparisons of DNA to determine if they are from the same source."

Anderson got Komansky to explain the reliability of DNA testing, allowing his witness to conduct a brief lecture on the development of the testing procedures and stressing the fact that a DNA match indicates that only one in several million, or perhaps one in several hundred million persons will have the same DNA characteristics.

Then, he asked the question everyone in the courtroom was waiting for. "Dr Komansky, what conclusion, if any, were you able to draw from comparing the three samples, the one taken from Mr Thrasher's body during the autopsy, the one recovered from the carpet sample in his office, and the one taken from the carpet sample from underneath the seat of the automobile belonging to Mr Givens?"

Komansky looked at the jurors. "I concluded all three samples, as you have described them, have identical DNA. This means they all came from blood belonging to William V. Thrasher, Jr."

The prosecution's next witness was Carlos Estrada, the security officer at the 815 State Building, where the offices of Golden, Wallace, Givens & Whitfield were located.

"Do you know Andrew Givens?" Anderson asked.

The small, wiry man looked quickly over to me, his gaze darting just as quickly away, back to Anderson, his home base.

"Yes, sir, I know him. He is the man sitting right over there in the dark suit."

"Did Mr Givens work in your building?"

"Yes, he did. I knew him because he came in and out after normal hours quite a bit, just like a lot of the folks who work there, they're always busy."

"Do you recall, did Mr Givens sign in and out on the night of July Fifteenth of this year?"

"If that's the night you asked me about already, yeah he did."

"Do you remember the times he signed in and out?"

"The exact times?"

"Well, what do you remember about the times he signed in and out?"

"I can't say for sure. It was pretty late when he signed out I remember that. Aren't you going to show me the book like you said you was going to?"

Anderson's face turned red. A reporter sitting on the front row behind him laughed out loud. A young man sitting on the front row in the jury box broke into a broad grin.

"May I approach the witness?" Anderson asked.

Garza nodded.

Anderson handed the witness a blue notebook. "Do you recognize this?" he asked.

"Sure," Estrada said, smiling, happy to be on safe ground. "That's the log book that we keep our sign-ins and sign-outs after hours. It's the one for this year."

"Please go to the page that covers July Fifteenth, Mr Estrada."

Estrada thumbed through the book. "Got it," he said.

"Does reviewing that page refresh your memory of when Mr Givens signed in and when he signed out of the building?" Anderson asked.

"Yes it does, thanks."

Estrada's answer prompted another loud guffaw from the row behind Anderson. Judge Garza rapped his gavel and stared angrily at the offending reporter.

Anderson forged ahead. "Mr Estrada what do you now remember concerning the times when Andrew Givens signed in and out of the 815 State Building on July Fifteen of this year?"

"I remember now, you know, now that I've seen it, he signed in right at seven p.m. and he signed out real late, at twelve-fifty-five a.m., that was actually on July Sixteenth."

"Thank you, Mr Estrada. I have no more questions," Anderson said as he returned to sit down next to a smirking Arnold Weiss. Turning the screws can be great fun, even when you're sitting second-chair.

Mark went right to work. "Mr Estrada, didn't you say you have a lot of folks coming in and out after hours where you work?"

"Yes. That's right."

"Well, you mean to say you actually can remember way back in July to a specific date and a specific person?"

Estrada looked at Anderson and smiled. "I might not have, except the police came and asked me and I remembered it then, that is why I remember it now." Rehearsal was paying off.

"How long was it after July Sixteenth when the police came and talked to you?"

"Oh, it was only two or three days. Nothing more than that," Estrada answered, still smiling over in the direction of the prosecutor's table.

"Well then, let's see. Sir, do you still work at the 815 State Building?"

"Yes, I do."

"Were you working there three days ago?"

"Yes, I certainly was, it's my job."

"Do you remember who any of the people were who signed either in or out after hours three nights ago that would have been Thursday, December Tenth?"

Estrada hesitated. This wasn't part of the rehearsal.

"Well, for example, do you recall if Mr Del Wallace signed in or out that evening?"

Suddenly, Estrada's eyes brightened. "Why, yes I do. I believe Mr Wallace, he's one of the partners of Mr Givens, signed out after hours. In fact, I'm positive he did because we had a conversation, about how this trial was starting. I told Mr Wallace I was going to have to testify."

Mark continued, "Sir, do you remember what time it was when Mr Wallace signed out last Thursday night?"

"Uh, not exactly. I know it was last Thursday but exactly when, I'm not real positive."

"Do you still have that log book in front of you?"

"Yes."

"Please review the entries for December the tenth, Mr Estrada."

Estrada paged forward and read one of the pages. As he did, his eyes lit up.

"Have you had an opportunity to review the entries for that date?"

"Yes," he answered, smiling again.

"Does reviewing that entry refresh your recollection as to when it was that Mr Del Wallace signed out of the building?"

"It sure does. I remember now it was ten-thirty in the evening. He stayed real late that night."

"Are you sure Mr Estrada?"

Estrada nodded emphatically. "That's what I remember and yes, I'm sure. I watched him sign out and it was at ten-thirty."

"That's all I have, Mr Estrada. Thank you."

Garza instructed Anderson to call another witness.

"The state calls Steven Golden," Anderson announced.

My former partner entered the crowded courtroom and shuffled slowly toward the witness stand. He tottered up the aisle, a mere husk of the man he'd been just a few months earlier. Mark had warned what Golden was expected to say. Still, I couldn't help feeling sorry for him. His whole reason for being revolved around his law firm. A firm that was now in shambles, the harsh reality of that fact sucking the life right out of the man.

Golden seemed slightly reluctant to answer the prosecutor's questions and on one occasion when he glanced over to where I sat, I thought I saw just a hint of a wry smile. But just the same, Anderson got what he wanted: Golden met me in the office after normal hours, on the evening before Thrasher's murder. He did not remember seeing me leave, so I could have still been there when he and Fred Whitfield left the office after their meeting to discuss what to do about William Thrasher's threatened malpractice action.

Mark took Golden only briefly on cross-examination, asking if he remembered me saying I could be reached at the Cornwall if he and Whitfield wanted to speak with me. Golden stared vacantly past Mark. "No, I don't remember Mr Givens saying that."

The way the man looked, it was a wonder he remembered his own name. All I could do was hope the jurors drew the same conclusion.

The last witness of the day was Cynthia Simons, the office manager of Golden & Wallace, formerly Golden, Wallace, Givens & Whitfield. She was a big, sturdy woman, the kind that by her outward demeanor might just as well be wearing a sign saying, "I'm all business, bub, don't mess with me." She took the stand with the same confident, self-assured air she always displayed. I'd never envied her for having to work with a dozen demanding lawyers looking over her shoulder. But that didn't mean I liked her. She was usually an incredible pain in the ass.

Anderson asked if she'd brought the documents that had been subpoenaed by the State, and she said she had. He asked what they were and she told him she'd brought exactly what she was asked to bring, the records of out-going telephone calls from the firm for the month of July.

Anderson got the records admitted into evidence and then displayed the critical page on an overhead transparency.

"What are the meanings of those three-digit numbers preceding the telephone numbers that were called?" Anderson asked.

"Those numbers represent telephone locations in our office," she replied.

Anderson highlighted one of the calls with an orange marker:

07-16-032, 713-850-1687 -0035-0039. "Let's take this call. What does the 032 represent?"

"That is the location in our office where the call originated."

"Can you tell us, Ms Simons, where that telephone that has number 032, where is that phone located?"

Simons turned to the notebook she'd brought with her to the witness stand. "Yes, that would be the desk phone in Mr Givens' office."

"And the next numbers are the area code and number called is that correct?"

"That's right."

"So this means that a call was placed from Mr Givens' office to 713-850-1687, a local call to a number here in Houston, right?"

"Can you tell from that line the date and time when the call was placed?"

Simons stared at Anderson. "Why *of course* you can. That's why we have this system. So our billers can accurately charge the correct clients for their calls and be able to charge the appropriate amount of time spent on the call."

Anderson grinned. "Well, I'm not quite sure I understand. Can you tell us, Ms Simons, the date and the time when this particular call was placed?"

Simons gave her questioner another icy stare. "Why, certainly. The call was placed on July Sixteenth at twelve-thirty-five a.m. and it was completed at twelve-thirty-nine a.m."

Anderson walked over to the easel pad. "Ms Simons, you don't happen to know whose number this is that was called that night do you?"

She shook her head. "No sir, I don't maintain that sort of information. It would be up to the biller, in this case Mr Givens, or his secretary to fill in the client matter indicating how this call needed to be billed. We still have to circulate the calls to each biller. Pretty soon, we'll have our new system installed that will identify the matter to be billed, but even then, our attorneys will still have to review it for accuracy."

Anderson flipped through several pages on the easel until he found the one he was looking for. It said: "713-850-1687—private line of William Thrasher."

Everybody had the point now.

Mark got up to deal with Cynthia Simons. No, she didn't know who placed the call. Yes, it was possible that anyone who had been in the office at that time could have placed the call. Yes, it was true that my office had been the first one inside the reception room. But none of those points seemed to make much difference, and I hardly paid attention.

As Anderson announced that the State rested, I thought about Fred Whitfield. The man had done quite a job. I hoped he was roasting in a hot spot in hell.

# Chapter Thirty Five

Mark's choice for a defense expert was a good one. Desmond Cutler, retired FBI agent. He'd served in the field for most of his career and was top notch in conducting criminal investigations, particularly in death cases. More importantly, he'd also done a stint at the FBI's crime lab, serving as acting director for a couple of years during the organizational shake up following the demise of J. Edgar. Best of all, Cutler was a native Texan and he spoke in a plain, direct way that our jury would understand and hopefully appreciate.

When he got the chance to take a professorship in criminology at Sam Houston State, just north of Houston, he jumped at it. With his credentials, he was frequently asked to testify as an expert in difficult criminal cases, usually for the State. Thanks to Mark's charm, we'd been lucky enough to get him on our side.

As he took the witness stand, Cutler looked every bit the G-man—a grizzled bulldog in a conservative dark suit. He first described what he did to become familiar with the crime scene, explaining he'd been limited to a review of the photographs taken and the reports prepared by the investigating officers. He was in basic agreement with the conclusions drawn by The State's blood expert, David Matthews, except for the fact that Matthews had equivocated on the question of whether the murderer could have avoided getting blood on his or her own clothing. Cutler stated his opinion emphatically. The killer absolutely could not have done what was done in Thrasher's office without getting "quite a lot" of the victim's blood on whatever he or she was wearing at the time. He also testified that blood residues would be left on most clothing, even after professional cleaning, unless extremely strong industrial-grade solvents were used, and that such solvents were seldom used by commercial cleaners.

Mark then directed Cutler's attention to the suit and shirt I had worn. The police had picked them up from the hotel when they came back from the laundry.

"Were you furnished with the clothes that HPD collected from the Cornwall Hotel?" he asked.

"Yes, I was."

"Did you conduct an analysis of those clothes to determine if there was any blood residue on that clothing?"

"I didn't conduct it personally, but I took them with me to the FBI lab up in Quantico, Virginia. I still go up there on consulting assignments from time to time."

"Did anyone from HPD know you were taking those items with you?"

"Yes, of course they did. I've done it for them before."

Out of the corner of my eye I noticed Albert Anderson glaring daggers at Arnold Weiss.

"Did the FBI lab analyze the clothing for blood residue?"

"Yes."

"And were you there at the lab while the tests were conducted?"

"Yes, that's right," Cutler answered.

"Did the tests reveal any residue of blood on the items of clothing that you furnished them?"

"No, they did not."

"Thank you, Mr Cutler that's all I have," Mark said.

Anderson sat across from us ashen-faced. We'd just punched a hole in his case and he didn't seem to have a way to plug it. He asked several innocuous questions, probably in an attempt to hide the fact that he really didn't have a legitimate basis for challenging Cutler. He finished his examination by asking Cutler if a reason for not finding blood on my clothes could be that additional clothing was worn over what the police had recovered at the Cornwall.

Mark objected, but Garza allowed an answer.

Cutler replied, "Sure, if somebody wore another garment, like a coat, a rain slicker, or something like that, it could account for blood not being found on anything worn underneath something like that."

Anderson smiled. "Thank you, sir. That's all I have."

After Cutler, Mark called Patrick McPhee, the manager of the Cornwall. With his Saville Row suit and erect, slightly aristocratic bearing, McPhee looked every bit the part of an English gentleman. Small wonder he fit in so well at the hotel. Mark got McPhee to identify two of the hotel's charge slips, the first established the time I checked into the hotel as six-fifteen on the evening of July Fifteenth, and the second established that a room service order had been delivered to my room after my arrival.

Mark asked if the slip told when the room service order was placed and when it was delivered. In a clipped British accent, McPhee replied that, unfortunately, it did not. All he could say was the order had to have been placed after the time I checked in and before the end of the evening shift at midnight, when the room service kitchen closed for the night.

"What was ordered and delivered to Mr Givens' room?" Mark asked.

"The charge slip for room service is for one steak sandwich and a carafe of bordeaux," McPhee answered.

"How long does it normally take room service to prepare and deliver those items?"

McPhee smiled. "We pride ourselves in taking very good care of our guests. Prompt room service is one of the ways we have of keeping our guests happy, so all of our orders are delivered within thirty minutes of the time they are received."

"Thank you for that information, sir," Mark continued. "But do you know what would be the shortest possible amount of time it would take to prepare and deliver this particular order?"

McPhee paused, his thin lips curved in a frown. "Well, it would have to be an estimate, but I'd say realistically the shortest time would be between twenty and thirty minutes."

"So," Mark said, "if Mr Givens got to his room at say six-seventeen, two minutes after he checked in and immediately placed his order for room service, the shortest amount of time within which he would have received the order would put the time at six-thirty-seven, is that right?"

"Yes, but I must say, I do not personally consider it very likely. Our kitchen is usually quite busy at that time. I do not believe it likely that we would have been able to prepare and deliver an order at that time of day in a mere twenty minutes. We're good, but we're not magicians."

"So you believe it would have been delivered later then six-thirty-seven?"

"Objection, calls for speculation," Anderson said.

"Over-ruled," Garza responded. "Answer the questions, Mr McPhee."

"Yes, I believe it would much more likely have been at the outer limit of our thirty-minute delivery policy."

Anderson conferred briefly with Arnold Weiss. Most likely, they'd missed the hotel's room service delivery on their time line. How were they still going to get me signed in at my office three blocks up the street at seven o'clock? Say I wolfed down my order, and rushed over to the office to get busy plotting Thrasher's murder? As McPhee had stated, that was possible, but not likely.

Anderson wrote furiously on his pad. He pushed a message in front of Arnold Weiss, glaring at his associate. Weiss studied the note and the color drained from his face. The blame for missing the significance of my room service order had just rolled down-hill.

Our next witness was Del Wallace. Del explained how he'd been my partner and that we had been and still were close friends, taking away the point Anderson could score about our friendship by stating it up front. Mark asked if Del still maintained an office at 815 State and if he was familiar with the after hours sign-in and sign-out procedures that the building's security force followed. Del said he was painfully familiar with them because he worked late on a too-regular basis.

"Then I take it you know Carlos Estrada?" Mark asked.

"The man who works the security desk at our building? Yes, I know Mr Estrada."

"Did you sign out after-hours on December tenth, that would be last Thursday?"

Del grinned. "Yes, I sure did."

"Was that because you needed to stay late at work that night?"

"No, it was because you asked me to do it," Del said, a mischievous twinkle in his eyes.

"What time was it when you signed out last Thursday?"

"It was at seven-thirty p.m."

"Are you sure about the time?"

"Oh, yes. I'm very sure. I made special note of it just like you asked me to."

"Was Mr Estrada working the security desk at the building when you signed out?"

"Yes, he was there. I went out of my way to speak with him. I gave him a good chance to remember me."

"If Mr Estrada testified that you didn't sign out until ten-thirty last Thursday night, would you say he was mistaken?"

"Yes, I would have to say he is definitely wrong, if that's what he said."

"Thank you, Mr Wallace," Mark said.

Arnold Weiss stood. Anderson was actually allowing his helper to take a witness.

"Mr Wallace," Weiss began, his Adam's apple bobbing, "how is it you say you're certain you signed out at seven-thirty when the building log book states that you didn't sign out until three hours later?"

Mark almost laughed out loud.

Del smiled. "Sir, I know I signed out at seven-thirty. I wrote ten-thirty in the book just to prove a point."

"What point was that Mr Wallace?" Weiss asked, his bottom lip trembling.

"Just that our building security man, Mr Estrada, can't remember what he says he remembers, that's all."

Arnold stood at the lectern open-mouthed. Garza prompted him, asking if he had anything else. Sweat popped out on the young man's brow. He glanced questioningly over to Albert Anderson who refused to look at him, staring instead at a blank sheet of paper.

"No further questions," Weiss croaked.

Giggles from press row led to another admonishment from Garza.

We'd put another hole in the prosecution's case. I hoped it meant the score was tightening up.

When Mark announced his next witness would be Elaine Turner, Anderson immediately objected and asked Garza to excuse the jury. "She's been in court throughout the trial, judge," Anderson said. "She can't testify. We invoked the rule."

Judge Garza looked down from the bench and shook his head. "No sir, Mr Weiss *mentioned* invoking the rule, but according to my notes, neither side ever did."

"That's right, judge," Mark agreed, smiling over at his suddenly red-faced opponent.

With the jury back in the box, Elaine approached the witness stand and was sworn in by the clerk. In response to Mark's questions, she informed the jury that she worked for me, first at Golden-Wallace and later when I opened the office out on Jackson Avenue.

"Miss Turner," Mark asked, "did you ever know if Mr Givens kept a spare set of keys, including his car key, at his office?"

"Yes, he did. He kept extra keys to the office, his house, and car in a box that was always in the middle drawer of his desk."

"As far as you know, was that set of keys in his desk at the State Street office on July Fifteenth of this year?"

"Why, yes, they were always there, as far as I know. Andy, uh, I mean Mr Givens, never used them. He just wanted them there in case he needed someone from the office to take his car to run an errand, or go out to his house to pick something up when neither he or his wife were at home."

"Did Mr Givens on occasion ask you to take his car to run an errand for him?"

"Well, it's happened a few times, not very often, but, yes, I've done that."

"And on those occasions, did you use the set of keys that Mr Givens kept in the middle drawer of his desk?"

"Yes."

"And when you've gone to get them have the keys always been in that box in the middle drawer of the desk?"

"Yes, they have."

"Do you know, has Mr Givens ever made it a practice to lock the middle drawer of his desk?"

"No, he hasn't. In fact, when I first began working for him, I remember asking if he wanted me to keep his desk locked. He laughed and said he didn't know where the key to that desk was."

"Do you know, did he keep the door to his office locked?"

"No, none of the individual offices have locks on them."

Mark nodded. "That's enough about locks, and car keys, Miss Turner. Let me ask you this, did you have occasion to speak with Mr Givens on the morning of July Sixteenth?"

"Yes, I'm the one who told him about Mr Thrasher being killed."

"What was his reaction when you told him Mr Thrasher was dead?"

"Objection," Anderson shouted. "Calls for hearsay. Also, a conclusion by the witness, not a statement of fact."

The judge shook his head. "No, I'll allow it. The objection is over-ruled."

Elaine looked into the jury box, just as Mark had instructed. "Well, he was shocked, just like everybody else. I could tell just by talking to him."

"Did you see Mr Givens that morning?"

"Yes, I delivered some things to him at his hotel and then we walked back to the office together."

"Would you please describe for us, Miss Turner, how he appeared to you when you saw him that morning?"

Anderson was back up, shouting, "Your honor, objection! This witness hasn't been qualified as an expert on what can be deduced from how someone appeared. The very basis for the question is to give her a chance to say she doesn't think her boss is guilty."

Garza frowned. "It seems you're making their point for them, then, Mr Anderson. Your objection is over-ruled."

Anderson sat down, slamming his legal pad on the table.

"Counsel, watch yourself," a stern-faced Garza admonished.

Elaine continued to look at the jurors. "He was very upset. It was very plain to me, he couldn't believe what had happened. I thought he was close to being in a state of shock."

That was laying it on pretty thick and I hoped Mark would stop the music soon. Just the same, the folks in the jury box seemed to be enjoying the show. They paid rapt attention to her every word.

Mark thanked her for her testimony and announced he had no more questions.

Anderson was on his feet immediately. "Now, Miss Turner, how old are you?"

"I'm twenty-six," she said, her green eyes boring a hole through him.

"And you've worked for Mr Givens for how long?"

"Almost four years, ever since my graduation from the University of Houston."

"And during that entire time you've been his *personal* secretary?"

"I am, and always have been, ever since I started working, a *legal* secretary."

"Did you have any special qualifications that you possessed at the time you took your job with Mr Givens?"

Elaine shook her head. "No, not really. I was proficient with a word processor and must have scored well on the tests I was given, but no, I really didn't have any practical experience."

Anderson smiled. "Now, Miss Turner, you are not married?"

"Objection. Not relevant," Mark said.

"No, I'll allow it. Answer the question, Miss Turner," Garza said.

"That is correct," Elaine said, returning her attention to the jury box.

Albert Anderson stood and pointed at me. "And during the time you and Mr Givens have worked together, isn't it true you've developed a personal friendship?"

She gave Anderson an icy stare. "Yes, of course we have."

"Hasn't your relationship with Mr Givens developed into significantly more than a friendship?"

Mark objected again, and Garza over-ruled him again.

"I'm not sure what you mean, but yes, our friendship is more than it was."

Anderson remained on his feet and pointed at me again. "And Miss Turner, haven't you and Mr Givens engaged in an intimate sexual relationship?"

"Objection!" Mark shouted.

"Please answer the question, Miss Turner," the judge directed.

Elaine turned red-faced. "I don't see what business this is of yours, but yes, we have."

"And Mr Givens is married, is that correct?"

She shifted in her chair and glared at the assistant DA. "He's separated. We didn't become, uh, as close as we are, until long after that happened."

"And you care for him very much, don't you Miss Turner?"

"Yes, of course I do."

"You'd do anything for Andrew Givens, wouldn't you?"

"Objection!" Mark shouted again.

Anderson smirked. "I'll withdraw that last question, Miss Turner, I'm finished." He glanced over at our table and smiled as he turned to walk back to his seat.

Mark leaned over and whispered, "Damn it, Andy, you should have told me."

His words stung. I knew he was right.


It's easy in this business to let yourself become extremely critical of people's performances on the witness stand. It's the ultimate in Monday morning quarterbacking. But my experience those couple of days in December changed all that. Every practicing trial lawyer should sit in that chair with his or her tail on the line, and a lot of that second guessing would come to an abrupt halt.

Direct was easy enough. We'd been over the outline several times. My years as a trial lawyer working in Washington for the government and then in private practice in Houston. Being hired by Thrasher Industries in a big important case. Going home the day the Thrasher trial ended and learning that Monica wanted a divorce—thus explaining what I'd been doing staying at the Cornwall that night. Going back to my office, signing in at a few minutes after seven. Leaving and signing out approximately twenty minutes later, after retrieving my trial notebook and having a brief conversation with Steve Golden. Explaining that someone had to have changed the sign-out time recorded in the security log. Returning to the hotel and ordering room service. Finding out the next morning about Thrasher's death. Meeting with the police and resigning from my law firm that same day, concerns over the malpractice suit and Thrasher's death having caused my partners to request that I leave. Looking in each juror's eyes, telling them no, I did not kill William Thrasher.

When it was over, Judge Garza called for lunch recess. To me, only minutes had passed. Actually, I'd been on the stand for over three hours.

Mark came to me smiling. "Andy, you did good. Just remember the hard part comes next. Keep it up."

Elaine, Mom, and Dad sat with me in the otherwise empty courtroom, lending their support. I felt like a fighter between rounds. Being peppered with advice and encouragement, knowing soon enough it was me who would have to go back into the ring.

That afternoon, Anderson covered every aspect of the Thrasher case, in his usual methodical style. Yes, I did know Thrasher's private number and yes, I had on occasion used it. No, I did not know any way that a late-night visitor could have gotten inside the security door at the elevator on Thrasher's floor without someone on the inside opening it.

Yes, I was aware that Thrasher kept a baseball bat—a gift from the Astros up in his office. Yes, it was correct, I was six feet-three. Yes, I knew that Thrasher was considering filing a malpractice lawsuit against me for the way the W.D.S. case had been handled.

Toward the end of the afternoon, Anderson changed direction. "Mr Givens," he asked, "do you own a raincoat?"

"I do," I said, wondering what this was about.

"When is the last time you've seen it?"

I couldn't remember and said so.

"Would you describe the raincoat that you own?" Anderson asked, wearing a smug look.

"What I'm thinking about is a tan trench coat," I said.

"Where was it last time your remember seeing it?"

"I'm sorry, I just don't remember," I said, glancing over at Mark, who looked back poker-faced.

"Did you keep your raincoat at your office, Mr Givens?"

I tried to think. "Sometimes, I might have. I don't wear it very often."

"It's been rainy for the past several days, hasn't it, Mr Givens?"

"Objection," Mark barked.

"Withdrawn," Anderson said. He stood and walked around the table to the jury box.

"Have you worn your raincoat at all during the trial of this case?"

Mark objected again.

Garza overruled. "Answer the question, Mr Givens."

"Have you worn your raincoat at all during the trial of this case?" Anderson repeated.

"No, I have not."

Anderson raised his arm and pointed at me. "Mr Givens isn't it true that on the early morning of July Sixteenth, you wore your raincoat when you went to William Thrasher's office for the purpose of killing him?"

"No," I answered, trying to maintain control.

"Isn't it true that you wore your raincoat on that occasion knowing that you intended to kill William Thrasher with the baseball bat in his office and you knew you needed to wear something over your business suit that would permit you to get back inside the hotel without doing so in bloody clothing?"

Mark jumped up shouting an objection.

Garza quieted the ensuing commotion with several raps of his gavel. "The witness will answer," he said.

I looked at Anderson. Standing there in front of a blow-up of the bloody mess in Thrasher's office, smiling in self-proclaimed triumph.

"No, that is not true. I did not kill William Thrasher." I looked at the jurors. Did any of them believe me?

Anderson glanced up at the clock behind the table where the courtroom deputy was seated. "Judge, it is almost four-forty-five," he said. "I suggest that this might be a good place to stop for the day. The State will be prepared to wrap up its cross of Mr Givens in the morning."

Garza nodded. "All right, Mr Anderson. We'll see you all back here at nine o'clock tomorrow morning."

As soon as possible I went to Elaine. "Do you remember that raincoat? I haven't seen the thing since I don't know when."

Elaine nodded. "It should be in the back of the receptionist's closet at Golden - Wallace. It was there for quite a while. At least since last fall. It kept getting in the way in your office closet, so you asked me to put it someplace and I did."

I hurried to the phone at the clerk's desk, hoping to find Del in the office. He was there and I asked him to go look. A few minutes later he came back on the line.

"Andy. I'm afraid there's no raincoat in that closet."

"Okay, thanks."

I told Mark. "This is chicken-shit," he said, "but I'm afraid we're gonna hear more about that coat."

Mom and Dad stood at the rear of the courtroom. Walking toward them, I turned back and said, "Mark, I'll call you about getting together this evening."

He nodded wearily. "Okay, I'll be at the office."

We were pulling into the driveway when Elaine turned to me and said, "Andy. I'm sorry, I forgot. I checked messages during the afternoon break. Nathan Junell called. He left word that he wants you to call him. He said it's vital that he talk to you this evening."

At my desk I dialed the number Elaine had given me.

A voice boomed on the line, "Yeah, what is it?"

Unless I missed my guess I was talking to Junell's body guard, the hulkster.

"This is Andy Givens," I said. "Senator Junell is expecting my call."

"Just a minute," he replied and I was put on hold.

A few minutes later, Junell came on the line. "Givens, how're things going for you in that trial?"

"It's about over," I said. "We'll know soon enough."

"Well, you have my best wishes, son."

"Senator, I appreciate the call. Is there something I can do for you?"

"As a matter of fact, there's something I believe I can do for *you*. I realize this is coming at an awkward time, but I have someone who you need to see this evening."

"Sir, I've got a trial going on over here. I'm sorry, but I've got to go to my lawyer's right after dinner."

"Now, please listen. I'm telling you, this is something that *will* make *a lot* of difference to a lot of people. I can't talk about it. I promised I wouldn't until my man meets you personally. But it has to be tonight. That's just the way it is."

Driving ninety miles to Port Arthur right in the middle of my own murder trial? I started to say no, but what if Junell really had something? "I'll have to call Mark Watson," I said.

"Tell you what," Junell replied. "You said you're having dinner and then meeting with your attorney later?"

"Right."

"I'll send Brad over. He'll pick you up and drive you and Watson to see me here at my office. When we're finished he'll drive you back. That'll give you and your attorney plenty of time to work. My limo is set up for that kind of thing."

"Why are you doing this?"

Junell chuckled. "You'll see, and Andy, I promise you, you definitely won't be disappointed."


It was one-thirty in the morning. Mark got out of the limo sporting the same wide grin he'd worn all the way back to Houston. "That was wild," he said.

"Yeah it sure was," I agreed. I still didn't believe what had happened at the office of Senator Nathan Junell. It put a new, disturbing light on the Centennial lawsuit. If I made it through the Thrasher mess, at least I wouldn't have to worry about being charged with suborning perjury. But as I watched Mark head for his car I couldn't help wondering, how were Vincent and Sylvia Caponi going to handle the news?

## Chapter Thirty Six

The last day of the Thrasher trial passed in a blur. Anderson completed his cross-examination getting me to admit to having a temper and a loose tongue. From my own lips the jury learned about the threats I made to two people, both since Thrasher's death, one of whom was dead, the victim of an as yet unsolved murder. Better to admit those sins and attempt to explain them than have the esteemed Judge Campbell and Joseph Hartson crammed down our throats.

Detective Springer was the only rebuttal witness called by Albert Anderson.

"Now, Detective Springer, earlier you testified you served search warrants at Mr Givens' home, his former residence, occupied at the time by his wife, Monica Givens, and at his former office on State Street, did you not?" Anderson asked.

"Yes, that is correct," Springer replied.

"And you testified those warrants each specified a search for items of men's clothing?"

"Yes, all of them did."

"Why was it important to search for those items?"

Mark objected. "Lack of foundation."

"Sustained," Judge Garza responded.

Anderson smiled. "All right, tell us, Detective Springer, what was the reason for including items of men's clothing in those search warrants?"

Springer grinned, the righteous cop bringing the sleazy lawyer to his knees. "We had reason to believe that Mr Givens was involved in William Thrasher's murder. As I believe I testified earlier, we found large quantities of blood at Mr Thrasher's office. That led us to search for clothing that might have been worn during the commission of the crime which might have blood stains or other evidence of their being worn at the time the murder was committed."

"Were there any specific items of clothing you were looking for?"

"Yes. We looked for articles of clothing which could have been worn over other clothing. Sweat suits, cover-alls, topcoats, raincoats, those sorts of items."

Anderson pursed his lips. "Did your men find a man's raincoat at any of the locations which you searched?"

"No. We were told Mr Givens owned a raincoat and we thought it was odd that we didn't locate it, but we never did."

Mark was on his feet. "Your honor, objection. That statement wasn't responsive to the question and there's no way a question could possibly be framed that would permit that sort of answer."

Garza nodded. Glaring at Springer, letting the jury know what the dective had done was wrong, he said, "Ladies and gentlemen, you shouldn't have heard that. You are instructed to disregard everything the witness just said after the word 'no'."

*Sure.* As if that would do any good.

Anderson announced the close of The State's rebuttal case and a sickening realization hit home. My guilt or innocence meant nothing. It still boiled down to what the jury believed—how far those people were willing to go, one way or the other. Anderson practically strutted back to his chair, appearing every bit the man who knew he'd gotten the job done.

On closing argument, Mark covered two main points. First, that the prosecutor's time sequence made no sense. How could I possibly check in at the hotel, order room service, wait for it to be delivered, and then get over to my office three blocks away, all between six-fifteen and seven o'clock? Second, he emphasized the shadowy figure behind the wheel of my car that night, saying that it could have been anyone and that fact alone was what cast the shadow of reasonable doubt over the entire case.

Then, he reminded them of my testimony. "Andy Givens took the witness stand and explained to you in his own words exactly what happened on that night last July. He answered every question that I and the prosecution put to him, forthrightly, and honestly. He was able to do that, ladies and gentlemen, because Andy Givens doesn't have anything to hide. He was able to do that because he didn't kill William Thrasher."

Mark looked into the jury box, scanning each face. "I'm going to finish now," he said, still looking at them. "In just a moment, Mr Anderson will address you for the State. I won't get another chance to speak with you to answer everything he says. So I ask you, as you listen to what he has to say, just remember, the time sequence, when Andy checked into the hotel, ordered room service and got his room service order. When he signed in at his office building. He didn't have time to do all of those things. Someone changed the sign-out time on the log. That same person is the one who took Andy's car keys and used Andy's car to go to William Thrasher's office and kill the man. But whoever that was, it definitely wasn't Andy Givens. And remember, we can't see who it was who was driving that car in and out of the garage that night either. That fact alone raises a reasonable doubt. That's what reasonable doubt is, ladies and gentlemen. Don't convict a man of this serious crime when the prosecution hasn't met its burden. Reasonable doubt permeates every single aspect of the prosecution's case. Because it does, for that reason alone, you have no choice. The law *requires* you to find Andy Givens *not guilty*."

In contrast to Marks's isolation of key pieces of evidence, Anderson seemed determined to cover each piece of the State's case, arguing that, in its totality, the evidence was overwhelming. The video showing my car going in and out of the garage, Thrasher's threat of a malpractice suit that stood to ruin my career, the phone records, the office building security logs, my fingerprints in Thrasher's office, my height being in the range of people who could have delivered the fatal blows, Thrasher's blood in my car. The evidence pointed to only one person: me.

Summing up, Anderson said, "You saw Mr Givens testify. He is a clever, well-trained lawyer. He is accustomed to convincing people with the speeches he makes. Ladies and gentlemen, don't let him fool you. His conduct in this very trial proves he doesn't deserve your trust. What did he do? He brought his best friend, and his lover, in here in a shameful, pathetic attempt to try to pull the wool over your eyes. If you take each piece of this evidence that we presented to you, and add it to all of the other pieces, you will conclude there can be no other explanation. Andrew Givens killed William Thrasher. You must find him guilty."

I watched the jurors closely as Anderson closed. As they filed out of the courtroom, they looked ready to do what they'd just been asked.

We didn't get a verdict that evening. Judge Garza let the jurors go home at a little before nine o'clock to pursue further deliberations the following Monday morning. That left us to wait the weekend. Mom kept us well fed, teaching Elaine some of my favorite recipes. While they cooked, Dad and I took long walks along the tree-lined streets near Rice University. None of us talked about the trial.

"It's in God's hands now," Mom said. "That's a good place for our fate to be."

On Monday afternoon, we finally got the call. The jury had a verdict. When we got to the courtroom, Mark, Albert Anderson, and Arnold Weiss were seated in their usual places. I joined my lawyer as Elaine helped my parents re-claim their spots on the first row behind us. Moments later, Judge Garza took the bench and called in the jury. The foreman, Lonnie Morris, the man from the funeral home who Garza seated after our *Batson* motion, handed the verdict form to the deputy who delivered it to the judge.

Garza examined the verdict looked at me and said, "The Defendant will please stand."

I got up, with Mark at my side. My knees were like water, my heart rose in my throat. The judge handed the verdict to his clerk and instructed her to read the jury's decision.

The clerk looked at the sheet of paper and read, "In the charge of murder in the first degree for the death of William V. Thrasher, Jr., we the jury find the defendant, Andrew C. Givens, not guilty."

In the brief instant of ensuing silence, she looked at me and smiled.

Mark pounded my back. Elaine and my parents rushed around the rail. Garza said something, I'm not sure what, the courtroom already was filled with the din of competing voices. Reporters shouted questions, vying for position in the line that rapidly formed leading to the door. I shook Mark's hand and then I stood for a long time hugging my mother, my dad, and Elaine all at once.


We celebrated that night in a private room at the Cornwall. My parents, Elaine, Eddie, Mark, and Judge Garza's courtroom clerk, a cute young thing who'd caught Mark's attention during the trial, Mitchell and Susan Knight, Del and his wife, Charlotte. Most of us, myself included, were less than enthusiastic about being there. We were worn out, numbed by the experiences of the past several weeks. But Mitchell Starlarski had insisted. We *had* to get together.

The long table was covered with a white-linen table cloth and was decorated with red place mats and beautiful Christmas china and candles. Lights from a fully decorated spruce tree set up in the far corner of the high-ceilinged ornate dining room sparkled brightly. We were served a splendidly prepared meal, accompanied by delicious wines. As we ate, Mark stood to propose the first of many toasts.

"To Andy Givens," he began. "It's far more difficult to represent an innocent man, and Andy, this was the most difficult case I've ever had. Congratulations, my friend you got what you deserve."

I returned the toast. Then, Mark and I both toasted Elaine and my parents for their help and support.

Just the same, our celebration was forced. There were a lot of people out there who still believed I killed William Thrasher. On the six o'clock news, Anderson was interviewed, saying he still believed the State put the right man on trial. A middle-aged woman named Emily Dorch, one of the jurors who'd glanced at me suspiciously throughout the trial, also was interviewed. According to Mrs Dorch, the jury initially voted eight to four in favor of a conviction. She took credit, along with Lonnie Morris, for convincing the eight who were in favor of a guilty verdict to reconsider. But she made it clear, everybody on the panel still believed that somehow I was involved in Thrasher's murder. Nevertheless, they concluded the prosecution had failed to meet its burden of proving guilt beyond a reasonable doubt. To make matters worse, the news anchor announced that sources inside HPD were confident an arrest in the Fred Whitfield murder was anticipated in the near future. A small bone for a public that didn't like to think a guilty man was being allowed to walk free. Mark offered a toast to Mitchell and Susan, for the party they'd gone to the trouble to throw. Dad toasted Del and Charlotte for being such good friends to stand by his son when he needed them the most.

Finally, Mitchell got up. "To Susan Knight," he said, "the most beautiful and the most wonderful woman I know. A woman who, despite those qualities, might be in line to have her head examined, because earlier tonight she agreed to marry me."

Everyone applauded while Susan blushed. Right on cue, Christmas carolers hired by the hotel came in after Mitchell's speech. Mitch sent a waiter for champagne. The women left *en masse* to go to the powder room to do whatever it is that they do when they disappear the way they always seem to do right in the middle of festivities.

I stood to stretch my legs and wandered over to admire the tree, decorated with miniature packages wrapped in gold and silver paper. Christmas. I'd spend it with my family in Tennessee. Elaine and Eddie were headed for San Diego to be with their folks. I'd tried all afternoon to convince Elaine to change her mind and come to Sandy Creek, offering to then go with her to see her parents. But she'd politely refused, saying she had to go with Eddie.

Del came to stand next to me. "Well, pal, it's over," he said.

"Yeah, I guess it is."

"Do you think they'll ever figure it out?" he asked.

I shrugged. "I don't know. They said on the news that they expect an arrest in the Whitfield case. I guess that means they think they can prove I hired Charles Lucas. And that's right after that woman on the jury announced they all thought I did it, but the DA couldn't prove it. I'm afraid there's going to be more where this came from."

Del nodded sympathetically. "It's just not fair. You know, the time Whitfield told me he wasn't so sure you were the one who killed Thrasher, he also told me he planned to go to the Judicial Commission about Fritz Taylor and Otto Loring. He thought that deal smelled to high heaven."

Thinking about Whitfield made my stomach turn. The man was dead, and the man who'd killed him was dead too. Now, there'd never be a chance to prove Whitfield was responsible for Thrasher's murder.

"Do you think he actually went to them?" I asked.

"I don't know. If he didn't, I'd be surprised if Steve Golden hasn't gone himself. Even though he's wanted so badly for the whole mess to just go away, he seemed so damned shocked when I mentioned to him the other day what Fred told me about Taylor and Loring being pals. I wouldn't be too surprised if the old man tried to do something about it."

I made a mental note to speak with Golden. Maybe with the verdict in, he'd change his tune. When the women returned, I took Elaine's hand. Tomorrow we'd go our separate ways, at least for a while. But tonight, we were together. That alone was reason to celebrate.

# Chapter Thirty Seven

I parked in an empty space in front of the apartment and walked with Elaine to her door. A few stars twinkled feebly, barely penetrating the ground light of the city. We stood outside, shivering in the cold night air.

"Coming in?" she asked.

I smiled. "Sure, I'd like to."

Elaine started water for coffee. I followed her into the living room and sat next to her on the sofa.

"I couldn't have gotten through this if you hadn't been with me. I'll always be in your debt."

She smiled and I pulled her to me, holding her in my arms The kettle whistled. She kissed me before going to tend it.

She came back with two steaming mugs. Handing one to me, she sat down in the Eames chair across from the sofa.

"Andy, we need to talk," she said. "A lot has happened over the last few weeks. We're going off tomorrow in opposite directions, and somehow, it just doesn't seem right."

"I know," I said.

"Well, I didn't plan to say it that way, but I did. I think it's actually for the best that we spend this time apart."

"I was about to get my hopes up that you'd changed your mind and decided to come to Tennessee."

"Oh, Andy, I'd really like that, but, I don't know, I guess I'm scared."

"Scared? What do you mean?"

"Andy, I'm afraid I've fallen in love with you. And I don't know where you stand. You've still got a lot to figure out. I don't want to push you into something you're not ready for."

"Elaine, I want this. The way I see it, I'm the luckiest man in the world."

She nodded. "That's how you feel now, but what happens when Monica calls again? She will, you know. After that, well, don't you see? I'm the one who stands to get hurt."

I frowned. "Monica? That's over."

"How can you be sure?" she asked. "Please understand, I'm not saying this to demand a promise. You're probably as sure as you can be. But you must realize, I'm not strong enough to make a commitment to you and then see you forget all about me the first time she comes calling."

I put my mug on the coffee table, and sat on the floor next to her chair. Reaching up, I took her hand in mine. "Elaine, I promise, that will never happen. I love you."

A single tear ran down her cheek. "I know you mean what you say, but I have to be sure, don't you see?"

The truth of the matter was, I was completely confused. "What can I do?"

"Nothing," she said, wiping her face on her sleeve. "That's why it's good for both of us to spend this time apart. I'll miss you, you know I will, but we both need time to think."

"Elaine, dear, isn't there anything I can do?"

She managed a smile. "As a matter of fact there is." Reaching out to me, she said, "Would you hold me some more?"

I was more than willing to oblige.


At the airport the following morning, I called Mark, just to say thanks one more time. When he came on the line he sounded worried.

"What's the matter, didn't you have any luck with the clerk?"

"Nah, nothin' that serious, pal. Somebody broke in our office last night. That's all. We can't find anything that's missin', so I guess I shouldn't worry, but it makes you feel kinda weird when you know somebody's taken this sort of interest."

"Well, is there anything I can do?"

"Yeah. Stay outta trouble for a while. I'm plannin on takin' that little clerk up to Breckenridge right after Christmas."

"Merry Christmas, Mark."

"You too."

I tried calling Vincent Caponi one last time too, but didn't get an answer. I needed to talk to him, but he didn't seem to want to cooperate.

"Come on, Andy!" my father shouted, worried that the plane would leave at any second, even though the boarding process was just beginning. We took our seats, Mom and Dad in the row in front of my window seat. The morning was bright and clear and we had an excellent view of downtown as we climbed northward on the way to Nashville. I craned my neck to look back as the city faded away.

The passenger sitting next to me opened his newspaper. On the front page of the *Chronicle*, the headline read, "LAWYER FOUND INNOCENT." A grainy, slightly off-focus photo showed Mark, Elaine, my parents, and myself, leaving the courthouse. I turned away, relieved to be leaving Houston behind.


Sandy Creek is a sleepy little town nestled on the bank of a small tributary where it feeds into the Cumberland River, just west of Nashville. A red-brick three-story courthouse with a white clock dome dominates downtown. A scattering of dress and gift shops, a drug store, furniture, appliance and hardware stores, are positioned around the square, ever-ready for the county's farmers and their wives to come to visit. The prominence of that building and of the men who practiced before the circuit and chancery courts inside were early influences leading to my decision to become a lawyer. As Dad drove past it on the way home, with all that had happened, I entertained thoughts of going back to burn the place down.

Christmas Eve, I went with my parents to the tiny white-frame church up on Stovepipe Hill, overlooking the town. Christmas Eve service was a family tradition and Dad groused during the short car ride about how his daughter and son-in-law should have brought their brood up from Nashville that afternoon instead of waiting until morning.

"Edward, that's enough of that," Mom cajoled. "You know the children are of an age where Christmas is important to them. They have the right to wake up in their own house not having to worry if Santa's going to be able to find them all the way up here."

"Well, the weather man said we might get snow tonight," Dad replied, undeterred.

"It's sure cold enough," I said. "It must be down in the twenties already."

"Eighteen degrees back at the house," Dad said. "I checked the thermometer before we left."

"Now, look at those stars will you?" Mom exclaimed. "If it snows tonight, it'll be a miracle."

We slipped into our pew, the third row from the front on the left side of the aisle, the same one the Givens family had used for at least the past fifty years. Stained-glass windows flanked the long, narrow sanctuary. An enormous cedar tree, over twenty feet tall, took up most of the area in front of the chancel, decorated with hundreds of tiny white lights, satin crosses, and white feathered doves. Candles burned brightly behind the pulpit and around the choir rail. Mrs Esther Beale, director of the Sandy Creek Methodist Church choir ever since I can remember, led the choir down the aisle to *Come All Ye Faithful*. The congregation stood and sang along.

Brother Phillips gave his regular Christmas Eve sermon. Christ in the Manger. The hope and the promise of His birth. I knew it by heart. Everyone there did, but no one seemed to mind. The little church was packed, just as it always was on Christmas Eve.

Outside, it became eerily quiet. When the congregation began to file out after the service, a murmur of excitement came from the door. Huge snowflakes were framed in the light. The windows of the cars and pick-ups in the parking lot were already covered, and patches of white were forming on the lawn.

"There's your miracle, Sarah," Dad said. "I only hope that Libby and Rob are able to make it in the morning. That road from the Interstate gets mighty slippery."

As we drove back into Sandy Creek the snow kept coming down, rapidly turning the surrounding landscape a sparkling, wondrous white.

Christmas with the Givens family passed in its usual progression. Timmy and Abigale, the respective terrors of the first and third grades at Crockett Elementary, ripped open their presents with fixed determination, littering the entire room with piles of wrapping paper. They seemed only mildly interested in the actual contents in the boxes beneath the paper, pausing only for brief seconds before attacking the next package.

Dad carved and served the traditional turkey. Mom's giblet gravy, corn bread dressing, peas with water chestnuts, squash casserole, and cranberries rounded out the meal. By the time the pecan pie was served, most of us were screaming for relief from uncontrolled self-indulgence. The football games on television gave everybody the excuse to nap and to recover from the day's excesses.

I woke first, Dad still asleep in his recliner, the prototypical head of the American home. My sister, Libby, and her husband, Rob, were on opposite ends of the long sofa that ran the length of the wall in the den opposite the television. I looked around for Mom and heard water running in the kitchen. There she was, cleaning up for round two, the only one of us who never seemed to rest.

"Great dinner, Mom," I said, giving her a hug as she stood from loading dishes into the washer. "Where're the kids?" I asked.

"I put them upstairs. They were pretty worn out. Libby said they were up at four, anxious about Santa coming to visit. Then, they saw the snow. It's been quite a day for them."

I glanced out the window. At only three-thirty, it already was beginning to get dark. The thermometer outside read sixteen degrees. "It's going to get cold tonight," I said.

"Afraid so," Mom agreed. "The weatherman says we might get another three or four inches before this front pushes through and then there's another one coming that's tracking right behind."

"Remember Libby's senior year?"

She nodded. "Of course I do. How could I forget? You kids, out of school for almost a month. We haven't had anything like it since."

"I think I'll go out for a while."

"You be careful. It's slippery and old bones don't mend as fast as young ones."

I laughed. "My bones aren't that old."

Outside, the only sound came from the occasional sigh of the pine trees as the wind gusted. The sky was a dark, steely gray. An occasional snow flake fell, either blown off the trees, or maybe the weather report was right and more was on the way. I made my way up the steep hill behind my parents' home. Reaching the crest, fields and woods stretched out on the far side, covered in a mantle of white, reminding me of a scene from Currier & Ives. As heavy snow began to fall, my thoughts returned to the situation waiting back in Houston.

What about Elaine? Everything she had done, standing with me when almost no one else had. Offering her constant encouragement. Refusing to allow my dark, ugly side to win out. Demonstrating her caring and affection with repeated acts of selflessness. What had her brother said that night at her apartment? "If she ever risks letting herself love again, she'll never stop." Had she allowed herself to risk loving me? Or was she still holding back, worried that Monica might come between us? I couldn't blame her if she was. She'd seen how desperate I'd been to convince Monica to take me back. And how could I really be sure? The objective, bluntly honest character who every now and then showed up in my thoughts told me maybe Elaine was right. Maybe I wouldn't know myself until the time came.

I probably didn't deserve her, but I had to find a way to convince her the risk was worth taking. Even if it proved as impossible as catching the snowflakes that swirled around me, I had to try. Although I was prepared to do all I could, I couldn't help thinking, under the circumstances, was this the right thing? Fred Whitfield was in the ground, those pitifully lonely red bud trees in the Pasadena Cemetery his only company, the authorities still seeking to charge me with his murder. Charles, Dog-Man, Lucas notwithstanding. And even if that never happened, what were the chances of erasing the stigma that promised to stick with me for the rest of my life? Was dragging Elaine Turner into that sort of future really fair?

At least my problems weren't as bad as what Vincent and Sylvia Caponi would soon face. I hadn't been able to reach them to let them know what I'd found out at Nathan Junell's. Their instincts about the parties responsible for their son's death were well-founded—what those lousy bastards had done, just to win a lawsuit. But they still didn't know the details. I would have to tell them soon.

The wind rose, and the snow turned to hard, grainy sleet that slanted into my face and stung my eyes. Leafless branches of nearby trees rattled and, in the distance, shadowy ghostly shapes danced in the wind.

I thought of Vincent and Sylvia in the airplane on our way back from their son's funeral, clinging to each other with such profound sadness, and of what Vincent had promised.

"You were right, Vincent," I said. "They'll pay for this. You can count on it."

I was walking up the driveway to my parents' home, my thoughts returned to the trial, when it hit me. I didn't like it in the least, but suddenly I knew who'd killed William Thrasher. The problem was, I had no idea how to prove it.

## Chapter Thirty Eight

On New Year's day I caught a late afternoon flight to Houston. The plan was for Elaine and I to meet at the airport. My flight got into *Hobby* an hour earlier than hers, so I found a seat near a television in the airport lounge and watched Syracuse and Notre Dame playing for the national championship in the Orange Bowl. The place was nearly empty, just a couple of guys down at the far end of the bar watching the game.

I was on my second Bud Lite when a new customer came in. A big, powerfully built fellow with a weathered face and rough, work-hardened hands. His eyes were blood-shot, probably from too much bringing in the New Year.

He stared at me, giving me a thorough inspection, so I tried to keep sight of him out of the corner of my eye, while still concentrating mainly on the television. It was a pretty good game. A few minutes later, I felt a heavy hand on my shoulder.

"Hey, ain't you that guy who was in the paper, 'bout a week ago?" he demanded.

I didn't reply, just took another sip of my beer.

"Listen, Mac," he persisted. "I'm talkin' to you, understand?"

I swiveled around on the barstool to face him. "If it's the same to you, I'd like to watch the game and finish my beer in peace, okay?"

He peered at me out of rheumy, eyes. "Yeah, you're the guy. Don't know what this world is comin' to when scum buckets like you are out walkin' around free as a bird. I tell you, it ain't fair, you damned big-shots can buy off anybody you please, an' that ain't right."

I stepped off the stool, keeping it between me and Mr Nice. "Look, I don't want any trouble from you."

"What're you gonna do? Kill me?"

His warm, stale-beer breath spewed his words of hate. I stood my ground, knowing what was coming. He reached back, ready to take a swing, and I moved just beyond his reach. He swung wildly, and when he missed he almost toppled over the barstool between us. While he was still off balance, I grabbed his wrist and pulled him the rest of the way down. His head banged on the bar counter. I pinned his arm behind his back, holding him there, twisting the arm further up toward his neck every time be tried to pull free.

"Mister," I said, "I'm going to let you go, you hear me? And when I do, if you want some more, I'll be happy to oblige. But if you take my advice, you'll just stay calm right where you are, while I walk out of here."

I waited a few seconds more, applying increasing pressure. Finally, he nodded and said, "Okay, damn it. You're breaking my friggin' arm. Lemme go."

I eased off and let him up. Reaching into my coat pocket, I tossed money onto the bar, and nodded to the bartender who stood frozen in his tracks right across from us. Welcome back to Houston, Andy Givens, we've got special ways to deal with folks like you.

Elaine was one of the first passengers off her flight. When she saw me, her eyes brightened and she hurried the rest of the way to where I stood waiting at the end of the jet-way. I pulled her to me and we kissed.

"Did you have to wait long?" she asked.

"Not very," I said, leading the way to the baggage area.

The man from the bar stood at the carousel, apparently waiting for luggage. He spotted me headed in his direction and looked around wild-eyed.

"Did you see that guy?" Elaine asked, pointing at the man beating a hasty retreat out of the baggage claim area. "He didn't pick up a bag, maybe he was planning on stealing people's luggage."

"Do you think so?"

"Well, then he looked like he was afraid of something," Elaine continued.

"Yeah," I said. "He did look worried didn't he?"

On the drive from the airport, Elaine rested her head on my shoulder. "I guess we've got a lot to do to get ready for the sanctions hearing on Monday, don't we?"

"Yes," I said, smiling. "And there's something about the hearing you need to know."

"Andy, if you don't mind, can that wait 'til tomorrow? I'd just as soon enjoy the rest of the evening without having to worry about Caponi and Centennial."

"Okay," I said, pulling into the parking space in front of her apartment. I retrieved her bags from the trunk and followed her inside.

"Coffee?" she asked switching on the light over the stove in the galley kitchen.

"Only if it has brandy in it," I answered.

I carried the luggage upstairs, then returned to watch Elaine pour generous dollops of Hennesey's into oversized coffee mugs.

"Andy, I think I must've left my purse on the front seat. Is your car locked?"

"I don't remember. I'll go and get it."

I went back to the car and retrieved Elaine's purse from the floorboard. Back inside, the downstairs lights were off. A faint glimmer of flickering candle light came from the head of the stairs. I heard Elaine, humming along with a familiar old tune on the radio, and I climbed the stairs to join her.

# Chapter Thirty Nine

I sat with Vincent Caponi at one of the two large dark wood conference tables positioned inside the bar in Judge David Lowenstein's courtroom. At the other table were the usual cast from the defendants. Joseph Hartson and his associate, Carl Hopgood, Fritz Taylor, Alton Giles, William Mossberg, Nelson Tucker, and the others.

Vincent Caponi drummed his fingers on the table, his dark eyes darting anxiously around the room. He was still shaken by what I'd told him when I finally contacted him the night before.

"What if he's lying?" he asked.

"If that's the case, we're in a lot of trouble." Before I could say more, Judge Lowenstein entered the courtroom. He got right to business. "Are the parties prepared to proceed with the Defendants' motion for sanctions?"

Hartson and I stood and announced that we were.

"Very well," Lowenstein said. "Mr Hartson please call your first witness."

"We call Tommy Duncan," Hartson said. He glanced over at our table, just as arrogant as ever.

Tommy Duncan, on the other hand, was completely out of character. No more Mr Jovial. The poor man looked about as nervous as anybody I'd ever seen walk into a courtroom. Under the circumstances, I didn't blame him.

Hartson asked Duncan preliminary questions establishing he was a *former* employee of Groves State Bank, that in a deposition taken in this case, he had testified that his boss, Anthony Mason ordered employees of the bank to spread the word that the Caponis were Mafia and that their savings association was going under because the Mafia was siphoning off most of the depositors' money.

"That testimony, which you gave in your deposition, was it true?" Hartson asked.

"No sir, it wasn't," Duncan replied.

"Why was it that your testimony was not truthful?"

Duncan hesitated, glancing up at the judge.

"Why did you lie, Mr Duncan?" Hartson demanded.

"It was Roberto Caponi and his father, Vincent. They said I had to tell those lies or my family would be paid a real unpleasant visit by some of their friends from over in New Orleans."

"Was that the only reason you lied?"

In a high-pitched whine, Duncan answered, "Well, it was the *main* reason."

"What do you mean, Mr Duncan?"

"Well, on top of threatening me and my family, Roberto Caponi gave me a manila envelope with twenty-five-thousand dollars cash in it."

Hartson slowly shook his head. "What is the truth of the matter, Mr Duncan, did Mr Mason order you to tell your bank customers that the Caponis were related to the Mafia?"

"No sir, he did not," Duncan replied, straightening in his chair as he warmed to the task.

"Did Mr Mason order you to tell your bank customers that Centennial Savings was about to go under?" Hartson asked, pressing the point.

"No sir, he didn't order that either. Like I told you, I only testified the way I did because of the threats. And I want to say I didn't want their money. I never asked for it and I didn't spend so much as a single dime."

"Well now, Mr Duncan, what about the memorandum from Mr Mason to the employees of Groves State? Did you write the handwritten note in the margin?" Hartson asked, showing Duncan a copy of the memo that Roberto found that afternoon in my conference room.

"Yes sir, I did, but I need to explain. Just like I told you, it isn't true. Mr Mason never ordered me to say those things about the Caponis and their company."

"Then tell us, Mr Duncan, why did you write that note in the margin?" Hartson tapped his fountain pen on the lectern. He was enjoying his role immensely, dragging the so-called truth out of poor Tommy Duncan.

Duncan shifted uneasily. "Well, it was what Roberto Caponi insisted I do. He said it was actually his lawyer's idea. Said we needed some sort of physical proof to back up our story."

Hartson looked over at our table. "Did Roberto Caponi tell you the name of his attorney who came up with the bright idea of fabricating evidence?"

Duncan glanced over at me and quickly looked away. "Yes, sir. He said it was Andrew Givens."

Hartson puffed out his chest. He stared at me, and with a tone of abject disgust said, "Pass the witness."

I stood and took Hartson's place at the lectern. I looked over at him sitting there at counsel's table with his cronies and made a show of adjusting the microphone to accommodate my greater height.

"Mr Duncan, I want to make sure I understand," I began. "You're saying Mr Anthony Mason, the president of Groves State, never told you to spread the word that the Caponi family had Mafia connections and their company was about to fail because the Mafia was pulling all its money out, and that you only testified that way at your deposition because you were threatened and bribed, have I got that right?"

Duncan stared at me and said, "Yes sir, that's right."

"And, Mr Duncan, have I also got it right that you falsified a document to corroborate the story that Vincent and Roberto Caponi wanted you to tell, and they told you that part of the scheme was something *I* suggested to them?"

"Yes sir, that's what I'm saying."

"Tell me, Mr Duncan, when did the Caponis contact you to make the threats you say they made?"

"Uh, I don't have a good memory for dates, but it was just a few days before my deposition."

"Were the threats you say they made communicated to you in a face-to-face meeting?"

Duncan nodded.

"Sir?"

"Yes, I'm sorry," he replied.

"Where did this meeting take place?"

"Uh, well, they came up to me in the parking lot across from a restaurant where I go to have lunch sometimes in Port Arthur. A place called Frank's."

"And this was at lunch time just a couple of days before your deposition?"

"Well I'm not sure of the date, but it was in the same week when I gave my deposition here in Houston."

"And both Roberto and Vincent Caponi were there?"

"Yes, sir, they sure were."

"What kind of car were they in, do you remember?"

"Uh, I'm not really sure. It was big and black, a Town Car I believe."

"Now did the conversation where the threats were made, did it take place right there in the parking lot?"

"Yes, they came up to me and we talked, standing right there next to my car."

"And, who did the talking? Roberto or Vincent?"

Duncan leaned forward. "Why, I believe the old man, sittin' right over there," pointing at Caponi, "he and his son both did the talkin'."

"You *believe* they both did?"

"No, I'm sorry, just a figure of speech. I'm sure."

"And Mr Duncan, you also said something about an envelope that Roberto gave you that had twenty-five-thousand dollars in it. Is that right?"

"Uh, yes, sir."

"When did he give you the envelope?"

Duncan thought about this one for a while.

Judge Lowenstein asked, "Mr Duncan, do you understand the question?"

"Yes, sir, I'm sorry," Duncan replied. "He went back to his car and got it and brought the envelope back and gave it to me."

"Now when was it that you falsified the document, the one that you said they had you write in a note in the margin?"

Duncan looked down at his feet. "Uh, that came later, the day before my deposition, in fact. Roberto Caponi called me and had me meet him at the Hyatt where I was staying getting ready to be deposed. He came up to my room that night at the hotel."

"And that's when you say he told you that falsifying the document was my idea?"

Duncan's glance shot past me, to the defense table. "Yeah, that's right."

"When you say you had your first meeting with the Caponis in the parking lot across from Frank's, did you report that to your employer?"

"No, sir, I didn't."

"Did you report it to the police?"

"No, I didn't."

"Why not?"

"I was afraid, for my family, everybody knows those Mancusos ain't nobody to mess with."

"Mr Duncan, I'm going to ask one more time. Think about it carefully. Has everything you've testified to here today been the truth?"

Tommy Duncan looked right at me, calm as could be. "Yes sir, it's all true and sir, I have to say this, you know it's true."

I sat down. Vincent Caponi wrote on his legal pad, 'I need to speak with you now!' I nodded.

Hartson was back up taking Duncan on re-direct. "Mr Duncan you testified that you no longer work for Groves State?"

"That's correct," Duncan answered.

"When did your employment with that institution end?"

"Right after the day they took my deposition. Mr Mason told me I was fired right then and there."

"Has anyone told you that you will get your job back for testifying in court as you have today?"

Duncan shook his head. "No, sir, there's not a chance of that. I wish there was, but I know Mr Mason."

On that note, Hartson finished with Duncan.

"Anything further?" Lowenstein asked Hartson.

"No, judge, that is all we have," Hartson said, casting a contemptuous glance in my direction.

"Mr Givens?" Lowenstein prompted, "are you ready to proceed?"

I stood. "Your honor, I would like to take ten minutes to confer with my client. Then we'll be ready."

Lowenstein frowned at me, drumming a pencil on his desk top. He wasn't pleased with the delay. Just the same, he said, "Very well, we'll take a recess until ten-thirty."

Outside the courtroom, Vincent Caponi and I sat at the far end of the hallway.

Vincent's dark eyes glistened. "Andy, I can prove I wasn't with Roberto over in Port Arthur. I think I'll be able to prove that Roberto wasn't there either."

"How?"

"I've got Sylvia for most of the time, and two days before that deposition, we had a creditors' meeting in the bankruptcy. Remember? Roberto and I were both there from mid-morning until late in the afternoon."

"They'd just put Duncan back on to say he already said he wasn't sure about the exact day and Vincent, you should know, the court probably won't give Sylvia's testimony a lot of weight."

"What about Elaine? She can testify how Roberto found the document with Tommy Duncan's note on it *before* you even scheduled his deposition. That's what I remember you and Roberto both telling me the night we went out to celebrate, remember?"

I'd already witnessed how Elaine's testimony could be impeached. It hadn't been fatal the last time, but that didn't mean Lowenstein would find her convincing. I explained my concerns, but Vincent was determined to convince me to go with the inconsistencies in Tommy Duncan's story as our defense. I understood why. I really did. But too much rode on the outcome to take the risk.

"Vincent, you know we can blow them out of the water. Probably put an end to this right now. We've got to do it the way I explained."

Caponi stared at me. "Andy, what you are asking, I told you, I would go along only if it was the only way. I have to think of Sylvia." He paused, took a deep breath, and sighed. "Are you certain?" he finally asked.

"I'm afraid we have to. We can't take the chance."

Vincent Caponi stood and shuffled away. He'd aged by years since the day of his son's funeral. A few minutes later he came back, stared at me intently, and said, "Very well, go ahead."

I smiled and shook his hand. "I'll call you first. That will give Elaine time to get the show going."

Caponi nodded and headed toward the courtroom. He paused at the door and looked back over his shoulder his dark eyes questioning one more time the decision he'd put in my hands. I didn't blame him. It took a strong man to do what he'd decided.

I stopped at the pay phone and called Elaine. Then I went inside.


An hour later, Vincent Caponi left the witness stand. He'd performed well, denying all involvement in bribery or threats made to Tommy Duncan, holding his own with Hartson during a heated cross examination.

As Caponi came to sit next to me, Lowenstein asked, "Mr Givens do you have additional witnesses?"

I nodded. "Yes, your honor we have one more witness."

"Very well, let's proceed," Lowenstein instructed.

"We call James Weeks," I said.

The sound of muffled whispers came from the direction of the defense table. Hartson was leaning over to question Carl Hopgood. He was his usual smug self. Not the least bit worried. Good. He was about to get a big surprise.

James Weeks, a thin, ebony whip of a man, entered the courtroom and walked slowly down the aisle. He was dressed in a black suit, black tie, crisply starched white shirt and polished black shoes. At his side was Nathan Junell.

Junell went with his client up to the witness box. "Mr Weeks is represented by counsel," Junell announced. "I want the record to reflect that."

Lowenstein nodded. "Senator Junell, it is so noted on the record. If you would like to take a seat during your client's testimony, why don't I have my law clerk get one for you? You can sit right over there, next to the jury box."

Junell smiled at the judge and lumbered over to a padded leather chair the clerk pulled up for his use. After Weeks was sworn and seated, I began taking the bankers' conspiracy apart.

"Mr Weeks, are you employed?"

"Yessuh. I work for First Texas Republic Bank over in Beaumont. I'm the bank's driver, pick up customers for meetings at the bank, take Mr Carroll Carter 'round in the bank's limo. Been doin' it for the past fourteen years."

"Thank you, Mr Weeks. Do you recall ever bringing Mr Carter over to Houston in the bank's limo?"

"Yessuh, I do."

I was distracted by the sound of papers hitting the floor. Carl Hopgood was in a state of panic. Lunging for a file he'd knocked to the floor, he succeeded in knocking Hartson's notebook off the table too. The young man's face was ghostly white and beads of perspiration popped out on his forehead. He grabbed a legal pad and began writing furiously.

"Mr Weeks," I continued, "when was the last time you remember bringing Mr Carter over to Houston in the bank's limo?"

James Weeks glanced quickly toward Nathan Junell, who nodded his massive head.

"It was in November, on a Friday, I believe."

"Where did you take Mr Carter?"

Hartson stood. He held a sheet of paper in his hand, a scribbled note from Hopgood. "Your honor I fail to see the relevance of this questioning. Mr Carter's movements are not at issue in this hearing. It is the Caponis and their counsel who have the explaining to do."

Lowenstein looked at me. "Counsel?"

"Mr Carter's movements on that Friday afternoon are extremely relevant to this hearing your honor and, with just a couple more answers by Mr Weeks, that will become apparent to everyone."

Carl Hopgood stood next to his boss, his hands trembling. "Judge, could we, uh, maybe take a brief recess? There is some, uh, information that I need to share with defense counsel."

Lowenstein scowled. "A witness is testifying, counsel. When his direct examination is completed, I will consider your request for a recess, but not in the middle of the stream. Do you understand?"

Hopgood nodded weakly and slumped back into his chair. He whispered to his boss, possibly filling him in on the truth, maybe just making up whatever dumb story he could come up with on the spur of the moment. Either way, whatever he said caused Joseph Hartson's face to turn red.

"Where did you take Mr Carter?" I repeated.

"Uh, a couple places. When we got to Houston, first off we went to the bank building down on Louisiana. I waited out on the curb and thirty or forty minutes later, Mr Carter come back with that fella' over there." Weeks pointed in the direction of the defense table.

"Which one of the gentlemen are you pointing out?" I asked.

"It's that one the judge was just talkin' to. Carl Hopgood's his name," Weeks replied.

"Did Mr Carter and Mr Hopgood get into the limo?"

"Yessuh, they sure did," Weeks said.

"While they were in the limo together did Mr Carter and Mr Hopgood speak to each other?"

"Yeah they did, you know that. Idn't that what you got me up here to talk about?"

Hartson leaped up. "Judge, Mr Carter is the President of First Texas Republic. Mr Hopgood is his lawyer. Anything they said to each other is protected from disclosure by the attorney-client privilege."

The judge looked at me. "He's right. Mr Givens, don't ask the witness what Mr Carter and his lawyer talked about."

"Yes sir," I replied. "Now, Mr Weeks, did you take Mr Carter and Mr Hopgood anyplace else that afternoon?"

Weeks leaned over in the witness chair. "Well, it was actually just about time for lunch but they didn't want to go to a restaurant. Mr Hopgood had me drive over to Sam Houston Park and told me to pull in the lot next to the visitor's center."

"How long did you park the limo in that lot?"

"Oh not much more'n ten minutes. Mr Carter and Mr Hopgood, they stayed in the limo and waited and talked."

"Could you hear what they said to each other?"

Hartson was on his feet again. "Objection, judge. Mr Givens is asking the witness to testify about a privileged communication."

Lowenstein frowned at me.

"All I'm seeking to establish at this time is that Mr Weeks heard the conversation. I have not asked him to reveal what Mr Carter and his attorney said to each other."

"All right. Mr Weeks, do you understand? Do not tell in your answer the substance of what Mr Carter and Mr Hopgood said to each other."

"Yessuh, I understand," Weeks replied.

"Could you hear what they said?" I asked.

"Yeah I could," Weeks said, looking at me with a sheepish expression. "They shut the glass partition, you know the one that slides up and down between the driver and the passenger compartment. But Mr Carter, he left the intercom on, and with what they was talkin' about, I just didn't turn it off."

"Are you sure you didn't turn the intercom on so you could over-hear their conversation?" I asked.

"No, suh," Weeks replied, arching his bushy eyebrows. "I'd never do somethin' like that. Besides, even if I'd wanted to, you can't even activate the on-switch from the driver's side. Mr Carter, he'd been talkin' to me, giving directions, and he left it on. I don't know why, I guess he just forgot about it."

"Did you pick up any other passenger while you were in the lot at the park?"

"Uh, yessuh. Mr Hopgood opened his door and let Mr Roberto Caponi in."

Murmurs of surprise sprang up throughout the courtroom. Judge Lowenstein pounded his gavel.

"Are you certain it was Roberto Caponi who got into the limo?"

"Well, that's who I figured out it was. I turned around and got a good look at him as he got in. He sat on the seat facing me. Hopgood and Carter was on the seat with their backs to me. It was the same guy who you and Mr Junell showed me a picture of that night right before Christmas over in lawyer Junell's office. And they called him Roberto, and said his daddy was Vincent Caponi, so with all that, I'm sure that's who it was."

"What did they discuss with Roberto?"

"Well, Mr Hopgood, he done most of the talkin'. He started out tellin' that Roberto fella' that he and his daddy was in big trouble for bribing Tommy Duncan. Roberto told them he didn't know what they was talkin' 'bout. He hadn't bribed nobody and then he said Hopgood got him there by sayin' he had proof that his daddy bribed Tommy Duncan. Anyway, Roberto ask Hopgood where was the proof? Hopgood and Carter started laughin' and Hopgood, he told Roberto he had it all wrong. That Roberto was gonna *have* to testify that he bribed Tommy Duncan and made Tommy write up a fake document."

Hartson was on his feet shouting, "Judge, this is *absurd*! It is highly improper to permit this kind of slanderous, fabricated testimony to get a bunch of already proven extortionists off the hook."

Lowenstein glared at Hartson. "Counsel, in case you've forgotten, I'm the judge in this courtroom, and I'll not tolerate any further attempts by you or your colleague to derail this hearing. Do you understand me?"

"Judge," Hartson pleaded.

"Sit down, Mr Hartson," Lowenstein commanded.

"What did Roberto Caponi say after Hopgood told him that?"

"He laugh and say no way he ever say those things."

"Did he say why he wasn't going to say what Hopgood wanted?"

"Yessuh. He say it was all a pack of lies and they never get him to say that sorta b.s. Then he ask Hopgood if this wasn't all his idea, and if it was, he said it wasn't gonna work."

"What did Mr Hopgood say then?"

"Oh, he jus' kept laughing and chucklin'. It was confusing, why he was actin' the way he was, but Mr Carter he was chucklin' too, and he usually don't laugh about much of anything. But all of a sudden, Mr Hopgood, he got real serious and told Roberto he was right. Nobody bribed Tommy Duncan, except for Carroll Carter and that was to get Tommy to say what he and Carroll Carter wanted him to say—that and a nice job workin' at Texas Republic. Then, Hopgood told Roberto he was gonna have to say whatever they told him to, and if he didn't, then his momma and daddy would just have to find out what it was that Roberto and his little friend, Sammy Lopez, liked to do to each other. After that, Mr Carter, he started laughing his head off, and he ask Roberto if he want to see the pictures they had of him with Sammy. He said he found that sorta thing disgusting, but maybe his folks would be more understandin'."

Hopgood was busy melting into a puddle. He and Hartson both received stony, disbelieving stares from their co-counsel. Nelson Tucker stood and left his place at the table to sit in a chair just inside the bar. Others soon followed suit. The sight of those folks distancing themselves from Carl Hopgood, Joseph Hartson, and the venerable firm of Marshon & Davis was really quite remarkable.

"What did Roberto do after that?" I asked.

"He didn't say nothin'. I looked at him through the rear view mirror. I'll never forget that, long as I live. That boy, looked like his life was over right that minute."

I walked back to my chair. Vincent Caponi sat at the table staring straight ahead, tears running down his cheeks.

"What did Carl Hopgood and Carroll Carter say to each other after Caponi left?" I asked.

"Attorney-client privilege," Hartson objected.

Lowenstein stared at him and shook his head. "Mr Hartson, you must realize, we're quite a ways beyond that. Your objection is over-ruled."

James Weeks thought for a minute. "They start laughin' an' giggling like two school boys who jus' pulled some kinda childish prank. Hopgood asked Carter what he thought when he told that little queer about showing pictures to his mamma and daddy. Carter laughed and said he was afraid the boy was gonna mess his pants and he was glad he didn't, 'cause it mighta taken a while to get the smell of that faggoty wop out of his limo. It was real mean what those men did to that boy and then how they said those things and laughed about it like they did."

The last questions were for Nathan Junell. The only pay-off he'd requested for delivering the testimony of James Weeks.

"You know what your boss and his lawyer were doing was wrong, didn't you?"

"Uh, yessuh, I did."

"Why didn't you come forward and report what you heard before today?"

Weeks glanced quickly over to Nathan Junell. Then he looked back to where I stood at the lectern. "Well, I know I should have. But I was scared what they might do to me. If they was willing to play as rough as they did with Roberto Caponi, what do you think they'd be willing to do to a black man like me, or my wife, and our children? I guess I didn't because I was afraid."

"What made you change your mind?" I shot a glance toward the jury box where Nathan Junell was puffed out like a bull frog.

"Well, it was botherin' me real bad. I couldn't sleep. Didn't want to have nothin' to eat. And it got worse knowing how that young man had gone and killed hisself right after Mr Carter and Mr Hopgood got through with him. Finally, I just had to talk to somebody. So I goed to see lawyer Junell. He saved my parents' home back when my daddy was hurt workin' over at the Fina Plant. We'll never forget what he did for us back then, so I went to him and told my story. He promised me, there wasn't nobody gonna hurt me or my family for tellin' the truth and as the Bible say, it's the truth that sets a man free. Well, next thing I know, I was meetin' with you and Mr Junell over in his office right before Christmas. I knew then what I was gonna have to do and I ain't even worried about it all that much. The hardest part was to keep goin' in to work at the bank, drivin' Mr Carter and his wife to Christmas parties and all."

"Thank you, Mr Weeks," I said. "No further questions."

Judge Lowenstein stared angrily at Joseph Hartson. "Mr Hartson, do you still want that recess?"

In a bare whisper, Hartson answered, "Yes judge, we do need a few minutes."

When the hearing reconvened, the other defense lawyers sat at chairs inside the bar, but they remained away from the defense table. Hartson was on his own. Hopgood was missing, apparently banished by his boss. But for a man who was nearing a state of shock, Hartson actually did pretty well. Only not well enough to avoid the one final trap I'd set.

"Don't you realize Mr Carter is a highly respected member of the community over in Beaumont? Don't you see, he is going to climb up there in that chair you're sitting in right now and refute everything you've said? Mr Weeks, it will go better for you if you just go ahead and admit how you've been lying, believe me, it will."

"I don't think Mr Carter'll say I'm lying," Weeks replied. He sat ramrod straight and stared matter-of-factly at Hartson.

"Why is that?" Hartson asked, making the cross examiner's fatal mistake, akin to asking the witness why he is sure the defendant bit the plaintiff's nose off when he didn't see it happen, only to hear the answer, "Because I saw him spit it out."

"Well, suh," Weeks began, "after the first couple of minutes, while they was still waitin' for Roberto Caponi, I reached down and flipped the record switch. That recorder, it was Mr Carter's idea. He was always worried that a customer he took around in the limo would someday say he'd made a loan commitment or agreed to a work out or somethin' like that. He only ask me to switch it on a couple of times. Anyway, I got all of it from that point to the end on the tape."

Hartson stood at the podium staring at the witness in utter disbelief.

"I got a copy of the tape with me if you like to hear it," Weeks offered.

"That tape doesn't have any place in this proceeding," Hartson said, a tone of desperation overriding the bravado of his words.

"I think it does," Judge Lowenstein declared.

Hartson slunk back to the defense table.

This was the moment I had relished since that night when I first met James Weeks. Just the same, I couldn't help but feel just a little sorry for Hartson. I was certain he hadn't known what his client and his own associate were up to. At least I chose to give him that benefit of doubt.

By the time the tape was played to its end, Lowenstein was more angry than I've ever seen a judge. He took several moments to compose himself, scribbling notes on his docket sheet. When he finished, he looked out across the cavernous court room, his face drawn, a hint of disbelief glimmering in his steely eyes, obviously shaken by the knowledge that his court had been abused by heretofore respected members of the federal bar.

In a firm but somber voice he announced, "The motion for sanctions against Plaintiffs, Centennial Savings Association and Vincent Caponi, and their attorney, Andrew Givens, is denied. I am referring the matters brought out at this hearing to the U.S. Attorney. I will expect all parties involved to cooperate fully and completely with her in any investigation of criminal wrong-doing that has occurred."

Hartson stood and approached the podium. "Your honor, if I may, I just want you to know, I didn't know anything about this."

Lowenstein glared at him for a moment, then got up and walked out, leaving Hartson facing an empty bench.

I leaned over to Vincent. "It's over. None of them will dare try to go forward after this."

Vincent nodded and managed what passed for a smile. "It's not over, Andy. I still have to go home and break the news to Sylvia. That will be the most difficult thing I've ever done."

"Want me to come along?"

Vincent took the handkerchief from his breast pocket and wiped his eyes. "Yes, I would consider it an act of great friendship if you'd come out to the house with me."

Elaine stood at the other side of the table, waiting. "Andy, Mr Tucker asked me to see if you'd have time to visit for a few minutes."

Nelson Tucker was the dean of Beaumont trial lawyers, a true gentleman and a man of honor. Just as I'd expected, the forces were lining up with him, the renowned master of compromise. As the defense bunch silently filed out, it was easy to see, there was no fight left in them.

I took the time to visit briefly with Tucker, explaining my need to go with my client. I promised to call him soon. Then, we left the courtroom.


Later that night, Elaine went with me to the home of Vincent and Sylvia Caponi. Hopefully, being there counted for something. As Sylvia cried for her lost son, the enormous tragedy of his death weighed heavily on all of us. The poor boy. He'd been too ashamed and too afraid of letting his parents know what he was to risk seeing them again.

# Chapter Forty

I sat across from Del Wallace in his office, my first time back since the day after William Thrasher's murder.

"Like a drink?" he asked. "We've still got some stuff down in the conference room from our Christmas open house."

"No, thanks. I'll pass. Trying to cut back some—a New Year's resolution."

Del got out of his chair and began pacing. Finally, he said, "Are you sure you want to do this? He's been acting pretty weird."

"Yeah, I've got to."

Del shrugged. "Okay, suit yourself. He's down there where he always is."

I walked down the corridor to his office. The door was closed, so I knocked. A muffled "come in," came from the other side.

I stepped into the dimly lit room. Del had warned me to be prepared, but I was still shocked by the changes in my former partner. Normally fastidious in appearance, his hair was disheveled, and his suit was stained and rumpled.

"Andy," he stammered.

"Hello, Mr Golden."

"Uh, congratulations on the trial. I'm happy for you, I meant to call to tell you but …."

"Sir, we need to talk, don't you think?"

"Well, uh, certainly. If there's something you want to discuss, I'm happy to visit."

"I appreciate that," I said, pulling up one of the chairs.

In a voice that was tired and weak, matching his withered appearance, he asked, "What is it you want to talk about?"

"I suppose you know, sir, after William Thrasher's murder, I became convinced that Fred Whitfield went out there and killed him, and tried to pin the blame on me."

Golden nodded. "Yes, Del explained that to me. But I hope that's not why you're here. It won't do any good to dredge up the past. Fred's dead. Thrasher's dead. Nothing will change that."

"Maybe the past can stand a little more analysis. I've been hoping the police would re-open the Thrasher case, but my lawyer tells me they still think they put the right man on trial. I have to tell you, it hurts, having people still believe I'm a murderer."

"Andy, I wish it was different. I truly do."

"What do you think, Mr Golden? Do you think I killed William Thrasher?"

"Well, there was a time, but now I don't know."

Golden sank further into his chair. For several moments neither of us spoke. Finally, he said, "Will you join me in an armagnac?"

I nodded.

"Please," he said, gesturing toward the liquor cabinet. "Be generous."

I went to the cabinet and poured into two large leaded-crystal snifters. I passed one of the drinks across the table to Golden. He raised his glass. I put mine down on his desk.

"Why did you do it?" I asked.

He stared at me through glassy, feverish eyes. "Do? I don't understand."

"Sir, you went out to Thrasher's office that night, didn't you?"

Golden dropped his head. Then nodded slowly. "I wasn't about to allow that blow-hard, snot-nose to ruin what I'd worked for for my entire life. A malpractice case, the humiliation of it. Just imagine. The reputation of the firm, *ruined*."

"They're lots of malpractice cases brought these days, that's no justification."

"Not against *my firm.* You do understand that don't you?"

"No sir, I don't."

"I went out there to convince him to give us a chance to set things right."

"Yes, and you called him from my office, took the key to my car, and drove it out there, didn't you?"

"I knew you had his private number on your rolodex. It was late and when I couldn't reach him at his home, I took a chance that he still might be at his office. When I talked to him and he said he'd wait, I remembered my car was in the shop and I thought about the key in your drawer. You said you were staying at the Cornwall, so I guessed your car might be in our garage."

I sipped the armagnac, feeling its smooth, fiery taste. "What about my raincoat? You took that too, didn't you?"

Golden nodded. "I realize it looks like I intentionally tried to pin the blame on you. But that isn't what happened. I didn't even know that raincoat belonged to you. It had been in our reception closet for months. And it was pouring that night. If your car wasn't in the garage, I was going to have to find a cab."

"You thought you might take a cab when you were planning on killing a man? Come on, sir, I'm not buying that."

Golden's jaw dropped. "Andy, I had no such intention. And if you're telling me the truth that you didn't kill Thrasher, I might as well let you know, I didn't do it either."

I shook my head. "You expect me to believe you, after you've admitted you went out there that night?"

Golden stared at me. "You've got to. When I got to his office, Thrasher was already dead. The first thing I thought was, somehow, you'd gotten out there ahead of me, had an argument and that you killed him."

This was becoming more preposterous by the second. "If Thrasher was dead, how did you get inside the door at the elevator?"

"He told me he'd prop it open so he wouldn't have to keep looking for me. The door was open, just the way he said it would be."

"Mr Golden, your story doesn't hold water. If you really didn't kill him, why didn't you simply call the police?"

He looked at me with such shock, you'd think I was the one who had gone insane. "Andy, I thought you'd done it. At first, I thought that was far worse than the malpractice claim I'd worried over. And then I panicked. I picked up that damned baseball bat. Then I had to find a towel in his bathroom and clean it off. I was afraid to leave it behind, so I stuffed it in a pocket of your raincoat. I didn't know I'd gotten blood inside your car. I burned the towel and your coat in my fireplace. Even though I was convinced you were the guilty one, I never tried to prove it. Don't you remember? When I testified at your trial, I could have done a lot more damage if that had been my objective."

I'd lost my patience with the man. "Why are you lying to me? You know, there's a lot more to this than mere coincidence."

"Andy, I don't know what you mean."

"Come on, Steve. The security records. If you didn't intend to frame me, why did you change the time on the sign-out sheet to show that I was still in the building when you called Thrasher from my office?"

Golden stared down at his desk top. He reached for the brandy snifter but only succeeded in knocking it over, spilling the drink across the green-felt blotter on his desk. He looked up, what little color he had completely drained from his face. "Don't you see? I had to. I believed you were guilty and I needed a way to prevent ruining the reputation of the firm. After it was over, we could say, we made a mistake about Andy, he was the problem, but the firm would still be here, still strong, still intact."

I sat there staring at the pathetic little man. Off in his own twisted world. How did he feel, now that someone else knew his secrets? "It didn't stop with Thrasher, did it?" I asked.

Golden stood and shuffled around his desk to sit next to me. "I realize you don't believe me. If I were you, I probably wouldn't either. But so help me, I had nothing to do with Fred Whitfield's death. As for what I did, going to Thrasher's, thinking you killed him, and changing the security log the next night, Andy, all I can say is I'm sorry. Once it started, I didn't know where to stop."

I didn't know what to say.

"What do we do now?" he asked.

"I think we'd better call Randle Hughes, okay?"

"Yes, I suppose it's come to that."

"Do you want me to call?"

He chuckled mirthlessly. "Yes, I'd appreciate it. But could you go down to your old office? I'd like to have a few moments alone."

"Del is here, too, Mr Golden. I'll try to contact Randle from there."

Moments later, Del Wallace sat at his desk, stunned speechless.

"Have you got a number for Randle?" I asked.

"Yeah, in my rolodex," he mumbled. He still wore a vacant stare. "I'd have never suspected Steve Golden of anything like this," he said.

Me either. Steve Golden. A man of impeccable integrity and honor. A man above reproach.

"What are you gonna do?" Del asked.

"Call Randle Hughes. I'm pretty sure Steve's ready to confess. And if he doesn't, I'm going to call Lieutenant Puryear.

Just then, a muffled popping sound, like a firecracker going off in a deep well came from down the hall. Del and I glanced quickly at each other, then ran down the corridor.

We found Golden slumped in his chair, a small hole near his left eye. A stream of red ran down his face and pooled in his lap. One of the Sam Houston pistols was on the floor next to his chair.

"I'll call an ambulance!" Del shouted, hurrying back the way we'd come.

"You'd better have them send the police, too," I said. Steve Golden wouldn't be needing a lawyer after all.

It was almost mid-night when I got home. I opened the back door and felt my way through the darkness of my office, still not believing what had happened. Steve Golden. William Thrasher's murderer and Fred Whitfield's too. The only light on in the house was at Elaine's desk. She'd left a note there saying she'd gone to her apartment. She thought she was coming down with a cold, and had some mega-vitamin C tablets there that she needed to take.

I picked up the phone to call her, but before I finished dialing the number, a light flashed on the console indicating someone was using the line in the conference room. She must have changed her mind. Or maybe she'd already left and gotten back. Either way, her being here was a relief. We needed to talk. I hadn't told about my suspicions concerning Golden. As Del had pointed out just a little less than an hour earlier, now, with the old man dead, and having never confessed, in all probability we never would determine what really happened in Thrasher's office that night.

The double doors to the conference room were closed. I pulled one of them open and stepped inside, expecting to see Elaine at the telephone. Instead, the room was dark and a tall, thin man's silhouette was framed in the faint moonlight coming in from the windows on the far wall. Elaine sat across from me, her eyes blocked from view by shadow, but I could see her hands were bound behind her and a wide piece of adhesive tape covered her mouth. As I headed toward her, the man put the phone down and pointed a pistol at my chest.

"Hold it right there, Givens," Alton Giles said. "Your little friend and I, we were beginning to wonder if you'd ever get here."

"What's this about, Giles?" I said, taking a step closer.

He braced the pistol level with both hands. I stopped, but he continued to point the gun at my chest.

"I came for this," he said, gesturing toward the video tape on the conference table. "Some day, somebody might get smart enough to look at the rest of this and if it goes back far enough, or ahead far enough, they might realize my car went into Thrasher's garage that night too. But it didn't come back out. Not until the following afternoon. You see, I was with him all evening. He told that little mouse of a woman who worked for him that I'd left and then he sent her home so we could continue our business without any interruptions. But when she volunteered at your trial that I'd been there meeting with him, I knew I had to get my hands on this just to make sure."

"You Giles? I don't understand." Out of the corner of my eye, I noticed Elaine was gradually working her hands free. I needed to keep Giles talking. Keep him doing anything that would buy time.

Giles chuckled. "That client of yours. He must have been quite a pain. But he was very clever. When he came to me with the proposal that I should convince my client to settle, offering to pay me a nice commission in the process, I found him extremely creative. But then, the bastard renigged. He thought that damned jury he said you liked so much would give him a lot more. Fritz Taylor had his buddy, Judge Loring, ready to direct a verdict and put your case on ice in the court of appeals if the settlement didn't go down. When Thrasher backed out, Fritz told Loring to go ahead and pour you out."

"You mean you and Thrasher had a deal?"

His thin lips twisted in a contemptuous smile. "Why Givens, you shouldn't be shocked. You knew the man. He had no scruples. Absolutely none."

"But what about you, Giles?"

His smile widened. "Me? Well, they say every man has his price. I simply discovered what mine was."

"What was it? I'd like to know," I said. Elaine was getting closer to freeing her hands.

Giles frowned. "That's immaterial. But after Loring's directed verdict, when Thrasher called wanting to try to put the deal back on, he wound up offering a three-hundred-thousand dollar down-payment. All in small bills too. I waited while he drove out to his house to get the money. He got back at around ten or so, still trying to cut himself a better deal. The man really was dense. Couldn't understand how, with Loring entering the directed verdict, it was going to be difficult to convince W.D.S. to pay him so much as a dime. He was a sorry bastard. Givens, you have my sympathy for having to put up with the man. I was about to take the money and go, but then, that old man, Steve Golden called. Thrasher actually invited him to his office. Right in front of me. Said if I couldn't come through, he'd see what he could get out of your firm's malpractice carrier. I figured the pig-headed son-of-a-bitch was so unreliable I'd never see another dime, so before I left, I hit him with that damned baseball bat he'd been fiddling with all evening. As long as I live, Givens, I'll always remember that feel. It was like splitting open a ripe melon."

"And Fred Whitfield? Why did you kill him?"

Giles edged a step closer to me. "Yes, there was Whitfield too. Somehow, he found out about the relationship between Fritz Taylor and Otto Loring. He called me to say he intended to take it to the judicial commission. I couldn't risk a full-blown investigation by those folks, certainly not with Whitfield urging them on. So I hired that fellow Lucas." He paused and chuckled again. "When the paper all but named you as the chief suspect in Whitfield's murder, Lucas came up with the idea to kill you too. He said that would be the end of any police investigation. Especially if he could make it appear that you shot yourself with the same gun used to kill your former partner. I told Lucas about your trip to Chicago. By the way, that's when our firm bowed out of the

W.D.S. negotiations. I didn't want to be up there knowing what Lucas had planned."

"This isn't going to work, Giles. They'll catch you for sure."

He shook his head. "Givens, you are naive. I've learned so very much. For one thing, I know, and you should know too, the police are very stupid. They'll most likely conclude pretty much what Lucas had planned." He glanced briefly at Elaine. "Only this time, I'm afraid they're going to find a murder-suicide."

She almost had it. Just a few more seconds. But Giles had been more observant than I thought. He cut his eyes toward her and said, "Now, Miss Turner, if you've gotten your hands free, you can help me tie Andy's. I'm going to shoot you first, just so he can watch, and I don't want him to give me any trouble when I do."

I took another step toward him, but he still held the gun leveled at my chest. "It's no use, Givens. Now kindly come around to the other side of the table."

I did as I was told, hoping somehow I could get between the two of them before rushing Giles, giving Elaine at least a fleeting chance to get away. As I reached the end of the table, Giles following me on the opposite side, I noticed a movement on the floor. Ivory creeping from a space between the boxes stacked high at the end of the room. Giles, didn't see him and stepped on his tail. Ivory screeched like a banshee. Giles took a startled step back. He glanced quickly down. I ran at him, throwing a crude body block. The pistol fired just as my shoulder hit him in the chest, driving him backward. He staggered against a row of the boxes. The ones on top toppled, pinning him against the conference table.

Giles seemed dazed and he groaned in pain as he tried to push the boxes away. I reached for the gun that had fallen from his hand. But as I did, the room began to swim and, as if in slow motion, I felt myself beginning to fall.

I woke in a strange place. The lights were dimmed, but in the far corner I saw Elaine and Eddie. He had an arm around her shoulder as they spoke in hushed tones.

"Are you okay?" I asked

Elaine and her brother hurried to my side. Both smiled expectantly. Elaine had tears in her eyes. I reached out to take her in my arms, but an excruciating pain made me stop.

She grasped my hand, leaned down, and gently kissed my forehead. This time, I managed to get my arm around her and pull her close. We held each other for a long time, until one of the nurses came in and made us stop. But Elaine wouldn't let go of my hand.

Smiling through her tears, she said, "The doctors say you're going to be fine. But you're not supposed to move."

"And you have to promise you won't step in the paths of any more speeding bullets," Eddie added.

"What about Alton Giles?" I asked.

Eddie gestured toward the door. "He's right down the hall with a cop standing watch. A couple of cracked vertebrae in his neck."

I looked up at Elaine and smiled. Then, I must have dozed off. They tell me I slept for a long time before I woke again.

# Epilogue

My lungs burned and my shoulder throbbed steadily where the scar from the bullet wound was located. For several more minutes, I attempted to maintain Del's pace. We'd gone almost five miles, a lot further than I'd run since the night I was shot by Alton Giles.

"Del, slow down I can't keep this up," I gasped.

He looked back and grinned, slowing his stride. "Better?"

"Yeah, thanks."

We jogged side by side. The sun, which was just coming up when we started, was shining brightly in a clear, early-spring sky. Vibrant azaleas and fragrantly sweet honeysuckle were in bloom, making our run through Hermann Park and up Sunset Boulevard a thoroughly pleasant experience.

We were on South Boulevard, on our way back to my office, when I finally had to stop. Even the slower pace wasn't one I could maintain for another mile. Del trotted back to where I stood, sucking in air under the always-impressive canopy of Live Oaks.

"Well, if you're going to be such a poor sport, I might have to find somebody else to run with," he said.

"I'll get back in shape," I declared.

Del grinned that sly grin of his. "Shoot, you say you are, but I hear you and Elaine are going off to some Caribbean retreat. You might come back in good shape, but it won't be from running."

"Well, I'll get in shape as soon as we get back, that's a promise," I said.

"Is the settlement complete?"

It was my turn to smile. "Sylvia and Vincent signed the papers yesterday."

"What are you guys gonna to do with all that money? The rumor is you don't exactly need to work too hard any more, unless you really want to."

I laughed. "Del, I've already told you, we agreed to a confidential settlement."

I couldn't blame him for trying. If the shoe were on the other foot I'd try too.

"What are Vincent and Sylvia's plans?" Del asked, trying to crack the nut from a different angle.

"I'm not sure," I said. "They're going to spend some time at a friend's ranch out in New Mexico. Try to regroup. Nathan Junell wants Vincent to re-open Centennial Savings. He's even offered to become an investor in their first project. But honestly, I don't know what's going to happen. Neither is close to getting on with life. They're still focused on Roberto. Busy blaming themselves. Sylvia says she knew Roberto was different, and she suspected he might be gay, but she never gave him the opportunity to discuss it with her."

"What about Vincent?" Del asked.

"I don't know if he knew or thought he knew. He won't talk about it at all, other than to say how he feels responsible because his son preferred to kill himself rather than reveal what he was."

Del looked down and kicked a pebble with this toe. "Wow, it must be pretty hard to have to live with guilt like that."

"Yeah it must be."

When we got back to the house, Elaine had coffee and bagels waiting. We sat to eat and she showed us the morning paper. "JUDGE AND PROMINENT HOUSTON LAWYER INDICTED IN FEDERAL PROBE." Del and I quickly scanned the article.

"They got 'em both," I said. "Guess I never thought it would happen."

"I didn't either, not at first," Del said. "But then I heard that Otto Loring panicked when the suggestion was made that the investigation might extend beyond mere bribery of a public official, and might get into the murder of Fred Whitfield. Apparently, when the old boy heard that, he started singing like a meadow lark, admitted to taking a few thou' to put the Thrasher case on ice in the Court of Appeals. Hell, by the time he was done, he even gave them the goods on his buddy, Fritz Taylor."

"Another shake-up at a big Houston firm?" Elaine asked, alluding to the quiet departure of Joseph Hartson from Marshon & Davis.

The word was, Hartson would be lucky to avoid disbarment, even though no one had, as yet, been able to prove he was actually in on the scheme hatched by his client and Carl Hopgood.

Hopgood, by the way, was already toast, facing a certain stint in a federal corrections facility for extortion, bribery, and tampering with evidence in a federal lawsuit. The same thing went for Carroll Carter and poor, dumb Tommy Boyd Duncan.

As for Alton Giles, he was in the county jail awaiting trial for the murders of William Thrasher and Fred Whitfield. According to Mark Watson, Albert Anderson was slated to try both cases for the State.

The news about Judge Loring and Fritz Taylor got Del excited. He made a quick exit, eager to get downtown to find out about the latest scandal to rock Houston's legal community.

I took one last glance at the headline and finished my coffee. Then I went upstairs to take a shower. I kept thinking about Joseph Hartson and Fritz Taylor and wondered what they were doing, how they were holding up, now that it was their world that had suddenly turned upside down.


It was late afternoon. I opened a chilled bottle of sauvignon blanc and took it and a couple of glasses out back where Elaine sat on the lawn, playing with Ivory. I filled the glasses, handed one to Elaine and we toasted silently.

I reached down and scratched Ivory's head and ears. He rolled over on his back, begging for more.

"I haven't seen much of you lately, pal," I said.

"Yeah and he's missed you, too," Elaine observed.

"Well, I haven't been around much and when I have, I haven't paid him enough attention."

"Promise you'll always treat me better than your cat."

I smiled and said "I promise," and we kissed.

Through an open window we heard the phone ring.

"I'm expecting a call," Elaine said as she stood and brushed grass from her jeans.

"Let it go. Whoever it is will leave a message."

"I told Eddie to call when he got back from his trip," she replied, heading for the still ringing phone.

"Tell that worthless brother of yours no, he can't come with us to Barbados."

Elaine turned and smiled, then she ran up the stairs, shouting back, "Yes, of course we'd love to have company on our trip, Eddie. Andy will be thrilled to hear the news."

Moments later, Elaine came back out onto the steps. Voice shaking she said, "It's for you."

"Unless it's Nelson Tucker saying he's coming over to deliver the money in person, tell whoever it is I've gone on a long trip."

"No," she said, a tone of insistence mixed with worry in her voice. "It's Monica. She wants to speak with you right away."

I looked to where Elaine stood in the doorway. The sun was about to set and its reflection off of the window panes blocked her face from view. What could I do to convince the woman I loved so very much? Suddenly I had it. I smiled up at her and said, "Tell her I'm not in."